SUMMER'S BLOOD

SUMMER'S BLOOD

IRON AND EARTH
BOOK ONE

SARA T. BOND

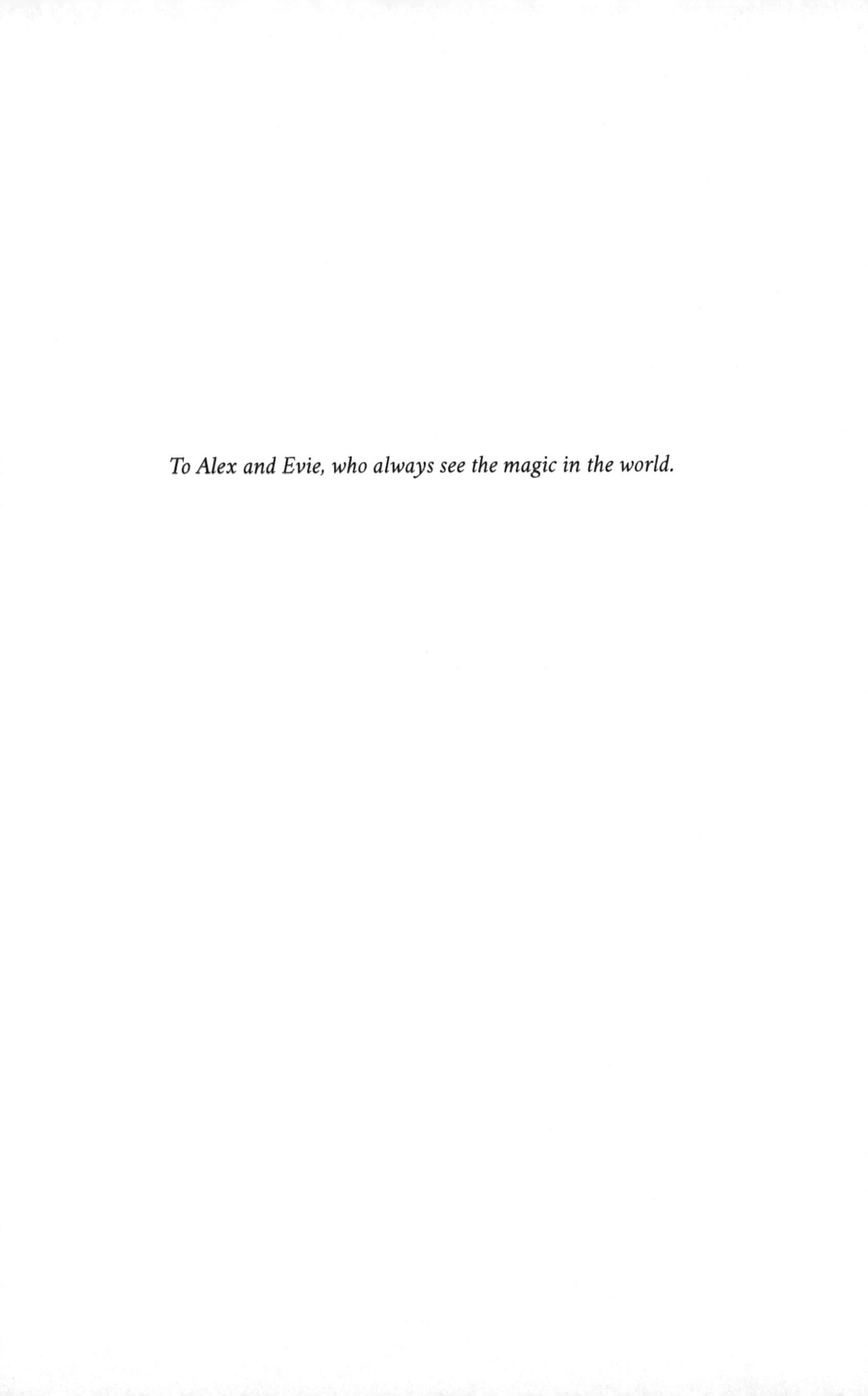

To Alex and Evie, who always see the magic in the world.

CHAPTER ONE

Hunting was illegal at the Greenwood Knoll, and everyone knew it.

The Knoll was a designated place of sanctuary for anyone—fae and human alike—who might stop in for a drink before or after crossing between the worlds. It had been that way for over two hundred years, and while that might not be long in the memory of some of the immortal creatures that visited the watering hole, it was more than long enough to expect every drunk from Buckhead to the Eternal Realm to know better than to seek prey among the patrons of my pub.

If that wasn't enough, it was also posted at both entrances and above the bar itself.

Apparently, the incubus in front of me was either illiterate or had a profound death wish.

He was in full predator mode and not even trying to hide it. Charm and pheromones were dialed up and directed at the human woman seated beside him. She was young, brunette, pretty, and working on her third vodka martini at three in the afternoon on a Thursday.

Anna—or Hannah, or whatever her name was—was a new regular

at the Knoll, which was unusual for a human. Though it was not unheard of for humans to know about the fae, it was still rare enough that having one as a regular made me slightly uncomfortable. And yet, this particular human had plopped herself down at my bar at least five times in the past month and left each time with a different fae. Always male, always attractive.

I shook my head. This human was playing a dangerous game, and she didn't even get to see how dangerous. With a human in residence, the protective magic of the Greenwood Knoll was in full effect. The glamour wards kept her from seeing the true nature of any of the fae in the establishment, so she couldn't even see who was about to prey on her, what manner of creature was likely to suck away at her life force. If I let things continue with the incubus, poor Anna/Hannah might find out exactly what it feels like to be on the wrong end of the food chain.

"Hey, Shiv." Mikka Balaur rounded the far edge of the bar from the kitchen. She slid into place beside me, leaning against the barback by the cash register, crossed her arms over her chest to mirror my pose, and leaned over conspiratorially. "Argus says to deal with that sooner rather than later." She nodded to the incubus who was not-so-sneakily moving his hand higher and higher up Anna's thigh while she giggled and sipped at her drink.

"Though," Mikka continued, "Varon and I would be happy to take care of it." She waggled her eyebrows and grinned, baring all her teeth in a show that was much more threat than mirth.

I laughed. Mikka and her twin brother Varon acted as security for the bar, and I'm pretty sure Mikka lived just to rough up patrons who violated the rules of the Knoll. She and Varon were drakes, a fire fae species related to the dragon, and as hot-tempered as they were fiercely loyal.

"Are you so eager to set fire to this place again?" I teased. "We just cleaned up from karaoke night last week."

Last Saturday a group of maenads had gotten drunk and convinced a banshee to sing an Adele song. The place had fallen apart. No fewer than three patrons tried to kill themselves with butter knives, and when Varon moved to turn off the speaker system to minimize the damage of the banshee's profound heartbreak, a mob had attacked him. Argus had been ready to call off karaoke night all together, but I managed to convince him that it was our number-one money-maker. When in doubt, always appeal to a barkeep's greed.

Still, I knew Mikka was right. The incubus was a problem. I could taste his magic, bright syrupy citrus, sweet and sticky, with an undercurrent of something nutty: almonds, I think. It was thick in my throat, cloying and strong, which meant he was really pouring the magic on.

I sighed. It didn't matter if the prey was as willing as it seemed Anna was. The rules of Sanctuary were immutable. Human or fae, all were safe here, and it was my job to make sure of it.

"Fine," I sighed. "Let's take care of it." I reached behind me for my glass of Malbec and took a healthy swig. The earthy bite of the spicy red wine suited my task: grounded, firm, a tiny bit angry and assertive.

As I walked toward them, the incubus whispered something in her ear, and Anna laughed with her full body, leaning forward and almost knocking over her cocktail. As she righted it, she lifted her gaze and smiled like we were old friends.

"Siobhan! Have you met my new friend Lloyd?" She gestured to the incubus. His warm smile didn't quite reach his eyes as he stiffened and sat up straighter. "Lloyd was just telling me the best story about this Fuath he knows."

"A Fuath? Really." Seeing as Fuath were water spirits that had a special fondness for drowning mortals to consume them later, I had a hard time believing Anna might find them amusing. But to each their own. "Maybe another time. Lloyd, was it?" I snorted a bit. Usually fae in the seduction business tended to pick more currently fashionable names, and Lloyd seemed more appropriate for a middle-aged line cook at an all-night diner than for a sex fae with a chiseled jaw and perfectly coiffed honey-blond hair. "I need a word."

"Actually, we were enjoying ourselves," he said, a poorly faked southern accent dripping from his lips. "But I'd love another round. Martinis, gin for me, vodka for her."

"Lloyd," I drew his name out, layering sugar and venom on the word. "I wasn't asking. End of the bar. Now." I nodded my head toward the kitchen as Mikka slid around behind the couple and placed a hand on Lloyd's shoulder. "Excuse us, Anna."

"Hannah," she corrected, never losing her smile and seemingly oblivious to Mikka's sudden presence. "It's Hannah. And it's no problem. Y'all can stay put. I need to use the little girl's room anyway." She slipped off her bar stool and gave Lloyd a quick peck on the cheek. "Just don't leave without me, okay, honey?"

When she'd gone, I gave the incubus an even look. He knew what he'd done.

"Look, I wasn't hunting her." His accent disappeared almost as fast as his fake smile.

"Uh huh," I said.

He tried again. "We were just talking."

I gave a single nod to Mikka. She tightened her grip on Lloyd's shoulder, and I could see the air start to shimmer around her hand. She'd turned up the heat on him, literally.

Lloyd began to sweat. "We're in a bar, for Mab's sake! You're supposed to pick people up in a bar."

"Pick people up. Not prey on them, Lloyd. I've been able to taste your magic for the past half hour, and if you crank it up any more, I'm likely to gag on it." The syrupy almond sweetness of his magic was turning bitter with his stress, giving me a nasty aftertaste.

He sneered at me, posturing aggressively to hide his fear. "I did nothing wrong. You're just angry because she's a pathetic human, like you."

"Half human," I corrected. I was getting tired of this. If he was going to get racist with me, then I was going to have to spell it out. "You violated the Old Laws of Sanctuary, Lloyd. You hunted, using your fae abilities to draw prey to you. Had you just talked, had you just flirted, you'd be within your rights with her, human or fae. But the second you turned up the juice, you violated the laws."

"But they're just pheromones!" The skin around Lloyd's hazel eyes tightened into fine lines, and I could see the sweat beading on his upper lip and around his hair line. "It's an instinct. A natural reaction. To any pretty girl. It just happens!" An edge of hysteria crept into his voice.

"If you can't control yourself, then I recommend finding your drinks and other enjoyments elsewhere."

"But!" Lloyd tried to stand up, but Mikka's fiery grip on his shoulder held him firmly on his stool. "You're the only solitary bar in the city!"

I smiled wanly. "Then go swear allegiance to the Courts, or try your luck in the human bars, because you are no longer welcome at the Knoll." I gestured toward the door where Varon had been carefully watching the scene. He unfolded himself from his slouched perch on his stool and came to mirror Mikka on the other side of Lloyd. Each with a hand on a shoulder and an elbow, they lifted him off his seat and steered him toward the door.

"You can't do this! I didn't do anything to her!" Lloyd continued to protest as the twins half-carried, half-dragged him to the door. "She wanted to go with me!" With a seamless and thoroughly rehearsed series of moves, Varon edged the heavy oak door of the Knoll open with his left foot, Mikka braced her right foot against the other side of the jamb, and together they swept their arms back and out the door, sending Lloyd sailing out over the wide front porch, down the stairs, and into the gravel parking lot.

Before anyone in the bar could even hear him land with a skitter of rocks and curses, the door fell shut, Varon silently swung himself back onto his barstool, and Mikka made her way back to me, grinning like a hyena the whole way.

Spontaneous applause erupted from a pair of maenads in the middle of the great room, and a trio of clurichaun in the far corner chuckled to themselves. They were all regulars and loved seeing someone get tossed out.

Mikka brushed her hands off. "That was fun. Think we'll get any more to throw tonight?"

"It's Thursday, Meek," I said with a sigh. "Probably not."

Mikka's smile dropped away. "What's the matter, Shivs? You usually love when we take out the trash for you."

She was right. Normally, tossing the bums to the curb was the highlight of any night, or slow afternoon, as it were. But things hadn't felt normal around here for a few weeks. I looked at the maenad pair, sticking close together in the center of the room where they could be seen by anyone who walked into the bar. The trio of clurichaun had arrived as a group, and they would likely leave as a group: one car, one destination. No one was taking the risk of traveling alone these days.

I shrugged as I removed Lloyd's empty glass from the bar. "I don't know, maybe we shouldn't have thrown him out. Maybe we should let him call a friend or something."

"Why in Mab's name would we do that? He broke the rules. He gets tossed."

"Yeah, I know. But it's been almost a week, and there's no word from the new waitress, and I just don't want to be responsible for—"

"Oh, no," Mikka sighed. "Not you, too."

"What?"

"Jocelyn's fine. She's a maenad, you know. She probably just got caught up in some new lover or hobby, and she'll show up in a day or two, besotted and full of energy. Seriously, everyone needs to stop worrying so much. The Knoll might be an institution, but it's not the only option out there. Maybe they moved on to another bar. Or another city. Or gave up drinking. No one is hunting our fae, and there's no one picking people off one by one. Atlanta is a perfectly safe place for us."

"You say that," I said, but didn't elaborate further. I didn't need to. She knew the facts as well as I did. No fewer than seven of our patrons had, over the course of a year, stopped coming to the Knoll, and no one could account for their whereabouts. Three maenads, a handful of dryads, and a few recent immigrants from Fairy all had just stopped coming to the pub, stopped talking to their friends in the community, and had, by all accounts, disappeared. No sign of them here or in the Eternal Realm, according to those who had missed them.

And that didn't even include the no fewer than four waitresses we had hired who disappeared within a matter of days or simply never showed up for their first shift. We had just hired a new girl to help with my days off and busy weekends, and I hadn't heard word one about her since Argus offered her the job last week.

Of course, I knew as well as anyone the fickle and ephemeral nature of some fae. A maenad seized by mania could in a single week fall in love, get married, fall out of love, and burn the unlucky husband's house down. A sylph could change lifelong allegiances with nothing but a shift in the breeze, and an ala who had taken upon herself to possess an unlucky truck driver could find herself cross-country before she checked in with her family back home. But when the mania faded, the breeze settled, and the truck stopped its frantic flight or ran out of gas, everyone always checked in. Even in the solitary community, without the allegiances of Court magic and politics, we valued our chosen family. There were too few of us left for someone to simply vanish.

Maybe two or three patrons of my bar could disappear without any word. But not seven. And certainly not the dryads.

I shivered, thinking of the abandoned oaks at the edge of the property. Anais, the dryad who had tended to them, was among the missing, and from the day of her disappearance, her trees had lost leaves, branches, and now the very roots were beginning to rot.

The brunette human returning to the bar put an end to my thoughts of dead fae and deader trees. I put a new vodka martini in front of Anna, er, Hannah as she slid into her barstool.

"Where'd Lloyd go?" She frowned as she reclaimed her spot at the bar.

"He was asked to leave," I said. Look at me, playing the diplomat. "Your martini is on the house. And Hannah?"

She had looked a bit crestfallen but promptly smiled at the free drink. "Yeah, sweetie?"

She was so young. So innocent. I always felt a bit bad for the humans who ended up at my bar. She had no idea that my regulars could flay, flambe, and filet her and keep her alive for the whole thing. "Be careful in here. This isn't the kind of place you're equipped to handle."

Hannah jutted her chin out and sat a little straighter. "You don't know what I can handle." As strong as she appeared, her voice wavered. That sign of unease, of weakness was enough for me.

"You're right," I said, giving her the benefit of the doubt. "You're probably a very tough human. But that's all you are. Human. No matter how charming, young, or fertile you are, you wouldn't survive a day in my world."

Her supple rose lips pulled together in a pout, that no doubt felt to her a very serious expression. It made me want to kiss her and slap her in equal measure. This stupid, vulnerable human. She should run from here. Get back to her own world. She had that option. Not everyone did.

"For your information, I have handled more than my share of fae." She straightened her shoulders and pulled herself to her full height. "I'm here every week, and none of you seem all that scary."

What a foolish, brave girl. She had come to play in a pool of sharks, to swim with the predators. She fancied herself an equal, secure in her own confidence. She didn't know how powerless she was. How could she? She'd only been able to see what the fae allowed her to see. If she only knew what we really were.

Maybe someone should show her.

I could give her that at least.

I shook my head and dropped my chin to my chest. Argus would fuss at me later, but what I was going to do was for this poor girl's own good.

I took a deep breath and shrugged my shoulders, letting my own glamour fall first. It took some effort; I was working against the wards of the Knoll and my own instincts. Keeping a glamour in place was second nature to fae in the human world. Even half fae like myself. It was our first and greatest defense in this realm, allowing us to hide in plain sight and masquerade as harmless humans.

I concentrated and pushed at the thin layer of magic surrounding me and my appearance. The glamour crept down from the top of my head, sliding down my dark hair, removing the mask of human frizz and dark dry curls to reveal sleek and wild coils, shining like obsidian corkscrews erupting from my head. They caught the light with every movement, shining from within in perfect spirals of purest onyx. The glamour oozed down off my shoulders, dropping the dull, acceptably human light brown skin tone and revealing the shining topaz I was born with. I spread and wiggled my long, tapered fingers, admiring my golden talons for a minute. I knew what I looked like: eyes flashing like dark citrine, thick rose-colored lips in an unleashed grin, and an aura of a lion at rest, a tiger waiting in the grass, a panther perched in the treetops.

If only she knew I was just as harmless as she was.

Hannah gasped and flinched into the backrest of her barstool. Her eyes wide, she turned around to look at the bar with new eyes as I dropped the veil of the Knoll itself, showing her exactly who she'd been drinking with.

The maenads at the central table sparkled like sunlight through a cask of mead. Their laughs had gone from infectious to undeniable, as their magic bubbled through their voices. It was intoxicating, effervescent as prosecco and as deadly as air through an IV. The tastes of pear, green apples, and an array of night-blooming flowers surrounded them.

In the corner, the three clurichaun sat unmasked. What had appeared as middle-aged working men, rough around the edges and a bit unkempt, revealed themselves to be sharper and more feral. Gone were the smiling brown eyes and inoffensive generic white skin. Their faces and arms were now mottled with the colors of pinot noir and chardonnay. Hands that had been unremarkable now sported long thick nails of oak, and the brown and black hair that adorned their heads were spotted through with grape leaves of various hues.

And at the door and the edge of the bar stood the most terrifying creatures in the bar. Mikka and Varon, the drake twins, steady and assured in their power. Though even in their true forms they looked ordinary in every aspect, with their dark brown hair, chestnut eyes, and Mediterranean olive skin tones, the heat that radiated from their auras marked them anything but human. The haze around them shimmered with menace and danger, and as Mikka smiled at the wide-eyed human, her eyes lit up from within with a dark, smoldering flame.

Then—of course she couldn't resist—Mikka snapped her fingers and opened up her palm, revealing a ball of fire and plasma roiling around like a miniature sun that had been doused in gasoline. Flames licked upward as Mikka grinned like a pyromaniacal goddess.

Hannah swiveled back to face me in terror. "You can all wield magic like that?"

"Well, no," I said, letting my exuberant and free grin fade into a chagrined pout. "Mikka's a drake, a fire fae, and—" I cut myself off. I didn't need to explain my magic, or lack thereof, to this human. I could see I'd made a mistake. There was fear on her face, as there rightly should be. But there was something else, something I had seen far too often in my long life.

Disgust.

I sighed. "Finish your drink, Hannah. Try not to stare. Then go get in your car and drive away. The world of the fae is not safe for you." The wards around the property would confuse any who might try to follow Hannah as she drove away. And if she stayed away from the fae after this moment, she might live a safe and happy life. It was the most safety I could offer her. It was all I could offer anyone.

CHAPTER TWO

I grabbed my ever-handy dishrag and turned my attention back to my job. The clurichaun had empty glasses, and they'd be wanting another round. Beer before six. Wine after.

It was a comforting ritual to all of us in these uncertain times.

I pulled the tap back on the brown ale and watched the glasses slowly fill one by one.

"You think someone should escort the human home?" Mikka was suddenly standing behind me, ostentatious fireball gone, watching the petrified human sip at her martini in silence.

"She'll be fine," I said, shutting the tap off and grasping the beer mugs by their handles. "The wards will keep anyone from following her. And I don't think she'll be back after our display."

"Pity."

Halfway around the bar, I snapped my attention back to Mikka and caught the subtle flame on the edges of her pupils. "Uh uh. No. Don't even think about it."

"But she's cute," Mikka protested. "She's got a great ass and has that whole innocent, powerless, I-can't-fight-my-way-out-of-a-pixie-cuddle-puddle thing going on."

I couldn't help myself. I laughed. "Cute. But no. Mikka, you have terrible taste in girls, and going for the weak ones is only going to get one of you hurt. Perhaps fatally."

I delivered the beers to the waiting clurichaun, who let up a cheer of thanks before I returned to Mikka. She was still pretending to pout. "Can I at least hook up with the maenads again? Brynn? Or Carissa? She's cute." Mikka waggled her eyebrows suggestively at one of the maenads at the center table, who to my horror smiled and waved back.

"Absolutely not!" I smacked Mikka's hand down. "Stop dating my regulars, Meeks. You can pick up a stray next time one comes in. Just make sure she's house-trained this time."

"That was one time!" Mikka protested. "How was I to know she was molting? Harpies usually stay home that time of the year."

Poor Mikka had been picking feathers out of her carpet for weeks.

"At least she wasn't a basilisk. You know, they shed their—"

"Stop!" She placed her hands over her ears. "I don't even want to hear it." She walked away, back toward the kitchen again, an extra swing in her swagger. She was no doubt heading back to charm a snack from Meara the cook and tease Tobin the dishwasher. The floor was too quiet for her at this hour. She'd emerge when the happy hour crowd started to pour in, ready for some excitement.

She was the complete opposite of her brother, who perched on his stool, taciturn and moody over by the door. I waved at Varon to get his attention, and he flipped a lock of thick black hair out of his narrowed eyes as he acknowledged me.

Bless his heart. That one could land in the middle of a lilin orgy and still turn a cold shoulder. He was so committed to his role as the dark, brooding drake, I frequently wondered how he and Mikka could be related, let alone twins. Drakes and dragons were supposed to be fiery, intense, passionate. Varon could give a Winter Queen frostbite.

With a smile, I gestured behind me to the bar, asking if he wanted anything, but he just raised his eyebrows. He was working. He wasn't about to compromise his focus with alcohol. He slouched back onto his stool, letting his hair fall back into his face, giving the impression that he was bored or napping.

A low voice spoke from behind me. "Send a Milagro over to him, and tell him I insist."

I turned to see my boss looming over me. Argus was a full-blooded dragon and stood at a considerable six-foot eleven. "One for you as well?" I said, already reaching for the back-shelf tequila.

"Double."

"Everything okay, boss?"

"Fan-fucking-tastic." He rounded the edge of the bar and took the stool at the edge closest to the kitchen. I poured the tequila, one for him, one for Varon, and one for myself. I placed one in front of the boss man and waved at Varon to fetch his own. He glared at the pair of us but stomped over, shot his tequila like a good boy, and then returned to his stool at the entrance.

I tapped my shot glass against the one Argus lifted, then dutifully knocked it back. The smooth fire of it warmed my belly. "So, what happened to snuff your flame?"

"Jocelyn."

"Who?"

He shook his head. "Newest waitress? Maenad that was supposed to start yesterday?"

I should probably remember her name, if I was going to devote time to worrying about the missing waitress. She was supposed to be covering for me, after all.

"Right. Jocelyn," I said. "She just up and disappeared, too, huh? Just like Anais." I darted a nervous eye at the heavy oak front door. The missing dryad had donated the wood herself, gifted it to Argus over a hundred years ago. She'd never have just up and left without leaving word.

"Yup. She never showed. I had to man bar last night, and Kaia covered the floor alone."

Kaia was our main waitress and would be in soon. She had worked at the Knoll for a good ten years already, and I knew she had been hoping the new hire could fill in for her on occasion, too. "Did Jocelyn at least have a good excuse?" I asked.

"Nope. No call, no messages. Just a complete no-show." Argus shook his head. This was the third no-show in the past month. "It shouldn't be this hard to hire a good waitress."

I wondered vaguely whether we should add the no-show wait staff to the tally of missing fae in the area. But I kept that to myself; bringing it up would probably not lighten the mood.

Instead, I smiled at Argus. "You're welcome to go bus some tables, if you like. I'm sure Tobin would prefer to lurk in the dish-pit all night instead of venturing among the regular people."

Argus gave me a look that would fry a lesser person. His eyes flashed with scorn, and a thin line of smoke escaped out through his right nostril. "Careful, Siobhan. I'm not in the mood."

The air around him began to shimmer as his heat rose. I had a hard time believing that a no-show waitress would leave him in a mood to flambe, but I knew better to push it when he was already smoking. Never poke an angry dragon. With my biggest smile, I winked at him and pushed the Milagro his way. "I'll leave you the bottle, then."

I turned to go check on the back of house before we got busy. Tobin, our hobgoblin bus boy, and Meara, our kikimora cook, would both be in the back prepping food, clearing taps, and generally avoiding anyone up front. I could save a lot of stress if I could get them anything they might need before we got busy.

I didn't make it to the kitchen before I felt the heat growing at my back. "Siobhan. We're not done."

Damn. I knew that had been too easy.

I slowly turned back around with a winning smile on my face. No sudden movements, keep the mood light, keep the boss happy. "What's up, Argus?" Yup. Nice and easy. Nothing contrived in the way my voice jumped in pitch at the end there.

He gestured to Hannah as she slunk past Varon and out the door. "Why did you show that human the truth? Why lower the glamour for her?"

Of course he knew. Argus knew everything that happened in his bar. I would have sworn there were cameras or spells monitoring the place, except I'd been here nearly fifty years and never seen evidence of any kind of surveillance.

I grabbed a cloth and began mopping up an imaginary puddle of something on the bar, avoiding his eyes. "I don't know. I guess I thought, if she was going to spend time among the fae, she deserved to know what she was dealing with. To protect herself."

Argus sighed. "Siobhan, we've talked about this. As harmless as humans seem individually, they are a real threat when they are armed with truth. You have to be more careful with them."

"But she was being hunted. Here, in the bar. She couldn't even know what kind of danger she was in. Not really. I figured if she saw what she was up against, she might be able to defend herself. Or run."

Argus shook his head. "It was too risky, Shiv. I know you empathize with them, but you could have dealt with the incubus and helped her without turning it into a confession of what you are."

I recoiled as if he had hit me. His words struck something deep and sparked my own fire. I threw my rag down on the bar top and glared at him. "And just what am I, Argus? Huh? What exactly? How about someone who knows what it's like to be helpless and hunted by those with actual magic? Who feels all too human sometimes? Too powerless."

He looked at me steadily for several beats, letting my words stand alone in their wasted breath. "No. You're someone too often compromised by her over-pronounced sense of justice and by her deep insecurities. I understand you wanted to reach out to her. I even understand why. But that doesn't give you the right to do what you did, to put everyone else here at risk." He leaned forward and made sure I was looking directly at him. "And baby girl? You've never been powerless."

I closed my mouth, my eyes hot, and my cheeks enflamed. "It's almost sunset. I'm going to go open the Gate." Ignoring the fact that dusk was at least three hours away, I stormed out from behind the bar. I pushed past Mikka, who emerged from the kitchen, snacking on some fried green beans. "Cover tables until Kaia gets here," I called over my shoulder, then marched past Tobin in the dish-pit and ignored Meara's call from the walk-in refrigerator. If Argus was feeling so full of sympathy and wisdom, then he could deal with them.

One push out the back door onto the pub's expansive back porch, and the humidity of the early summer afternoon engulfed me. As I leaned out against the wooden railing, I gulped in the thick heat and let it fill my tight lungs with its familiar languidness. The hot press of the air overwhelmed the heat of Argus's comment and criticism, cutting off the anger and shame that gripped my chest.

I knew he was probably right. I shouldn't have revealed myself and all of the bar to Hannah. We kept glamours in place for a reason. The fae's ability to hide in plain sight was what had kept us safe among the humans for millennia.

And yet my old frustrations of being forced to hide what I was had pushed me to the rash and reckless decision. I'd spent most of my life hiding one side of myself or another, trying to pass for something I wasn't or wasn't enough of. I was too fae to walk down the street without a disguise and too human to possess any real magic. I couldn't summon flames or speak to the trees or unleash the winds or rains. I could only taste the magic of others, and how useful was that really?

Still, it didn't give me the right to remove the scales from a human's eyes. I was risking everyone in the bar, everyone Hannah might come across later. It had been impulsive and ill-conceived, and no matter how I might try to justify it as for her own protection, I knew it had been for my benefit.

If she, a human, had willingly accepted the fae as we truly were without glamours to make us palatable, normal, less than, then maybe she could have accepted me: both the fae part as well as the human.

Her recoil and disgust was proof that it wasn't going to happen. Not with her.

I sighed into the press of the late afternoon. At least that bigotry might keep her alive.

It didn't matter how much Mikka insisted to me that the city was safe. The fact still remained that several of my favorite regulars were no longer regularly showing up. Anais's abandoned trees confronted me every time I drove in to work, but there were other holes in the bar.

Kari and Hina came to mind; the two maenads were gregarious, karaoke regulars, and often egregiously outspoken in their criticism of the Summer and Winter Courts. I had thought those two were on their way to organizing a march on the Summer palace earlier in the year, the way they carried on after a few rounds of drinks. They were all about power this, artificial scarcity that. Then within a week of each other, they had stopped coming: no karaoke, no happy hours, no Sunday brunches.

There were rumors of more who'd disappeared, fae who skirted the edges of our society, passing from the Eternal Realm to here in the Iron. Those fae who might not have close ties to anyone in town or might just be passing through, but they'd been noted and then missed. A sylph or fire fae who'd just arrived through the Gate might have stopped in for a drink at the Knoll, and then was never seen again.

It was enough to unnerve my customers, and so it was enough for me to pay attention to.

Maybe it was time to re-up the wards.

I made a mental note to ask Argus about the magical protections on the Knoll and our grounds. Then I remembered I was mad at him and huffed in frustration.

"Thought you were going to man the Gate," a low voice said.

I turned to my left to find Varon leaned up against the railing a few feet down from me. He was not looking at me, his attention drifting instead along the edge of the property line of the Greenwood Knoll. The large pub had a deep covered porch that circled the entirety of the building, with an expansive lower deck a few feet below filled with tables, wicker couches, and Adirondack chairs that faced out to the Chattahoochee River and the tree line that enclosed the property.

The path that led to the Gate seemed to hold Varon's attention, as his eyes narrowed for a moment. Then he turned his smoldering green gaze to me and raised a single eyebrow.

"The Gate will hold until I'm slightly less enraged." I folded my arms and leaned back over the railing.

"You're not enraged," he said without moving from his post, his attention back out past the river. "You're disappointed."

I gawked, ready to transfer my anger to him, but looking at his steady profile, I knew he was right. Everyone around me was right. I hated how young and naive it made me feel to have the people around me naming my emotions and interpreting my reactions while I spluttered and flailed. It made me feel that my response to things was invalid or unwarranted.

"Thanks," I mumbled. "That's helpful."

Varon didn't react to my sarcasm. "For what it's worth, I've asked the Far Darrig clan to watch our perimeter for a few weeks."

I turned and blinked at him. "The redcaps?" Redcaps were a particularly fearsome species of fae, known for their territoriality and their willingness to shed blood. If Varon was calling in such serious reinforcements, he either had some major favors to trade with or he was willing to assume the cost of their backup because he thought it worth it.

"I still think there's a reasonable explanation for most of the disappearances." He turned to me then and stood at his full height. "But I trust your instincts." He moved toward the door, but as he passed me, he put a hand on my shoulder. The heat from his touch spread down my arm and back, settling some of the anxiety that pulsed through my insides. He squeezed and leaned in to speak in my ear, his breath warm and familiar. "You don't owe anyone anything."

In an instant, he'd slipped back into the bar without a sound.

I closed my eyes and groaned.

I knew deep down that he'd meant every word to be supportive. Varon was the watcher of the bar; he missed nothing and understood everything. He'd seen my reaction to the human almost becoming victim in my bar, my desire to help her, and my hurt at being called out by Argus. Varon had meant to assure me that I didn't have to prove myself. That I was enough just as I was. Half human, half fae, with or without active magic.

Still, his assurances had the opposite effect. It made me spiral a bit more into my thoughts. I may not have had to prove myself to anyone here at the Knoll, but a huge part of why I was here, why I was a Keeper, was because I did owe something. I owed it to the community, I owed it to my heritage, and I owed it to myself. I had a job to do here.

And I should probably get to it.

CHAPTER THREE

The cicadas buzzed louder than ever as I pushed myself off the rail and hopped down the wooden steps to the lower deck and then into the grassy backyard of the Knoll. Rolling my shoulders, I pulled a glamour back around me like a security blanket, settling into a comfortably human look as I stomped down the pebbled path. I probably wouldn't encounter anyone else at this time of day, but it was second nature to assume my normal human camouflage.

To my right and left, the fire pits and assortment of teak chairs and tables sat empty in the mid-afternoon. Soon, the assorted solitary fae of Atlanta would be reclining around the fires, drinking, and seducing each other with alacrity.

At this hour, though, only the cicadas were mating.

The Chattahoochee along the edge of the property appeared still and calm, but I knew just beneath the surface, it pulsed and pulled at the edges of Atlanta, bringing breath and power to the city just as any living body of water. I let it ground me, restore a taste of the magic within and around me.

At the bank, I followed the bend of the path that ran parallel to the water and then disappeared into the trees along the northwest edge of the Knoll's property. The pine, oak, dogwood, and sycamore trees closed in around me as I walked, and I could feel the power of the Greenwood Gate as I approached. It knew I was coming, and it called to me.

Within a few hundred feet, the winding wooded path opened onto a clearing that was as familiar to me as the main dining room of the Knoll.

The glade was less than fifty yards across, extending down toward the edge of the river and encircled by thick trunks and undergrowth. Blackberry bushes occupied most of the north edge of the space, while honeysuckle vines and wild azaleas took up the southern edge. The ground was covered with various mosses instead of grass, and it gave the impression of a thick emerald carpet.

In the center of the clearing stood the Greenwood Gate.

The Gate Between Worlds was the connection point between this, the Iron Realm, the realm of the humans, and the Eternal Realm, the realm of the fae. Through the arch of the Greenwood Gate, anyone could pass from the human world to Fairy, moving across two different dimensions as though one were walking through a simple doorway between rooms.

One would expect it to be grand and impressive, signifying its consequence with its presence. It should be imposing, towering over mortal and immortal alike, trimmed with crystals and jewels, speaking of wealth, importance, magic. After all, the Fairy Gate stood astride the veil between the mortal and immortal worlds. It held all magic at bay on one side and partitioned all growth and change on the other; all immortal, unchangeable potential lay beyond, and the inevitability of death and life here. It was the only crossable boundary between our worlds for hundreds of miles in this realm, and I had always felt there should be something remarkable about that.

Instead, it was plain. It seemed to be composed of well-worn riverstones piled up by hand in a crude stone arch. Stretching the width of four people, the tight transverse of the curve held the slick riverstones in place without any visible mortar or adhesive. It was large, sure, but not really extraordinary. There were no signs or plaques, no indications at all that this single landmark was anything more than a hastily constructed walkway for getting from one part of the dirt path to another.

If a mortal stumbled across it, they would likely be confused why there was a stone doorway to nowhere, but they would continue on their way, none the wiser. Even if that normal human tried to pass through it, nothing would happen. It was a portal to nowhere: strange, but ultimately forgettable.

But even a fae that had never visited this particular pathway would recognize what it was by the markings along the inside of the arch. Ancient sigils were subtly carved into the face of the rocks, deep magic that I'm not sure any fae alive could fully explain or replicate. It didn't matter what they said; these sigils spelled out the Way to Fairy, and they were awakened with blood.

Awakening the Way was why I was here.

I stepped up to the archway and pulled the small blade I kept concealed in my back pocket. My knife served many purposes: stripping foil from wine bottles, slicing citrus peels for garnish, and letting my own blood flow to open the Greenwood Gate.

I wasn't just the best bartender at the Greenwood Knoll; I was also an avowed Keeper of the Gate. That made me an ambassador for those coming through the Gate, but it also meant I was responsible for opening the Gate daily to allow magic to pass freely through the realms.

And that required a sacrifice of magic and blood.

Lifting my knife to my left forearm, I ignored the vulnerable veins at my wrist and around my elbow and chose a fleshy part of my arm to make a shallow cut in my flesh. Blood immediately welled up to the surface and pooled before dribbling off to the sides of my arm. I dragged my index finger along the stinging cut, gathering blood, before swiping it along the edges of the doorway, tracing the outlines of the stones with the sigils. I'd learned long ago I didn't need to trace the sigils exactly; they could be activated with just a few drops of blood freely given.

Dragging my finger along the etched stones on either side of the archway, I spoke to the Gate. Technically, I didn't have to say anything, I didn't even have to think anything. I could open the Gate with nothing but the magic in my blood.

But most times, I imagined the Gate could hear me.

"Hey, sweetie. Time to shine." I stroked the smooth riverstones with my finger, tracing their curves as they connected, their symbols and forgotten language like braille under my fingers.

The Gate responded with a shiver. As my blood soaked in, a ripple spread from the edges of the doorway, crossing the empty space between and undulating for a span of seconds before shifting inward. The empty space contracted and snapped into place with a power that I could feel and taste. The feel was like an electric shock, waking my cells with a power that was alien and more familiar than my own breath. It was like waking up, or getting a jolt of adrenaline. My entire body vibrated with energy that was both concentrated and diffuse.

The taste of it was green and alive, like a shot of wheat grass and gin. It was floral and botanical but more full of life and potential than anything you could consume. It lived as it crossed my tongue, and it danced through me, happy to visit with someone it recognized.

"Good to see you, too." I took a few steps away from the archway and sank down into the moss. I crossed my legs and let my cut arm hang to the side, the blood flowing freely, an offering to the Gate.

I closed my eyes and breathed in, accepting the life and power and potential it wanted to offer me and giving it the sacrifice it demanded.

Even without active magic, soaking in the power of the Gate at this proximity made me feel like I was full fae, like I could take on the world. The pure possibility of the magic that flowed from Fairy into this world and into me made me feel almost pure blooded. It was exhilarating, like an infusion of energy. Sometimes it left me feeling drunk with potential, buzzing with a euphoric high.

The blood loss, though, could make my head spin. Even as the Gate offered magic, it exacted a cost. I wasn't entirely sure what all it took from me. Stronger fae with active magic always noticed their abilities diminished for a day or so after opening a Gate. Sylphs who could conjure hurricanes could only manage a small breeze; fire fae who regularly stoked bonfires were resigned to lighting candles and smoking embers.

I had no active magic to sacrifice, so the cost was negligible. Still, the process could leave me dizzy and in need of an espresso if I held the Gate too long.

Twenty minutes should be enough for today.

It was just past midday, and there shouldn't be too many fae attempting to cross between the worlds. Those who opened the Gate for themselves chose crossings at dawn and dusk, avoiding the heat of the day and the midnight hours, when the crossings seemed to take more of a sacrifice. Most common fae opted to cross through when the Gate was already open, accepting the sacrifice of the one who created the way through. This meant they were at the whim and availability of the Gate Keepers.

I knew some Keepers across the country opted only to open once or twice a week. We at the Greenwood Knoll went above and beyond to open twice a day: at dawn and dusk. It was part of what made Atlanta a prestige destination in the Iron Realm.

I leaned back on my hands and focused on the sting of the cut in my arm, on the blood that trailed down to my wrist and into the ground. My skin itched with the urge to heal. Every fiber of my flesh that had been split apart tingled, reaching out to its mate, trying to find resolution, healing. After this many years as Gate Keeper, it took more intention to keep my wound open than it took to heal it.

After waiting a few minutes, I concluded that no one was coming through the Gate this afternoon. I tried to focus on the drone of the cicadas, to fall into a meditative state and keep my blood sacrifice flowing. The bright heat of the day beat down on me, and I could imagine a languid state settling upon me like a blanket, drifting and coating me with silence, with the peace of doing my duty to my community.

This was my calling. I should find peace in it. I was giving back to the people I was born to serve. I released magic from Fairy, let it pass through the Gate and filter to the people of our city. I might not be powerful or have great magical gifts to lead my city, but I was able to serve them.

Usually that thought brought me peace. Today, though, it just left me agitated.

Something was happening to the fae in my city, and instead of doing something about it, I was lounging around soaking up magic like it was sunlight and I had a vitamin D deficiency. There had to be something more I could do than sit around and bleed. Maybe I could try and track down the missing fae, see if Mikka was right and they were following some whim. If she was wrong and something had happened to them, if there was a danger threatening my people, then I should face it.

Right, I snorted. *Me and what magic?*

I sucked in an irritated breath and nearly choked on the thick wetness of the air and the unmistakable taste of death at the back of my throat.

It was as dank as black mold and as sweet as rotten meat. I gagged on the gritty sensation of black ash and stale air on my tongue, coating the back of my throat, and raining down my esophagus. Death was near, and it was fresh.

I turned away from the Gate, looking for the source. The sickly sweet taste was stronger by the river. Branches and tree roots jutted out into the water from the birch, oaks, and magnolias.

There.

Ahead. Something was floating in the water. The source of the taste.

Not thinking, I started running toward the strange shape I could just make out through the trees at the edge of the banks. Maybe I could help.

My boots sank into the soft earth as I got closer to the water's edge. Then I saw it. All of it.

Tangled in the half-submerged branches of a fallen pine tree. Blue fabric, black hair, bloated and spongy golden skin. Open, sightless orange eyes. Djinn.

His throat a gaping, bloodless wound.

Dead.

No.

Murdered.

Only when that final word worked its way up out of my throat and settled fully in my mouth did I begin screaming for help.

CHAPTER FOUR

I don't know how long I screamed or how loud. I just knew I was alone with the body, then help arrived.

Varon was the first to come running, with Mikka close on his heels. They each held a huge ball of flames in hand, ready to go to war, but they pulled up short when they saw me standing by the edge of the Chattahoochee River.

Exchanging a look, the twins doused their flames and moved cautiously to my side. Varon continued past me and stooped down by the body, while Mikka came and put a steady hand on my shoulder. "Are you okay?"

"It's a djinn," I whispered, unable to take my gaze from the body. There was a dull film gathered over what should have been fiery gold of the djinn's eyes. The flame snuffed out, he was left with a watered-down amber, the color of cheap beer: more water than lager.

Long black hair floated around his face, clinging to the branches his body was lodged against. His blue shirt was torn in places; his black pants twisted about his legs. The golden skin of the djinn had been rendered dull and lifeless, like a fuzzy peach that had been dropped to rot on the ground beneath the tree, or an oxidized copper pipe, left out in the rain for decades of neglect. It was spongy and soft and bloated.

I'd never seen a dead fae before. If his eyes had been closed, he might have looked human, but even in death, he was unmistakably fae. "He's dead."

"I know." Mikka gave my shoulder a small squeeze. "Let's go back to the bar." She guided an arm behind my back as she lifted me to my feet—I hadn't even realized I'd fallen to my knees—and carefully steered me away from the river and pointed me toward the path beyond the Gate.

I realized belatedly that in the minutes that had passed, my arm had healed and the Gate sealed shut again. Lifeless. Like the djinn in the river.

"But I have to help him," I protested weakly, my voice raw and scratchy. How long had I screamed for help? I couldn't take my eyes off him, floating, bloated. The skin of his neck wound feathery soft and blanched along the edges. Would he feel as spongy as he looked? I shuddered, thankful I didn't have to stay here with the ashy, black taste of the fire fae's death on my tongue.

"You can't do anything here, sweetness." There was no malice in her words, just concern and regret.

"It's okay, Siobhan. We'll take care of it," Varon insisted.

"We?" I leaned back into Mikka's arms. I didn't want her to let me go, to leave me alone with the taste of death. Not that it mattered. I knew the feel of ash on my tongue would linger, no matter how far I got from the body.

"We," Argus said arriving at the head of the path. He ignored the body, his attention on me for the moment. "It's okay, Shiv." He put an immense hand on my shoulder and gave me a small squeeze. "Go back to the Knoll. Get a drink. Mikka will take care of you." Mikka nodded with a sympathetic smile.

Each of them stood around me, ignoring the body, carefully watching me for something. Signs that I was going to fall apart? Cry? Scream? All seemed like good options at the moment.

Instead, I returned Mikka's nod. "Okay, yeah."

I let her lead me away but got only a few feet before I wheeled back on Argus and Varon. "Someone should report this. We have to call this in."

I said "we." What I meant was "not me."

Beside me, Mikka stiffened, while Argus pursed his lips, and Varon cleared his throat. They all knew who we should report it to. And they all knew exactly why I couldn't be the one to do it.

The arm around me pulled me more insistently toward the path. "We will," Mikka said, soothingly. "Argus can call it in." She didn't wait for any assurance but began half carrying me up the path. "How does a glass of Malbec sound, sugar?"

I stopped fighting and let her steer me, stumbling only a little on the uneven ground. "No, wine is for relaxing. Or celebrating. Or socializing."

"Whiskey, then?"

I nodded. A hard burn could take the edge off whatever I was feeling. I reached past the unease in the pit of my stomach for the panic that would no doubt begin to bubble up, but my feelings were dulled. I should be panicking, shouldn't I? I'd found a dead body. A dead fae.

What did panic feel like, anyway? Was it numb? Unsteady? Erratic and irrationally terrified?

Whiskey. Whiskey was perfect for dealing with this. Wash the bitter taste of it out of my mouth.

The taste of ash and rot. Of fear and grief. Of rusted iron and stagnant, fetid water pooling in my lungs.

"Can we drink on the porch?" I asked in a small voice. I couldn't go inside or face customers yet. I needed space, clean air.

Mikka chuckled. "Yeah, we can do that."

She escorted me up the back steps and motioned to one of the cedar rocking chairs that faced the river. "Sit. I'll grab a drink and ask Kaia to keep holding down the fort while we take care of this."

"Oh, she's early," I said automatically, though I realized I didn't really know what time it was. The sun seemed lower than it should be. How long had I been out here? It might be getting close to happy hour. I should prep the well and garnishes. Get my custom simple syrups from the back. We had new specials this week.

I frowned. How could I worry about drink specials when there was a body at the Gate? This meant serious trouble.

As a bartender and a Gate Keeper, I wasn't just commissioned with pouring drinks and opening the Gate to let the magic flow between the realms. I was also supposed to protect the peace. The Gate, the path, and the Knoll were sanctuaries; they were safe spaces for all who crossed between the Iron Realm and the Eternal Realm.

At least they were supposed to be.

A dead fae this close to the Greenwood Gate was beyond troubling. The Deep Laws were supposed to protect all travelers. Politics, personal squabbles, power struggles between the many factions of our kind were put aside when approaching and departing the Gate.

My only hope was that the poor djinn had been killed elsewhere and just happened to wash up near the Gate. Unhappy coincidence I could deal with.

Because the alternative would mean trouble.

Self-contempt rose up like bile from my stomach. There was a dead djinn in the river, and I was fretting about the political fallout. I was my mother's daughter.

I stood and spit over the edge of the railing.

"Djinn left a taste with you, didn't he?" Mikka said, emerging back onto the porch with a whiskey in either hand. "Rinse it out with this."

"Thanks." I accepted the drink and took a healthy swig, rinsing it around to chase the bile and ash. As I swallowed, the smooth burn of the smoke and peat eased the clenched tension out of my throat.

Glass in hand, Mikka leaned against the wooden railing, her back to the river, and looked down at me, staring at the place in the woods where Argus and Varon were no doubt dealing with the body. Would they struggle with pulling the body from the branches? Would they have to close his eyes? Would the body be cold as no djinn should ever be?

"Stop thinking about it," Mikka said. "It does nobody any good to dwell on death."

"Tell that to my tongue," I said, taking another swallow of liquid fire.

Mikka took her own sip. "What did he taste like?"

"Like iron and ash and rotten vegetables."

"Huh," Mikka said, drawing out the poor imitation of a word, and took another sip.

I waited for her to say more, but she kept her tongue. "Huh, what?" I prompted, standing up and leaning back against the rail to mimic her position.

"Nothing," she said, before tipping her glass back and draining her whiskey in one gulp. "I'm going to go man the door until the men-folk come back. Take your time, sugar." She squeezed my shoulder and smiled before pushing off the railing and propelling herself through the door.

I appreciated her giving me space to process, but if I spent any more time on this porch, I'd just end up obsessing over the body and what it meant. It wasn't up to me what happened from here. Argus was going to deal with the details. He'd report the body, get it taken away before it caused trouble with the evening crossings or tonight's happy hour crowd.

All I needed to do was get back to the bar, prep for the night rush, and try not to mentally connect a dead fae to the missing dryads, maenads, and assorted waitresses who never showed up for their shifts.

Denial ain't just a river in Egypt.

I didn't get past the kitchen before a voice snarled out, "Siobhan!"

Meara, the Knoll's cook and resident kikimora, was clearly not happy about something.

Meara was a genius in the kitchen. She made the best hearty stews in the South, so thick you could stand a spoon up in the middle of the bowl. Brunswick stew, burgoo, jambalaya: she made them all. She'd recently embraced the modern culinary movement toward small plates of snackable food with creative twists on Southern culture, like her collard green quesadillas and mac-n-cheese egg rolls. She was always happy to try something new to impress our clientele.

At the moment, though, Meara was anything but happy. Lips turned down under her beak-like nose and arms crossed as she fumed by the kitchen door, I could almost picture her as the stereotypical swamp witch.

"Meara," I said, almost relieved. Angry cooks I could deal with much more easily than I could dead djinn. "My love, whatever is the matter?"

"The hot sauce I special ordered from the Queen of New Orleans. It has been three weeks. It still has not arrived, and I cannot make my burgoo without it. I put it on the weekend menu because you promised it would be here by now."

She had been talking about that burgoo for at least two months after she had visited her sister up in Louisville, Kentucky. She insisted that the dish was made all wrong in the Iron Realm, but only because the humans didn't have access to the right spices and root vegetables. There was a pepper that grew in parts of Fairy that would do perfectly, and the head cook at the Queen's palace in New Orleans made a hot sauce from it.

"I'm sorry, Meara. Delivery sheet said it arrived this morning. Milo signed off on it and everything. Could you have overlooked it? Mis-shelved it?"

Meara bared her teeth at me in a purely instinctual reaction to frustration and anger. She quickly tucked them back away behind her lips. She did not like to be second-guessed. "If I had touched it at all, I wouldn't have lost it. If it arrived, which I doubt it actually did, it never entered my domain. I know where everything is in my kitchen." She narrowed her eyes. "Including the missing rue, feverfew, and extra crastum root you've been nicking at the end of your shifts. Don't think I don't notice."

I had the good sense to blush and drop my gaze. I had been taking the crastum root to make a tea so I could sleep without dreaming. Old recipe from my mother's kitchen.

Then again, I shouldn't have to apologize for anything. I was the one who had placed the orders for the extra root, and I was paying for it out of my cut of the tips each night. "I'll ask Milo if he shelved the hot sauce somewhere else. It might be in the cellar or behind the bar. He might have thought it was a new bitter. I'll keep an eye out, okay?"

Meara sniffed but turned back to the kitchen. "When Varon finishes disposing of the body by the river, you send him to me. I will make up a substitute menu item for tonight, and he is the only one of you who will tell me the truth about its brilliance."

I pursed my lips. I appreciated her need for an honest food critic, but the way she casually admitted to knowing about the dead djinn by the river made me worry how fast word was spreading. I didn't think this was news that should get out immediately. If it got out to our clientele, it could cause a panic or political complications. Or worse, it could stop people coming to the Knoll.

And I had a mortgage to pay for.

CHAPTER FIVE

It didn't take long for things to get crazy at the bar. It was only a Thursday, and we always managed to maintain a regular group, but this was a bigger crowd than normal. Friday would be busier, and Saturday would be packed for karaoke night, but we had more than enough people to keep us moving. Plenty of our regulars showed up for a few hours of relaxation, and despite no one coming through when I was manning the Gate, there was a fresh batch of travelers who came through later on their own and stopped in for a drink or two.

Argus personally escorted the newest visitors from Fairy, who were beyond pleased when the gruff owner offered to pay for the first round of cocktails. He then told me that Varon would be along shortly and that everything had been taken care of before he retired to his office upstairs.

I just managed to grab his arm before he dashed up the stairs behind the bar. "You're going to report it, right?" I needed his assurance.

"Yes, Siobhan. I am going upstairs to make a report now. I don't imagine it would be good if the news got to the Queen through gossip and hearsay. It will go through all the proper channels, I assure you."

"Good, good," I mumbled, relived he was going to take care of it so I didn't have to. "Thank you."

His annoyed look softened as I released his arm. "Baby girl, stop fretting. You just worry about having a good Thursday. These people are thirsty. And most have nowhere else they can go for a good time around here. You show them that even if we're their only choice, we're still the best one."

I beamed up at him and saluted. "Yes, sir, boss. You can count on me."

He didn't return my smile, as the skin around his eyes grew taut. "I know I can."

"Hey boss?" I called up at his disappearing back.

He stopped midway up the stairs but didn't answer and didn't turn around.

"Don't worry. Whoever did this, whoever hurt that guy? You'll find them. And they'll burn for what they did."

He turned around at that and regarded me solemnly. "They will at that." Then without another word, he disappeared up and into his office.

Nothing left for me but to do my job.

Several elementals had arrived and promptly grouped up by type. The sylphs congregated with other air spirits, dryads and diwata and other tree spirits circled a distant table, and the metal and earth workers pulled together in a corner nook. Homeworkers, like the brownies, dobies, hobs, and a few monaciellos, took up residence near the hearth and sent occasional representatives to the bar for liquid reinforcements.

Alden, Cormac, and Baerd, the three clurichaun who had so gleefully cheered the ejection of Lloyd the incubus a lifetime ago, had welcomed another pair of their kind: Gair and Leland. They had a bottle of whiskey in the center of the table, and it looked like they'd need another one before the night even got going. Gair waved at me with a smile, and Leland smacked him before he whispered something to the table. They all ducked their heads and began a heated discussion that required a new round of whiskey pours. They were really going to make it a Thursday.

It wasn't just the regular solitaries in tonight, either. Several sidhe and Court-affiliated fae sat in their fancy dress and sipped at whiskeys and bourbons. They should have looked out of place in their rose-petal and fern-leaf robes, but as more and more glamours dropped as the night went on, as the fangs and tails and pointed ears emerged, their refinery added to the visual feast.

The solitary maenads attracted my attention the most that night. Okay, they attracted my attention most nights. They were not only gorgeous and vivacious, as creatures of Dionysus, they had a taste for wine and sex and fun. The maenads were my most faithful regulars.

Dozens of maenads lived in Atlanta, and I always had at least three or four of them in the bar at any one time. They were among my best tippers, and about half of their troupe had worked here at the Knoll, at one point or another. Almost every one of them had been fired for being unreliable with collecting payment for the drinks they served or for failing to take seriously their duty to the sanctity of the Gate, but at least they had brought an enthusiasm to the job.

Or at least to the wine part of the job.

The three maenads from this afternoon had expanded their group by at least four times their original size. The new arrivals had pulled together a few heavy wood tables and piled up gifts of various sizes on one of them. It looked like we were hosting a special occasion, and that meant even bigger tips.

I grabbed two bottles of champagne from the fridge under the bar. A good vintage, from a year with alternating heavy rain and heat waves that produced some high-quality grapes. The average customer wouldn't appreciate the subtleties of the wine, but the maenads always did.

"So, what are we celebrating here, girls?" I placed one of the bottles in the middle of the largest table and displayed the other to Talisa, one of the original four girls from this afternoon and a leader of the group.

"Perfect!" Talisa exclaimed, already unscrewing the wire cage over the cork. "See, I told y'all my girl would take care of us."

The group talked excitedly amongst themselves, but they all kept trading looks that seemed to center on one girl I didn't know well. She sat there with a beatific smile as she absorbed the energy they fed her.

I looked at her, and then at the hands she clasped protectively over her stomach.

"No!" I said, filled with the same excitement. It was contagious.

She nodded enthusiastically as her smile grew wider.

Tears sprang into my eyes. "Mab's blessed womb! You're pregnant?" I didn't bother keeping my voice down.

The maenads erupted into squeals of delight, and there were spontaneous hugs all around. Patrons around us broke into applause, and they spread the word quickly.

"Oh, honey!" I popped the cork, passed the bottle to Talisa, and flew to the pregnant maenad, sweeping her into a hug. "How wonderful!" I squeezed her about the shoulders, avoiding anything lower, careful to protect the precious life within her. A fae baby. To a solitary fae. I couldn't believe it.

It had been years, maybe even decades, since I had seen a pregnant fae outside of the Courts. The idea of a fae nurturing, birthing, raising a child beyond the Court's breeding program? The possibility filled me with so much hope, I couldn't help the tears that cascaded down my face and onto the pregnant woman's shoulders.

"I'm sorry," I said, pushing away, and swiping at the stains my blubbering left on her floral silk dress. "I don't even know your name."

"Semele. Semele Tyne," she said shyly. "But call me Mellie, please, Your Highness."

I cringed. "No, no. No royalty here. If I can call you Mellie, you call me Siobhan. Or Shiv. Please."

"I will, Siobhan. Thank you." She seemed genuinely pleased as she maintained her radiant smile.

"I'll be back with glasses for all of you. And can I get you anything special, Mellie? Are you craving anything? Meara is a brilliant cook, and I can mix up anything to drink. Non-alcoholic if you prefer it." Alcohol and inebriation didn't affect the fae in the same ways it did humans and was probably perfectly safe to drink while pregnant. But anyone who has tried for seventy plus years for a single child often chooses to take as few risks as possible.

"I'd love some pineapple juice, actually, if you have it? With three limes. And some peanuts? If you have those? Boiled peanuts?"

I laughed as she leaned into the cravings cliche. "I can do all of that. Meara keeps a pot of peanuts on slow cook on the back burner all day. I'll send Kaia over with a bowl."

My feet barely touched the ground all the way back to the bar. A baby! It had been so long.

The fae of the Iron Realm might slowly be going extinct.

But, not tonight.

Mellie's birth wouldn't be because of the Court-sanctioned breeding programs. It wouldn't be through careful curation of mating partners, assessed for potential fertility and virility. This woman wouldn't have to pledge herself to a political system just in the hopes of one day having a child of her own.

She was a maenad, a free spirit, a solitary fae, and a patron of the Greenwood Knoll. No, her child would be free.

That called for celebration.

"Attention," I called as I climbed atop a step stool behind the bar. "In honor of the new mom-to-be Semele Tyne, for the next half hour, all beers are on me!"

Such an enthusiastic cheer went up from the crowd that I was sure only half of it could be for the free drinks. Kaia and Mikka, both beaming themselves, rushed back behind the bar with me and lined up pint glasses to fill.

The next hour was a rush of filling drinks and tallying the eventual cut to my pay at the end of the night. Everyone took advantage of the celebration, getting multiple refills and toasting Mellie and her unborn child. Luckily, to offset some of that, there were multiple tips dropped in the large jugs at the ends of the bar. Much of it in the form of Fairy coin.

A huldra newly arrived from the Eternal Realm leaned over the bar as I was filling his third pint of the hour. His race was a type of incubus, known for their shapeshifting abilities, and as he talked over the bar, his eyes kept distracting me as his pupils contracted from narrow cat's eyes to snake slits to the all-encompassing black of horse eyes. He was so drunk by then, I didn't know that he noticed his inability to hold form. Or maybe he was just that excited.

"You can believe it? A real fae child?"

"Yeah," I said, laughing a bit as his heavy Fairy accent became more pronounced with his inebriation. "It happens here from time to time." I didn't add that I couldn't think of a time it had happened without serious intervention.

"Nothing is better! This is why my sister and I come here. Life is possible. The Winter Court? They deny it. Say this world pollutes our heritage, our Magic. But Life?" I could hear the capitalization of his words as he spoke, and I smiled at his enthusiasm. "Life makes every sacrifice worth it."

"You wanted a lager, right?"

"Kellerbier, if you have it?" His eyes shifted again, leaving a pale cloudy cast to them. "My grandfather taught monks how to preserve their yeast in the beer."

Every fae had their own tale of ancestors teaching the humans something special. As though the fae were the only good thing to happen to the people of this realm. "Uh huh," I said, tugging on the draft pull for the Franzikaner. It wasn't quite the barrel-fresh beer he was looking for, but I wasn't about to waste my good stuff on free drinks for already wasted fae. "Enjoy, sweetie."

Without looking up from the glasses I was eager to put in the washer, I turned my body to the next thirsty customer. "What can I get you? Only the beer is free, and only for about," I checked the ancient clock above the fireplace, "seven more minutes."

"Shiv, if you serve me beer, I swear I'm reporting you to the Court for violence against nobility."

I snapped out of my autopilot mode and focused on the fae in front of me. "Shiro! Hi!"

Shiro Harada was not only a regular and a good friend of mine; he was also a scribe for the Summer Queen of Atlanta and an official member of Court. And he was one of my oldest friends.

He described himself as a Canadian mutt, but he was anything but. Pureblood fox fae back through four generations, he was one of the most perfect specimens of vulpine beauty. His mother was a kitsune who had moved to Canada from Osaka back in the 1930s to marry and mate with a great grandson of the trickster fae, Reynard the Fox.

His lineage made Shiro one of the only true-blood fox fae in the western world, yet he was always shy to claim it. He took a scribe job at Court when he could have been a major political player and often spent his downtime slumming it with the solitary fae at Greenwood.

"Karaoke isn't until tomorrow," I reminded him as I turned to grab the amaretto and cognac for his French Connection cocktail. "And if you haven't brushed up on our duet, I may never forgive you."

"And I may never forgive you for making me play the simpering love interest in a movie musical," he replied, his dark eyes narrowed and accusatory. He was always complaining about my choice of musical duets, but straight-forward rock duets were too played out.

"At least it's not Paradise by the Dashboard Light again," I countered as I poured the ingredients for his cocktail and began to shake it up.

"Paradise is a terrible duet, Shiv. It's like twelve minutes long!"

"It's not even nine," I said, handing him his properly bittered French Connection. "And we got a standing ovation the last time."

"Only because you're serving everyone's drinks."

I wrinkled my nose at him. "Possibly true, but it's not nice to point that out."

He shook his head and laughed before sipping his drink. "New cognac?" I love that he knew immediately.

"Got a new distiller with connections with the Paris Court. They've never done wide distribution, so I only have a small batch for you, but if you like it, I'll order more."

Shiro sniffed. "Parisian? The Bordeaux Court has better vineyards and distilleries." Still, as he took another sip of his drink, his bourgeois sneer softened. "Though I suppose this has merits."

I snorted and moved to fill another drink order that came in from Kaia. Two local lagers, a mead, two wines, and an Amaretto Sour. I wrinkled my nose at the cocktail but quickly got to work. Two beers, wines and mead were quickly ready. The Amaretto Sour order was more complicated. Was this a guest newly arrived from Fairy or someone who'd been in the Iron Realm for a hundred years? Would they be expecting something with easy, commonly processed ingredients or something more herbal?

The fact that they went with an Amaretto Sour insinuated they'd been in the United States for at least a few decades. They'd likely be expecting something easy, slightly almond, but sweet. I figured I'd split the difference with a decent Amaretto liqueur, some prepared lemon juice, simple syrup, soda, and a hefty orange slice. If they expected sour mix and cherries, well, they'd have to realize they were in the wrong bar.

I mixed the drink, no doubt grimacing through the whole thing, given Shiro's reaction.

"That looked like it physically hurt you."

"It did," I admitted.

I still poured it into a rocks glass with a nice clear round globe of ice and put it on a tray with the other drinks. Kaia came to collect with a wince that said she knew exactly what I was going to say.

"If they don't like it, tell them to order a rum and Coke next time. I'm not doing that again."

"Got it," she said, taking the tray and whisking it away.

I turned and gave Shiro my full attention again. "All right. Why are you really here?"

He pouted. "I can't just be here to enjoy a drink with my favorite fairy princess?"

I shook my head and glared. He was the only one allowed to call me princess still, but that didn't mean I had to like it.

"Fine," he admitted after another sip. "I'm here with a request. From the palace."

I sighed. Of course. He was here on official business. From my mother: the Summer Queen of Atlanta.

And if she wanted something from her wayward daughter, that meant more trouble. As if my day wasn't trouble enough already.

CHAPTER SIX

Luckily, I didn't have to answer a summons from Illythia, Fairy Queen of Atlanta. Mother or not. Even if she still didn't accept it, I was solitary. Had been for nearly sixty years.

"Not interested," I nearly snarled at him. "And I have half a mind to reclaim that drink. That's good cognac."

Shiro pulled his drink in close to his chest to protect it. "Shiv, it's not like that. It's not an order. It's just a request. A favor." He almost choked on the word.

"Awesome," I said. "Then it should be easier to tell Mother why I said no. I don't wanna." I wasn't being petulant exactly. Okay, maybe I was. But if the Summer Queen comes around asking favors, it usually meant it was something I really didn't want to do.

"It's not from your mother. The Queen…" He stumbled over his next words. "Her majesty doesn't know I'm here. I'm here on behalf of your sister."

Oh. That might change things. For a number of reasons. First, the fae will contort themselves in any number of uncomfortable ways to avoid placing themselves in another's debt. We don't ask favors lightly, and asking for one indicates either desperation or a complete disregard of self.

For my sister to ask a favor, Bryony must either really need my help or was showing an olive branch and might be willing to repair our relationship.

"You may continue," I said magnanimously.

Shiro continued. "I'm here because there's a group of dignitaries arriving through the Gate tomorrow, and I need you to help me welcome them."

"Not going to happen." I wasn't going to play politics, even if that got Bryony in my debt.

"The dignitaries are not Summer fae," he quickly amended. "They're here on a diplomatic invitation, but they are from the Winter Courts."

That pulled me up short.

"Huh?" I couldn't help the verbal confusion that came out of my mouth. Interactions between the Summer and Winter Courts were frosty in the best of conditions, and as a result, most summits between emissaries happened on neutral ground in Fairy. Visitations between delegations on a rival Queen's territory required skilled diplomacy. Court politicians would take weeks of negotiations, pageantry, and gifts to smooth travel for low-level envoys.

I leaned over the bar and lowered my voice so that Shiro had to lean in to hear. "So, I'm guessing Bryony needs a neutral ambassador? Harmless solitary welcome party and all that?"

Shiro's guarded expression relaxed. "Exactly. I knew you'd understand."

I snatched the drink out of his hand and pulled away from him. "Fuck off, Shiro."

"But," he began.

"Let me stop you. Bryony wants me to help her avoid tension with the Winter Court, because technically I'm unaffiliated. I'm still Illythia's daughter, though, and everyone knows it. So it's not the grand gesture she thinks it is."

"But—"

"I'm not finished." I took a deep breath and looked at the people who sat to either side of Shiro. I knew perfectly well that by now every word we said was going to be common gossip by the end of the night. While I might have insisted certain news be reported through official channels, it might not be wise to spread this knowledge quite so widely.

Then again, it might be better if everyone here knew there was a serious threat in our city.

"We found a body by the Gate this afternoon. I. I found a body. It was a djinn, and his throat had been cut." My voice broke, and I had to swallow.

"I know," Shiro said quietly. He reached across the bar with his palm open. I placed my hand into his, eager for touch in that moment. He closed his other hand on top of mine and looked at me entreatingly. "Are you okay?"

I nodded a little shakily and wet my lips. "I'd never seen a dead body before. I mean, I've known humans who died. But not a fae. And never so…violently."

He understood what I meant. He gave my hand a small squeeze. "I imagine it was quite unsettling."

"Yes," I said and squeezed his hand in return. "But I think it's more than that. A body near the Gate has troubling implications."

Shiro frowned. "You found the body at the Gate itself?"

"Well, no," I admitted. "He was in the river. Caught in some branches."

"So, he could have just washed up on the shore," Shiro said. He dropped my hand and shrugged. It seemed so simple.

"I want to think that. I do. But it didn't taste right." I ran my tongue over the edge of my teeth, tasting it again: ash and water rotted vegetation. And iron. "Iron," I said out loud. "The body tasted of iron." I took a sip of the drink I had confiscated from Shiro to wash it away.

"Iron? Like blood?" Shiro said. "That makes sense. You said his throat was cut."

"No, blood tastes of copper," I insisted. The difference was subtle, but when one of your only magical skills relies on your sense of taste, you learn how important nuance is. Copper is the metallic taste when you suck on a paper cut or lick a penny; it had an astringent tang or sourness to it. Iron was the taste of a rusted pan or an old spoon, and was duller and more bitter. "And he had no taste of blood. He had no blood to taste." I didn't realize that was true until I said it, but now I was certain of it. The djinn body had no blood in it when I found him.

"If he was in the river, and his throat was cut but there was no blood, then that all tracks with him being in the water a long time. Siobhan, he probably just washed ashore there." Shiro stood up straighter. "And there's certainly no reason that this poor djinn's death should have any influence on you helping me with these Winter Court dignitaries."

He held out a hand for his drink, and I gave it back to him. "What if there's more to it?" I was unwilling to let it go. Something wasn't right. "And," I continued, "what about the missing fae? Several of my customers have gone missing. Argus has reported every one, and the Summer Court has done nothing about it. Mother hasn't even publicly acknowledged that there's anything going on, which keeps most of the city from knowing there might be a problem."

"Okay." Shiro sipped his drink, and I could practically see the wheels turning behind his shifting eyes. "What if, and I can't make any guarantees until I relay the request back, but what if I can guarantee that the Court will look into that issue if you help?"

"You think Mother will suddenly act on this just because I agree to welcome some high and mighties?"

Shiro snorted. "Her Majesty does not need to bother herself with small matters. No, Bryony can ask the Knights to investigate."

I frowned. Bryony had sent Shiro. Bryony was controlling the Knights of the Court. Bryony was asking a favor.

My sister might be heir to the Atlanta throne, but she shouldn't be wielding that much power already.

That meant Mother was having one of her episodes.

Now the need for me to come tend to visiting dignitaries became apparent. If Mother was beginning to succumb to the Fairy Queen's madness, then Bryony would be covering the administrative duties of the Court. She probably figured I could pinch hit on sensitive diplomacy issues. Mother would be busy dissociating and fighting against reality while the forces that surged through her ripped at her sense of self.

I grit my teeth. "You could have led with some of that information."

Shiro's face lit up. "Wait. That's a yes?"

"What time is the meeting?"

Shiro whooped with a fist pumped through the air. The celebrating crowd echoed him, eagerly seizing on any enthusiasm. "Thank you, Siobhan. Seriously, thank you."

"What time?" I sighed, already regretting this. "Just don't say dawn."

He had the good sense to cringe. "I'm meeting them just after eight."

"Shiro Harada, you will owe me. If you're going to ask me to meet you at the Gate at eight a.m. after a shift here, I'm invoking Favor from you as well. Or you can personally tell my lovely baby sister to choke on a pixie wing."

He paused for a moment, considering the implications. If I invoked Favor, I could call on Shiro at any time and for any reason with a request he couldn't deny. The ancient fae laws that governed our powers, our long lives, our connection to Fairy across the worlds, also governed the force behind our words. It was ancient magic that constrained and empowered us in even measure.

Shiro must have really needed me because he nodded solemnly before saying the words. "Siobhan Cambry Illythia, by Mab's name, I grant you Favor. May Nour Sitra divide my soul should I deny your request."

The few fae who had continued to eavesdrop on our conversation fell silent in observance of the moment. Two even closed their eyes and no doubt reached out for their connection to their magic. I did it instinctively, feeling the protective warmth of my glamour about me and tasting the magic of those near me. There was a briny salt from a nereid, the fresh air of an iele, and the grainy wood of a pair of dryads.

Two steps to my right, and I pulled out a drawer beneath the computer slash coin register. A ceremonial athame awaited me on a bed of red velvet, cleaned and sharpened for any in the bar who should need it. It was rare that the need came from a bartender, but it wasn't completely unheard of. I grabbed the knife and walked back to my friend the Court errand boy.

"Mother name?" I demanded. I should have known it. I'd been friends with Shiro for the past thirty years, but I had never had occasion to learn his formal name.

"Lamond."

"How very French Canadian. All right, Shiro Lamond Harada, I accept your Favor. I will meet you tomorrow at eight. But if you use my bar again for official requests from the Crown, I will ban you from the Greenwood Knoll." I cut a small gash in my palm and extended both it and the athame to him.

"Understood," Shiro said. He cut his palm in return and clasped my hand.

We didn't so much shake hands as pull each other closer. The tension between our hands pulled on the other's magic, bringing our spirits into contact until there was a small overlap. Our words and our magic united into intention, where the promise bound us. It was like a string within our souls stretched out and wove itself into the other. Electricity and a vague hint of cinnamon, anise, and lemon crossed my tongue. It was like a licorice-and-lightning-forward hot toddy.

So long as the promise was unbroken, we would be connected. Our magic and connection to Fairy would be bound to the other, until the Favor was either satisfied or denied. At that moment, either our connection to each other would cease, or our connection to the other World would.

Few fae could survive that.

I hoped we had made the right decision.

As the licorice and lightning taste faded, I released Shiro's hand. He immediately took it back and rubbed it on the thighs of his jeans, while I took a swig of water to wash it away.

"See you at eight, then?" Shiro said, as he passed money over the counter to pay for his drink.

I thumbed through the cash. Two hundred percent tip, damn straight. "See you then."

He turned to leave, but I stopped him. "Oh, and Shiro?"

He spun with apprehension written all over his face. "You'd better bring me the biggest coffee you can find."

CHAPTER SEVEN

The early hour might have been torture, but the coffee did not disappoint. Shiro met me at the back steps of the Knoll with a tureen of French vanilla roast. I lifted the top off and took a big whiff of that comforting aroma, rich and warm.

"I thought you might prefer iced, given how hot it is," Shiro said. "But then I thought you might literally kill me if I watered down your caffeine."

"Damn straight," I said as I took a sip and promptly burnt my tongue. He was right about the weather though. The sun had barely been up for an hour and already it was topping eighty Fahrenheit. Atlanta summers. You can't beat the heat away with an ice wolf's tail.

"Shall we get this over with?" I said as the heat of the coffee scalded its way down my esophagus and made the oppressive heat of the surrounding air feel cool by comparison.

Shiro extended an elbow out to help me down the Knoll's back steps.

It was then I realized how horribly I'd underdressed for this meeting.

Shiro was the picture of sidhe royal grace. He had on silvery gray slacks with dark blue trim racing down the side topped with a blue tailored jacket with silver trim on it. Silver leaves adorned his epaulets, where delicate shining threads hung down, catching the early morning sun and dazzling the eye. His buttons were prismatic tourmaline, and he sparkled with every movement. His jet-black hair was styled up into a pompadour like a wave of night cresting over his head, and I could see more gemstones cuffed over the top forward edge of his ever so subtly peaked ear tips.

"Reynard himself would be jealous," I said, and punctuated my admiration with a small whistle.

He preened a little, lifting his shoulders up and back. "Thank you. You look, er, nice, too."

My denim skirt and silky blue blouse weren't winning me any style points. I didn't exactly have royal regalia in my closet, and there was no way I was going to the Atlanta palace just to pick up clothes for an escort errand. Hey, I wasn't wearing jeans as I normally would on a weekday morning.

I sighed. "Let's get this over with." Ignoring his offered elbow, I started off down the path in my sensible navy blue flats. I couldn't imagine walking down the wooded path in heels.

I snuck a look back and down at Shiro's footwear. Sure enough, his shiny boots had a small heel, and he was struggling on the uneven stones leading to the river.

Stifling a snicker, I picked my way down the path, past the river, through the woods, to grandmother's house we go. The clearing opened up, free of bodies but still tasting with the nearest whisper of ash and iron and rot. A few more sips of coffee and I could ignore it long enough to get through this little welcoming ceremony for our Winter visitors.

The Gate stood quiet and expectant as we approached. Shiro pulled a delicate silver knife from a holster hidden under his jacket. He checked the position of the sun to confirm the time while I glanced at my watch: eight on the dot.

Shiro lifted his palm up as an offering to the Gate and brought the tip of knife to lay it carefully against his skin. Then he stopped and turned the knife around to offer it to me. "Would you do the honors, Siobhan?"

I rolled my eyes. "How do you manage to turn something so mundane into something grandiose?" But I still grabbed his knife and shoved the huge tumbler of coffee at him. "Take this."

Placing the knife against my forearm, I slid the sharp edge, not the tip, over the meaty top side. The blood immediately welled up and began to drip down the side to splatter on the ground. "Cutting your palm is stupid," I scolded. "It hurts, it takes forever to heal, and you can accidentally sever tendons if you're not careful." I swiped a finger through the stream and wiped it along the stones. "Open sesame," I murmured, and shoved the ceremonial dagger back to Shiro before reclaiming my coffee. He wiped the knife clean and tucked it back away before stepping several feet away to stand at attention.

The Gate responded, the air between the stones already sparkling with a glow that was not unlike the prismatic reflections from Shiro's tourmaline buttons. It was shimmery, like oil on water, or the edges of a fire opal, not any one single color but a dance of many. The glow spread upward from the base rocks climbing slowly up to the tip of the arch, outlining a doorway. As the glow reached the top stones of the arch, it cascaded downward, like a waterfall flowing over the empty space.

The moment the waterfall of light touched the stones at the bottom of the archway, I could feel the power of the Gate sweep over me. "Hello, darling," I whispered as the flavor of Fairy washed over me: green, verdant, alive. It was like parsley and grass, like green olives and truffle oil, like mushrooms and wine.

On cue, the shimmering surface of the Gate wavered, and the delegation from Winter emerged.

The first pair to emerge were in formal suits like what Shiro wore. Their burgundy red jackets had stark lines around the collar, heavy epaulets, and gold trim. Their ice-white faces were equally imposing, with strong square jaw lines, aquiline noses, and steely pale eyes. They looked so alike I had to assume they were from the same bloodline. Though, to be fair, that happens a lot in the Winter Court.

The next two visitors were dressed in white robes that were embroidered along the hems with what looked to be deep purple snowflakes, icicles, and gemstones. They each had long white hair, though one was pale as new-fallen snow, while the other had skin of deepest umber. They were both beautiful and completely androgynous.

The final two to emerge were less intimidating. At least in appearance. They were not matched as the preceding pairs had been. One appeared to be a petite woman with chestnut brown hair and a delicate feminine face, all soft lips and dewy cheeks. Her partner was only slightly taller, with close cropped black curls, full laughing lips, and large black eyes. He moved with almost a bounce, while she seemed to float along beside him. They seemed like kids off on a field trip.

The power emanating from them belied any thought that they were young or harmless in any way. I was nearly knocked back from the presence of them as they passed into this realm. My breath caught in my throat, and I wanted to fall at their feet.

Mab's tits.

I wanted to fling my coffee at Shiro and run for sanctuary back at my bar, but I schooled my face into impassivity. These weren't just visiting dignitaries. This was a Winter Queen, passing into a Summer Queen's region.

And here I was greeting them in a denim skirt and flats.

I was going to kill that fox the second I didn't think it would cause an inter-realm incident.

The first four members of the Queen's entourage swept to either side of the Gate to flank the young Queen and her consort.

Shiro swept into a low bow. "Greetings, your Majesties. Welcome to Atlanta. I am Her Majesty Queen Illythia's emissary, Shiro Harada. I trust your travels were uneventful."

The dewy-faced young Queen laughed, a sound like ice breaking under foot. "As easy as gliding through mist." She grasped at her partner's arm with an excited tug. "Darling, didn't you know a Harada once?"

He smiled at his Queen indulgently. "Karata, my love. Karata. And she is still part of the Cailleach's Court. An occasional consort, I believe."

"Yes, yes." The Queen waved a hand about, dismissing the correction as if it were a mosquito buzzing about her. "But who is this?" Her eyes alighted on me and grew wide. I felt pinned to my spot as if a wild tiger had just sighted me and declared me lunch.

I lowered my eyes, bowed my head and dropped a very slight curtsy. I was solitary and technically did not need to show obeisance to any royal fae. But I also didn't want to offend and have her freeze my blood in my veins. "Your Majesty. I am one of the Keepers of the Greenwood Knoll and Minder of the Gate. I welcome you to the Iron Realm and offer you sanctuary as you travel through this region."

"Yes, yes." She waved her hand again. "Greenwood Keeper, but who are you?"

"Majesty? I am merely a barkeeper, and solitary. I am no one," I said, not wanting to give her my name.

"Your name, child," her partner snapped. "Before she loses patience."

I sighed. I couldn't deny a direct command like that. "My name is Siobhan Illythia."

"Illythia's royal half-breed! I knew it!" The Queen was delighted at this news, clapping her hands. "I know your brother."

"Many do in the Winter Court," I said as casually as possible. It would not do to have her focus on Dariel at the moment.

She didn't seem interested, though as she began to pace around me, looking me over, less now like she was going to eat me than she was going to dissect and probe at me to find exactly how I worked. "They say you don't have magic. Is it true?"

I bristled at her insult, even if it was closer to true than not. "Begging pardon, Your Majesty, but many half-human fae in this realm are born with a number of magical abilities."

"But not you." Her eyes narrowed as she got in close and stared me down. "They say you are more human than fae. That is why you were removed from your Court. The eldest daughter of the grand Illythia is practically powerless."

That was dangerously close to a challenge on Mother's power in her own region. I couldn't let that stand. "No one of Illythia's line is powerless, Majesty. I assure you of that."

Shiro wisely chose that moment to step in. "Siobhan is a well-respected member of the solitary community of this realm, and an avowed Gate Keeper. She and her unique gifts may be of great use to Your Majesty in your investigation."

I started at Shiro's mention of an investigation. He had said nothing of why this Winter Court was here, other than a meeting with my sister. The number of things he had failed to mention grew, and I was beginning to see why he was willing to owe me a Favor over this.

For her part, the Queen dropped both her predator act and her excited young girl persona in an instant. She was suddenly still and all-terrifying authority: cold and utterly ruthless. "Do not speak of what you do not understand."

The air crackled with raw power, like an electrical storm in a blizzard. This tiny childlike creature was as dangerous and volatile as any force of nature. She was a Fairy Queen, and she wasn't about to let us forget it.

Fairy Queens were more than political figureheads or legislators for local fae society. They were the conduits through which Court fae pulled magic. Whether a Gate was open or closed, Fairy Queens maintained constant contact with Fairy, serving as bridges across which magic could pass freely without obstruction. In their own way, Queens were embodied Gates, themselves, constantly imbued with power beyond what any normal fae could control.

Fae who had pledged themselves to a given Court gave up a great deal to easily wield their magic in this realm; they opened themselves up to their sovereign, giving her access to everything they did with the power that flowed through her. Their Queen could access a fraction of whatever magic they wielded and cut it off, or increase it at her whim. A sensitive Queen could feel any time one of her subjects pulled magic through her, and with a little concentration, she could access her subject's emotions, and sometimes even thoughts.

Most Queens recognized that unfettered access as the curse that it was. As conduits for huge communities, Summer Queens were often connected to hundreds of individual fae, all pulling on Fairy magic, constantly flooding their conduit with power, emotions, thoughts, and voices. If a Queen was not careful to protect herself from the onslaught of information and power that flowed through her at all times, she could easily lose her mind.

It was why neither Shiro nor I was surprised by this Queen's erratic mood shifts. Shiro bowed his head and accepted the castigation for overstepping his bounds.

"You," she turned and commanded me now, "as a leader of the solitary here, you may assist me."

"Oh," I said, amused at her misunderstanding. She was from the Winter Court; it made sense that she wouldn't understand how things worked outside her region. They didn't get out much. "Thank you, but, actually, I'm not a leader. See, the whole thing about the solitary is that we don't bow to leaders. It's in the name. Solitary. Solo. We do our own things."

I knew it was stupid the second it came out of my mouth. Maybe I could get away with mouthing off in my mother's Court. Even to some of the other Queens of this realm that knew me.

But this was a Winter Queen. By her Court's own beliefs, she didn't interact with solitary fae often. She probably never interacted with humans, and likely thought mixed race fae were an aberration. To have someone, especially someone like me, reject her authority in even small ways was a gross insult and not to be tolerated.

"You do not bow?" she said in a low voice. "As powerless as you are, you should know your place." She let out a harsh single laugh, and the sound of it whipped across my skin, snapping against my cheek with a sharp cut.

My hand flew unbidden to the place where she'd cut me, and I pulled it away to find a smear of blood.

That bitch. She'd cut me? Eldest daughter of Illythia?

What I wouldn't have given for an ounce of my mother's power in that moment.

But she was right; I didn't have any way to lash out magically. I could do nothing but taste the freezer burn bitterness of her pique as it touched me.

And something I bet she couldn't do.

I reached up to the stinging slash on my cheek and wiped it clean. As I touched the wetness of my blood, I let the only active magic within me whisper to it. I awakened the energy of my cells and encouraged them to heal. Already the surface of my skin was mending itself. Rapidly the wound stitched itself back together beneath my blood, starting at the deepest layer of the epidermis she'd harmed and building back, cell by cell, atom by atom, until there was no evidence I'd ever been harmed.

All the Queen saw was me wipe away the wound she'd given me with nothing more than a wave of my hand. Her eyes widened in surprise.

Fae heal quickly, but no one else that I knew of could stitch themselves back together in quite the same way I did.

"No, your Majesty," I said. "I do not bow. To anyone. And I'm not entirely without magic."

The Queen's surprise gave way to a delighted smile that was wider and more terrifying than the last.

Oh, Mab's curse. I'd made a terrible mistake.

I'd just made myself interesting to a Fairy Queen.

CHAPTER EIGHT

Y ou heal," she said as softly and warmly as ice melting.

"Everyone heals," I pointed out. All creatures healed given enough time and blood. So long as a wound wasn't immediately fatal, even full-blooded humans could heal from most injuries with rest. Though most fae healed a bit faster than humans, it was true that I healed faster than even most Queens.

I had always assumed that since I had no other powers, all of my innate magical ability was focused on just holding and restoring my body to its optimal state. It's not like I could use my healing abilities on anyone else; I'd tried.

"Illythia has been keeping secrets," the Winter Queen sang, reverting to her childlike persona.

"Lada," the Queen's consort said. "My dear, shouldn't we attend to our purpose here?"

Her head tilted like a confused puppy, as Lada's eyes flicked to one side and her gaze fixed into the distance, as if she were trying to remember why she was here in the Iron Realm in the first place. "Oh, yes. Our inquiry."

"Exactly," he replied.

"What is our inquiry about?"

He blinked at her rapidly, trying to figure out if she was toying with him or truly had forgotten. I had never envied the delicate dance of a Queen's consort. "Natara?"

At the name, the Queen seemed to shatter. It was as if she had been stabbed in the chest. Her shoulders caved forward, her chin fell to her chest, and her legs gave way beneath her as she sank to the ground. Only the swift action of her consort kept her from sprawling at our feet.

A low moan began emerging. No, not a moan. A wail. The Queen began to keen like a broken banshee. She was grieving.

"Natara," she lowed. "How? How could I forget? Oh, my sweet girl." She turned to her consort and clawed at him, scrabbling for a hold, pulling his arms about her, burying her head into his chest. "She hurt. So much. It hurt her. My sweet girl." Then she dissolved into tears.

The consort held her close and rubbed the back of her head, smoothing her glossy chestnut hair. "Shh, Lada. There was nothing you could have done. She was beyond your reach. There's nothing you could have done."

"Kiral," she said. "She couldn't heal. It was a slow death. Like the others. But she couldn't heal." She looked suddenly to me with desperation. "She wasn't like you. Mortal after all." Then she buried her head once again into her lover's shoulder.

"Shh, shh, I'm here." Kiral gave us a look of apology and then devoted his full attention to his Queen.

Shiro and I stood awkwardly. If we were used to erratic breakdowns from our Queens, that didn't mean we knew what was appropriate to do when they happened in our presence. I wondered briefly if we should leave, let this woman grieve alone. Shiro caught my eye and nodded back toward the path. He had the same idea. We'd fulfilled our duty. We could probably leave without insulting our visitors.

Or maybe we should wait to be dismissed.

Luckily, one of the dignitaries recognized our distress and stepped forward before we walked away. The dark-skinned ambassador stepped forward, their long white robes sweeping the ground as they bowed to us. "We thank you for your welcome. Queen Lada is staying at a commercial property in the city of Atlanta, and a conveyance is already arranged to pick her up near the Greenwood Knoll Sanctuary. I assume this path," they gestured to the path we'd taken to get here, "will lead there."

"Yes," I said. "It'll take you straight to the back of the Knoll. The parking lot is around the front."

"Very well. We will attend her Majesty." They bowed again. "You are free to go."

Shiro and I didn't wait for any further elaboration. We both bowed to the weeping Queen and her entourage and hurried away up the path, Shiro leading the way.

I waited until we were out of sight to smack Shiro as hard as I could upside his thrice-cursed head.

"What were you thinking?"

"Ow," he said, rubbing his skull but not slowing down as we put distance between us and the Winter fae behind us. "I was thinking that I needed a Keeper from the Knoll to greet a royal, and asking Mikka or Varon would have been a really poor choice."

"Why not ask Argus? It's his establishment. He owns the place and is the Lead Keeper of the Gate. Why in Mab's name did you not ask him to greet the ice-addled Queen?"

"For many reasons," Shiro said, still forging ahead, leaving me scrambling to try and keep up. "One, he isn't exactly the most diplomatic on his best days."

That was true enough. As unpolished as I undoubtedly came across today, I had diplomatic training, knew my Court manners, and could charm the wings off a pixie if I wanted. It just so happened that I didn't exactly *want* to most of the time. Argus, by contrast, was your typical dragon: brusque, short tempered, and frequently willing and eager to sneeze fire on anyone who insisted he behave by any expected rules of engagement. He could have caused an inter-realm incident without trying. I'd at least have to try. Probably.

"Two," Shiro continued, "he is aggressively solitary, rejecting any connection to the Court to which Queen Lada is paying a visit. He could easily have insulted the Queen I serve. If he had done that in hearing of a visiting royal and Illythia had allowed it to stand, it could undermine her standing amongst the Courts."

That was also fair. Mother and Argus had a hard-earned understanding between them. They'd coexisted in Atlanta for nearly two hundred years, and Mother was constantly forgiving his slights. I daresay her affection and past romantic history with my dragon boss was a part of that. But that wouldn't have mattered if he'd managed to insult or sully Mother's good name in front of this other Queen.

"And third?" I prompted.

Shiro sighed. "I asked him first, and he told me no."

I snorted. "You could have led with that."

"Doesn't negate any of my other points."

We emerged from the copse of trees to see the Greenwood Knoll up on a small hill, proudly looking out over the Chattahoochee. It was a handsome building, a two-story wood and stone construction, with its sweeping covered porches along the back and front that extended into uncovered decks along either side.

Firepits, Adirondack chairs, and game areas dotted the lawn. On busy weekends, you could find gremlins and redcaps playing cornhole with stregas and sylphs, while vila and valkyries debated kobolds and orges over friendly bocce games.

This early on a weekday morning, though, the place was quiet. Argus was, no doubt, still asleep upstairs in his private quarters, while Meara would be accepting deliveries and sorting through prep work for the busy Friday rush to come.

As we approached the back steps of the building, Shiro finally stopped and turned to me. "You're right. It wasn't fair to invite you into that with no preparation. I should have told you that we were meeting a Winter Queen and why."

"So why didn't you?"

"Because I was scared you would have turned me down as well," he said, shrugging. "I needed a representative from the Knoll to properly welcome a visiting dignitary from a rival Court. Especially given her purpose in visiting us."

I stepped past him and took a seat on the stairs, crossed my legs, and leaned back to look up at him. "And are you going to tell me what that purpose is?" I took a sip of my coffee and was pleasantly surprised to find it still warm. Shiro had brought it in the good thermos. "Does it have anything to do with a missing fae named Natara?"

Shiro nodded. "I hadn't known her name, but yes. Ostensibly, Queen Lada is here investigating the disappearance and subsequent death of one of her subjects. From what I have learned, Natara was an akila, a weather-controller, from Lada's home region outside Bucharest. She went missing after visiting a cousin here, a few weeks ago. Then last week, Lada contacted Bryony about the death of one of her subjects in our territory and demanded something be done about it."

I fumbled my coffee and spilled some of the hot liquid on my silk blouse. "How is this the first I'm hearing about this?"

Shiro raised a single eyebrow. "In what world does your sister, or your mother for that matter, announce diplomatic crises in public?"

Shiro was right. Mother might be erratic and reliable, and Bryony might be power-hungry and selfish, but they both knew how to rule a queendom. They protected their subjects, and they protected their power; threats to either one were dealt with quickly and quietly. Announcing the death of a Winter fae on our territory was not the way to instill confidence in anyone's hold over the city.

There was something else to it, though. "You said, ostensibly," I pointed out. "Do we have any reason to suspect the Winter Queen is lying about her subject?"

Shiro pursed his lips, but he didn't say anything.

"I see," I said, though I truly did not. I could imagine reasons Lada would have lied about one of her subjects dying in Atlanta. The murder of one of her subjects on another Queen's land could give her leverage against Mother to demand reparations or justice against the ones who committed the crime. She could be looking for that leverage. Or she could want access to Atlanta for another reason. If Mother was incapacitated and Bryony was the one running things, Lada could be taking advantage of a power vacuum.

"Siobhan," Shiro said, warningly. "I can see you thinking. Stop. This isn't your fight. Whatever is happening with the Winter Queen, it's not your problem."

I frowned at him, the acid of my coffee churning a bit in my gut. "You're the one who invited me into this. Plus, she's in my city, and you don't trust her. That's enough for me to get involved."

"No, it's not," Shiro said. "You're solitary. You can't just insert yourself into Court politics because you smell blood in the water."

"But there *was* blood in the water. What about the dead djinn in the river?"

"Actually, you specifically said there was no blood in the body."

I glared and sat forward on the steps. "You know what I mean. This has to be related. Lada comes here over a dead fae; I found a dead fae in the Chattahoochee. If her dead subject is related to the body or to the missing solitary fae of the past few months, then I have every right to be involved."

He straightened his spine and looked straight ahead before speaking in a emotionless voice. "Whatever has happened to your solitary patrons must be dealt with by the solitary alone. The official stance of the Court is that it is not responsible for the activities or whereabouts of those who occupy Queen Illythia's territory but have rejected her gifts."

His cold words hung like frost between us for several moments before either of us were willing to speak. I wasn't sure if he had schooled himself to such dispassionate response, or if he truly didn't care one way or the other about the solitary fae of his region.

Then again, he'd lasted nearly eighty years longer in the palace than I had. Perhaps in that time, he had learned how to steel himself entirely against the needs of anyone outside of his Court.

"Is that the edict of my mother or of my sister?"

He said nothing.

I sighed, angry and disappointed. I knew he was just repeating what he was told, what he was required to say, but that didn't make it hurt any less. "I think you should go."

He didn't try to defend himself or argue with me. He simply

nodded agreement and turned to walk around the Knoll to the front parking lot.

Shiro had nearly rounded the building when he stopped and called back to me. "If I am able, I will speak to Her Majesty about your customers. Perhaps the Winter Queen's visit will spur her to some action."

"Despite my sister's edict?"

Shiro pursed his lips again. He was playing a dangerous game here. He had undermined Bryony's order but had not disobeyed her. Besides, his loyalty was still to the Queen, not her heir.

"Thank you," I said as I gained my feet. "And I'll see you tomorrow."

He looked confused for a moment.

"Karaoke. And don't you forget you and I are up first. So don't be late."

He moaned. "Seriously, can't we pick a different song?"

"No. It's my week, and you're doing the musical number. And if you complain again, I'll make sure my great Favor is you singing the entire catalog of the Beatles B Sides. No hits. Only the weird shit. For the next six weeks."

I didn't wait for a reaction as I turned and bounded up toward the Knoll to help Meara in the kitchen with deliveries.

CHAPTER NINE

As much as I love karaoke night, Friday night might be my favorite night to work the bar at the Knoll.

Fridays are the day that all the human-passing fae are done with the work week. They're able to let their figurative hair down, drop the glamours, and finally be themselves among people who understand them. They are also frequently flush with cash from payday, so they're very willing to share the wealth in the form of exorbitant tips.

I accepted a fifty for bringing the clurichaun by the hearth a fresh bottle of five-year Macallan Scotch and told them they are some of my favorite customers, before rushing off to bring the ten-year bottle to Daione Sidhe sitting at the big table in the middle of the room. The clurichaun were naturally protectors of wine and spirits who would appreciate the bottle more, but chances were good the Daione Sidhe who all worked in human corporate culture would tip better.

It was no matter to me. I was happy just to keep my customers happy.

And there was a table of maenads throwing a baby shower in the middle of my bar.

I guess word had spread, because the group had grown since last night. About four tables were pushed together around a central throne where Semele, er, Mellie held her own court. She had about six different kinds of juice in front of her, snacks of every kind that Meara could come up with, and a mound of presents lined up and ready for her to open. The word had spread throughout our small community in the past day, and tonight was turning into a community-wide celebration of the maenad mother-to be.

Just as I was bringing another three bottles of champagne to the table, the door opened and a cheer went up. I craned my neck to see who had arrived and was delighted to see Talisa, the frequent leader of the maenads, pushing one of the biggest and most elaborate baby strollers I'd ever seen.

At first glance, it seemed old fashioned with a flat-bed egg seat with an extendable canopy, but it was so sleek and modern, it was obvious this was a premium luxury item. Black fabric stretched tight over the frame, and rose gold trim accented every curve and joint. The bed of it and the extra-large storage basket underneath were overflowing with beautifully wrapped gifts, and Talisa also juggled a humongous bouquet of peonies and ranunculus.

"Thierry Kellan sends his apologies for not being here himself," Talisa said with much fanfare as she swept into the room and delivered the stroller, gifts, and flowers to Mellie. "But he sends his best wishes and promises a much more elaborate celebration as you near the baby's arrival."

My eyes widened in surprise. Thierry Kellan was the most powerful solitary fae in the United States, if not the entire Iron Realm. Reclusive, eccentric, and nearly as influential as a Queen, he'd built up one of the most interesting reputations. He had arrived in the Iron Realm at the turn of the 20th century and had refused to pledge himself to any Queen. Instead, he had established businesses, estates and investment vehicles, and community outreach organizations, aimed at solitary fae. He owned several companies, including the real estate behemoth that employed most of the maenads on the east coast.

Despite his considerable influence in human and solitary circles, Thierry had been careful never to overstep any Queen's authority, and it was reported that few of the people who worked for his companies actually knew him personally. But his name was one of those ever-present forces in fae circles.

He operated out of New York, and as far as I knew had rarely visited Atlanta. But if Talisa was bringing gifts from him, perhaps he had taken a more personal interest in our city.

The maenads all squealed in excitement as they descended upon Mellie and the gifts. I struggled to get out of the way, quickly opened the bottles of champagne, and set them into the waiting ice buckets on the tables the maenads had claimed.

Talisa somehow squeezed out of the crush of excited women and grabbed my arm before I could get away. "Hey, Shiv, thank you for accommodating all of this." She waved to the madness of women passing around gifts, shaking them, and venturing guesses as to what was inside.

"It's my pleasure," I said.

"Mr. Kellan asked me to pass this along and say he'll cover any expenses incurred as a result of the celebration." With a wink, Talisa passed me a small black credit card. "That goes for everyone at the bar, not just our little group."

"That is incredibly generous of him," I said, more than happy to continue bringing out the good stuff as long as the maenads wanted to continue celebrating. "Please pass along my thanks to Mr. Kellan." I slipped the card into the inside pocket of the short black apron tied around my waist and moved to go back to the bar.

Talisa grabbed my arm, sending a thrill of heat through me. "Hey, actually, do you have a minute? There's something I need to talk to you about."

I looked around at my bar. We had a larger than usual crowd, even for a Friday. It seemed everyone who had heard the news wanted to be a part of Mellie's baby shower. Everyone seemed to be in high spirits, but there was something else: an undercurrent of uncertainty and fear in everyone but the maenads. The regular group of clurichaun, including Alden, Cormac, and Gair were huddled once again in a tight group, whispering and darting glances about the room. A table of dryads and sylphs were sipping at their cocktails, barely talking, with arms clasped about them or leaning forward, avoiding eye contact. Even the usually gregarious hobs and brownies were more subdued tonight as they kept close together.

I had little doubt why everyone was on edge.

With Argus helping out behind the bar and Kaia manning the floor, I could spare a minute or two to talk with Talisa. "Yeah, give me a minute to put this card away, close out a few of the sidhe at the bar, and deliver another round to Gair's group in the corner, and I'll meet you out on the porch?"

"That'll take more than a minute," Talisa said with a smile. "Say fifteen? And if you need help running anything to tables, let me know?"

I gave her shoulder a squeeze. I'd forgotten she worked here many years back. Granted, she had only lasted two weeks because she kept getting caught up flirting and drinking with her friends instead of running drinks. But she had become one of our most loyal customers and was always a welcome face.

"Thanks, but I can run the drinks. You go get some air. Or grab a glass of champagne with the girls. There are some extra glasses on the table, and I brought out your favorite."

"The Le Crown?"

I nodded.

"Good thing Mr. Kellan is paying! We'll have another few bottles," she laughed, and she dashed away to grab a glass.

I ducked behind the bar and first slipped Kellan's no-limit corporate credit card into the curse-protected drawer under the cash register. If anyone tried to steal from our register, they would suffer itchy boils and bad luck until they returned every cent they stole with 10% interest. If they stole from the hidden drawer underneath, their hand would catch on fire and could not be extinguished both until the stolen items or cash was returned, and the bartender put it out with milk. Which was only stored in the walk-in fridge in the kitchen.

I had just stepped up on the step stool to reach a bottle of eighteen-year Glenfiddich when I heard a friendly voice call my name.

"Gair," I said, pleasantly surprised to see the tall red-headed clurichaun waiting on the other side of the bar. "You just saved me a trip. This bottle is for you and the group if y'all still want it."

His bright blue eyes lit up. I usually only brought out the eighteen-year for them when they asked for something special. Most of the time, they couldn't afford it. The majority of their group worked in blue collar jobs as laborers and tradesmen. Gair had the highest paying job of them, working as an adjunct professor of politics at Emory University. "Really? We just got a new bottle."

"You're celebrating Mellie's baby shower, right?"

He swept a hand through his wavy auburn hair and looked over at the crowd of giggling and squealing maenads, then over at his group of wine and barrel-colored brothers. "Yes?"

"Good answer." I passed him the bottle. "Compliments of Thierry Kellan, provided you toast the baby-to-be and lay out an offering for Mab and her daughters."

He accepted the expensive liquor reverently. "I'll do you better and lay out an offering for Kellan his own self."

I wagged a finger at him and tried to look stern. "Don't invite any curses on us with your blasphemy, now."

He gasped and held a limp-wristed hand to his chest in horror as he affected the deepest southern belle accent I'd heard from him. "I would never blaspheme his corporate majesty, Siobhan. I thought you knew how seriously I take the holy role of gold and infinite credit accounts in this realm. Why, to have you question my reverence for the wealthy muckety-muck of our kind is downright hurtful."

"All right, all right," I said, laughing. "Take your bottle before I charge you instead of his muckety majesty."

Gair's blue eyes twinkled as he winked and lifted the bottle in a toast before disappearing back into the crowd.

That task done, I printed out a few bills, accepted a handful of coins and several credit cards to close out a few customers, mixed up a few of the cocktails that came through from Kaia, and then tapped Argus on the shoulder as he filled a half dozen pint glasses with the kolsch we'd just added to the draft menu.

"Hey, I'm going to take a five out back."

"Better make it ten," he said without looking up.

"Huh?"

"You're going out back with Talisa," he said, shifting glasses without disrupting the stream of golden liquid flowing from the tap. "She can never get to the point in five minutes."

"Fair enough," I agreed. "Back in fifteen."

"Oh." He smirked as he switched glasses again. "You're planning to flirt."

"Will you stop that?" I smacked the arm that wasn't manipulating pint glasses. "You don't know everyone as well as you think you do. I'm not going to flirt. We're going to talk."

He snorted and a small wisp of smoke puffed out of his nostrils. "That's what Mikka said right before she and Talisa started seeing each other the last time. Their 'talk' lasted two months." He flipped the draft tab off and started moving the pint glasses to the bar top for Kaia to take to the floor. "Have a good talk then."

I rolled my eyes and pushed past him.

Talisa wasn't on the back porch when I got outside. There were some lilin flirting and laughing along the railing with a few humans they'd brought along for the evening. I scanned them but didn't taste any overt notes of magic. There was a lot of touching and intimate looks passed around, but no one seemed to be in a predatory mood. Just out having a good time on a Friday at the local fae bar.

The other side of the porch just had a few elementals, paired off in small conversations at tables and rocking chairs. But no Talisa.

There. Down by one of the fire pits in the yard. The fire was unlit, given how warm the evening was, but she was leaning back in one of the chairs, her feet braced against the circle of flat stones as she tilted her head up to the stars.

"Hey," I said, taking a chair next to her.

"Hey, you." Talisa didn't turn her head to me, but kept looking upward. She had one of those classically beautiful profiles. Her forehead dipped to a nose that sloped gently upward before dropping away to lips that were almost thin if they weren't so full of expression. Just now they were opened slightly, as if in awe, of the sky above us.

I looked up and saw little to be in awe of. We were too close to the city of Atlanta to see many stars, and the few wispy clouds above us were little more than ink stains on the light pollution. But, still, it was nice to take a moment of silence with a pretty girl.

Closing my eyes, I took a deep breath of the fresh, green wet taste of the river below us, the comforting wood and beer taste of the Knoll behind us, and the subtle notes of strawberries and balsamic vinegar from the maenad beside me. After the day I'd had and the madness of the bar tonight, it was nice just to breathe in what was around me, to feel someone also being present in the moment. Blindly I reached out and felt the warm, softness of her hand grasp mine.

I could feel her looking at me, but I wasn't quite ready to give up my other senses and open my eyes. "I don't think you called me out here just to appreciate this moment of stillness," I said. "Though, if you did, thank you."

"You're welcome." I could hear the smile in her voice as she gave me a small squeeze. There was a thick pause, as if there was something she wanted to say. I released her hand and sat up, eyes open and intent on her.

Talisa's hazel eyes were cast away from the sky now, far away, over the Chattahoochee and beyond. Her lips were pursed and down-turned, and immediately I wanted to reach out and grab her hand again, offer her comfort.

"Hey," I said, instead, leaning forward and toward her. "What is it?"

She smiled weakly and shook her head. "I don't know. It might be nothing. But then you found that body…" Her voice trailed off.

I knew it. "You're thinking about your girls."

Talisa had been part of her maenad troupe for nearly a century, and while they had no official leader, she had taken on a maternal role with most of them. She was the first one they called when any of them needed a ride home from the Knoll or needed advice on a latest infatuation. She was always the one they called when they were having a great time and wanted to share the moment with their sisters. Talisa was the girl you called in good times and bad, and she was always willing to be there.

She bit her lower lip and nodded, her eyes filling with tears. "I know I should be thinking about that poor guy in the river. About his family and whoever lost him. But, Siobhan, you know so many of my girls have gone missing. It could so easily have been one of them."

I understood her worries. The maenads were a flighty bunch in a good year, and having one or two disappear for a few weeks on a manic episode as they fell in and out of love with a project or a person was not unusual. Talisa herself had disappeared in the 80s when she'd fallen in love with Kiefer Southerland. She'd taken the Greenwood Gate to Fairy, found a Gate that that opened to Los Angeles, and had spent several weeks as extras on his various movies. When she'd finally gotten his attention and kissed him at a party, though, she'd hated the way his lips felt against her teeth and returned as quickly as she'd disappeared. The entire time she'd been gone, she had been in contact with her maenad sisters here, sending messages through travelers to and from Atlanta, so they never worried about her.

That was true about most of the fae who frequented my bar. They were here because they needed companionship, needed other souls in their lives, and not just to consume. It's too easy to disappear from this world if you don't have somewhere you can touch base, share a drink, and find connection. Even the local redcaps clan contracted with us on occasion, if only to remind the rest of us that they were here, waiting to pick off the weakest among us should we give them the chance.

Safety in numbers might have been another motivating factor for sticking together and checking in with each other.

If Talisa was describing any of her very closeknit troupe of maenads as actually missing, it meant they hadn't just gone off to follow a passion or mania. They had disappeared without contact. Without a trace.

As tears began to trickle down her cheeks, I got up off my chair and knelt in front of her. "Hey, sweetie." I reached out for her hands, holding my palms forward in front of her. I didn't have her consent to touch her, even in comfort, so I left my hands open. If she wanted my comfort, she would take it.

She stared at my unguarded palms a few moments, then laid her hands in them. I immediately squeezed, trying to push as much warmth and comfort and security into her as I could. If she had let me, if I could have reached inside her to heal this hurt, I would have. Seeing this vibrant, loving, passionate woman hurt made me want to rip something apart and stitch everything together at the same time.

"Talisa, it will be okay. Just because we found that djinn by the river, that body, well, it doesn't mean that your girls aren't okay. It doesn't." I squeezed as hard as I could without crushing her fingers. "They are just missing, right? Just because you haven't heard from them, just because they forgot to send word, they could still be fine." I knew my words sounded empty. I had nothing to offer beyond the press of my fingers, the empathy of my words. "How many?"

"Four." She looked again to the river.

I followed her gaze. I wondered if she pictured her friends, her sisters, floating in the river like that poor djinn. Their hair tangled with sticks and leaves, their skin bloated and gray, their eyes lifeless and dull.

"Hina, Ariana, Jessa, and Jocelyn."

"Jocelyn," I muttered. The name was familiar.

Talisa sniffed. "She was so excited to work with you. With Mikka. I'd told her how wonderful y'all were. How you'd show her how things worked, how to make friends in the city, how to be solitary. Just like you did for me."

Jocelyn, right. That was the name of the girl who was supposed to work with us at the Knoll. The new waitress.

"She was nervous, though," Talisa continued. "She'd never been away from the Court before."

Oh, no. That broke my heart a bit. The poor girl—Jocelyn, her name was Jocelyn—had been newly solitary. For whatever reason, she had broken her connection with the Court and had severed herself from her direct source of magic from Fairy. She'd been cast out among the solitary misfits and had needed a place to belong. Talisa had probably recommended her to Argus, to us at the Knoll. We could give her a job, a way to connect with a community of like-minded solitary fae. To realize she could have a life outside of the Court.

"Do you think," I said, "maybe she went back to the Court? Could she have changed her mind?"

Talisa shook her head vehemently and pulled her hands away from mine to wipe at her cheeks. "No. Her mother was solitary and was one of my girls, too. Jocelyn had been talking about breaking away from Summer for years. To be closer to her mother. To be free."

I opened my mouth to say something. To say that I understood how she felt, or if not, to say I cared.

But Talisa stood then, brushing at her pants and walking away from the Knoll. "I'm sorry. Fretting about my girls isn't why I asked you out here." She turned and looked at me, her cheeks stained with tears and her eyes glistening. "I wanted to say that I think my girls' disappearances, the body you found, the unrest with the Courts. I think it's all connected. And I want to help stop it."

I stood and took several steps forward, my hands tingling with the need to reach out to her, to touch her again. Pressing my hands to my side to avoid giving myself away, I nonetheless took another step toward her. "What do you mean?"

"I don't know yet," she admitted, closing the gap with a tiny shuffle toward me, her eyes never leaving mine. "I just think it's too much of a coincidence that everything seems to converge here."

"You mean, the Knoll?"

"Yes. So far as I know, the Knoll was the last place any of—"

I cut her off with a raised hand as something ripped at the instinct in my gut. "Wait."

She frowned and scoffed a little.

"Sorry, but something's wrong."

Her annoyed frown turned into an expression of worry. Darting her head around, she looked for whatever had disturbed me.

Green, alive and verdant and intoxicating. It nearly knocked me over with the intensity of it. And underneath, a sickly-sweet rot. Death and life in one breath.

The Gate was open, and I could taste it from here.

Something was wrong.

And there, in the sky above where I knew the Gate waited, the sky shimmered with the iridescence of Fairy.

"Get Argus," I shouted as I ran past Talisa and down the path toward the Gate. "Something is wrong with the Gate."

CHAPTER TEN

I could feel it. More than I could see it or even taste it, I could feel the open Gate. There was a powerful, fluctuating otherness as the magic seeped into this realm. It was tangible in the air, like I could reach out and grab a handful as I ran, seize the chaos and wield it like a weapon.

The magic moved, flowed like the river beyond the Gate, a coursing stream of possibility and power all around me. Shimmering with a green-tinged purple, it raged with potential like a typhoon before it hits shore, an impossibly still tornado, a wave forever growing and cresting but refusing break and drown us all. It was a threat, a promise, if only I would open myself to its power, let it in and release it.

It was too much. Such power should never be released all at once; it could drown this city.

Keepers existed to control the flow of magic, to release the pressure valve of the Gate little by little. Someone had opened a floodgate, and I had no idea how.

As fast as I ran toward the Gate clearing, a force barreled past me, and I knew from the smoked pipeweed and brine taste that Argus was as terrified as I was.

Within a few steps, twin balls of heat closed on my heels. Mikka and Varon were there in an instant, moving faster than they had any right to. Varon blew past me to catch up with Argus, but Mikka matched my pace.

"What happened?" she said as easily as if we were standing around the bar.

"No idea," I huffed. "All at once I could taste it: Fairy all around me. Then I saw the sky. It looked like—"

"Like the surface of an open Gate," Mikka finished, pointing up. The purple green glow had expanded and loomed exactly over us.

"How?" I didn't have any answers. Only horrified questions. It was like the sky had been ripped open and Fairy had leaked through.

Looking up, I stumbled over a tree root, and Mikka caught me. I was holding her back as she matched pace with me. "Go." I waved her ahead as I felt a stitch growing in my side. I would never be as fast as a dragon or a drake, and she could do more good at the Gate than helping me dodge roots and loose stones on the path.

She nodded and was gone in seconds, disappearing through the trees. I slowed even more when she was out of sight, gasping, and clutching at my side. It was less that I was winded than that the effect of the magic grew as I approached. The verdant taste of parsley and mint and grass mixed with a heady botanical richness that left me floating and infused with energy and life. It left me with a feeling like I was on the edge of panic without any of the anxiety—like my entire being was operating at its extreme, ready for anything.

It was exhilarating and terrifying, wonderful and awful.

It wasn't right.

In the clearing, the Gate stood open and bleeding into this realm. The shimmering surface seemed to pool out in all directions, as though the riverstone archway was merely a suggestion for its opening. I could see the stones, standing where they should be, but they were obscured by the overflow of Fairy essence, wavering and clouded as if they were several feet under water or seen through fog or smoke.

The Gate seemed to recognize me as I approached, and it seemed for a moment that the pools of visible chaos stretched toward me. I wanted to go to them, to touch the surface of that potential. I'd been through the Gate countless times, but this felt different, alien to what I knew so familiarly. Would it be gaseous or liquid? Would it resist me with surface tension, or embrace me with a caress?

I took a step toward the light, and the ground squelched beneath my feet. The moss around the Gate was wet, sodden with thick liquid. I knelt and put my hands down into the thick press of the moss and lifted fingers wet with sticky red. Even in the purple light, I could see that it was blood.

And it was still warm.

Stumbling back in horror, I remembered, too late, that I had followed friends to this spot. Argus, Mikka, and Varon were here.

Where?

I scanned the clearing, unable to see anyone. Had they touched it? Had they passed through the Gate?

"Siobhan," Varon called. Still in this world, then. I pulled myself away from the arch, circled wide around the gaping wrongness of the uncontained magic, and saw Varon gesturing to me from the other side of the Gate, near the river. Careful not to get near the wavering edges, I went wide around the arch and found Argus and Mikka kneeling over a figure, prone on the ground.

Another fae, body sprawled on her back, eyes open but unseeing, even as she gasped in shallow breaths. Her wrists were both slit, and Mikka was trying to staunch the bleeding on the left with the t-shirt she'd torn from her own body.

"Stay with us," Argus exhorted softly, trying to get the woman on the ground to focus on him as he clutched her right hand, trying to lift it above her heart, to stop the flow of life from her body. "Hey, you're not done yet. Stay with us."

I sank to my knees as I recognized her.

Nyssa.

Her red hair was still a blazing copper, and her open eyes still a bright moss green. She was one of Mother's. One of the family. Had been. Once upon a time. An earth sidhe. She had supported the gardens and warmed Mother's bed for generations before she left a few years ago to attempt to start her own family.

These days she was a regular at the Knoll.

She attended karaoke last week. She'd sung Pat Benatar. Love is a Battlefield.

Now she was dying on the ground before me.

I choked back the well of emotion that filled my throat and noticed the dagger that was stabbed into the red Georgia clay beside her. That and an almost empty fist-sized bowl that was stained with the same liquid saturating the ground before the Gate. Nyssa's life's blood.

"Oh, Nys," I said, sinking down beside her. I wanted to grab her other hand, to push my own warmth and life into her, to stop her dying, but I could see despite Mikka's efforts, despite Argus's exhortations, she was all but gone already. There would be nothing else I could do.

Hot tears fell from my face, and I wept.

Nyssa had been a fixture at Court in the 30s, when I was still a part of the royal succession. She'd been Mother's lover for a time, and her friend for years before and after that. She'd helped me through the heartbreak of my first love. Poured wine and let me cry when my first girlfriend had left Court for a suitable marriage and potential children. She'd been the first one to assure me that procreation and the continuance of our line was not always going to come before genuine emotional connection. Even if she'd eventually left Court herself for that very reason.

I hoped she had found that emotional connection. I regretted that I had never asked her. About her partner. About her efforts to have children that had never been fulfilled. I had never given her enough thought after I left Court myself. Had never reached out to connect with someone who knew me, cared about me as a child.

Now I wouldn't have the chance to ask. Her eyes were distant, and though she was still warm, still alive, the blood that had flowed moments ago was already beginning to slow to a trickle.

"I'm so sorry, Nyssa." I knelt down close to her ear, unsure if she could hear me, or if she was already too far gone. The taste of juniper, pine, and lemon of her magic was fading, as an iron flavor began to creep across my tongue. We were losing her. "I'm so sorry."

I didn't even know everything I was sorry for. That she was dying, murdered in such a cruel way. That I didn't have the magic to stop it. That I hadn't been a part of her life. That I didn't care enough when she was vibrant and alive and here to ask anything about her beyond what she wanted to drink and if she was doing well. That none of it mattered and she was going anyway.

Her breath began to hitch, and her unseeing eyes shed tears. She grew taut, her legs and arms spasmed once, twice. Then she stopped, her breath gone in a last sigh. I watched as the last vestiges of color and life immediately began to fade from her already cooling body. The bright copper of her hair faded to a dull bronze. The milky cream of her complexion became a dull chalky clay. Every last bit of life and magic passed away from her.

Soon, Nyssa was nothing but a body.

And the Gate began to close.

The violet glow of Fairy that had leaked into the Iron air around us began to seep back down into the stone archway. Like someone had pulled a plug and it was being drained from this world and safely back into the one beyond. The iridescent glow flowed downward, once again a waterfall, passing down to where it belonged.

Argus, Mikka, Varon, and I watched, stunned, as the unnatural magic that leaked into our world faded. It blurred around the edges, and within moments, the magic and light of it too passed completely away.

The Gate was closed, and the night was silent.

CHAPTER ELEVEN

Argus and Varon again remained behind to deal with the body. That's what she was. Nyssa, the confidante, the soil genius, the loving friend, was nothing more than a body now.

Another body by the Greenwood Gate.

I tried to impress the horror I felt on Argus as he closed Nyssa's eyes and gathered the tools around her. "We can't go on saying nothing about this!" I paced in front of the Gate, closed and dormant, and no longer a temptation. "This is two bodies in two days. If everyone connects them to the missing people like we have, there's going to be a panic."

"There's not going to be a panic," Argus said softly. "Because you're going to go back to that crowded bar and tell everyone we are going to keep them safe."

I stopped pacing and took several rapid breaths as I considered my boss, who had apparently lost his mind. "I am? Me?"

"You." His word was final. Argus didn't follow up with any instructions of exactly what I was to tell our customers, what I was to do. He gestured to Varon, and they began gathering the things that surrounded Nyssa's body: the bowl, the dagger, a handful of herbs and stones.

"Boss," I persisted. "I can't lie to our customers. Something horrible has happened here. It's happened before, and I can't now promise it won't happen again."

Argus stopped what he was doing. His back was to me as he investigated the now quiet stones of the Gate, but he turned and faced me. "Siobhan, you have worked with me nearly eighty years now. I have never once asked you to lie on my behalf, and I won't start now." He looked down at his hands that were already red and sticky with blood. Nyssa's blood. "But for tonight, all our people need to know is that even though the sanctity of the Gate was violated, it is closed, and they are protected. There will be time to mourn Nyssa, but that will come after we protect our people. And we will protect them all."

Something in my floating gut settled in that moment. Whatever had happened, Argus was here. He would protect us. He would handle the messy fallout of this moment, like he had always done.

All I had to do was go to the bar and let everyone know.

I could handle that.

Mikka accompanied me on the slow walk back to the Knoll.

While I considered exactly what I would say to my patrons, Mikka's eyes darted every which way up the path. She was my ever-present bodyguard, and I was thankful to have her. I wanted to reach out and let her know by touch how thankful I was for her, but I didn't want to distract her, so I kept my hands to myself as we found our way back to the Knoll.

Talisa was waiting at the far edge of the trees. I was surprised she hadn't followed me farther up the path or run for help, but I was thankful she was there. She rushed to me, and while I thought for a moment she might throw her arms around me, she stopped herself and merely reached out for my hand. She stopped before grabbing me and let me meet her grasp. I did, thankfully, and gave her hand a quick squeeze.

She took the desperate way I clutched at her hand as an invitation to move in closer. She didn't try to embrace me, but she brought her forehead to mine. I couldn't quite bring my eyes up to meet hers, closing them and accepting the comfort of her being close to me.

"Are you okay? Siobhan," she said, squeezing my hand with more urgency, "what happened out there? What was that in the sky?"

I shook my head, still trying to figure out how to explain what I'd seen. I didn't want to have this conversation multiple times. I would go into the bar, make an announcement, shut things down, and then figure out how to deal with this. "I'll explain in the Knoll." I had meant to come across confident, steady, and like someone she could trust to handle this. I'm afraid I came across as shaky, scared, and not at all prepared for whatever was about to happen.

But she accepted it. She stood straight, gave my hand a final squeeze, and stepped back so I could get into the bar.

The path, though, was already crowded with worried fae. Those who had seen what had happened to the sky, who had seen the Fairy magic that had ripped through the horizon over the river, had summoned others.

"Siobhan," several voices called. "What's happening?"

"What's going on?

"Thank Mab. It's over."

"Shiv, are we safe? Should we go back inside?"

"Hey, Siobhan, can I close my tab?"

I ignored all of them and pushed my way through everyone and up to the steps.

"Inside, everyone," Mikka said, following my lead and ushering people into my wake. "Siobhan will speak to everyone at once." She began shooing curious people who were looking down the path. "Come on. Inside. We'll explain. In the Knoll."

The crowd followed, ushered behind by Mikka.

Once inside, without a thought of what to say, I stepped back behind the bar, grabbed my trusty step stool, and climbed up on top of the polished wooden surface. Argus would scold me for putting my muddy shoes on the top of his bar, but I figured he had more impor-tant things to think about right now.

"Can I have everyone's attention?"

At once, the music cut off. I snapped my attention to the sound system behind the bar and saw Talisa had switched off my iPad that controlled the music. I nodded my thanks and turned my attention back to the crowded and nervous bar.

"Everyone, I'm sorry to do this, but I'm afraid the Greenwood Knoll will be shutting down early tonight."

There was an immediate outcry, though it didn't sound angry. Rather, many of the voices bordered on shrill, shaky, and scared. Argus had only shut down early on a weekend a handful of times. Always it was because there were circumstances that made things dangerous for his customers.

Some of the people close to the door ducked out and disappeared, but most of the crowd settled down and waited for me to continue.

If only I knew what to say.

I opened my mouth and, thankfully, words came to me. "I owe each of you the truth. The lights many of you saw out back were, in fact, Fairy. Something happened tonight at the Greenwood Gate."

This time there were outcries and tears. The idea of something happening to one of the Gates between the worlds, well it was impossible, unfathomable. As far as any of us knew, the Gates had stood for hundreds of years. Ever since Nour, granddaughter of Queen Mab, had separated this Iron Realm from Fairy, we had known only the Gates as our bridge to our homeland. If something happened to the Gate, the people in this room would be lost.

I continued, carefully picking my words so as not to lie nor obfuscate the truth. Contrary to the stories, fae can lie with the best. Falsehoods come easily to those who rely on glamours and hiding in plain sight to exist amongst humans who would be terrified if they knew the creatures that lived among them. It's precisely because of our need to lie constantly out in the world that I find it so hard to do when it matters. Lies leave you vulnerable, exposed, and I was vulnerable enough at the moment.

There was no way I could tell the entire bar everything.

But it was my duty to be as honest as possible. "Tonight, the Greenwood Gate, the passage between this world and Fairy, was violated. We do not know exactly what happened, and the consequences of this violation of our crossings is still undetermined, but Argus is investigating and will be working with the Summer Court to determine the extent of what happened and what it means for our community. Whatever we learn, I can assure you, as a Keeper of the Gate and of this sanctuary, I and Argus and Mikka and Varon will do everything we can to restore the Gate and the safety and security of this realm we all call home."

I paused then. It felt wrong to say nothing of how the Gate had been violated, and the fae who had died, bleeding out and holding the Gate open with her life's blood. Nyssa deserved to be mourned.

I had said nothing but truth, though. It might be enough to soothe my customers.

"To make sure that we can do that, I hate to do this, especially tonight." I looked at Mellie and her baby shower guests. "I'm truly sorry to cut this all short, but for your safety, I'm going to have to close the Knoll early tonight. Your tabs have been covered by the generosity of Thierry Kellan, so no need to close out with me. If you need rides, we will be happy to help arrange those for you."

I paused again, looking at the sea of scared faces. For many of the fae who were gathered here tonight, we were their only safe space. Most of us had turned our backs on the Court, either unwilling or unable to accept the safety and security they offered in return for our unquestioning fealty. For them, the Greenwood Knoll was the only place where they could be themselves, unafraid to show their true faces and to let loose. If there was danger out there, if there was a threat to any of us, we here at the Knoll owed it to them to be the safe space they expected.

"One more thing," I added, as people started new, more apprehensive conversations. Everyone fell instantly silent, waiting for me to continue. "We will be bringing in additional security and will be reinforcing the wards on the property. If we can make sure each of you can be safe when you are here, when you seek sanctuary, then we will be open tomorrow evening for karaoke. We will, of course, keep our doors open, regardless, for those who need refuge. But I promise, to the best of my ability, we will do all we can to be the Sanctuary this community needs. Now and always."

With that I climbed down from the bar and started responding to requests for rides. Argus retained a regular taxi service manned by a family of shadowmen and women who usually worked karaoke nights to get our over-exuberant singers home discretely and safely. It only took a single call from Mikka, and the Hendleys were quick to show up in one of their sleek black Mercedes sedans, SUVs, or vans.

By the time Argus and Varon returned, we had only a few stragglers finishing up their drinks. Talisa had taken the lead with her maenads, packing up gifts for Mellie, and they had been among the first to clear out. She'd promised to check in with us at the Knoll later tomorrow to see if we needed any help with prepping for the inevitable rush we would experience if we opened for karaoke.

"I can prep the bar, help Meara in the kitchen, whatever you need. Between the scared, the curious, and the opportunistic, you're going to have every last solitary fae in the city coming out here the second they can."

I had a feeling she was right. I thanked Talisa for the offer, gave her a small kiss on the cheek, and promised to let her know if we needed her help. "For now, though," I said, "you just make sure Mellie and your girls get home safely."

She nodded solemnly. No matter what, she took care of her girls first.

Almost everyone else followed their lead, and despite my assurances that their tabs would not be held against them, nearly everyone made it a point to leave sizable tips. That surprised me, though maybe it shouldn't have. The fae were a small community in a big, antagonistic world. We tended to care for one another in any way we could.

That responsibility for my community had me pushing forward, through visions of blood-soaked moss and lacerated wrists, unseeing eyes and water-bloated faces. I'd spent most of a century without ever coming face-to-face with death. Now the Morgana herself seemed to be shadowing me.

I wondered which of my customers she would come to claim next.

I looked carefully at each face as my customers walked out my doors. I had a responsibility to each of them, to notice them, see them, serve them.

I was a Keeper. I kept the bar, providing comfort, courage, and compassion. I kept the Gate, offering safe passage, defending the sanctity and neutrality of this space, this way station. I kept the peace. I kept counsel, that belonging to others and, more often, my own. But most importantly, I kept this community together.

Protecting and serving the people who came into this place and looked for everything from fellowship and friendship to an escape or an excuse, was my entire calling. I'd been born to serve. It wasn't in the realm of the Courts as my mother had imagined, but I was still serving my community, with or without the firm grip on the reins of power I had been taught was necessary.

It didn't matter if the people here were loyal to me or to my cause. Summer, Winter, solitary, we were all one. We were connected by heritage, by the realm we shared, by the magic we recognized, even if we wielded it in different ways. Half human, quarter fae, whatever. We were connected.

I served them all.

And I owed them a safe place to gather.

Finally, there were just the clurichaun left. Gair, Alden, Cormac, Leland, and Baerd all sat around their usual table in the corner, finishing off the last of their bottle. I couldn't blame them for staying to the end. It was a nice bottle of whiskey, one meant to be savored and appreciated. Though the mood wasn't as jubilant as it had been when they opened it, they were still seeming to enjoy themselves.

So engrossed in conversation, they didn't even look up as I approached. "Hey, y'all. You're the last ones here, and I need to clean up."

"You heard the lady," Gair said, pulling a credit card out of his pocket. "Time for you freeloaders to pay up." They laughed, knowing full well he'd refuse to let his brothers chip in.

"The Macallan was already covered, Gair. I told you that. Payment is square for the night."

"Oh, yeah, right," he said, frowning at his brothers as they tapped at their glasses and avoided my eyes.

"What's up, y'all? I've never seen any one of you take so long to get through a bottle of whiskey, let alone five of you."

They passed another round of uncomfortable looks across the table. Finally Leland spoke up. "We was wondering—"

"We weren't sure—" Cormac interrupted.

They stopped and let the silence stretch again.

"Miss Siobhan," Gair finally broke in. "I know you were trying to keep everyone from panicking what with the Gate and all. But, well, with the body in the river yesterday, and the Gate trouble tonight..." He trailed off and looked down into his glass of whiskey. Then with a nudge from Leland, he met my eyes again. "Did someone else die at the Gate?"

I didn't say anything, but the look on my face must have given it away. The clurichaun all looked around at each other, grim-faced and nodding.

"That's what we thought," Gair continued. "Was it—was it someone we know?"

I nodded my head, unsure if I should tell them anything more. Argus had asked me to keep word of Nyssa quiet, but I couldn't lie when asked a direct question. I didn't have it in me.

"Was it Kari?" Baerd's voice broke.

"Kari?" She was one of Talisa's maenads, I knew. And come to think of it, she hadn't been with the girls tonight. I wasn't even sure when I 'd last seen her; it must have been a few weeks. "No, it wasn't Kari. It was a Summer fae, an earth sidhe."

Baerd's breath hitched. "Thank Mab." He took his glass of whiskey, knocked it back down his throat, and without another word, fled from the bar.

"I'll go after him," Cormac said, standing up and knocking back his own glass.

"We'll go with you," Leland said as he and Alden stood. Leland clapped a hand on Gair's shoulder and gave it a small squeeze. "Good-night, Miss Siobhan. Please be safe."

I smiled, a bit confused as the three men followed after their friend, leaving me with Gair, who sat back down at the table to explain. "Kari and Baerd were seeing each other up until about six weeks ago when she went missing." He sipped at the last of the whiskey and offered me a clean glass.

I sat down beside him but shook my head at the glass. "I had no idea. I'm so sorry."

"They were talking about getting a place together in the suburbs. Starting a family. But then she just disappeared." He set the glass down. "He thought she got cold feet and abandoned him. Or was seized with one last mania before settling down. He's been a wreck since yesterday, though."

I could imagine so. It was one thing to imagine a sweetheart had ghosted you. It was something else entirely if something terrible had happened to her.

"I'm so sorry," I repeated.

Gair just nodded. "We've been talking. The boys and me, and we wanted to extend an offer. We know you live alone. With everything that's happening, I, or rather we, wanted to offer to escort you home. To make sure you're safe."

He looked up then, and the sincerity in his bright blue eyes hit me harder than I anticipated. A well of gratitude rose in my throat, making it hard to swallow and pulling hot tears into the corners of my eyes. I'd been so concerned with protecting my people, I forgot that they were here to protect me too.

"Oh, no, Miss Siobhan," Gair said, flustered. "Aw, honey, I didn't mean to upset you."

I blubbered for a moment. "Oh, no. Oh no, you didn't upset me. Oh, you sweet man. Oh, bless your heart." I couldn't get a hold of myself. I babbled unable to find my words, to get a hold of my emotions. I had seen too much these past days. I wasn't prepared for kindness in the midst of having to hold it together. Sympathy, comfort—that was supposed to come after I had a handle on stuff. Not when I was just barely piecing together a coherent response to everything.

"I'll be fine. My home is well protected and warded," I assured him as I struggled to pull myself together. "Really. Thank you. So much. I —" I paused to sniff away a few more emotions than I was prepared to handle in the moment. "I don't know how to express how touched I am that you thought of me. But I won't forget it. If you keep coming back here and keeping me company at the bar, then that will be enough for me."

Gair stared at me long enough that I was sure he was going to say something that would make me cry again. Instead, he broke into a large grin. "Well, as long as you can keep getting Mr. Kellan Money-pants to pay for our drinks, I think we can keep providing sufficient enthusiasm and skill to drink them all."

"Gair," I said in a tearful laugh. "I have no doubt you can rise to the occasion."

He stood then, and I forgot that for all his attempts to diminish himself in normal conversation, he was quite able to back up his offer of defense. He wasn't overly tall, coming to just under six feet, but he stood as firm as oak casks. He was solidly built and compact with a thick, slightly unkempt auburn beard and wavy red hair that was overdue for a haircut.

He smiled warmly as he turned for the door, but before he could leave, I stopped him. "Gair. Can I—" I swallowed the tears that seemed to still trickle down the back of my throat, even as I'd wiped my face dry. "Can I get a hug?"

Gair broke into a grin, his red beard and mustache parting to reveal a full mouth of slightly wine and whiskey-stained teeth. "I thought you'd never ask me, lass."

He rushed forward and swept me off my feet in an embrace as he spun me around. I squealed in surprise and a bit of hysterical delight. It was just the right move to surprise me out of my heavy emotions. But as he settled me down on my feet, he held on tight, his arms wrapped warmly around me.

I laid my head down on his chest and breathed deep. Gair smelled of deep tannins, stone fruit, tobacco, and earth. He was like a rich red wine, with a wooded pine scent that surprised me. He didn't smell of

Christmas pine and nettles; rather, he had an earthy bark smell, like a mix between a forest after the rain and a sawmill.

Breathing deeply and slowly, I found my own strength again and stepped away from Gair's warm embrace. Still, some tears lingered as I blinked them away with a smile. "Thank you, Gair. I think I needed that."

"Of course, ye did," he said, a brogue coming through in his speech. "I'm only mad at ye for waiting so long to ask." He bowed his head to me, walked out the door, and left me with a lingering warmth inside.

"If you're quite done making that boy fall more in love with you," Argus boomed from behind the bar, "we have some talking to do."

I spun to find Argus, Mikka, Varon, and even Meara and Kaia grinning at me. I blushed furiously. "I'm not even his type."

Mikka laughed. "Seriously? Gorgeous, generous, kind, and funny, with thighs any fae would kill to have wrapped around them? Siobhan, you're everyone's type."

My blush only increased as Argus scowled.

"Knock it off, Mikka. Grab the tequila, Varon. And everyone pull up a chair. It's time to formulate a plan."

CHAPTER TWELVE

Argus chose a table at the center of the Knoll, gave us each a two-ounce fluted shot glass, filled them from an unmarked bottle of tequila, and waited until we'd taken a sip. Anything from Argus's unmarked stash was meant to be sipped, appreciated, and never shot back with disdain.

The tequila burned with a citrusy start and vanilla and caramel aftertaste.

"Things are not good," Argus said, stating the obvious. "Two dead fae, on our grounds, near the Greenwood Gate. They may or may not be related, but having their blood so close to the Gate has had some ill effects."

"What happened out there tonight?" Kaia asked, clutching her drink.

"We arrived to find a Summer fae, one of Illythia's good friends, dying by the Gate. What's more, the barrier between the worlds was open, and it was leaking out into our Realm. In my nearly eight hundred years, I've never seen a Gate do that, and I don't know what it means."

The way he described it sounded so benign. But it had been so unnatural, like Fairy was an ink stain spreading across the fabric of the Iron Realm. It had seeped into the sky, an oil slick across reality, magic polluting the mundane. It didn't belong here, but it had called to me.

"I will take Varon in the morning to test the functioning of the Gate, see if there was any permanent damage." He took a sip of his drink and allowed everyone to take in the news.

"What about Nyssa?" I asked, thinking of the poor woman who bled out before my eyes.

Argus considered before speaking. "A fae died this night. Her name is known to us, and we will repeat it. Tomorrow we will acknowledge the loss so that her family may mourn. We will also report the death to Summer. Her Court will investigate, but I imagine they will come to the same conclusion I have."

"Which is?" Mikka pressed him.

"That her death was either an unfortunate accident or a suicide."

Everyone at the table fell into horrified silence. Suicide among the fae was not completely unheard of. There were rumors of fae who had lived for hundreds of years growing tired of life; they'd experienced so much and were unmoved by novelty. Or perhaps they had outlived loved ones or had failed to acclimate to modern life. They may choose to end their lives rather than continue on alone or lost in time.

The idea that one as young as Nyssa would seek an end was almost an impossible one. Every person I knew with a fraction of fae blood in them recognized how precious life was. Our numbers were so small, our people so scattered. The idea of one with family and friends and so much to live for taking her own life was not one I could fathom.

That left the other option Argus offered. "An accident?"

"I can see it," Varon said, looking thoughtful.

"I can't. How could someone accidentally slit their wrists?" I stared around the table. Kaia and Mikka both looked as confused as I felt, but Argus, Varon, and Meara all seemed to understand.

"It's not common," Argus said, "but I have heard more reports of young solitaries holding the Gate open at odd hours. They go in pairs, so one can hold the Gate with blood, while the other soaks up as much magic as they can. It can be dangerous if they are not prepared to staunch their blood flow or if they are overtaken by the euphoria of standing in the flow of Fairy's magic. It is possible Nyssa offered a sacrifice to open the Gate and it got away from her."

Meara made a noise in the back of her throat.

"What is it?" Argus said, instantly attentive.

"I am missing some things from the kitchen. A special hot sauce made with mallan leaf, as well as rue, feverfew, and crastum root." She frowned at me. "I know the crastum, but rue and feverfew can loosen the blood. Slow healing. And mallan leaf creates visions."

Varon sat up with a dangerous look in his eyes. "Someone has been through the kitchen?"

Meara shook her head. "My wards are better than that. No one comes into my kitchen without me knowing it. But some things haven't been delivered that I ordered."

"I'll speak with Milo and Tobin." The hobgoblins mostly kept to themselves and avoided the public when they unloaded deliveries and took care of the dish pit. But they were also the ones most likely to know if anything had failed to arrive. Tobin at least was meticulous about his checklists.

I couldn't believe what I was hearing. "So that's it? Nyssa killed herself? The djinn with the slit throat was just an accident? The near dozen of our customers who have disappeared are just a coincidence? We just let it all go?" I was on my feet before I knew it.

"Sit down, Siobhan," Argus said patiently. Mikka reached out with a soothing touch on my arm and helped pull me back into my seat. "I'm not saying that we ignore what is happening by attributing the easiest explanation. I would hope you know me better than that."

Chastised, I reached for my tequila and took a larger sip. "Okay, so what are we doing?"

He took a breath. "We are going to protect the Knoll. Our first responsibility is to our patrons, and they need to know that this is a Sanctuary, no matter their allegiance. If our customers are going missing, then they are going to doubt our ability to keep them safe. And I will not deny we have had customers disappear. Anais. Rylan. Kari. Jocelyn."

At my blank look, Mikka hissed under her breath. "Mab's tits, Shiv. The would-be waitress."

Argus continued. "I can't imagine that every disappearance is connected. Fae come, and we go as we please. Some of us are more prone to wanderlust and mania than others, but given what has happened over the last thirty-something hours, we have to take seriously that there may be a real threat to our people. Especially given what happened tonight. Even if there have been accidents, fae are dead. We don't know exactly how, and I certainly don't know why. But I intend to figure it out." He raised his tall shot glass to his lips and eyed me over the top. "We need more information, and we know where to find it."

I knew exactly where he was going with this. Maintaining eye contact, I started to slowly shake my head. "Uh-uh. No. Nope."

"If anyone knows what's going on and can give us answers—" Argus started.

"No. No way."

"No one else can even get in the front door without an invitation."

"No, Argus," I said, finding my feet suddenly under me. I slammed my hands down on the table and leaned over to glower at him. I couldn't even believe he was asking me this. "I'm not going."

Everyone else avoided joining the conversation. Kaia suddenly found the ceiling interesting, while Mikka and Varon looked only at each other. Only Meara was brave enough to join the conversation.

"She is right, Gus. There's no promise there is any help. We are alone in this as in all things."

I sighed and squinted at Meara. "That's not exactly what I was saying, Meara. We can ask for help, but—"

"It is decided, then." Argus didn't wait for me to finish. He stood, finished his tequila, and began to walk out of the room, while he announced over his shoulder, "Since we are closed, Siobhan, you can go to the palace tonight."

"You are out of your mind," I said, following quickly after Argus as he made his way back behind the bar. He was already laying out the dirty glasses on a plastic dish rack and tossing silverware into a bin. "You want me to go to Court? To the palace?"

"Where else would we get the help we need?" Argus pushed past me with a full rack and went to the kitchen.

I followed closely. "Anywhere but there! We have friends," I insisted. "The Grey Meranti did our original wards. She can come and refresh them. Give us something new?"

"She is already coming in the morning," Argus said, not looking up as he lifted the rack of glassware over my head and headed for the dish pit in the kitchen.

"Oh," I said, grabbing the silverware and following him. "And what about Obelia? She may have some truth magic? Or lie detection? She's the most accomplished encante in the entire country. She can get us information. And what about Thierry Kellan? He's got several friends who come here. Why shouldn't he come and help protect his people?"

"Yes. We can call on all of them," Argus agreed as he pushed the glass rack into the industrial washer. "I think we can say the situation is dire enough."

I dropped the silverware into the next plastic rack, waiting for the washer. "Then, that's fine. We have plenty of help. We don't have to go to Court."

He closed the washer and locked it, activating the first rinse cycle, before turning back to me. "We do." And he walked back past me, through the door to the bar. We both ignored the fact that everyone else was sitting still and listening to every word.

Argus walked to the far end of the bar to grab the rubber mats along the floor behind the bar top. He grabbed one, then the other, without giving me any more explanation.

"Argus, you can't ask me to do this. There's no reason."

He didn't bother looking at me as he pushed past and back to the kitchen, where he dropped the filthy mats on the floor of the kitchen before grabbing a hose. "There is. Mab's name, Siobhan, the Gate was open. With a dying fae's blood. The Gate requires a small blood sacrifice, but a death? No wonder the thrice-cursed thing bled through. That much life force given to open it? I am surprised it closed at all."

He grabbed the hose connected to the faucet and turned the water pressure up before spraying down the mats.

I raised my voice to be heard over the sound of the water. "And if it wasn't an accident? If it wasn't a sacrifice? Argus, she could have been murdered."

"Yes," he finally admitted, switching off the hose. "And she was one of your mother's. She never disavowed the Queen, nor gave up her connection to Summer. If anyone is going to be motivated to help her, it is the Queen who felt her die."

Oh.

Oh, no. Poor Mother.

As the conduit for her subjects, a Queen was connected to her fae any time they were drawing on their power. Whatever had happened to Nyssa, she had been connected to her magic when she died. I had been able to taste it on her: the juniper, pine, and lemon fading as her life ebbed. Mother would have felt that, as the Summer sidhe had pulled upon her Queen's connection to Fairy and offered her sacrifice to the Gate. Her Queen was the prism through which her magic was refracted. As she had accessed her own magic, her Queen would have awakened to its touch, been able to reach out to her, sense her thoughts, her emotions. Her death.

Mother would have been connected to Nyssa at every moment she suffered. She would have felt every second of her subject's power until it was severed by her death.

I had no other excuse. Argus was right. Someone had to go to the palace. "Can't you go? Or at least go with me?"

A laugh escaped him, as he turned his big brown eyes toward me, his brows furrowed. "Oh, baby girl. I wish I could. But me, going to the Summer Court? Even if there wasn't a threat to the Gate, with dead fae on my property? There are too many political implications that I simply do not want to face in this century."

He was right, I knew. Argus was more than just a Gate Keeper. As proprietor of the Knoll, he was one of the de facto leaders of the solitary fae. He had incredible personal and political power, and because of his perpetual proximity to the Gate, he had access to all the magic he needed whenever he needed it. He was one of the few who could offer Sanctuary to those who ran afoul of the Summer or Winter Courts, and he had sheltered many who had incurred the Queens' wrath.

Without an invitation, any visit to the palace could be seen as antagonistic. As the daughter of the Queen, I could enter freely, with or without explicit leave.

Argus continued his argument as he walked back into the main room of the Knoll. "Illythia should be notified about violations to the Gate. And we must express condolences for her loss. One of her own died tonight. She deserves comfort."

He was right. And if she was in mourning, she might be moved to do something about what had happened. She might investigate what was really going on. She might even be able to tell us what had really happened to Nyssa.

"And you can follow up with your new friend, the Winter Queen. She's supposed to be at Court tonight for an informal gathering."

I balked. "Absolutely, not. I'm not walking into that."

"Walking into what?" Mikka asked from the floor. She and the others had stopped blatantly eavesdropping as she and Kaia swept the floors and Varon stacked chairs on top of tables.

Argus grinned at the twins. "An informal gathering between Queens."

She and Varon snickered. They knew as well as anyone what an "informal gathering" was at the palace. There would be a lot of political posturing, a lot of alcohol, and entirely too much nudity and merriment.

"Have fun," the twins sang out in chorus.

Morgana take them both. I was going to the palace.

CHAPTER THIRTEEN

Both the Greenwood Knoll and the Atlanta Summer palace were right off the Chattahoochee River, so someone new to Atlanta would have thought it easy to travel from one to the other. If you'd lived in the city for any amount of time, you would have known better.

The river wound through and around the city in unpredictable ways. Or rather, the city built itself up in a frantic attempt to avoid the river in every way possible. Atlanta was built as a hub for the iron rails. Train routes from ports along the Southern coast like Savannah and Charleston converged on the Georgia capital and branched off to the west and the north. The city hub, then, was several miles from the river near train depots, and as the city grew, it did its best to skirt away from the roadblock of the often muddy and overflowing Chattahoochee.

Only decades after the city was already established did the wealthy and privileged decide that they wanted places on the water and began building their mansions along the river. They took the choice places high above the water, on hilltops and past sweeping yards that provided buffers between the unpredictable stream. The lower, wetter parcels of land were left for commercial enterprises and public parks. And the Greenwood Knoll.

To travel from my humble bar and the Greenwood Gate where any lowly fae could cross between the worlds to the immense palace of Atlanta's Summer fairy Queen, you had two choices. You either grabbed a royally chartered boat and were paddled upstream a mile, navigating both natural and magical obstacles, checked in with the guards at the property line, and then were carried across the grounds past the hounds, to come in through the river entrance. Or you drove.

Driving in Atlanta was its own mythic obstacle. No matter what time of day it was, there was always traffic on the interstates thanks to two separate curses placed on the roads. The first was placed on the city by a tribe of ghillie dhu, angry when their grove of maple trees was bulldozed in the 50s to build an interstate exchange known as Spaghetti Junction. The other was courtesy of a single boggart whose cozy hidey hole in a depot warehouse had been the first place torched when William Tecumseh Sherman sacked the city in the Civil War and burned the place to the ground. No one could hold a grudge quite like a boggart. He'd cursed the interstate downtown connector at the place most locals knew as the Grady curve. It didn't matter how many cars were on the street at any one time; he could turn the freeway into a parking lot whenever the mood struck him.

Together, the Atlanta curses served to ruin any driving experience that took major roads through the city. Unfortunately, the best way for most people to access the Summer palace was to take I-285 to the Riverside Road exit, make your way past the parade of mansions, climb a steep wooded drive, and park at the Concordia House. The large facility served the greater Atlanta area as a spiritual retreat, with meditation courtyards, access to the nearby Chattahoochee River, and meandering paths through the nearby woods. Petitioners to the Court had to visit the Concordia House, get a visitor's pass, and then travel down the longest and most winding paths to access the Summer Court palace by foot. It was a way to be available to the greater fae public but make sure only those who truly wished an audience ever got near the private home of the Queen of Atlanta.

I knew a better way.

About half a mile before the Concordia House, I turned my seven-year-old Honda into the private driveway of one of the many castle-like mansions. It loomed over me, dimly lit with lights hidden behind sculpted bushes and in the manicured lawn. Cut stone imported from Italy stacked three stories high, a four-car garage, and columned entrance all clustered around an ostentatious fountain with a statue of a nude woman that was too familiar for comfort.

All in all, it was rather garish, even for this neighborhood.

I stopped before the large wrought iron gate and reached for the call box that leaned conveniently over the edge of the drive. I pressed the seven rapidly three times, then tapped the three. At a beep, a deep female voice answered. "You do not have an appointment. Please come back through the normal route."

"Siobhan Cambry Illythia. The lost sparrow returns. Tell Mama Bird to clear the nest."

"Confirm, please." Apparently the voice on the other end wasn't amused by my wit and made up access code.

I sighed, deeply, so she could hear me through the intercom. "Rain falls without a sound to hear, but the grass still drinks deeply."

"Code confirmed. Proceed." All business tonight. Way to set the tone for a touching family reunion.

The gate in front of me split, and the dual wrought iron began to slide apart slowly, as though pulling against a gravity that wanted them held together for all time. I inched forward, ready to be in and out by now, and annoyed at the delay. The moment I cleared the edge of the track of the doors, the gate snapped shut in an instant.

Yup. It was good to be home.

I drove along the polished stone path toward the house. It was big enough to house four three-generation families comfortably, and I knew farther back on the lot was a four-thousand-square-foot pool house and a separate carriage house with a studio above. It was unnecessarily big and gaudy.

I'd seen bigger.

Shaking my head, I continued down the driveway, through an

archway of the main house, past the carriage house to my right, and kept on through acres of grass, down the winding path. The polished stone under my wheels gave way to smaller pebbles that jostled my already strained suspension all the way to the bank of the river. The drive veered sharply to the right and skirted another garden wall of stone that ran parallel to the slow running current of the Chattahoochee. The wall ended at the property edge at a bank of trees, but I kept going off the pebble drive onto a path of pine needles and soft soil. Georgia pines, birches, and red oaks crushed against my car, threatening to punish my paint if I veered. Ahead a solid wall of trees stood sentinel as the road ended. There was no visible pathway.

I floored it.

The glamour faded as I passed through the trees and emerged on the other side, safe at the back entrance of the Summer Court palace: a long, carefully manicured tunnel between the pines to the most carefully guarded property in Georgia.

My heart leapt as my stomach dropped. Coming home never produced anything less than the wild exhilaration of return after a long absence combined with the crushing dread of having to face every reason I had left.

The Summer palace. My childhood home.

I slowed as the tunnel of trees gave way to sprawling lawns framing the brick facade of the building that loomed from its perch on the hill. The palace was bigger and grander by far than the ugly stone mansion I had passed at the entrance, but it felt more proportional. It was a palace, after all. Every room had a purpose.

The river-red brick, the white trim, the custom windows all stood assured and confident, nothing to prove and everything to back up its size. It was what Kensington Palace aspired to, with more humility and presence than should be possible with hundreds of bedrooms, a dozen different banquet halls, and a solarium that put most city botanical gardens to shame.

Up from the river, the back of the property shone, lit from a million carefully selected points. The garage on one side of the property could warehouse two dozen cars, with spots for several dozen more on the far side of the building. My mother had several Teslas, a Maserati, two different Lamborghini models I never learned the names of, and a handful of older cars that visitors were always impressed by. I couldn't tell you what they were. There was a red one, a few black cars, and a pretty green SUV that had terribly uncomfortable seats, but my sister loved to drive it.

The pool shone like a sapphire in the middle of the backyard, and even from a distance, I could see several bodies dashing and swimming and lounging about in and around it. The separate ponds were surrounded by ferns and trees, and it gave the impression of a grotto or an oasis. Multiple cabanas and tents surrounded the pool deck, and while some of the curtains were drawn, many were not, despite the vigorous activities of those within.

Discrete was not a word many fae were familiar with. Especially not the sidhe of the royal courts.

I averted my eyes from the frolic in the pool and kept to the drive along the edge of the property, swinging wide around the party in the back, and brought myself to the front entrance. Might as well come in the traditional way.

I stopped my Honda at the bottom of the grand staircase, parking it without ceremony, but left the keys in the driver's seat. If anybody wanted my old car out of sight, they could move it.

Brick steps loomed above me: twenty-seven, I knew. I had learned to count descending and climbing those steps to the front drive. I'd taught my little sister to do the same.

I wonder if Bryony still silently counted them as she descended to receive guests, or if she still tried to skip every third step when she was in a hurry getting back up to the house.

Probably not. She was grown, now.

Royal.

As I reached the top step, I stepped confidently before the illuminated twelve-foot doors, waiting for them to sweep open before I even knocked, revealing an elegantly robed courtier, the night's chosen greeter, ready to usher in welcome visitors and turn away those the queen did not wish to admit.

The doors stayed stubbornly shut.

It was the theme of the night.

I raised my fist and pounded three times, hearing the sound echo on the other side of the door. Still, no response.

"Hello?" I called out, feeling stupid. There was a party actively happening in the back yard; they knew I had arrived, had actually let me in through the gate, and they were going to make me wait?

Someone was making a point.

I huffed and stewed on the front stoop. Oh, for just an ounce of power. I would blow these doors open, storm inside, and let them know what happened when they refused a daughter of Illythia.

As quickly as it rose, the fire of my anger snuffed out, suffocated by a rising shame. I may not have inherited my mother's power, but I guess I still held a portion of her pride. I didn't need Mother's power to open a door. I didn't need to blow it down to earn respect. I certainly didn't need the hubris that came with storming in and demanding it.

Instead, I reached out and tried the handle. It gave easily, and a small push ushered me into the gaping maw of the entrance hall. A deep sigh, and I stepped over the threshold, allowing the palace of the Summer Queen to swallow me whole once again.

CHAPTER FOURTEEN

The entrance of the palace glowed like a long smoldering fire: inviting, warm, and deadly.

Dark, rich hardwoods expanded in all directions: left to the meeting rooms and official business spaces of the Court, right to the more social rooms, including the theatre, the ballroom, the dining hall, and the library. Dual staircases encircled the back wall, with sconces casting low light to guide your steps up to the palace's private rooms. A bronze chandelier hung suspended in the mouth of the staircases, its lines deceptively modern, because I knew for a fact the piece predated the American colonies.

From a distance, I could hear laughter and voices raised, but here it was quiet.

That ended quickly with the clunk of heels running from the back hallway, the rhythm frantic and unsteady. A small blonde who was over four hundred, but appeared only twenty by human standards, appeared from between the twin staircases. Magdalene, my mother's personal valet, stumbled as she saw me standing there, and she tried to draw herself up as dignified as she could while panting for breath.

"I'm so sorry, Your Highness," she gasped. "You weren't supposed to be here already. Then I thought you'd come through the back or the kitchens. So I was stationed with the porters for your bags." She pulled up short and began to look behind me. "Still in the car, then?"

"What are you talking about, Mags?" I frowned. "I'm sorry I didn't call ahead, but it was important."

"Of course," she said, but I didn't miss that her eyes widened in a moment of confusion. As always, Mags kept her composure. A porcelain smile spread across her dewy face, as if she were genuinely glad to see me. That wasn't fair. I'm sure she was happy to see me. It was just always hard to tell the true thoughts of those who served in the palace. "Your sister is by the pool, entertaining her out-of-town guests. Her Winter Majesty expressed a special wish to see you when you arrived. Shall I fetch you a towel and a cocktail?"

I shook my head, still slightly confused. "No, thank you. I was actually hoping to talk to Mother?"

Mags blinked a few times, but she gave no other indication that I had surprised her. "Certainly, can I convey you to your rooms?'

"No, I need to speak with her directly."

"Certainly, Your Highness. She will be ready to receive you in the morning."

"Mags," I said, exasperated. "I am not staying the night. I have karaoke tomorrow at the Knoll. Can you just let Mother know I am here?"

Mags shook her head sadly. "I'm afraid her Majesty is entertaining guests. Alone. Upstairs. I can arrange an audience before noon."

The fact that Magdalene was willing to wake Mother that early was an indication that her private audience upstairs was not to be disturbed under any circumstances.

"Thank you, Mags. You made offer of a cocktail and towel?"

She looked relieved and beamed at me. "As you wish, your Highness. I will prepare a private tent at the pool side as well. What would you like from the bar?"

"Can you tell Ianna I'd like a cedar-smoked negroni?"

"It's Pietro tonight."

I frowned. I'd forgotten that Ianna was taking weekends off to spend with her new lover. They had plans for a family.

Like Kari and Baerd. Nyssa and her partner.

"Right," I said evenly. "Pietro knows what I like. Tell him something dark and bitter?"

"It would be my pleasure." She left back the way she had come, her heels clacking, no doubt expecting me to make my own way down to the pool.

As I had led her to believe was my intention. But Mags should have known to follow my words more closely. I let her draw her own conclusions, but never indicated I would actually go down to the pool to meet with my sister and her guests.

When she disappeared from sight, I went directly for the right stair.

I didn't care if Mother was servicing the Oona herself upstairs. I had no interest in playing the pretty princess down by the pool with the Court's hangers-on and guests. I wasn't here to play politics or to join the games of power and privilege.

Mother was the one I had come to see, and I was going to get this whole Mab-cursed ordeal over with.

Besides, I had to make sure she was okay. If she was in one of her episodes, if she was suffering after what happened to Nyssa.

I had to make sure she was okay.

I scaled the grand staircase and went down the east corridor to the private quarters of the palace. To the west were the guest rooms, the meeting and playrooms for those visiting the palace for official and personal reasons. A dozen different rooms were sumptuously decorated with king-size beds, private baths, and anything guests might need for personal preferences. Dryads and nymphs needing plant life or earth could find their feather mattresses replaced with beds of richest soil and an array of complimentary ferns and potted greens. Water fae like selkies, alven, or kappas would discover their rooms humidified and water-logged, with extra-large pools installed. There were also rooms to cater to different kinks and more particular preferences of the palace guests.

The private quarters of the palace were off-limits without explicit invitation, though. I was reminded of this before I got past the first set of doors. Two fae stood, one on either side of the hallway. Even though they had no visible weapons, they were hardly unarmed.

I recognized them both. Keenan had been assigned to my nursery before he'd been promoted to Queen's security, and he'd always been one of my favorite guards. Rhys, on the other side, had been assigned to me from puberty until I left Court, and we'd taken to each other's beds off and on throughout my thirties.

Pulling up short, I didn't hide the fact that I was delighted to see them both. "Rhys? And Keenan? I can't believe Bryony was so thoughtful. Are you to be my escorts?"

They traded a look. "No, Your Highness," Keenan said carefully. "I wasn't given notice you were coming to Court tonight."

"Oh," I laughed. "I'm just at the palace. I'm not 'at Court.' Mab forbid." I put heavy finger quotes around Court.

Rhys smiled at that. They knew exactly how I felt about politics and official functions.

"No," I continued. "I'm here after hours to visit with Mother."

Rhys and Keenan exchanged another look. An "after hours" visit could mean so many things, and they'd heard more euphemisms than most.

But, ew. She was my mother.

"Mags will be bringing up a special cocktail from Pietro in a few minutes," I added, quickly. "Can you ask for an additional drink when she does so? I'm thinking smoke and mirrors. Mezcal and citrus something?"

"Argus got you into the tequila, huh?" Rhys teased. They had come to karaoke one night a few years ago, and they still hadn't forgiven me for the hangover I'd inflicted with several margaritas and then a ride home to my place.

"I can still teach you to appreciate the good stuff, darling," I said, moving closer. Rhys's eyes were a gold-flecked hazel, and they smelled of cucumbers and musk.

"Yes," Keenan interrupted. "We know exactly what kind of taste you give Rhys for the finer things." He narrowed his eyes. "What do you need in private chambers that you can't get by the pool decks?"

"Well," I said carefully. Then I swallowed. Once again, I struggled to lay out the truth. I didn't want to lie for the same reasons humans avoid it. Lies hurt people, create mistrust, and break down relationships with people. With life spans that often exceeded a hundred years, getting into the habit of telling falsehoods can leave you alone and friendless within a few decades. Not to mention, you then have to remember all the lies you told along the way and keep them straight. Mother had taught me to be as honest as possible with everyone. With those I knew, respected, and had affectionate feelings toward, it was all but impossible to speak in any but the most truthful terms. "I'm here to see Mother."

"So you said," Rhys reminded me. "Is Her Majesty aware of your visit tonight?"

"She will be when you let me in." I gave them my most winning smile, and Rhys returned it with interest. If Keenan wasn't there, I could have easily sweet talked Rhys into stepping aside for a little play time in a private room. And then letting me in to see Mother. But Keenan would have to be convinced. "I have some information for Her Majesty on a matter of her interest. And of interest to a prestigious guest."

They looked at each other. I was taking a gamble that the Winter Queen's visit was mostly secret, only because despite the Knoll being packed and rumors spreading there faster than whiskey at a cluri family reunion, no one had mentioned the words Winter or Queen in my hearing. My patrons were always pumping me for Court gossip, and no one had said brr to me.

As if I knew the first thing that happened at Court these days.

I pressed harder.

"You should probably let me past. I'd really hate for the lead to grow *cold*."

Rhys bit their lip to conceal a laugh, while Keenan rolled his eyes. "Yeah, we got it, Siobhan."

I narrowed my eyes. "No longer 'Your Highness.' How quickly we remember our familiarity." I put my hands on my hips. Rhys could probably tell I was teasing, but Keenan might take me seriously enough to let me through; he'd been with my family long enough, he knew exactly how short the patience of women in this house was. "Allow me to make this plain. Keenan, you will let me pass and speak to my mother, and I will enjoy the hospitality of her informal gathering as I choose, because you know full well I don't come here often enough these days to grant forgiveness for insults. And Rhys?" I raised my eyebrows as I wet my lips. I remembered the soft, questing touch of their lips, the flick of their tongue, the gentle and hungry way they always came to my bed. "Rhys, I hope you will make your way to the Knoll soon. It has been too long, and I would like to catch up."

Rhys missed none of my intention. "Let her through, Kee." They raised their hands instantly to wave off their partner's concern. "Her Highness is no threat, and obviously knows what she's walking into up there. If she incurs Her Majesty's anger, that is on her. If she incurs the interest of Her Majesty's guests, well," Rhys turned on me that hungry look I hadn't realized I'd missed, "well, then I'm sure Siobhan can handle that as well."

I couldn't help myself. Maybe it was the influence of being in the palace. Maybe it was panic at knowing what I was about to walk into in my mother's chambers. Maybe it was the fact that it had been too long since someone had looked at me the way Rhys just did.

I dashed forward before either of them could react and pressed an open mouth against Rhys's. I used my lips to force theirs wider, using my tongue to find their forked one, caressing that sensual notch, feeling them quiver against my need. Rhys welcomed my attention, pressing their body against mine, warm, hard, and strong. My knees felt weak as I drank them in. Rhys tasted of cucumber, juniper, and a spice like a sweet mustard.

Before I pulled back, I felt a flicker tasting me in turn. That forked tongue darted against my lips, snaking into my mouth with a promise of everything I knew they could do with that tongue.

If you've never dated a basilisk, I highly recommend it.

Stepping away with a lighter head and restored confidence, I gathered my resolve and stared Keenan down.

He scoffed. "I'm not going to fight that. I know better." He stepped to one side and pulled open his side of the large French doors that led to the palace's private chambers. "Have fun."

Rhys chuckled as they stepped back to open their door. "Save some fun for me?"

I licked the taste of them still lingering on my lips. "Gladly."

Then I took a deep breath and stared down the long hall of closed doors that waited.

Mother was at the end of that corridor. And she alone could grant me what I needed.

I looked back at Rhys. They smiled knowingly. They would definitely be coming to visit me soon.

All I needed to do was survive tonight.

I could do that.

I stepped into the private rooms of the Atlanta palace and bid farewell to the rest of my reservations.

CHAPTER FIFTEEN

Every step down that long corridor took me closer to her rooms at the end, and with every step, I could feel her presence more. It wasn't just that I was drawing nearer to my mother; I was coming into the presence of a Queen.

And she radiated magic.

It was how I knew what Lada was the second she stepped through that Gate. Queens had the kind of power that unmoored you. Merely being in the same room with one was like standing in front of an open Fairy Gate or inside a nuclear reactor. The residual power that emanated from them was intoxicating and terrifying.

Surprisingly, it was also tasteless. Though I could taste nearly every other fae creature's magic individually, most Queens contained so much magic it was hard to discern a single way to describe their power. I'd have an easier time describing light or heat or life, for it was all of these and more.

As I approached Mother's bedroom, my heart began to pound and my blood heated in my veins. Spots appeared at the edges of my vision, and a chill pimpled my skin. The proximity to such power, the possibility of tapping into it. It called me. I was bred to this power. Her blood was mine, her abilities as familiar to me as breathing. The magic of Fairy knew me as one of its own, and through my mother, it saw me as one of its chosen, one of the few who could wield its full power as a conduit.

No.

I shut down the call. I wasn't here for that. I wasn't part of the Court world anymore. I was not a Queen. I would no more pledge myself to a hungry jungle cat than I would pledge allegiance to the Summer Court. Not that there was much difference in the outcome. No, I would never serve as future conduit for the Fairy realm.

I'd given that up. I was solitary, now. I would live with the limited magic I carried with me. No more. No less. Let the Courts carry on with their power struggles and their political games. It wasn't my world.

Not anymore.

I pushed myself to the end of the hall, past my old rooms, and up another decorous staircase with carved wood balustrades and elaborate chandeliers hanging at every turn. Finally. I faced the double doors that lead to my mother's private chambers. Only a single guard stood there.

Lyris. Mother's Captain.

Her presence on door duty did not speak well to Mother's state. As the newest Captain of the Queen's Guard, Lyris oversaw every placement of guard on the grounds, every detail of visits off grounds, and every element of my mother's personal, bodily security. If she was the one stationed outside of Mother's room at this hour, things were even worse than I had imagined.

Not bothering with preamble, I hurried to give Lyris a hug.

If it had been anyone else stationed outside of Mother's rooms, even Rhys or other former lovers, I would have hesitated. But Lyris had been my personal guard when I'd been a member of the Court. She'd been there when I was born and had been at my side from the beginning. Even as I gained more staff and attendants, the tall, sturdy Nordic blond Valkyrie had been by my side every time I left the palace. She was a constant in my life.

She was more than a bodyguard; she was an auntie the entire time

I was with Court. Leaving her when I emancipated was almost as hard as leaving Mother and Bryony.

I couldn't help the tears that welled up as I hugged Lyris close. She hugged tighter, and just feeling her solid body against mine made me feel better.

"How is she?" I asked as we pulled away and looked at each other.

"Having a good time at the moment," Lyris said.

"And in the other moments?"

"Struggling." Lyris always did have a way of getting to the point.

"I need to see her," I said. I didn't think I needed to have more of a pitch to Lyris. Nothing I said would change her mind about letting me in the door; either she would open up, or she'd send me on my way.

"I wish you luck." Lyris reached behind her and pushed open the door to let me through.

I reached for her hand and gave her a quick thank you squeeze before stepping over the threshold into Mother's private chambers.

The double doors opened on the sitting room, an intimate area with a full-size leather couch, love seat, two armchairs, thick wooden coffee table, a fireplace big enough to roast a pig in, and a full bar along the inside wall.

I briefly considered a fortifying shot of her most expensive Reposado before I stormed the rest of the way into Mother's chambers but knew the gesture would neither fortify my courage nor even be noticed by Mother, so I passed.

I continued forward into the bedroom proper, my boots echoing on the deep, dark wood. She'd had them redone. There was a distinct striping to the dark wood that reminded me of zebras. I stooped and ran my fingers over it, feeling the slight imperfections that made it so beautiful. Macassar ebony, I'd wager, heartwood. Probably bought from the dryads of the trees themselves. She'd likely have to have a whole forest planted in Indonesia to make up for the floor in this room alone, but the dryads would accept the loss in exchange for a favor from a Queen.

The massive bedroom too was empty, aside from the tremendous bed that could fit ten full-grown adults. At least.

She wasn't in it. Nor were any of her guests.

She wouldn't be in her office if she was entertaining, as no one beyond herself or Mags was allowed in there. And her closet was off limits to anyone but her daughters and her lovers.

That left only one place for her to be.

I strode into the bathroom.

The bathroom was larger than the sitting area and the bedroom combined. White marble stretched across the space with plush rugs set out near a half dozen vanities, leading into Mother's lingerie closet beyond and set out in front of the tub. The tub itself dominated the center. It was the size of a small pool with multiple elaborate faucets at the corners. Columns extended up to the vaulted ceiling at each corner, and tables piled high with fruits, cheeses, and wines were placed next to each. The lights set deep in the bath provided the room with most of its illumination, though the rose-tinted color was diffused through the bubbles on the surface of the water.

And there, in the middle of it all, radiating power and lounging against the far edge of the porcelain with two fae on either side of her, was the Summer Queen of Atlanta: Illythia.

My mother.

She was luminous. Honey brown hair twisted up and pinned loosely on the top of her head, tendrils falling down around her face like she was a damned Greek goddess. Her caramel-colored eyes sparkled as she laughed at and touched the tawny woman on her left and wrapped her legs over and around the bronzed brunet man on her right. She was the picture of fae indulgence.

"Forgive me if I am interrupting, Mother, but I need to speak with you, tonight."

She looked up as if she had only just now noticed a fully clothed person had entered her sanctuary. "Siobhan! Well, this is a lovely surprise!" She turned to her guests. "Y'all, this is my other daughter." She was in full Southern hostess mode, and her accent sounded like a cross between Dolly Parton and Julia Sugarbaker.

"Yes, the half-human solitary." A svelte man with shoulder length, thick, black hair and intense black eyes, untangled himself from the lithe blonde he was wrapped around and carefully looked me up and down. "We were told of her, but we did not expect to encounter her." His English was strongly accented and sounded like hot caramel. He stood, revealing a tightly muscled body, trim waist, and a full erection. "I am Kanha. It is an honor to meet Your Highness."

I nodded and tried to keep my attention on his face. "I'm Siobhan. Uh, daughter. Not technically a Highness."

Mother reached out a hand to appreciatively rub Kanha's thigh. "Isn't he delicious? He's on loan from Queen Ishani in Chennai."

"It is my honor to represent my Queen," Kanha said, giving his full attention to Mother, as he sank back down into the water and his hands disappeared beneath the bubbles.

Mother leaned in to allow him to kiss her neck as she looked over at the two fae on the other side who had taken an interest in one another. The woman was leaned back, her breasts just surfacing out of the water, her head thrown backward, mouth open, as her partner arched over her, pressing into her again and again with soft grunts of passion. They were gorgeous together, his bronzed body over her deep sepia, they looked like a classical painting brought to ardent, lustful life.

"Calix and Eniola are new, but I have to say I am loving what they bring to my bed. And bath. And," Mother gestured to the blonde who had swum over to the snack table and was pouring herself a glass of wine, "of course, you remember Dulcea."

I nodded to her. "Lovely to see you again, Dulcie."

She smiled and offered the bottle up to see if I wanted some. "We've missed you, honey. Feels like ages since you've come to any royal functions."

I shook my head at her offer of wine. "Thank you, no."

"Well, you're here now." She extended a hand to help me into the huge tub. "Shall we make up for lost time?"

I shook my head harder and kept shaking it, trying to rid myself of the desire I felt for her, for Kanha, for everything Calix and Eniola were about. "No, no no no, that's not why I am here." Taking two large steps backward to put some space between me and the tub, I put my hands in front of me as if to ward off the call of losing myself to pleasure. The intoxication of a Queen's power also spoke to the basest natures of fae, and it was all I could do to resist the pull to sex. "Mother, I will wait in your sitting room. We have business."

"Oh, darlin'," she said, her eyes closed as Kanha moved against her, his hands still concealed in the water. "Don't get your knickers in a twist. Tell you what. If you ask nicely, you can borrow anyone you want and take yourselves somewhere more private. Dulcea has been talking about how much she misses you. And Kanha has—" She gasped as he did something I couldn't see under the water. "He is most eager to please. But no one's going to push you to do anything you don't want to do."

That wasn't the problem. Me not wanting. I did. I wanted to get in there with these gorgeous creatures and forget about everything else for a while. To forget the death I'd seen and the danger that still faced the people I cared about outside this room. I wanted to revel in life, in pleasure, in the potential for reproduction. It was in my nature.

I pushed it away. "No, Mother. I must speak with you."

"Can't it wait until tomorrow?" Mother said, already turning to reciprocate Kanha's attentions. "I have company." She kissed him briefly, before stopping and staring into the distance. "A redhead? Here? Go away. I don't have time for you."

Kanha looked to see who she was talking about, but Dulcea and I recognized the tone in her voice. She was speaking beyond us. No one had entered.

Mother quickly settled back into kissing Kanha, and he forgot the interruption as he dove into her affections with more rigor. It was up to me to stop things before they got away from us all.

"It's about Nyssa."

Her eyes flew open, and everyone stopped what they were doing as the sauna-like temperature of the room dropped. Dulcea stepped out of the tub and grabbed a robe as Calix and Eniola unwound and did the same. Kanha moved a small distance away but remained at hand to the Queen.

"Go."

It wasn't clear if she spoke those words to me, or to everyone else, but we all cleared out as quickly as possible. Kanha grabbed a robe like Dulcea, but Calix and Eniola fled the bathroom without even grabbing towels. I hoped they didn't slip on the wet floors.

I removed myself to her sitting room as I had said and waited.

CHAPTER SIXTEEN

I plopped myself on one of the black armchairs across from the almost identical leather couch and eyed the bar opposite me. That Reposado was looking better and better.

Before I could stand to pour a shot, though, the fireplace beside me roared to life as my mother came storming in. Thankfully, she'd pulled on a deep blue silk robe, and it billowed behind her as she blew past the couch and grabbed the very bottle I'd been looking at.

"Tequila," Mother said. It wasn't a question, so much as a confirmation of what we both wanted in that moment. She poured two glasses and swept back around the couch to hand me one and place the bottle between us.

Mother's robe was loosely knotted with a sash around her midsection, and a wide V of white, creamy skin extended from her navel up to a dazzling sapphire necklace she'd inexplicably put on to frame her delicate clavicle and vulnerable neck. My mother. Ever putting herself on display.

I just wondered who she thought her audience was.

"Well?" she said after she'd sat. She crossed her legs at the ankles and sipped her drink. Her hot rush of anger was not as apparent with her carefully controlled behavior, but I could feel the bite of it in the magic that seeped from her pores.

Best to distract her for a moment, then. "Mother, why did Magdalene ask me about luggage?"

She leaned back into the couch and cocked her head at me, confused as a labrador puppy. Her personality had shifted again. Gone was the coquetry of her Southern belle persona. Gone was the cold and dangerous anger she could unleash. Here were wide eyes blinking and clucking tongues. "But, did he not tell you?"

"He?"

She laughed a little and shook her head. "He truly tells you nothing." And she sipped her drink, staring off into the distance amused at her private joke.

This was familiar ground. "Riddles, Mother, riddles." The woman was absolutely incapable of straight simple answers to straight simple questions, a trait she shared with every fairy Queen I'd ever met. "You can't speak to people with half the conversation unspoken."

She smiled then, her eyes unfocused, as she shook her head causing honey brown tendrils to fall out of her haphazard updo. "Oh, my darling. There's so much of him in you. You should go visit, you know."

This was just peak Mother. I knew the "him" of this last statement had nothing to do with the "he" of her previous statement.

She was always half in and half out of any interaction, her statements completing thoughts she hadn't voiced, answering questions I hadn't asked, including people who weren't even in the room. Her bad conversational skills gave birth to countless conspiracy theories and intrigues in Court and was enough to try the patience of the most obedient of her servants.

It simply drove her daughters crazy.

I didn't have a mind to sit and puzzle out her meanings tonight. The heat from her anger-fire was beginning to stifle the room. It was too hot a summer to have a fire burning inside.

"Luggage? Answers. Or I'm leaving."

She brought the full weight of her attention to me, then. "Yes. Your luggage. I expected when I asked you to come stay with me for a few weeks, that you would have some clothes or personal effects that you wanted to keep close at hand." She picked up her glass and waved it. "Though I understand if you want to just go through my closet. We're still close to the same size. And your everyday things aren't exactly suitable at Court."

I was tempted to down the tequila in front of me. Or throw it at her. Anything to make sense of her. "What are you talking about? You never asked me anything of the sort. Why in Mab's name would I come stay with you for a few weeks?"

Her Renaissance face fell into a pout. "So you're not staying?"

I pursed my lips and bit them to keep inside the frustrated scream I could feel welling up.

"No, Mother, I'm here to talk—"

"I'm not asking," she interrupted. "I already told Argus. You must move back in. Your job is too dangerous."

I frowned, confused. As usual. "My job?"

"Of course, I wouldn't dare encroach on your burgeoning career." She had slipped back into her Southern Belle accent. "Barmaid is such a promising field for one of your caliber. You may continue to serve drinks here if you wish."

I stood. I knew it was pointless to try and talk to her as she slung casual insults. "Goodnight, Mother."

I tried to walk past her toward the door, but before I got past the edge of the couch, she had thrown herself at my feet, wrapped her arms around my legs, and was weeping.

"M-Mother," I started, exasperated at her histrionics.

"She was so warm. She kept me warm." Her shoulders heaved as she gasped the words to the floor and her fingers dug into my thighs.

"Who?" I said softly, knowing that while my mother was dramatic, she was not a great actress. Whatever she was feeling in this moment was real. To her.

"She was so alive. She warmed my bed. My heart. She was life itself. Now she is cold and distant. Of the earth. Now she will be in the earth. They took her blood. She watered the grounds one more time." She sniffed and laughed a little as she looked up. "Isn't it ironic? Don't you think?"

I ignored the fact that she had just quoted Alanis Morisette to me in the midst of one of her episodes. "Are you talking of Nyssa?"

She wept again. "Nyssa. She was so true. So open." Then in an instant, Mother changed. She stood in a rush, nearly knocking me over, and she glared with such venom and hurt, I thought she would burn me where I stood. "Open. Yes, daughter. She was open. You know nothing of that. You could open all doors, and you slam the one that matters most in my face!"

With that she flung a hand out toward the fireplace, and the expensive bottle of Reposado flew from the table into the burning fireplace. The inferno exploded outward in a rush of heat and light, and I cringed backward instinctively as the flames licked up the chimney and out around the lip of the hearth. Reposado was not high enough proof for that dramatic a display, so I knew she was doing that on purpose.

A shard of glass flew up and nicked me across the cheek in the same place the Winter Queen Lada had cut me. A thin dribble of blood started to flow like tears down my face before I realized what had happened.

Mother's eyes grew wide as she realized what she had done. "Oh, baby girl. I'm sorry." She reached out, but I instinctively cringed away. With her power blazing, she seemed seven feet tall, instead of the just over five feet she actually stood. In this guise she was terrifying, even to one who knew and loved her, and I stepped back. I regretted it immediately as the hurt in her eyes grew.

"It's fine, Mother," I assured her, raising a hand to my face. I pushed warmth and pulsed an instruction to my skin to repair, and the cut healed in an instant. Wiping away the blood, I smiled. "See? Nothing happened."

She seemed to shrink back down to size, a woman again instead of a Queen. "I didn't mean to."

"I know," I comforted her and wrapped an arm around her shoulders to steer her back to the couch. We sat together, and I rubbed her arms as the fire dropped away and the room grew colder. "Tell me about her. Tell me about Nyssa."

"She loved me. Even when she left. She didn't leave. She brought her partner to me. I liked him." She leaned her head on to my shoulder, nestling in like a child seeking comfort. "She would have made a good mother."

I hugged her closer. "She would have."

Mother seemed to cave in on herself, curling in to protect her core. "She died. Here." And she tucked her hands into a ball and brought them in to her chest. Pulling in her knees, ignoring the fact that her robe barely covered her, she hugged herself, protecting the ball of her hands at her center. "The cold rushed in as her spirit rushed out. She didn't even scream. She was silent as she died. Empty and cold." She sobbed and moaned for several seconds.

Then suddenly she was still. As if her grief had spent, she uncurled herself, let her hands fall limp to her lap and looked at me solemnly. "May Diana receive her."

"And Morgana mourn her," I responded, invoking the twin goddesses of death with her.

Her eyes widened, and she turned her gaze into the distance. "He smells of ferns and mushrooms," she said dreamily. Then another part of the room seemed to catch her attention, as her voice rose into a shrill cry. "I won't. I won't, and if you make me, I'll strip the air from your blood." And another. "Sleep, sweetness. Sleep and dream of me." She reached a hand to caress my cheek. Then her gaze focused again, and she saw me. "Siobhan? You're here?"

"Yes, Mother." I put my hand over hers still resting on my cheek and reassured her. "I'm here. I'm right here."

I wanted to press her on the details of Nyssa's death: what she had thought, who was with her, what she had felt. But it would have been cruel. Mother was breaking with reality at an alarming rate. She was channeling multiple people in just a few short minutes. Her activities in the bath should have kept her tethered to her body longer. I worried that the trauma of Nyssa's death was exacerbating her madness.

"It's gotten worse, hasn't it?" She knew the answer, but I nodded a confirmation. "Your sister has noticed, too. Asks me to rest. Up here." She frowned, pulling her cupid's bow lips into that perfect pout again. "She's just trying to hide me away. She's embarrassed."

"No, Mother," I said. "You know she's not." If Bryony had been keeping Mother to her rooms, it was for diplomatic reasons. If the Court, if any other royals, saw that she was nearing her breaking point, if the voices that came across the conduit were seeping into her conscious thoughts, things would not last long for her. The magic that surged through her would burn her out. It would corrupt her thoughts, break her from reality, and, like all the Queens before her, she would succumb to the magic that made her.

Which made me ask, "Mother, how long has Kanha been sharing your bed?"

Her eyes twinkled, and she shifted her robe about her, letting the satiny blue of it swish on her thighs provocatively. "He is divine. You really should take him for a night." She grabbed my hands as if we were girlfriends at a sleepover. "He can do the most amazing things with his—"

"How long, Mother?"

"A few weeks," she said softly. "He was a comfort blanket."

"A what?"

"After Cassius died, Ishani sent—"

"Cassius is dead?"

Mother didn't dissolve into tears. She simply considered the news she had shared with me and agreed with what she had said. "Um, yup. A few weeks ago. His breath was stopped. He reached for me. In his final moments. But it was too late for him." She frowned, her eyes darting around, as if she were waiting to feel whatever emotion would seize her next. Then she shrugged, the moment passed.

"Mother, I'm so sorry," I said, feeling grief for her, even if she was numb in this moment. Cassius had been with Mother's Court for upward of ninety years. He'd visited her bed for even longer. She had loved him quite dearly, and Bryony and I had spent many nights with him reading, playing cards, and enjoying him as one of the constants in an ever-shifting Court.

The reaction, or rather the lack of reaction, Mother had to his passing was yet another note of concern.

If Ishani had sent one of her fae to warm Mother's bed soon after his passing, it meant there was something bigger at play. Ishani was only Queen of Chennai, a powerful Queen in India, to be sure, but not as influential as the Queens of Mumbai or Delhi. She was to Mother as Mother was to Mairwen in New York, or Ludivine in New Orleans. Or even Gwendolyn in Boston. She was, forgive the expression, a lesser Queen currying favor.

If the Queen of Chennai was sending her favorite lovers to Mother's bed, then things were worse and far more complicated than I had even imagined.

The only questions I was left with were why no one had said anything, and what else didn't I know. "Mother, I need you to answer me honestly."

"I would never lie to you, pumpkin." She sat up and lifted her chin, defying me to ask what I would. Then I lost her again as she glared at the table. "*Melanerpes erythrocephalus relinquo mea acer pseudoplatanus.*" She blinked several times and looked back at me. "Sorry."

I repeated myself patiently. "Mother, how many Summer fae have gone missing or died in the past few months?"

Her gaze went blank again, but instead of looking out and losing herself to the voices that intruded, this time she seemed to turn inward. Several seconds passed before she answered, and then her voice sounded hollow, as if coming to me from somewhere far away or down a deep tunnel. "The cold ones. Summer set, and they feel Winter's breath. Breathless, two of them, frantic for air. Angry, scared. Fire. Sweating and charred. Ashy breath, chalk and fear. Wet. Krianna. She was wet. Vashti, too. Hot wet falling. Slipping. She promised. The Way. She promised. Wet stains wash away. Open doors. Lets the heat out. Close them. You'll catch a death. Nyssa."

She snapped herself out of the trance with the last word, suddenly lucid again. She grasped for my hands, and her nails dug into my wrists. "Siobhan, you said you had news of Nyssa." Her tone was utterly at odds with her grasp on me; she clawed at me as if she were desperate to stay on solid ground, but she sounded as if she were asking about the weather.

"Mother, I'm so sorry to tell you this, but she's—"

"Dead, yes I know. I felt her die. Like the rest." She smirked. "It's why I needed a party. A pick-me-up. You know how sad I get." She stood then and picked up our empty tequila glasses. "I don't think I can handle any more losses this year."

I tried to think of what she had said, but the words were so unclear, the message so garbled, I couldn't tell how many Summer fae she had felt die. Three she had named: Nyssa, Vashti, and Krianna. And there was Cassius. And it sounded like at least two or three more. Suffocated, burned, drowned, or like Nyssa, cut open to let their heat, their life just spill out. Six, seven? More?

And that wasn't counting the solitary fae that I knew had gone missing. Were they dead like Mother's Summer fae? If not, what had happened to them?

"Why haven't you done anything? Or at least said something? Let people know what is happening?"

She sat still, looking once more into the distance, and I wondered if I had lost her again. But then in a small voice, she answered, "We did not want to cause a panic."

We, she said. She meant Bryony. Of course, Bryony would have looked at this politically. She may not be sitting on the throne, but if she was running things in the midst of Mother's madness, then she would be the one who would be accountable. But she was just acting as Queen; she wasn't the Conduit, and as such, no matter how much the Court listened and followed her directives, she wasn't the true Power. Until Mother stepped aside and passed the Queenship to her, she had to do what she could to consolidate and protect her authority.

"Mother, how long have you known about this?"

In the same small voice, she whispered, "Three months."

Seven fae in three months. Three months.

I felt sick to my stomach. This threat had faced her people directly for three months, and she had said nothing to her Court, nothing to the solitary fae in her community. How many deaths could have been prevented if we had even known there was a threat?

And how long had it been for us? When had Anais vanished? I didn't remember seeing her since before the spring, and it was already nearly midsummer. Four months or more that my own people had been disappearing.

Nothing had been done. Nothing was being done to protect anyone in this city.

"Mother, you have to do something."

She spread her hands helplessly. "What would you have me do? Bryony has had my knights investigating. They have found nothing. No clues that link the deaths. No evidence that any of it was real outside my head until, well, this week. Only what I—" She stopped and swallowed, her eyes closing as she shuddered. "What I felt when they died. It might not have been real."

"But now you have confirmation. Nyssa is dead, Mother. It's not just in your head. I held her hand as she passed."

The look that crossed her face was so pained, so conflicted. There was relief, that what she had known all along, that what she had felt was real and not just in her head. There was grief, for the women she had loved, the fae she had cared for were gone. And there was guilt, for she had not stopped what had happened to them. She had washed her hands of things, and it had only made matters worse.

She patted my hand and nodded reassuringly. "It is okay, darling. We will speak to your sister. We will protect the Summer."

"And what of the solitary? What of the Winter victims?"

She cocked her head like a debutante cocker spaniel. No one performed confused innocence quite like my mother. "What of them?"

Bringing the palms of my hands to my face, I roughly rubbed away hot tears of frustration and anger and desperation. "Mother, the Summer fae are not the only ones affected by this. My people are disappearing. Lada is here because one of her fae died in Atlanta. A Winter Queen in your realm, Mother. She wants answers, as do we.

And if you won't lift a finger to help any of us, we at least deserve to know enough to protect and defend ourselves."

She merely blinked rapidly, as if the words I was saying were not in a language she understood. "Darling, what are you talking about? There's no Winter Queen in Atlanta."

CHAPTER SEVENTEEN

Between Lyris at the door, the private quarters entertainment, and the increasingly obvious conduit madness, I should not have been surprised that Mother was left in the dark about Queen Lada's visit.

Yet the fact that the Queen of Atlanta, the conduit of the Greenwood Gate, was ignorant of a visiting royal, spoke to more complicated politics than I wanted to deal with tonight.

"Oh," I said, unable to offer anything more intelligent to backtrack what I apparently should not have shared with her. "Um, what?"

I was worse at lying that I'd even given myself credit for because she immediately became more lucid than she'd been all evening.

"Darling, pumpkin, honey bun." With every endearment her tone got more dangerous. "Is there a Winter Queen at my palace? Why?"

"I don't know the details, Mother," I said, regretting that I had said anything. "I was just told she was here for an informal gathering with Bryony tonight."

Mother broke into a peal of laughter. "Oh!" She giggled again. "Oh, honey. You mean Lada? She hardly even counts!"

I took a deep breath, though whether it was in relief or frustration, I truly did not know at this point. "You know her?"

"Bryony visited her in Romania a month ago. They had a lovely time, and she mentioned they might want to see each other again." She patted my hand. "Pumpkin, you worry too much. I know I didn't have as many Queen friends as I could have, and that's my fault. Us old guard get so touchy, you know, when it comes to territory and loyalties."

"Believe me, I know," I said not so quietly.

She pursed her lips and raised an eyebrow. I was probably pushing it with the backtalk. She had always granted some latitude when it came to her daughters; to her, we were still young women, stretching our wings. Never mind that I was well past my century, and Bryony into her late eighties; in the scope of Mother's long life, we were mere teenagers.

"If you're worried about her visiting," Mother graciously continued as if I had not spoken, "then you should go down and see them both. Lada's a lovely girl. And that beau of hers? Kiral?"

An immediate chant went through my head: *please don't tell me you've had him already. Please don't tell me you've had him already.*

"Well, I hear she guards him very closely. Doesn't share at all. Can you imagine?" She sounded absolutely scandalized at the idea of monogamy, but she just rolled her eyes. "What a waste."

"I'm sure Lada and Kiral don't think so," I said carefully, and earned another pursed lip of disapproval from Mother.

"Go," she said, tired of my disapproval and judgment. "Go see if you can have fun with the children by the pool. And ask Lyris to send in some fresh faces. And Kanha. I want him back."

It took all of my strength and discipline not to roll my eyes right back at her for that.

She was so intentionally blind to what was happening. Her fae were dying, her daughter was inviting foreign Queens to her domain, and rivals were potentially sending their spies to her bed. But I guess if Kanha did a sufficient job of keeping her tethered to her body with orgasms, all could be forgiven.

"Yes, Mother," I said, reserving my tone. I stood to leave, but she reached out and grabbed my arm before I got too far. I tensed, ready for anything: a plea not to leave, a curse, another break with this reality.

"Siobhan?" Her voice was suddenly small. Her affectations and walls were down, and her Southern accent gone. She almost sounded as she had when I was a child in the nursery, raw and real. "I love you, sweet girl. Please be safe. I don't…" She swallowed. "I don't know what I would do if anything happened to you."

I started to speak, but I didn't know what to say. It was so rare that she was vulnerable with me. That she was real. "Thank you, Mother. I will be careful."

"Beware open doors. The fall is long on the other side."

I blinked, not sure she was still talking to me, or if she was, what she could mean. "I'll be careful," I said again.

She released her grip on my wrist with a look of such relief, I had the feeling she thought I'd said something more than I had.

"Have fun tonight, Mother," I said.

"Oh, I plan to." She stood in a fluid motion, letting her robe fall open at the neck as she shrugged a shoulder slowly, luxuriating in the feeling of the silky fabric against her skin. "Kanha has the most talented—"

"Goodnight, Mother," I said, as I fled her room.

I gave Lyris the most perfunctory instructions about keeping an eye on new additions to Mother's bed before heading for the back stairs.

I passed the hall that led to Bryony's chambers, and the ones that led to my old rooms. Stifling an urge to go check the state of them, I moved as quickly as I could to the stairway that led directly to the back balcony and the pool beyond.

A floor down, and I fled out the glass doors. The landing stretched nearly the entire length of the house, from the stairway to the private royal wing of the house, along the entire back ballroom with its twenty-foot-high ceilings, to the stairways to the guest wing. I emerged on the west side of the building and looked out over the vast property.

The pool was center stage, an oasis of green and blue lit lagoons around a central oval. There were a number of large cabanas with privacy curtains and couches and beds scattered about, with a number of tall broad-leafed plants and ferns near the water to offer privacy and secrecy if one should desire it.

Tonight, though, most of the people seemed to be in and around the main pool. There were at least two dozen bodies lounging, swimming, and congregating at the edges, and another dozen seemed to be occupying open cabanas and lounge chairs. There may have been even more, but in the dark of midnight and the closed cabana curtains, I couldn't be certain. And that was laying aside that some people might be out in the gardens, inside at the bar, or upstairs in the much more private rooms.

I didn't really care who was there, where, or why. I wanted only one.

And tasting the intense sharp but sweet tang of vanilla in the air, I turned right to her.

Of course, she was looking right at me.

My little sister, Bryony Aislin Illythia. Full sidhe daughter of the Queen of Atlanta, thirty years my junior, but, magically, my superior. Mother never disclosed who might have been Bryony's father, as was her every right, but she assured to all that, even though her first born was half human, her second daughter, at least, was full fae. Not that there was ever any doubt; Bryony had exhibited her gifts before her second birthday. She could manifest most of what she desired, could control three elements, and had assumed four different personal forms before she could even speak properly. Compared to most fae, she was a prodigy; compared to her half-human sister, she was practically a goddess.

And no matter what she did, her magic always tasted of pure vanilla bean to me. It really turned me off to that late twentieth century trend of making all candles and lotions and shampoos smell of the shit. It always seemed like cocoa that couldn't quite commit to the goodness of chocolate.

Meeting her gaze, I lifted my hand to wave to my little sister. No doubt, she already knew I was here, so seeing me on the balcony should not have been a surprise.

She did not return my wave as she returned her attention to the person beside her.

Swallowing my pride, I reminded myself, I wasn't here to play politics. I didn't have to pay obsequies or offer up pleasantries to anyone. I wasn't a fairy princess; I'd left that idea behind me long ago. My only loyalties were to myself, the Greenwood Knoll, and the people I chose to make a part of my life. I'd fulfilled my duty to all of them by telling Mother what I knew and giving her the rightful responsibility of protection of the realm.

Still.

I had accomplished nothing.

Mother wasn't equipped to help us. She wasn't even equipped to help her own people. She was incapacitated by the Queen's madness, and it would only grow worse in the coming weeks. In her current state, she would not even be able to properly mourn Nyssa, let alone inform her family and attend to the rites for returning her body to Fairy. That was if she even remembered her death in the morning.

I had to talk to the only one in this house who could actually do something about the mess in Atlanta.

That fact propelled me down the two stories of stairs and into the very gathering I'd been hoping to avoid.

Scanning the crowd as I descended, I couldn't see Lada or her consort Kiral, but they could be behind one of the lagoons, in one of the cabanas, or just outside the reach of the strategically placed lights, opting for some privacy.

I did recognize one face. Or rather she recognized me, as I descended the stairs.

"Siobhan?" Talisa came running up to me from the side of the pool. She had eschewed the complimentary bathing suits, bikinis, and trunks in the cabanas, opting to swim nude, and the sight nearly took my breath away. Her honey-amber skin was soft over curves in all the places I liked them. She had strong calves, wide hips and thighs, a waist that nipped in just enough to a soft, luscious middle, with modest breasts and a long, noble neck.

I smiled down at her full lips, peaked nose, and dark green eyes. "Well, hello. I didn't expect to see you here," I said as I took the last few steps down to the pool patio.

She lifted her lips, and I took them in a soft welcome kiss as I dropped off the last step. She tasted of strawberries and mint with a hint of balsamic vinegar. That intense a taste of her, and I knew she'd been using her magic recently.

"Hello, yourself," she responded, delighted at my greeting. "I was worried after the way I left you..." She let her sentence trail off.

"I'm pretty sure I was the one kicking everyone out of the bar," I said, smiling. "Did your girls get home safely?"

"I tucked Mellie in myself," she said. "Was everything okay with the Gate after I left?"

"We didn't find any more bodies, if that's what you mean," I joked. Then when her eyes widened, I realized that the dead body was not part of what I had announced at the bar. I'd said the Gate was violated, but not what caused it.

Discretion, thy name is Siobhan.

"Dammit," I said, out loud. "I shouldn't have said that."

"No, no," she said. "Don't worry. I won't tell anyone. But was there really a body at the Gate?"

I nodded, not trusting myself to share more than I should.

"Wow. We speculated, the girls and I, but when you said the light in the sky was that the Gate was opened, and then it shut, well, we mostly figured it was just an unexpected opening. Like some important guest coming through. And then lo and behold, there's a Winter Queen visiting." She smiled like a selkie at a water park. "Have you seen her?" Talisa started looking around at the cabanas and the more private lagoons around the pool area.

"Not tonight, no," I said. "I came hoping to talk to Bryony."

Talisa's gaze turned immediately to my sister, who was lounging on a teak and silk-webbed recliner and speaking to a man standing over her.

"By all means. Don't let me keep you," Talisa said, immediately respecting my situation and stepping aside. She reached for my hand as we walked across the poolside, though, and leaned in close to whisper in my ear. "Can I get you alone at all tomorrow?"

I bit my lip as her hot, breathy voice tickled my ear and stirred things inside me. "During or after karaoke?"

"Bit of both?" She smirked as I pulled away.

"I might find a moment," I said. I turned and brushed my lips, butterfly soft against her cheek. "Wait for someone to request Bohemian Rhapsody, and I can get away from the bar for at least five whole minutes."

"The thrill of wooing a bartender," she laughed. But she spun away and skipped to a nearby cabana, her soft, round ass bouncing.

Mab's kiss, I groaned. I did not have time to lose my head over a girl right now.

I couldn't waste any more time. I stalked over to Bryony who was regally reclining in a red two-piece bathing suit that showcased her long, athletic body. She had not inherited Mother's famous curves, but her body was toned, strong, and lean. Her shiny golden hair was twisted up off her neck and secured in a deliberately messy chignon with ornate silver combs.

She was speaking to a very pale man, with white-blond hair and shockingly blue eyes. His green bathing shorts were smaller and tighter than was the modern fashion, but he was at least dressed.

As I approached, Bryony looked up with a cool but unreadable expression. "Siobhan, Mags told me you were here. She left your drink there." She waved at a table set a short distance away. "It's a bit watered down after you took so long to get down here. How's Mother?" Always so good with the pleasantries.

"Mother is well taken care of," I said, ignoring all of the unsaid things in her statement. I walked over to retrieve my drink. A sip revealed that the ice had melted too much, and the boulevardier was indeed watered down. But I drank it anyway. "I'm not here to be social tonight, I'm afraid."

"Of course not. I never imagined you were," Bryony said simply. Anyone listening—and there were plenty of those scattered at nearby chairs, in the water, and standing around their aspiring Queen—would have missed the heat under Bryony's words. I knew her well enough to know she was furious. Whether that was at me or someone else, I'd have to figure out.

She swept her feet to the side of her chair and stood in a fluid move that spoke of strength and power. Looking down at me with a smile that didn't extend to her eyes, she sighed. "Shall we remove ourselves for a few moments for some privacy?"

It wasn't a question. She swept her arm out and indicated a large blue and white striped cloth cabana a few feet away.

"Forgive me, Marius. Family calls. We can resume our conversation later this evening?"

The man she was speaking to nodded and bowed his head to her. "I would be honored, Your Maj—Your Highness." He then retreated to the pool and several very interested fae who began questioning him about what he'd learned from the ersatz Queen and her prodigal sister.

Bryony, for her part, didn't look anywhere but straight ahead as she ushered me ahead of her to the cabana. She flung the curtains of it shut behind her, and before I could wonder how much privacy a few panels of all-weather blue and white canvas could afford us, she made a motion with both hands like she was a conductor cutting off the orchestra. In moments, the inner walls of the cabana began to shimmer with a silvery blue light; she'd soundproofed us, as all sounds from outside were cut off and a cloying taste of vanilla bean coated my tongue.

"How dare you?" She advanced on me, all five foot nine inches of pure faerie rage. "How dare you waltz in here, in the middle of delicate negotiations, without warning, without permission, without anything but the self-righteous stick up your twat that drove you from here in the first place?"

"Wh-what? Bry, I just came here to—"

She waved at me, as if to silence me with the same magic trick she'd used on the cabana, but it was nothing but her imperiousness at work.

"To tell me what, exactly?" She put her hands on her hips and pursed her lips, waiting a half second for an answer. "That the Gate opened all over the Atlanta skyline? I could see it across the river from my bedroom. I know what Fairy looks like."

"But—"

"The body of one of Mother's many cheap girlfriends was found at the scene. Yes. I know."

"And—"

"And it's the second body in as many days, and you're worried about several other wayward solitaries missing over the past few weeks." She sighed her eyes and shook her head. "Honestly, Siobhan, do you think there is anything that happens in my city without me knowing about it?"

"Yeah, actually," I interrupted before she could really get going. "I think there is a lot that goes on here that you don't know about. Like the fact that people are scared that the local Court doesn't care about them as people go missing. That they don't feel safe here in the Iron Realm. That the solitary fae in your city may be sacrificing themselves to get an ounce of power from the Gate just to protect themselves."

Bryony lifted her chin. "They're welcome to pledge themselves to Summer if they want more power. Now, if that's all you came to say—"

"It's not. If you know everything that is going on in 'your' city," I obnoxiously put quotation marks around the possessive, "then why is it still going on? Why haven't you done anything about it? Why aren't you investigating? Where are the proclamations, town criers, anything to get the word out so people can protect themselves even if you are going to sit here on your royal ass and do nothing?"

She rolled her eyes. "Proclamations? Really, Siobhan? So long as the news came from the palace, your people wouldn't care if I said Atlanta was burning and all Fairy was invited to the swog roast over the flames. They'd insist it was propaganda to control more of their lives and ignore it."

"You can't blame the solitary for not trusting the Courts when they withhold information like this."

"For Mab's sake, Siobhan, the Court isn't responsible for everything that happens."

"Clearly, you're not responsible for anything that happens. Unless there's a big naked party to host, you can't be bothered."

She opened her mouth to scream back at me but stopped and took a deep breath instead. Then she blinked her pretty green eyes and offered a cold, mechanical, completely royal smile. "You may leave. You made it abundantly clear years ago that you don't want responsibility for this city or its inhabitants, and you don't get to come in here and tell me how to do things. I know everything I need to know about what has happened at the Greenwood Gate and your little pub. I am doing more than you know. I have brought in resources to help get to the bottom of what is happening."

"Resources?" I scoffed. "You mean like the insane Winter Queen?"

"Yes! Lada lost someone on our lands, and—"

"Did Ishani the Chennai Queen claim that, too? Or was her lover someone you blindly invited to Mother's bed?"

Her eyes flashed, and I thought I had finally pushed her too far. I'd seen her call the lightning between an ex-lover's neurons and fry the sense out of him from the inside out when she'd caught him with one of her maids. She'd drowned the maid in her own personal thunderstorm.

But she had better control these days. She simply pressed a hand to the space between her eyes and started to rub, as if I were giving her a headache she really didn't need right now. "Kanha is a diplomat, and a good one. And Mother needed the comfort after Cassius. Especially after what happened to Nyssa. Think, Siobhan. When the Gate ripped open that much, when Mother's girlfriend did whatever she did to herself, she opened the Gate too far. Mother collapsed. With that much power rushing through her, I'm surprised it didn't kill her. She was screaming and ranting like I've never seen before. Why do you think she's being placated with four lovers at once? And as Ishani told me, Kanha has experience grounding a Queen on the verge of madness."

"I hadn't realized," I began.

"Of course, you hadn't," Bryony snapped, her control rapidly fraying. "You don't bother to come home unless you need something, but you're more than happy to criticize those of us here dealing with real problems." She took a breath. "Look, I love you. I would be happy to visit with you. But not now. Not tonight. Put your mind at ease. Magic flows between the realms. For now, the Conduit is unbroken, and she's as happy as she can be with her mind fracturing into several realities at once."

She stopped there and swallowed. She and I both knew that was what awaited her as well. It was what had awaited me when I had been the heir. No matter the power that came with serving as the Conduit, few could deny the price was steep.

Straightening her steel spine and lifting the neck that would one day support a crown, my sister tried again. "The Gate works, Nyssa's body is already being seen to, Mother is well-taken care of, and there are forces at work that you know nothing of. You'll be fine to hold your karaoke night and enjoy your blissful world of ignorance at the bar. But you have to leave. I have some delicate diplomacy to take care of, and unless you are interested in wooing either Lada Cassimira or Thierry Kellan to peace between our realms despite whatever is happening to our aggravatingly independent subjects, then you don't belong here tonight."

She didn't wait for me to argue but reversed her silencing motion to release her spell and stalked from the cabana, leaving the blue and white canvas flapping behind her.

CHAPTER EIGHTEEN

I couldn't bring myself to flee immediately. I sank down onto one of the lushly padded lounge chairs and let my head hang down in dismay.

There were few times I'd ever felt this helpless. Fae in Atlanta were going missing, dying, being murdered or, Mab forbid, killing themselves, and instead of helping me, my sister mocked and dismissed me. I couldn't do anything to help. I was useless.

And as of tonight, that wasn't even my most immediate crisis. Mother was succumbing to the Queen's Madness, and Bryony was using the opportunity to consolidate her own power by inviting the biggest foreign powers she could find.

Not only was she feting a new Winter Queen, but she was forging alliances with one of the most notorious solitary dissidents in the United States.

Thierry Kellan was in town? He was here, at the palace? I guess that explained his sudden interest in funding parties at the Knoll. He must be building his own coalition of support in the city.

And either Bryony had more faith in her own desirability, or she'd leveled up as a diplomat in ways that were not at all apparent to me. Regardless, she was acting as the Queen, when Mother was still alive and well upstairs, and no one seemed to raise so much as an eyebrow about it."

Worst of all, Bryony had very clearly let me know that I was useless to address any of these things. Without magic, without power, without political influence of any kind, I might as well just go back to my bar and sing a happy tune, because nothing else was likely to do good.

The whole point of being solitary was existing apart from the politics of Court. I had my bar, my Greenwood family. I had my regulars and some I might even call friends. But I didn't have resources. I didn't have powerful networks or connections. I was alone.

I'd never regretted that before.

Running my fingers up along my temples and into my hairline, I tugged at the roots of my curls, easing the tension headache that was building along the sides of my head. I should have known better than to come to the palace. I was as useless as a selkie in the desert.

"That bad, huh?"

I released my head and looked up to see Talisa poking her head in the open flap at the front of the cabana.

"You could say that," I said dejectedly. I scooted over to indicate she was free to join me if she wanted.

She took the invitation and stepped in, now dressed in a navy-blue sundress that swung along her thighs as she rushed to me, bare feet slapping on the rough stone tiles. She sank down next to me and pulled me into a hug. "Whatever she said, I'm sure she didn't mean it." Talisa cradled my head on her shoulder and rubbed my back soothingly. "She's got a lot on her plate tonight, and I'm sure she was just lashing out."

I nodded, utterly unconvinced.

"Seriously, sweetheart. Thierry tells me she's been wining and dining him all week. She doesn't have the first clue what's happening to the missing and now dying fae in her city. She's worried it shows weakness just as she's getting ready to ascend."

With a start I pulled my head from her shoulder. "Ascend? Already?" Mother had been in a bad way, but she hadn't lost touch with herself entirely yet. She was erratic, but so were all full Queens. Usually when Queens were ready to abdicate, there were more signs than she'd shown.

"That's the rumor," Talisa said carefully. "I'm sorry, I shouldn't have said anything. Thierry just…" She trailed off.

"What do you know of Thierry Kellan?"

She shrugged. "He owns my real estate company. Or rather he owns the conglomerate that owns the holding company that owns my real estate brokerage." She laughed. "He's come through Atlanta a few times, and all of us girls have had dinner with him. But he seems to be here for more than an appearance this time. He has a week of meetings scheduled, including with the palace." A crease appeared between her brows, as her voice lowered to an apologetic whisper. "He mentioned a change of regime that he should properly observe."

"Mother's not ready to give up yet." I insisted on it. I wasn't ready to say goodbye permanently. Not yet. If she abdicated, Mother severed herself from the Gate, she stepped out of the way of the power that passed from Fairy to Earth, and passed on the job of conduit to her heir. She had described it to me once thus: the local Queen is the dam that stands before the river of Fairy magic that wants to come through the Gate. She holds back the flood and allows it to pass to those to whom she is connected; some of the flow spreads to the surrounding lowlands, but she is the main channel through which the water passes.

When she abdicates, there must be another dam to hold the power back, or it will overwhelm the region, destroying all lives in its immediate path and damaging those close enough to feel its effects. The new dam is constructed, tested, and when ready, the old dam is removed. Though this can be done in a controlled way with redirected currents, feeder streams, and controlled letting of the waters, usually, the old structure is destroyed, consumed by the floods that rush past as they are released.

Abdication meant the old Queen's death. And usually the onset of the new Queen's madness.

I could lose half my family in a single moment.

Distractedly, I wondered if anyone had told father. Or my brother Dariel.

I wasn't ready.

Talisa saw me worrying my bottom lip with my teeth. She reached up a hand. "Hey," she said softly and rubbed a petal-soft thumb over my lip. "Don't do that."

Without warning, my mouth began to tremble under her touch. The traumas of the past few days, the growing fear and anxiety, the inevitable stress of speaking to my sister who never even bothered to try and communicate with me like I was a person, it all mounted up, and an avalanche began, starting with the tremble in my lip.

I would not cry in front of Talisa. I would not cry.

The first tears slipped out anyway.

"Oh, no. No, no, sweetie, don't," Talisa said, her voice low, and husky. She smoothed her finger from my lips across my cheek and cupped my face, her fingers light and warm against my jawline. She scooted closer and brought her other hand to my opposite cheek. "Siobhan. It's okay."

"Is it?" I said, ashamed of the break in my voice, as the tears blurred my vision.

"Shh," she said, as she moved closer, leaning her forehead against mine.

I blinked furiously as she pulled me in, holding the back of my neck lightly but firmly. She spread her fingers so some found their way around my neck while others reached up under my hairline. A soft press, and she pulled me closer, shushing over my sniffles.

"You're not alone," she whispered, as she angled her lips upward and laid a soft kiss on the side of my mouth. "It's okay." She kissed my cheek. "You're okay. You're one of the strongest people I've met."

I pulled away just enough to tilt my chin up and look her in the eyes. She met me, her green eyes steady and warm.

"I'm not. You don't even know me. I'm not strong."

"You are," she insisted. "Siobhan, you are incredible." Then using her gentle but insistent grip on the back of my neck, she pulled me toward her. Her lips received mine, pressed, and coaxed them open with a sigh, just enough for our breaths to merge, as I gasped in the strength she offered me. Her lips tasted of two ripe strawberries, still dusted with a rich balsamic glaze and the merest hint of mint. I grounded myself in the scent, the flavor of her.

To be fair, I did more than ground myself. Like my mother before me, I dove into the physical luxury, the present moment and the insistent touch of her skin against mine. Seizing the lifeline she offered, I near dragged her down with me, so desperately did I cling to her. I inhaled and savored everything she was willing to offer.

Reaching up, I wrapped my arms around her, pulled her close as I experienced every sensation: the rich, heady scent of her; the sound of her breath, light and eager; the hungry press of her thin lips and comforting hands. I let her envelope me, hungry for the protection of her arms, proof against everything that waited for me outside the cabana.

Too soon, Talisa pulled away, breathless. "Not here," she said. She was right. A cabana at the palace wasn't safe, or private, or anywhere I wanted to spend more time than I needed to.

She lifted a hand once again to my cheek, checking my face, looking for what, I wasn't sure. Maybe she was seeing if I would break down in tears again. Maybe she was seeing just how hungry I was for more, whether I wanted to taste all of her.

She must have seen what she wanted. All at once, she smiled, and the wicked sparkle in her eyes made my stomach flip. I reached for her again, but she stopped me by catching my hand. Bringing it to her lips and flipping it over, she laid a wet kiss on my palm before turning her intent gaze back to me.

"I left my car at the Knoll," she said hungrily. "If you take me there, I can follow you home?"

Unable to find my tongue for a few more seconds, I merely nodded and grabbed her hand as she led the way out of the cabana.

CHAPTER NINETEEN

I don't even know how we got to my car after that. We found Talisa's shoes at the poolside and scooped them up before we wove through ferns and stone paths, avoiding other people as much as we could. The next thing I knew, I was opening the door as she tumbled into my car, refusing to break eye contact as she did so.

Wanting to feel the feather-soft but electrically undeniable touch of those lips again, I nearly dove into her right there, but I restrained myself and closed the door. I had to pause for a fortifying breath as I walked around the rear bumper of my Honda Civic.

Looking up at the building that loomed beyond us, the imposing brick and gargantuan size of the palace and all the threat it contained within, my heat chilled. If I took tonight with Talisa, it wouldn't fix everything my people were facing. In the morning, I would still have to do something. I would have to call up Argus, Mikka, and Varon, tell the Knoll we were on our own. It was up to us to protect the solitary fae of Atlanta. That the Court was too busy doing whatever it is they do to protect their own power.

If anybody was going to spread the word, organize the solitary fae to their own defense, and get to the bottom of what was threatening all of us, we were going to have to do it ourselves.

But I looked at the silhouette of the redhead in my front seat. The way the lights around the building captured the soft curve of her shoulder, the wispy wave of her hair. I thought of the attentive way she kissed. The concern and fierce protectiveness she had shown me in a vulnerable moment.

Tonight, that was enough.

I slipped into the car.

"Hi," she said, almost shyly.

"Hi," I replied with the same tone. I couldn't help but giggle. Between us we had nearly two hundred years of experience in intimacy. None of it made any difference in those first few moments together.

Her laugh echoed mine, as she reached for my hand. "And here I was happy at the chance of getting to sing with you at karaoke. This is much more my style of duet."

I laughed harder, as I started the car, shifted it into gear, and twined my fingers between hers. "I hope you can harmonize," I teased.

"I have perfect pitch."

Something tightened deep within me at her challenge, and I squeezed her hand harder, before pulling the car out of the palace parking and pointing us toward the woods.

Seeing the confused look on her face, I realized Talisa didn't know the back way off the grounds. I grinned mischievously at her and took off faster than I should have. A quick fishtail as we spun off the driveway and onto the gravel had her squealing in a way that tightened my stomach further. I aimed for the exit that was invisible thanks to the royal glamour in place, and I barely let my foot up enough to actually turn away from the river and up the path only I knew was there.

Talisa saw what I saw: we were about to leave the edge of the property and crash into a line of Georgia pines. She clutched at my hand and began to press down on an imaginary brake on the passenger side as she braced with her other hand against the roof of the car.

We passed harmlessly through the glamour and came out on the wide path up through the woods and the private property beyond the palace.

I slowed down as her fear broke in hysterical laughter. "Oh, Mab's curse, I thought you were going to…I don't even know! I had no idea what you were doing. Oh, for Mab's sake. Of course there's a back way in."

"Sorry," I said, barely able to talk through my giggles. "I never get to surprise anyone with that." I lifted her hand, still entwined in mine, to my lips. "Forgive me?"

"I'll make you pay for it," she laughed back, her eyes flashing as she challenged me before she looked around at where we were.

"I can't wait," I said, enjoying as her panic gave way to delight.

I slowed down considerably as we passed through the private residence and out onto Riverside Drive before heading toward the interstate. Talisa leaned back, her hand warm and relaxed in mine as I pulled us onto the on ramp.

It was late, well after three a.m. at this point, but I-285 was never entirely empty. It formed a perimeter loop around the sprawling city of Atlanta, stretching from six lanes at its narrowest to twelve at its widest, and it was often the easiest way to get around the city without hitting any of the cursed central highways. Sporadic cars zipped past us, flying at nearly eighty miles per hour, while I kept us at an easy sixty-five in the middle lane. Even the occasional semi-truck passed inside, going much faster than they should, but probably eager to get out of the city before rush hour began in the next three hours.

When bright headlights came in my rearview mirror as we crossed I-75, I didn't think much of it. Not at first. Then, when the high beams came on, I was just annoyed.

"Go around," I muttered, before dropping Talisa's hand and flipping the rearview mirror up to avoid being blinded. Then I realized the much larger vehicle wasn't moving to pass us. It had matched our speed, directly behind us.

"What's the matter?" Talisa said, turning to look behind us and immediately squinting and putting a hand up to shield her eyes. The vehicle was larger than my Civic, a truck or SUV to judge by the height of its headlights. As it began to inch closer, I increased my speed to get away from them. "What are they doing?"

"No clue," I said, already putting on my turn signal and moving into a farther right hand lane. I wasn't going to speed up any, but I could move out of their way and let them be on their way.

The car moved with us, bearing down even harder.

"They're too close," Talisa said.

"I know." I could hear the fear in my voice before I even felt it. "We only have two exits left." I wasn't sure if I was trying to convince myself or her, as I clutched both hands over the edge of the steering wheel and darted constant glances at the rearview mirror.

I hit the turn signal and started to move over. That's when the truck gunned its engine and rammed into the back of us.

One moment I had full control of the car, then the wheels beneath us fought me in every direction. We lurched forward, and then the rear of the car pulled violently from side to side. At these speeds, I knew we were in danger of going into a full spin and flip as my tires squealed, but I held off slamming the brakes as my instincts insisted, and somehow held the wheel steady as my tires fought to grip the road.

As I found equilibrium and my Civic slowed its fishtail, I saw that the same headlights were still behind us, and already closing the gap. It was going to ram us again.

"Hold on," I shouted as I pulled hard on the wheel and swerved for the exit we were already passing. I almost lost control of the car again as we crossed two lanes, bumped over rough pavement, and jumped onto the exit ramp.

Talisa was screaming beside me, but the only way I could help her was to get us off the road.

I turned to see if the truck attempted to follow us, but I only saw taillights and heard the engine roar as the pickup sped away down the perimeter highway.

Safe for the moment, I allowed us to roll to a stop at the red light at the top of the ramp onto Paces Ferry Road. Clutching the steering wheel, I gasped for air before slamming the parking brake and ripping the seatbelt off of me. I twisted out of my seat and turned to check on Talisa who was wide-eyed and pale.

"Are you okay?" I grabbed at her upper arm to turn her toward me.

She blinked rapidly several times, her mouth gaping as she tried to find words. "They—they did that on purpose! They tried to run us off the road! They were trying to kill us!"

"Yeah," I agreed. "I think they were."

"Why?" she screeched. Her eyes were huge, but her pupils had shrunk to tiny pinpricks of black, and the taste of balsamic strawberries overwhelmed me.

"Oh, no, Talisa, hey, stay with me." I reached across her for her other arm, trying to connect with her. Fear had her reaching for her natural defense mechanisms, and that meant nothing but trouble for me. In their most vulnerable moments, maenads had access to incredible strength, boundless energy, and almost impenetrable physical and magical defenses, but to touch that power, they passed into a manic state that was incredibly contagious. Maenads had been known to bring entire crowds to ruin with a single panic attack.

In an effort to keep herself safe, Talisa could cross over into a state where she didn't know what she was doing or who she was doing it to, and she could pass that mania to me with a touch. Only I wouldn't have her same defenses.

I either had to get her under control quickly, or menacing pickups running us off the road was the least of our worries.

"Talisa?" I reached for her face, bringing a palm to her cheek. She flinched, and I wasn't sure she saw me, or even knew I was there. The taste of strawberries grew. She was breathing rapidly, nearly panting, choking down breaths, and her gaze was fixed far beyond me. "Hey," I said and cupped her face between my hands. I tried what she had done to me only a short while earlier. I rubbed a light thumb over her bottom lip, trying to find that intimacy, that soft, delicate moment that would let her know she was safe. The way she had done for me. "You're okay. Right? It's okay. You're so much stronger than this."

The words that she had used on me weren't hitting the same way.

Still her breathing was too fast, bordering on hysteria as she gasped and fed on her own fear.

"Oh, Mab help me." I leaned over the seat and planted my lips on hers, desperate to stop her breath from accelerating any further. I inhaled and tried to steal her breath, to still it, for just a moment.

A muffled question pushed between my lips, and panicked, she started to pull away. I loosened my hands on the sides of her face, letting her know that she could leave at any moment. But I still leaned into the kiss, giving her as much strength and assurance and grounding as I could manage through lips that demanded nothing and offered everything.

Stay here, I willed to her. *Be here with me. Feel me. Taste me. I've got you. You are safe with me.*

By Mab's grace, she didn't pull away. She pressed back into me. Slowly, her breath lost the panicked edge, and she relaxed into my kiss.

I don't know how long we lingered in that moment, but a quick series of beeps from behind us forced both of our eyes open and made us realize we were parked at an intersection that even at three a.m. wasn't entirely abandoned.

"I'm okay," she said, breathily, catching my gaze for half a second before darting a glance back at the car behind us, beyond to the freeway, and then back to me. "I'm okay. I'm here. I'm here." She sank back into her seat and repositioned the seatbelt that had slipped from her as we kissed.

As the car behind us whipped around to pass us before the light turned red again, I slid back into my own seat and put my seatbelt on. I checked Talisa again, and saw her wrap her arms about herself, rubbing at them as if she were cold, despite the summer air. Reluctantly, I took the car out of park, flipped my turn signal, and waited for the now red light to turn green again.

We rode the rest of the way to the Knoll in silence. It took longer on the surface roads, but we passed almost no one once we were off the main byways, and that was fine by me. I took the gravel drive slowly, careful of kicking up rocks in case it might make Talisa uneasy. I pulled into a spot right next to her black Audi sedan and turned off the car.

The silence was oppressive as we both just stared ahead. My fear and spike of adrenaline had all completely faded, and I was left feeling drained. The last thing I wanted was to take Talisa home with me. I wanted to go home, pull covers over my head, and vanish into oblivion for a few hours.

A look at her showed that she was thinking something similar. She was picking at her fingernails and avoiding looking up. She had her white sandals pressed into the floorboards so firmly, I was sure she was still pressing an imaginary brake.

"Hey," I said softly. Still, she jumped at the sound, before looking at me with a weak smile. "Do you need me to take you home? Or call someone? We have the Hendleys still on call if you want."

Looks of distress, disappointment, and relief warred over her face. "I don't have to go home. We could still—"

"No," I said, cutting her off. "No, sweetie. We've been through something tonight, and I don't think either of us are in any state of mind for anything else right now. I know I'm not. If you don't want to be alone right now, I understand, and I will happily take you home. Or follow you. Or call you someone." I reached out and put my open palm before her, asking for her to put her hand in mine. She hesitated, but slowly reached out and laid her limp grasp in mine. "I'm not going anywhere. Tomorrow, I will be right here at the Knoll, serving drinks, and eager for that duet with you. But I think, tonight, I'm not ready to process what just happened, or anything that has happened this week. I think I need to be alone. To rest, to react, and to find where the new ground is. And then we can reconnect tomorrow or later this week. Is that okay?"

She looked at me blankly, but then nodded, her lower lip trembling. She unbuckled her seatbelt and got out of the car without a word. I likewise stepped out, but I didn't move toward her, just watched over the roof of my car as she closed the door of my Civic and moved toward her Audi, key fob already in her hand.

She had opened her own car door, and I thought she would leave without speaking further when she looked up and offered a weak smile. "Can we sing 'Under Pressure'?"

My laugh had a manic edge that I wasn't entirely sure was my own. "Appropriate. Do you want Mercury or Bowie?"

"You can hit the high notes. I'll sing Bowie." She smiled shyly. "Get home safe, Siobhan."

"You, too," I said as I watched her slide into her seat, close the door, and drive away.

I looked up to the lit rooms above the Knoll. Argus would still be awake. As a dragon, he slept only a few nights a week, and as a bartender, those were never on the weekend. If I wanted to talk, to tell someone what was going on, I could go upstairs, and Argus would listen, offer support and suggestions on what our next move could be.

But I was not a dragon. I was still only half fae, and right now, all my human side wanted to do was go home to bed. So, wearily, I sank back into my car and headed home.

I could deal with things tomorrow.

CHAPTER TWENTY

I had never seen a crowd like the one that gathered that Saturday. Argus put out word that the Greenwood Gate was safe, he'd had the wards reinforced by noon, and by five thirty in the afternoon, we were already well over capacity. Karaoke didn't start until eight. Hell, the song list didn't even start taking names until seven.

Izolda, the vila who was our VIP MC, was already overwhelmed.

"Siobhan, this is madness," she gasped over the edge of the bar, fifteen minutes after we'd opened. "I was worried everyone would keep away after I heard the news. But it seems like every fae in the state is here."

I passed her a rum and Coke with lime and shrugged. "Sorry, sweetie. Maybe it's safety in numbers? Or everyone wants to be here in case something else happens. So they can say they were here, too."

"Whatever it is, do you want me to start early? Maybe open the list now and start things up in twenty?"

"That would be wonderful. Yes, please." And then catching a glance at the group in the middle of the room. "Oh, and can you dedicate a song to Mellie Tyne? She announced her pregnancy before things got crazy, and I worry she might feel overshadowed by what's happened."

Izolda's eyes got wide in excitement, and a smile broke across her wide, thick-lipped mouth. "A baby! A solitary baby? Oh, that's wonderful! Of course, of course. Wow. A baby! I don't know what is special enough to sing for that. Oh, wow! Thank you for the challenge." She walked away with her drink but called over her shoulder, "Don't forget to sign up, too. I got you and Shiro first, but I won't be able to squeeze in anything for you last minute like usual."

I stuck my tongue out at her. Typically, I was so busy making and serving drinks, I would forget that I wanted to sing, too, and usually pulled bartender privileges to get on the list whenever it was most convenient for me. Besides the duets with Talisa and Shiro, I hoped to get a solo song in as well. After this week, I needed the release as much as any of my customers.

And there were more than enough of them. I recognized faces I hadn't seen in years, fae I'd been convinced had moved away or returned to Fairy or sworn fealty to the Court. In fact, several members of the Court were here, including Shiro and a crowd of daonie sidhe, and some of the emissaries I remembered as Mother's local ambassadors. They were supposed to cultivate good will with the solitary community by forging friendships and relationships that surpassed Court allegiances, but I'd seen few enough of them in the Knoll over the year to doubt their dedication to the job.

The solitary fae of Atlanta were much more well represented. Sylphs, dryads, ifrit, selkies, and nymphs took up the majority of the tables with groups of intermingling friends. Several Bean Nighe, Tighe, and Sidhe families took up one corner of the room by the hearth, while the usual crowd of elementals, lilin, kobolds, and gremlins flitted from bar to tables to the porches outside. And of course, Gary, Atlanta's only barquist, came out. He took up residence wedged between the grand fireplace and the karaoke set-up. Eight feet tall with horns of varying lengths all down the back of his head, black fur on every inch of his exposed body, and claws like dog talons tapping the edge of his beer stein, he would terrify any human who saw him without his glamour. But when he turned his blood red eyes and razor teeth to offer a smile my way, all I could see was an overgrown puppy as giddy and excited as anyone else in the bar. Thank Mab he didn't have a tail, or he'd be wagging it and knocking over people and tables alike.

The maenads commanded the central tables as usual, while my crowd of clurichaun were all accounted for at their usual spot. Cormac, Alden, Leland, and Baerd held down the fort in the closed-off corner, but Gair kept coming up to the bar to order directly from me. The fourth time he came to refresh one of his friend's drinks, I laughed at him.

"You know you can ask Kaia to run drinks for you. You don't have to keep fighting through the crowd every time one of you runs out of water."

Over his beard, Gair's cheeks turned as red as his hair, but he smiled down at me. "I don't mind, Miss Siobhan. I like getting the chance to stretch my legs and see your pretty smile."

It was my turn to blush. "Then by all means, keep coming to visit me. Another Macallan for Leland I'm guessing?"

He laughed. "Got it in one."

I poured the two fingers of scotch, neat for Leland, and passed the tumbler to Gair. His fingers lightly brushed mine as I handed him the glass, and I lingered for a second as a smoky plum and pine taste like a rich cabernet whispered across my tongue. I licked my lips and met his clear blue eyes. "Gair, did you just bestow luck on me?"

His cheeks flushed more furiously, and he pulled his fingers and the drink away. "Ach. Forgive me. I did not have permission."

"To give me luck?"

"To use my gifts with ye." Once again, his brogue came through. "I only wish to help."

I couldn't reach him across the bar, but I slapped a hand palm down on the wood, demanding he take my words seriously. "Gair, stop. You have nothing to apologize for. I am honored by any magic or luck you choose to share with me. Honestly, this sweek, I could use all the help I can get. We all could."

"Miss Siobhan, ye may have all ye want of me." He looked down but didn't blush this time. "The rest of them can wait." Then he looked up with a surge of confidence and winked at me before leaving with his drink. Or rather Leland's drink.

I craned over the edge of the bar and saw that both Alden and he were halfway through their drinks already. Biting my lip, I realized I was already looking forward to Gair's next visit to me in a few minutes. His interest was unexpected, but nice. I wasn't sure it would go anywhere, but then I had never thought about Talisa as a possible romantic partner either before this week.

Stressful conditions had bred stranger bed fellows.

I smiled in spite of myself to think of Gair naked, his solid, oak-cask frame, strong and firm. I wondered if he had red hair everywhere.

"Who are we thinking of naked?" Mikka bounced up behind me, scaring me enough that I almost spilled the hefeweizen I was pouring.

"What? Nobody." I blushed and topped off the drink before passing it over to the gray-haired gremlin grinning at me across the bar.

"I bet it's Talisa," she said, grinning as she nicked a luxardo cherry out of the bowl under the bar. "Rumor is you left the palace with her last night after private time in a cabana."

Looking over to the group of maenads at the center of the room, I realized Talisa wasn't with them. I scanned the room but didn't see any sign of her honeyed hair. She must not have gotten here yet.

"I knew it," Mikka laughed, grabbing a tray and putting glasses on it, as I grabbed a bottle of wine and started to uncork it. "You better tell me everything."

The cork stuck as I tugged. "What are you talking about, Meeks? You've been with Talisa. Many, many times. For the past several years. You've slept with most of the maenads in this bar. And the succubi. And incubi. And—"

"Okay, okay!" She put her hands up to ward off any more listing of her sexual partners, but she was mostly amused. "Yes, I know how she is with me. But I want to know how she is with you."

"I wouldn't know." I passed off the drinks and told her to take them to table twenty-three. She raised her eyebrows, curious to know more, but she didn't push it as she took the wine and glasses to the appropriate table.

Before I could reach for the next drink ticket or ask the next order along the bar, a voice called out over the white noise of the crowd. We didn't have microphones in the bar as they were redundant given our DJ's unique skills.

Izolda cleared her throat and changed the way it resonated, and everywhere in the bar, you could hear her announce, "One and all, welcome to the Greenwood Knoll." She had to pause as a great roar rose up from the crowd. She smiled and continued. "I know we're getting started earlier than usual, but things being what they are," she paused again for an outburst of nervous laughter, "well, we might as well make good use of the time we're given. So, an hour earlier than planned, let's kick things off with Shiro and Siobhan."

I didn't know where Shiro had disappeared to, but he was there waiting for me by the time I pushed my way out from behind the bar and up to the stage beside the large fireplace that took up the far wall.

He leaned in to hiss at me, "You came to the palace last night?"

"Yeah, not now," I said quickly, before Izolda extended her magic over to our voices, and the music started. She didn't create the music herself, but rather extended her influence over to her phone, ready with the backing music for our duet. For this song, though, we started in silence, with nothing but Shiro's voice.

He turned to me, in full performance mode. Shiro Harada was descended from a trickster fae, and his performance skills were second to none. In a moment, without a single chord, he slipped into character as he looked at me with longing and told me tunefully how much he wanted me. He might hate musical theater, but he came alive with the right songs. As the music crept in behind him, the bar went silent, all eyes on us. He poured himself into a longing that was forbidden, impossible, and undeniable. He was mesmerizing, and though every time we performed together he was incredible, tonight there was something authentic and vulnerable to his performance.

Despite the monitor with the lyrics highlighted in proper time, I almost missed my cue. Luckily, the song was in the low part of my range, and I sank into the pulling tide of the melody. I confessed how hard it was to escape our circumstances, no matter what our feelings might be, that the world didn't care what we wanted. A fragility crept into my own voice, as I insisted that our destinies were already written, and no matter what we had here in our safe space, the world outside would never accept us. Would never accept me.

I felt naked on that stage, as I wrapped my voice around Shiro's and the raw need he brought to the song. Our voices twined about each other like aerialists lifting higher and higher, until the song hit solid ground, and I ended it in the same acapella style with which Shiro had launched us.

A beat of silence enveloped us before thunderous applause shook the building. I smiled to Shiro, about to thank him for singing with me, but he had already turned away and disappeared into a group of sidhe and Summer Court fae who were waiting at the edge of the stage.

For a moment, I felt like an exposed nerve, standing alone on the stage with the aftermath of the song. But I quickly pulled myself together and accepted compliments as I made my way back to the bar. I slipped through the open gap between the bar and the back passage and brought down the oak shelf that kept overeager patrons from behind the bar.

Safe behind the wood and liquor, I took a breath and leaned against the inside wall, hidden in the shadows. Part of what I was feeling, I knew, was a result of Izolda's magic. She had a gift for pulling truth out of her performers, and I'd felt the exhilaration of singing from my heart on her stage nearly every week for over a decade.

There was something more to it tonight. I didn't know if it was the song choice, partner choice, or something inside of me tonight. I felt untethered, like I was still spinning over the song and the crowd and everything I needed to face. My mother and sister, the faceless threat outside these doors, the fact that I was powerless before all of it. It seemed to me that the stars held nothing but my own weakness before undeniable forces. I was written to be a victim, a pawn, a leaf caught in a gale and set adrift in my own life.

No matter what I wanted, I could do nothing but sit back and wait for something to happen.

"Hey," a soft voice said to my right. On the other side of the oak partition stood Gair, his blue eyes hooded with concern. "Are you okay?"

"Was the song that bad?" I joked, a strained laugh followed, even though I hadn't planned it.

"It was beautiful," he said evenly. "Heartbreaking. I feel bad for the iele who had to follow you." He gestured up to the stage where a raven-haired beauty belted out a pop ballad that had only ever dreamed of sounding so good. "All right, never mind, she knows what she's doing."

Laughing, I assured Gair, "I'm fine. Really. Izolda just has a way of making you feel a song."

"I think the credit goes to the singer. Or singers. Your partner? He is from the Summer Court, isn't he?"

"Shiro," I said. Seeing as he was surrounded by a dozen people, all wearing clothing entirely too fancy for karaoke night at the local watering hole, I didn't need to confirm that he was part of the Summer contingent. Each of the group was young, beautiful, and wearing a distinctive silver pin in the form of a fern frond. Court fae didn't always feel the need to identify themselves so blatantly. I wondered if it was a way to stick together. Safety in numbers, and all.

Shiro looked uncomfortable. I wondered if the song had gotten to him as well.

Gair leaned over the oak shelf and pitched his voice lower. "I just wanted to make sure you were well. You seemed upset when you finished singing. And I didn't know if it was because of this Shiro, or if there was something more."

His blue eyes were tender and patient, and his genuine concern about broke something in me. I almost lifted the wooden rail and asked for him to hold me again, to let my fears and worries melt away into his arms. His hug was like a shot of whiskey that warmed me through, easing tension and loosening the hold of my anxious mind.

But then I noticed his gaze drifted past me. I turned to see what had caught his eye and saw Baerd at the other end of the bar, heatedly arguing with a woman. She looked familiar as she laughed and tried to dismiss him, but as he grabbed her arm and forced her to face him, I recognized her. It was Hannah, the human who'd almost fallen prey to incubus Lloyd two days ago.

"Hey," I said, already pushing myself away from my corner. "I'll be right back."

Gair nodded in understanding, as he was already straightening as well. While he had to push through the crowd and go the long way around the bar, I was able to beeline for the arguing pair and catch the end of their conversation.

"If there's any chance," Baerd was saying, a furious desperation in his voice, "Hannah, you have to tell me."

"If I knew anything, I would. But I haven't seen—" She cut herself off. "Siobhan! Hey, I can't thank you enough for helping me the other day. With that incubus? I mean, I knew, but I don't know if I *knew*. You know?"

I assumed her babbling was about my removing the glamour so she could see the patrons of the Knoll for what we were. "Oh, yeah. I'm glad I could help. Is everything all right here? Baerd?"

He looked at me like a possum with his paw caught in a trap. "Nothing. I mean, we're fine." He nodded at me, and then he saw Gair coming through the crowd. He turned a narrowed look on Hannah and then melted away, disappearing amongst people pushing forward for a drink.

Gair arrived just as I lost sight of his friend's head in the crush.

"What was that all about?" Hannah tittered on her bar stool as she juggled a glass of wine from one hand to the other.

"Hannah, it's good to see you here again," I started again. "Is everything all right with you and Baerd?"

"He didn't," Gair began hesitantly. "I mean, he's had a lot of whiskey tonight. And if he said anything inappropriate, he's just had such a hard—"

"Oh, goodness," Hannah interrupted him, putting a hand onto his thick bicep. "No, no, nothing of the sort."

Gair let out a small sigh of relief and looked to me. I knew the love he had for his clan, and I shooed him away to chase after his brother. He hesitated only a moment before slipping away as well.

"Are all of you people like that?" Hannah asked, taking a sip of her white wine.

I ignored the "you people" in her statement. "What did you say to Baerd? He seemed pretty upset."

"You got that right. That poor boy is torn up." She looked back into the crowd, though I was sure Baerd and Gair had both gone back to their private table in the corner. "He said his girlfriend is missing?"

I nodded. "It's been a few weeks."

"Oh, bless his heart," she said, bringing her free hand to cover her mouth. "And with everything else going on? No wonder he's distraught."

This girl had me confused. What was she doing here? After everything she'd seen, I'd expected her to run for the hills. Now with the attacks on the fae at the Gate? Well, the fact that anyone was here was a mystery, but it was even more puzzling that a human with no power, no defenses would come calling.

I committed to a casual query. "What brings you in here tonight, Hannah?"

Her eyes widened. "I—I thought humans were allowed."

Maybe I wasn't as casual as I thought. "They are. We are. I just," I cut myself off. I didn't know how to explain without sounding bigoted.

It wasn't like she was the only human here. Several humans were in attendance, and some of my favorites were regulars. Jennifer was here with her longtime sylph boyfriend. They never missed a karaoke night, and even though she favored Shania Twain, Carrie Underwood, and Miranda Lambert songs, she was one of my favorite patrons. The second was David, a local man who accidentally wandered in one night about three years ago and happened to love the vibe of the place. He'd caught on quickly that things weren't what you'd expect in a typical bar, but he'd been treated so well, and the beer was better than what was on tap down the road, so he'd stayed and made lifelong friends with a group of boggarts and redcaps. Never mind the friends he made would outlive him by decades, for now they were happy.

Then there was Hannah.

"I just figured your last visit would have scared you off of this place for good," I finished poorly.

She quirked her mouth. "Why? Because y'all don't look so normal when your guards are down?"

"Glamour," I corrected.

"Whatever magic you use to appear normal or like the rest of us, it's a defense mechanism. Like camouflage. I'm not going to run away from that. If you've got defense mechanisms, it's because you think you're at risk. That you have to hide. From people like me. You think of yourselves as prey, not predators. I'm surprised you let me in here, into your safe space."

For a moment, I didn't have words. Then I saw a customer waving to me from the edge of the bar, and I realized I'd been down here too long for such a busy night.

"Hannah, I'm sorry. I misjudged you," I said. "Tell you what? You stay as long as you want. And your next drink is on the house."

She beamed at me and toasted me with her glass of wine. "And this is why you're the best bar in the city."

I laughed and hurried to the customer who was already growing impatient.

CHAPTER TWENTY-ONE

By the time I got to the guy, he was literally snapping at me like I was some kind of dog.

"Hey! You with the big hair!"

I pulled up short and brought a hand self-consciously up to my black coils. My hair was gorgeous, wild, and one of my favorite features. Big? Who did this guy think he was?

He was tall, generically good-looking in a human kind of way, with shiny brown hair cut to emphasize its thickness and wave. He was clean-shaven with dull brown eyes, and a nose that hooked slightly at the end over a tight, unhappy mouth. A Summer Court gancanagh, from what I could tell, and full of all of the swagger and entitlement of a sex fae who was rarely turned down.

He must have been new in town because the other love talkers, sex fae, and seducers in town knew better than to treat a tender or server at the Knoll with such disrespect. Then again, him snapping at anyone in the way he did was a bad sign about his character.

Choosing to overlook his behavior, I slowly walked over. He was already tapping the bar with impatience.

"What can I get you?" I asked, all smiles and courtesy.

Despite staring me down the whole bar until I got in front of him, he only spared me a brief second of eye contact before he turned away and over his shoulder, barked out, "Two mint juleps!"

"Ha!" I guffawed. "That's cute." At his confused expression, I explained, "That sort of drink is too expensive tonight." I asked the couple standing next to him what they'd like and quickly got to pouring them the lagers they requested.

The gancanagh wasn't done with me, though. He actually leaned over the bar and put a hand out like a railroad arm to stop me giving the couple their drinks. I was too stunned to react for a second, but then he spoke. "I can afford whatever drink I want, thanks, sweetheart."

If I could burn with a look, the man would have been ash before me. Instead, I smiled wider as I moved his arm and took the payment from the couple who were trading worried glances at the gancanagh. "No, you can't. The cost is too high for you tonight. Trust me."

Predictably, anger flushed his face red. "The fuck I can't! How much is a drink in this shithole anyway?"

"Depends on the customer, sweetheart." I became aware of several of my regulars around him quieting their conversations and directing their attention our way. They all knew how the Knoll worked, but since this poor fool didn't, I sighed and explained. "Tonight, if you want a beer, glass of wine, even a shot of liquor on the rocks, you're golden with cash, card, or coin. Even simple cocktails are fine. If you come on any normal night and ordered a specialty drink I can shake up for you, you can pay straight up for that, too. But tonight is karaoke night, and with everything that's been happening around here, and you being who and what you are, you can't afford a mint julep. Not tonight. Not from me."

"How much?" He scowled and dug into his pocket, bored with the conversation and unknowingly out of his depth.

"Put the wallet away. You've been to too many human bars." I looked up at the stage, where an encantada was finishing up her rendition of "Bohemian Rhapsody." With her ability to split her own voice into harmonies, she was obviously killing it. I signaled to Izolda. She nodded. "All right. If you insist. Head to the stage. You're up."

"What?" The gancanagh darted a look at the stage and then back at me. Clearly, not getting it.

"If you want your order, you have to sing for it. And I choose the song." I beamed at him. I had a good one.

"Ugh, forget it. Just give me two pinot noirs."

"Uh-uh. Too late. You pissed me off. No one serves you here until you sing."

He considered it for a moment and then shook his head. "No. No, you're going to pick some impossible song in a range I can't hit." He began to turn to his partner.

"George Michael, 'Faith.' It's a crowd pleaser, most people know it and still like it. No real vocal ability needed, but you have to want it. You have to live it up, up there. If you can pull it off, you'll have the whole bar singing with you. If not, you get thrown out by my girl back there." I waved to Mikka, who was already grinning hungrily.

The gancanagh frowned. "No tricks?"

He was fae and should know better than to question my integrity on a rightful task. "Fuck off, then." I raised my hand again to wave Mikka over. At least she'd have fun.

"Wait, wait. Fine. I'll do it." He began to walk toward the stage.

"Name?" I called after him, shouting over the applause for the encantada who had wrapped up with a resonant "Any way the wind blows."

"What?" He cupped a hand behind his ear and leaned forward.

"We have to announce you."

"Delano. Declan Delano." He began pushing people aside as he moved toward the stage, but he didn't get far enough away before I heard him mutter, "Half breed, bitch."

I sighed. There it was. And here I'd been willing to meet him halfway with an easy song. Now he'd manage to insult my hair, my bar, and now my half human heritage. Fuck him sideways.

I nodded to Izolda, who was waiting. She had been listening carefully, pitching her attention through the crowd to hear every word of our shouted conversation across the bar. She then turned to the crowd, closed her eyes, and brought up a spotlight over her own head to make the announcement. Never mind that there were no physical lights installed. Setting the stage was Izolda's unique gift.

"Gentle-friends and enemies." She spoke softly, but her voice resonated through the pub. "I have a special request from the bar. Please welcome to the stage, singing for his supper, Declan Delano."

The spotlight illuminated and tracked the broad-shouldered man as he pushed through the crowd to the stage. He walked up to Izolda, reaching out for a microphone.

Her eyebrows disappeared into her fringe of auburn hair as she shot me a look. This guy was too new to know there were no microphones. I was too pissed to even laugh at his discomfort. I lifted both hands up and made a diamond over my head. She cocked her head to the side. "Really?" she mouthed.

I nodded once, and that was enough. The easy sounds of Neil Diamond's "Sweet Caroline" began to fill the bar.

At first, Declan the dirtbag's face softened, as he realized he both knew the song and could easily sing it. Anyone could sing it. As he raised his voice, though, trying way too hard to imitate Neil's gruff but crystal-clear tones, he realized the crowd was not on his side. After all, "Sweet Caroline" could be a crowd pleaser in the right hands in the right bar at the right time. That was not this bar, not this night.

From the first, the crowd could tell exactly who Declan Delano was. He wasn't a karaoke lover who had had too much to drink and had taken on a song he knew better than to attempt. He wasn't a complete neophyte who chose one of the only songs he could sing along to. This was an interloper, who was trying to game the system to get what he wanted.

The fact that he had been called to the stage by the bartender? Anyone could piece together what had happened.

The boos started.

Even before he got to spring turning into summer, the patrons of the bar were throwing drinks, silverware, and even a shoe or two at him. With his arms lifted to shield his too-pretty face, he turned and ran for the back door, which Mikka was conveniently holding open for him.

It may have been the fastest I'd seen someone flee the Knoll.

I was still cracking up when Kaia came around the edge of the bar. "Guess he couldn't afford his drink." She gave me a quick peck on the cheek. "Hey, I need four noirs, two chards, and a two-finger of rum with rocks. And Argus is on his way and needs something from downstairs."

Argus kept his off-label drinks in the cabinets above and beside the main bar. The mid-level cabinets were the rare vintages: wines and scotches of advanced age, collectors items recovered from wrecked luxury liners, or infused drinks with magical properties. The top cabinet was locked and consisted of imports from Fairy with either incredibly rare and expensive ingredients or unique magical spells infused. The private cabinets in Argus's office and in the cellar were only accessible with permission from Argus, Meara, or me.

I started pouring the red wines. "Which bottle from which cabinet?"

"Private stash," she responded as she began pulling beers for another table.

"Really?" I was surprised Argus would open something from the private cabinets for this crowd. Though if he was on his way, maybe he was bringing a VIP, someone who could afford the upsell of a private cabinet drink.

She came over to whisper in my ear, "Oona's Tears." She was scandalized and delighted.

I goggled at her, my mouth agape. Oona's Tears were named for the original Queen of Summer, the daughter of Nour, the divider of worlds. She'd been the first to choose the Iron Realm over Fairy, and it was said her tears for her lost homeworld still gathered at the foot of the Gates, every time a Gate closed. This was nonsense, of course, as many enterprising young drinkers soon discovered as the dishes they left around Gates remained dry and empty.

But a careful distillation of ingredients harvested near Gates on both the Iron and Fairy sides produced a liquor that was reminiscent of an herbal gin that was both briny and delicious. It tasted to me of olives and rosemary with a creaminess that I had never placed. It also had the benefit of conveying mild euphoria, pain reduction, and perfect pitch: all magically induced.

I guess it made sense to offer that on karaoke night, but the cost was more than any but a handful of fae could afford. Argus assessed costs in favors and very specific magic, and most of the fae who came to karaoke night didn't have the talent, ability, or desire to offer Argus what he asked for. "Any idea which guest requested perfect pitch tonight, and who they're hoping to impress?"

Kaia laughed as she began loading up a tray with the martinis I'd finished. "No idea," she admitted. "But I can't wait to see who he walks in with."

That made two of us.

CHAPTER TWENTY-TWO

The primary entrance to the cellar was behind the bar. A large built-in shelf of wines pulled outward and revealed stairs that extended directly behind the bar and into the earth below.

As I pulled the shelf toward me, a titter of excitement went up from some on the other side of the bar.

"Ooh, look! Shiv's going for the good stuff."

"Nah," another voice responded. "You just tapped the mead cask again."

They laughed as I grabbed a high-intensity lantern flashlight and disappeared down the wooden stairs to the deep, dark, beautiful cellar. Within steps, the loud music, voices, and ambiance of the bar disappeared, and I was swallowed up by welcome quiet.

The heavy wooden stairs descended the entire width of the Knoll with wide, shallow steps that were always appreciated when I was carrying heavy cases of wine or liquor up from the depths. The temperature dropped as I descended, enveloped by the magically protected space, and I could feel my thoughts stilling, quieting, even as the sounds of karaoke disappeared above. By the time I reached the bottom, I was twenty feet below the floor of the Knoll and blessedly alone with my thoughts.

The space was wide and tall, and it extended well beyond the bar and kitchen, reaching deep underground beneath the parking lot and yard. Huge beams were evenly set to hold the thick hardwood ceiling high above, though I knew it wasn't wood that held everything in place. Thanks to some favors called in on its construction, there was no small bit of magic allowing such a deep underground cellar so near the river. The heavy wood and cool tiled floors created a cavernous feel, while the shelves and racks full of wines, ales, and liquors cluttered the walls and created aisles and aisles of dark glass, heavy oak, and various metal canisters hidden amongst the shadows.

As always, I lamented the lack of well-placed electric lights and had to content myself with old-fashioned oil lamps along the walls and my industrial-strength flashlight.

To the left and under the main floors of the Knoll were cheap metal racks full of the brand-named liquors, grocery store wines, general supplies for the bar, and shelves of dry goods for the kitchen. Along the back wall were the kegs and barrels of whiskey, beer, and a few of Argus's favorite wines. To the right were my favorite racks. These racks were custom ordered, cut wood shelving, designed to fit a variety of bottles, jugs, and casks of the finest spirits this side of the Fairy Realm.

As any good fae bar owner, Argus had sunk good coin in true live oak and cedar to protect his investments. The vows and the splintered spirits of the dryads of the many trees that housed his collection would cradle and protect what they held. Brandies, ports, whiskeys of every variety, red and white wines dating back to the beginning of last century, specialty brews with ingredients I couldn't even have imagined putting into a drink.

And along the far wall were the locked wooden cabinets, housing the rare, valuable, and magical substances Argus kept on hand for the most special occasions. Here were the potions, the spell-infused cocktails, the magical drinks that transported and transformed even as they delighted the drinker. The cabinets were about five feet tall, in a hard red wood that didn't remind me of anything of this world, that felt as soft as moss but harder than steel.

I pulled the key out from under my collar where it lay nestled on a chain about my neck. The key itself was a standard metal toothed key, looking like something you could buy off your local hardware store and easily bypassed with a good lock-picking kit or a cloned key. As most things at the Knoll, though, it was more than it appeared.

The key was tied to my magic, such as it was. It recognized me, and I it. When it was fitted into a lock, it didn't turn and disengage the lock with its teeth, pressing and releasing pins and levers. It only worked when it could take my magical signature and use those unique properties to whisper open the lock it was pressed into.

In a way, the key tasted my magic in much the same way I tasted other fae creatures'; we opened ourselves up to the power that touched us and used it to identify the user.

Making a mental note to ask Argus about who made his keys and the principles at work in their use, I fitted it into the proper cabinet and twisted it open.

Inside were several containers. Some were small wooden casks with corked openings, while others were animal skin receptacles, but most were colored glass bottles of elaborate design, shape, and color. Glass of red, green, purple, and blue, most of the bottles were geometric shapes, some configured as natural elements like animals and plants, while others were so uniquely crafted, I wasn't sure the glass hadn't whispered the shape into existence itself. Each was hollow, though, containing a special drink that I could serve in the way station and bar above us.

Argus had never taken the time to organize the singular substances in his private cabinets, though, so it took me three locked cabinets and five shelves to find the small collection of Oona's Tears he kept. They were prominent on the top shelf of the third cabinet, and two of the containers were almost empty. I added to my mental notes to consolidate the bottles and have Argus contact his supplier and place an order for two more bottles. I grabbed the fullest bottle for tonight, unsure if the big boss was granting perfect pitch to a single patron or multiple customers, and locked the cabinet behind me.

When the key locked in place, I realized that something didn't smell right. Or rather, it didn't taste right.

It tasted of wine and wood, a slightly spicy, earthy red and the barrel it aged in. That shouldn't be unusual given the amount of wine and spirits around me, but this taste was hidden between the air molecules, infusing them with magic.

"Who's there?" I called into the darkness beyond the locked cabinets. My voice sounded thick and muffled as it was swallowed up by the cavernous space.

The taste of it was familiar, comforting, and I stepped toward it, seeking it out.

In the back corner of the cellar was the old dumbwaiter that led up to the back storage building at the edge of the parking lot. It was where we received our deliveries. Each afternoon when they arrived, Tobin and Milo would load up and remove the spent casks and kegs to send back out for refills. Then they'd lower down the newest shipments of wine, beer, and assorted spirits from our wholesaler.

The taste of the magic grew stronger as I approached. It had the distinct flavor of plums and currants, tobacco, and wood. "Gair?" No, the wood taste wasn't pine. It wasn't oak, either, which is what all of our wine barrels were made of. Cedar, maybe?

Something scraped over the tile as someone moved ahead of me. Flicking on the lantern, I threw light over two people, one sitting, leaning against the wall beside the dumbwaiter, and the other hunched over, their back to me.

"What are you doing down here?" I demanded, before realizing that the one on the floor was Baerd. His thick curly black hair and grizzled chin were obvious even if his deep blue eyes were closed. It was Baerd's magic I had tasted.

Then Hannah stood and turned to glare defiantly as I approached. "Siobhan, go back upstairs. This doesn't concern you."

"Hannah?" I couldn't make sense of what was in front of me, even as she stepped forward, her hand lifted. The edges of the scene blurred as my body began to sway.

"It's nothing. You just had too much to drink," she said soothingly. "Go on back upstairs. You're up soon in karaoke, I think."

"Yeah," I said. She was right. I had a song coming up. What had I signed up with?

Why was Baerd on the ground? Why were his eyes closed?

"Baerd? Are you okay?" I squinted. There seemed to be two of him.

"Maybe you should get some water," Hannah soothed. Her hand on my elbow turned me around. "You really shouldn't overdo it when you're working, you know. What would Argus say?"

Argus. He'd sent me down here. I lifted the bottle of Oona's Tears in my hand. I should get that back to him. Stumbling through the aisles of bottles toward the stairs, I was thankful for Hannah's grip on my arm. "Thanks," I slurred, my tongue furry and big in my mouth. I rubbed it over my teeth, trying to figure out how I'd gotten in such a bad state so quickly. I couldn't even remember drinking tonight.

It must have been the red wine. My mouth still tasted of currants, smoke, and cedar.

But our wines were aged in oak.

The dissonance pulsed in my head, sending it spinning even harder, and I stumbled on the bottom step, nearly dropping the priceless bottle of spirits. I sat down hard and put the heavy glass bottle against the wall so I wouldn't knock it over.

Why did Hannah taste of clurichaun magic?

"Come on," she said, trying to pull me to my feet, even as I rooted myself harder on the bottom stair.

"But you're human," I insisted around the fog that was already starting to recede.

"Yes, we've established that."

"I'm half human, you know." My thoughts weren't following the path I wanted them on. That wasn't what I wanted to say. There was some other thought I should be pursuing.

"Which is why I'm trying to get you out of here." Hannah tugged me up again, but I pushed her away. "Siobhan, please. Just go upstairs."

The taste of earthy red wine pulsed. "But what about Baerd?" My head cleared further as the magic receded. That was it. The cedar and currants. "Why do you taste like Baerd's magic?"

She froze, her fingers digging in harder. "What do you mean?" Her voice was steady, but I could taste the fear that went through her. Suddenly the complex wine flavor of the magic soured into a vinegar.

As the taste changed, the effects of it faded from my mind. I wasn't drunk. I'd had almost nothing to drink tonight.

But inflicting drunken stupors was absolutely a facet of clurichaun magic.

It was all clear for a moment. I wrenched my arm from her and quickly fled back down the stairs and toward where we had left Baerd, slumped and unconscious against the wall. "What did you do to him?"

She caught me before I got far, spun me toward her, and punched me with a solid right hook. She used my own momentum to generate more force, and the impact of her fist with my face sent stars through my vision. I crashed back against a tier of bottom-shelf vodkas and rums, knocking several bottles to the ground where they shattered, releasing a smell of rubbing alcohol and toasted sugar. Dazed, I slid to the ground and sliced my hands on the shards of glass and soaked my jeans in cheap liquor.

Hannah loomed over me with a look of disgust and regret. "I knew I shouldn't have come tonight. Karaoke night is always too messy. But she insisted."

"She?"

Hannah ignored my question as she pulled on a chain around her neck and revealed a small blue bottle hanging hidden beneath her black top. She uncorked it, put her index finger on the mouth of it, and tipped it over. Then, she corked it back, concealing it once again under her shirt, as she took her index finger and dabbed a red liquid at the hollow of her throat, at both temples, and then touched it to her lips.

Stooping down, she then kissed me, gently but purposefully, and my head swam harder than before. "Let's see if that works a little longer." She stooped, close to me, her hand on my shoulder, as she let the magic pour between us, twisting her mouth in a wry frown. "I am sorry for this. Given your background, I had hoped you would join us. But the timing was never right to talk to you about it."

Her words didn't connect, as once again my mind seemed to be treading water and losing against a strong current. My thoughts swam, bobbed, and dove into drifting waters. I couldn't find equilibrium, and I knew that at any moment I would surely drown inside my own head tasting of red wine and cedar. "This magic isn't yours." My tongue was thick again, and I saw no less than three of the woman before me.

"Whose is it, then, Siobhan?" She pushed her face into mine, forcing me to look her in the eye, though my vision swam, and my blinks took seconds to help focus my gaze before I lost it again. "Who owns this magic? Is it Baerd? He was born to a pure line of drunk leprechauns. Does that make this magic his? No. He doesn't own the magic that he was born with. He borrows it through the Gate, through his blood. And he only gets to touch a facet of the raw potential that Fairy magic could offer. Fair!" She barked out a disgusted laugh. "It's not fair. None of it."

"It's—" I wanted to say so much. That it was complicated. That the vagaries of magic were utter bullshit. That the whims of fate denied the most deserving and rewarded the least in every walk of life. That I understood more than most that it wasn't fair. But all I could push past my increasingly addled mind was, "It's not yours."

That was the wrong thing to say, as she stood and loomed over me. "Is it yours then, princess? Or your mother's? Does it belong to the royal families who throttle and control the magic that could pass freely between our realms? That could be shared and put to better use?" She shook her head, and for a moment, I thought she might actually spit on me as I slumped in a puddle of cheap liquor and my own blood. "She was so wrong about you. You have no taste for change. For growth."

She walked away from me, and though I tried to stand, I could not get my legs under me. All I could feel was the warm thickness, dripping from my hands and arms as the glass around me cut my skin.

It took me entirely too long to realize I should do something about the blood leaking from me. I tried to concentrate on my wounds, but thoughts and control swam away, minnows in a pond, darting from the movement of thought. If I couldn't catch the damned fish, I couldn't heal. I would drown in a red pool.

Hannah returned, startling me, though I could not be sure if she had walked away seconds or hours before. She reached down to my neck and pulled a chain over my head. I couldn't think what she might want with my necklace. Or why she would rub it against my bleeding hands. I lifted a head that was too big for my neck to support it, and it lolled about, trying desperately to focus on her.

"You could have been a force for change, you know. You are from both worlds. Born a part of the system, raised in it, but someone who walked away from it? You stand at the edge but know the inside. That's power. But you're still weaving the web as you sit caught in its strands."

She touched my shoulder again, and my mind filled with cotton, my tongue grew moss, and my eyes watered. My head grew thicker, and I felt a warmth spreading through my body, even as my body began to shiver.

"I'm sorry for this. My knowledge of Baerd's abilities limits what I can do. Alcohol poisoning isn't the best way to die, but at least neither of you will feel the flames."

I gasped for breath to question what she meant about flames, but as I inhaled, I coughed in smoke. Trying to turn my head toward the smell, the flashes of light, I lost sight of Hannah. And still I choked as the smoke quickly filled the suddenly too small cellar.

If only I could focus my abilities on my brain fog, on the haziness in my mind, I could heal the blood that slowly seeped from my hands. I could repair the synapses in my brain that refused to fire, that refused to react to the smoke that was creeping into my lungs. Soon, I couldn't even cough as the heat and smoke filled the cellar around me. My body temperature began to drop and my muscles to seize.

CHAPTER TWENTY-THREE

"Shiv, sugar, come back."

From beyond the sea of dark, the voice was husky and full of emotion, like it would dissolve in tears in a moment. That wasn't right. Her voice was reserved for sly asides, unabashed confidence, and sexual innuendo. I had to stop it before it broke me.

"Don't cry, Mikka," I said, before choking on the dark poison in my throat.

Sitting up suddenly to get out the ash in my lungs, I immediately regretted it. My body ached from the seizures that had wracked me from my plummeting body temperature and alcohol poisoning.

But I didn't seize again, and my temperature was exactly where it needed to be. My head was almost entirely clear as I looked up from Mikka's lap and saw her saucer brown eyes, sleek black hair, and heartbreakingly vulnerable face.

"She's alive!" she screamed to someone away from us, tears dripping down her cheeks.

"Hey, Meeks. It's okay," I said, reaching up a hand to cup her cheek. I realized as I lifted it, that my hand was coated in blood. I flinched before discovering the blood was dry, and my hand was healed.

"What—" I started to ask.

"She's awake?" a voice demanded from a few feet away. "Bring her to me. I need her ability. Carry her if you have to."

Mikka didn't hesitate as she scooped me up in her arms and rushed me to the commanding voice against the cellar wall. She stooped down, cradling me carefully and keeping me from the hard cold stone floor as she knelt down beside a young woman who was radiating magic.

Lada the young Winter Queen reached out and snatched my hand, and the pull of her magic overwhelmed me. "Forgive me. I do not have time to bring you up to speed."

At once, my small, quiet world opened up into a million fragments. Power surged through me, and I felt like I'd touched a live wire. Everything that had been sleeping in me was instantly awake, and the synapses that had been so dulled by Hannah's stolen magic were firing so fast I thought I might burn out. A thousand voices and promises and prayers spilled into me, and though I couldn't hear them, I felt them, and all the awful want, need, desperation that lurked behind the power they pulled from me.

It was like my entire personhood had been ripped away, that my skin, muscles, bones had been flayed and there was something raw processing all that was demanded of me. I was too weak, too insignificant to support the need that screamed at the edges of my being.

Whatever was left of me in that moment found something small at the center of that power. It was a taste of caramel and apples, of a slightly salty sweetness that had a fresh bite, with a hint of black pepper on the back end. Somehow, I recognized it as Lada's magic, who she was underneath all that power that swirled through her. Even as I grasped for solid ground beneath me, steady currents, air to breathe, she was deep inside there, holding me to myself.

"I'm sorry," Lada whispered along our connection. She hadn't spoken out loud, but I heard her regret and sorrow through every cell of me. What's more, I felt what she didn't say. She wasn't sorry for using me in this manner or subjecting me to a power that emptied me out even as it suffused me with so much more.

She was sorry that she hadn't sought consent before inflicting this on me. She broke a part of herself because she hadn't asked my permission, but still she opened me.

The conduit between me and Fairy fell open, and my magic reached out beyond me, flowing out and through Lada. It was wrong, this feeling, and I grasped at the magic as it left my body. It wasn't supposed to extend beyond me. My power wasn't active. It couldn't be shared or applied to others. It was a part of me as much a function as growing my hair or digesting food or casting glamour. Pushing it outward felt wrong.

Or perhaps this only felt unnatural because I'd never been able to extend it myself, to flex that particular muscle. This was how magic worked for others, wasn't it? Their ability propelled by will and objective pressed outward and changed, moved things around them. Whether they compelled vines to grow or flung fire conjured from combustible elements in the air, they didn't change just themselves; they acted on the world.

Perhaps this was what magic could be. *Should* be.

My itching, questing magic crept through Lada and into the man she touched: Baerd. He was barely breathing; his heartbeat slowed almost to a standstill. But deep down beneath his breast, life still twitched, nested within him. If I could extend my power to him, I could help him heal.

But I had no control over my magic as Lada seized it and shoved it into that deep coiled thing inside of Baerd.

No, I wanted to cry, even as I was still left emptied and filled by Lada's touch. This was not the way.

Unable to control or direct my magic, I felt in awe as it tapped into Lada's connection to Fairy. It sparkled like fresh snow in the moonlight but burned like frostbite as it surged through me, past Lada, and into Baerd.

The tendrils of my magic expanded outward from the point where they were thrust, and they began to spin spidersilk thin threads of life. They borrowed some energy from Baerd's core, some from Lada's extraordinary strength, and some small amount from me, but I was shocked to feel them reach out further, questing along Lada's magic for more sources of life energy. It felt like it could extend to everyone in the room, drain them dry or heal them of every ailment.

Baerd's body suddenly seized, unable to handle the process of his body knitting itself back together. Though my eyes were closed, I could picture the power racing through his heart and lungs to force them into action. He pulled in air too quickly, and his lungs contracted, trying to reject the life-bringing oxygen. His heart beat too fast, and I could feel him faltering into arrhythmia.

No, I thought again, and I reached for my power. It might be Lada who passed my magic into Baerd, but the power was still mine to control.

I pulled it back from Baerd's life force, moving it more carefully to the injured parts of him. The cut wrists began to build up new tissue and close off the open veins. I convinced the bruise on his brain and along the back of his skull to pull back the blood that threatened to rush in and flood the area, repairing the vessels instead and releasing the pressure that built along his cranium. Slowly, I allowed the power to increase his heart rate, to bring more oxygen into his lungs, as his body slowly moved from trauma response into recovery mode.

In seconds Baerd was stable and breathing easily, though his eyes remained closed. He was alive. He was going to make it.

Lada must have realized it as well because I felt the intrusion of her magic retreat, leaving a sudden vacuum, where my self rushed in to fill the void.

I reeled against Mikka as Lada stood regally, brushing soot and ashes from her silvery blue dress. She turned away from Baerd and me gasping on the floor of the cellar and called out, "The fire is out, the lives are restored. Now, Argus, I want answers."

Until that moment, I hadn't realized Argus was even in the cellar with us. He stood a few paces back along the wall, arms crossed over his broad chest as he watched us with hot wet eyes. "The night is young, Your Majesty. Would you like a song and merriment first? My bar is at your whim."

Lada laughed like a whip through the moist air. "Something thematic perhaps? Like rain on your wedding day? Would that suit?"

"Isn't that 'Ironic'?" I said. She was the second Queen in two days to bring up that song.

My head spun, but I didn't feel like I'd nearly died or had my power ripped out of me. I felt strong and refreshed. That didn't seem like the right reaction to what had just happened, though, so I let Mikka help me to my feet, and even stumbled a bit for authenticity.

"It is ironic," Lada agreed missing the joke entirely. "I was promised an escape from my duties. A chance to taste the local color, get away from the pressure of investigating Natara's death. And I come here and find that killing each other is just what your people do."

She stepped over to her consort, who was waiting as silent as the grave beside Argus. Kiral's dark skin should have camouflaged him in the shadows of the cellar, but he glowed from within as much as his Queen. Together, they were their own magic-fueled light source: twin stars in a winter sky.

"I did warn against this," he said, leaning down to give her a kiss and stroke her cheek. It was a romantic gesture, but I could see as his eyes swept over her face looking for signs of fatigue, of madness. His Queen had just expended a great deal of energy in a realm not her own; she'd also channeled another fae's power directly, power that did not belong to her, did not belong to a subject of hers, and was not willingly given. He reached out to her hand, to give her a tether to her body, to the physical realm. He knew what he was doing; he was grounding her.

She accepted his touches and grasped his hand and leaned into his arm. "There is too much at risk to hide in a palace. Truth always hides in the underground."

While they tended to each other, Mikka squeezed my hand and left me to see to Baerd. I watched for a moment as she settled him into a comfortable position with his head pillowed on a balled-up burlap sack. She checked his pupils, his pulse, while I subtly tasted for his magic. There was the cedar and malbec, the taste that Hannah had stolen. It was weaker, like watered down wine, but it was there. It was his.

"Your Majesty." I heard Argus raise his voice before Lada grabbed my arm and spun me away from the victim on the floor.

"Look at me when I am talking to you," she demanded. A cold frost passed from her fingertips into my arms as the spiced caramel apple taste of her wet my tongue. I wondered for a moment why I could now taste her distinct magic beneath her Queen's power.

I lowered my head, though, and bobbed a small curtsy. "Forgive me, Your Majesty. I did not realize you had spoken."

Her grip tightened and pulled me up to face her. "I asked if you know who did this. Do you know who attacked this clurichaun and tried to set this way station aflame?"

"I do, Your Majesty. She attacked us both, and I think she may have stolen things from the private cabinets down here." I reached unconsciously for the key that usually hung around my neck when I was on duty.

Argus immediately turned around to check his stash. Any number of the bottles in there could be dangerous in the wrong hands. We'd want to know what was stolen.

"Name the fae, then. Let's be done with this. I am ready to hunt them and leave this realm on a high note." She giggled and cocked her head toward her consort. "You see? Because my chosen song ends on a high note."

"Clever," he acknowledged.

Suddenly concerned, Lada looked frantically around the cellar. "Argus? Argus? You still have the Oona's Tears, yes?"

He stepped back around the shelves so she could see him. "I hardly know why you would need it, Majesty. But yes," he said, when he saw her eyes widen, "that stash is untouched."

Lada nodded in relief, but I didn't fail to notice that in his answer, Argus had insinuated there were indeed things missing from his cabinets. That could wait.

"Let's get to it, then," the Winter Queen said, in high spirits again. She licked her lips. "I want to sing!" She did a little dance move, like she was getting ready to mambo there in the cellar. "We shall sing and dance on her killer's ashes. Natara would approve." She twirled and swung her skirts before stamping twice in front of me. "Does your impure blood make you stupid? Name the fae, girl. Have done with it."

Then she snapped her fingers.

And it snapped the patience in me.

"No."

The temperature of the cellar plummeted, and the tiles crackled around Lada's feet.

"No?" Her voice was surprisingly light and full of laughter for the dangerous anger that radiated from her. She seemed to tower over me, despite the five inches of physical height I had on her. "You will not tell me who attacked you?"

"I will not." I was proud of how steady my voice held. I don't know if it was the buzz of whatever Lada had done with my magic, or the power that she had channeled through me. Or maybe I was just tired of being pushed around by powerful people who looked down on me. But I wasn't about to help this bigoted Queen in her vengeance tonight.

"You deny me?" She took a step toward me, and I could feel my fingers and toes starting to ache with selective frostbite.

"I do."

Behind the Queen, Kiral and Argus stood dumbstruck, one with a look of interested confusion, the other a cross between concern and annoyance. Behind me, I could feel Mikka take a step forward. No matter what she thought of my actions in the moment, I knew she would protect and defend me.

"Your Majesty, I do not know if what happened tonight is connected to what happened to your subject. Until I know the circumstances better, and until I understand exactly why Baerd and I were attacked tonight, I will not be handing anyone from this city over to you for summary execution."

She stepped forward then and grabbed my chin, forcing me to look down at her. Her fingers burned my skin, and her eyes were full of fury. "You half-breed bitch. I could freeze your veins and cause your insides to explode out of every sorry hole in you. You would choose the side of one who left you for dead, just to defy me?"

I smiled, even though the act of moving my face against her fingers scalded me to the muscle. "Call me half-breed again. Let's see how far I go to defy you."

Behind me, a wall of warmth flared to life, and I knew Mikka had conjured a fireball to defend me. Without a thought for herself or anything else, she was ready to back up my threats.

And, then to my surprise, a bigger ball of light grew in front of me, directly behind Lada. Argus held a large column of flame directly behind Kiral, while his other hand rested on the consort's shoulder.

"Your Majesty," Argus said evenly, as if he wasn't threatening a Fairy Queen and her consort. "Your invitation has been rescinded this evening. You have violated ancient laws. You threatened violence against a Keeper of the Greenwood Knoll. What's worse, you threatened one of mine. Take your lover and leave. If you wish to try again next week, we can revisit your Celine Dion song at our next karaoke night."

For a moment, Lada's anger disappeared, replaced by shock. Then she released my face and doubled over in laughter. She stepped toward Kiral and pulled him away from Argus. Still laughing, she looked around at all of us.

"Oh, I doubted it was true. But clearly she was right! About all of you. The rot is in the Greenwood!" She pulled Kiral down to kiss him passionately and seemed to check him briefly for any injury. Satisfied, she turned back to me and sneered. "You are Nour's mistake and need to be brought to heel. I will especially enjoy teaching you the lesson your mother refused to: defying a Queen is defying Fairy itself. In Mab's name, you will regret fomenting the unrest you have nurtured in this shack. War against one Queen is war against us all. This seditious house will fall. And then I will have my dance."

She raised an arm, and in a whirlwind of ice and snow and a final frosty laugh, Lada and her consort vanished, leaving only a cold emptiness behind.

CHAPTER TWENTY-FOUR

The moment she was gone, Argus turned his flame on me. "Mab's twat! You are certainly Illythia's daughter." His face was full of anger and fear and confusion. "I want an explanation for that immediately, or I'm going to march you up to the palace and hand you over to the mad Queens myself."

Mikka scoffed. "You would sooner take up sobriety." She turned me around to face her. "Are you okay?" She checked my skin where Lada had tried to freeze me, but I had already healed it.

"I'm good," I said, still shaking with adrenaline and anger. I'd stood up to a Queen; she could rip my skin from my bones, shred it to fibers, and weave a cloak to wear on festival days, all while keeping me alive to make me applaud the way my blue veins brought out her eyes.

"Then would you kindly explain why you just antagonized someone who could bring our worlds crashing down around us?" Argus was biting back on his rage, and the cold of Lada's emotions was quickly chased away by his hot anger.

"Because," I said quickly, "telling her the truth would have been worse. We were attacked by a human wielding Baerd's magic."

Mikka's breath hissed in, and Argus blinked rapidly trying to digest my words.

"A human? Wielding magic?" Argus shook his head. "Was it perhaps someone with mixed heritage? Someone who could have fae blood?"

"Wow." I frowned at him, disappointed and not a little hurt. "Not the first question I expected you to ask. But you summed up pretty well why I wouldn't want Lada to find out the details."

"I didn't mean—" Argus began, but he quickly stopped himself. He took a breath and tried again. "I wasn't trying to imply anything about magic and blood purity. But," he paused and considered his words carefully, "human or fae, if someone is wielding another's magic, that is something we should all be concerned with."

I agreed, but I wasn't about to let him off the hook here. Fae were born with magic. Even those of us with a mix of human and fae heritage, we all had access to some power. Some of us, obviously received lesser gifts than others, but that was the nature of genetics, wasn't it? Some people got blessed with the ability to call down lightning, whisper thoughts into people's heads, and transform straw into gold, while others only got to change the color of their eyes and identify which particular cocktail their friends' powerful magic tasted like. It was unfair, but it was immutable.

Unless it wasn't.

"It was Hannah," I said. "The pretty brunette who's been coming in every few weeks and flirting with the hottest male in the bar."

"Ugh," Mikka said with an anguished pout. "And I thought she was cute." She wrinkled her nose at Argus. "Siobhan's right, though. She's 100% human. I've chatted her up a few times, and she's as magicless as they get."

"Not tonight," I said. "She was wielding Baerd's magic. I could taste it all over her, and she managed to inflict drunkenness and almost alcohol poisoning on me." I tried to think of the details of what had happened, but there was a haze surrounding my memories.

"She also managed to steal a few things from my cabinets," Argus confirmed. "But she left your key." He held up a chain and offered it back to me. The key was still sticky with my blood.

That was it. "The blood. She had my blood for the key. And I think, she had some of Baerd's. To access his magic. She had a vial of some sort, and she applied it to her lips." I wiped my mouth as I remembered she had kissed me before sending me into a stupor.

Argus made a noise in the back of his throat and stomped away out of sight. I could hear a wooden door open, then slam shut. "Here," he said, thrusting a change of clothes at me. Everyone kept a few outfits on hand in their lockers; you never knew when you'd spill red wine down the front of your white button-down or get knocked into a rack of bottom-shelf vodka and rum and left for dead. "Get dressed. I need you and Mikka to go back up and finish out karaoke night."

"Wait, what?" I said, accepting the clean jeans and black t-shirt. I wriggled out of my wet and sticky pants and slipped the clean ones on. "We can't just not say anything."

"Yes, you can." Argus surveyed the damage to his shelves, and I knew he was mentally updating his inventory. "And you will. We will not have a panic over stolen magic. We know who is responsible for what has been happening. We know what she looks like, and we will be watching for her."

I tugged the clean t-shirt over my head. "Then why not warn the others about her? About what she can do? If others knew where she was, they could help us find her. Stop her from doing any further damage."

"Or they will use it exactly as you feared Lada would: to turn on the humans among us, create suspicion and tensions that we don't need right now." He turned to look at Baerd. "No. No, I will stay here to take care of Baerd. When he comes to, I will get the full story from him. We will know how we should move forward, then. Not before." He walked up to me and put a hand on my shoulder. "For now, go serve drinks. Give a champagne toast to the maenad celebrating her pregnancy. On the house. Sing an extra song. Close down a bit late. Then we will regroup."

He addressed Mikka. "You will help her. As will Varon. Keep

things normal. Give everyone a chance to unwind and remind them that though they are solitary, they are not alone. They are safe with us."

Mikka nodded, accepting her role, but I wasn't convinced. "Argus, this isn't right. If Hannah can steal magic from fae, we have to—"

"We have to give our people a night to let off steam. They're already scared, *louloudi mou*. They saw what happened at the Gate. No one is under any illusions that things are normal. But the Queens aren't going to take up arms against us tonight. And our people need to breathe, to know they are safe, if only for the moment. I will not take that from them. Truth is important, but facts at the wrong time only generate worse fictions. For now, let them have the safety and assurance they deserve."

Despite his steady words, I knew Argus was anxious and scared about what faced us tomorrow. He never called me his flower except when he felt the need to comfort me. "Okay, boss," I said reluctantly. I could hold the fort for the night.

There was a symmetry there that unnerved me more than it reassured. Argus wanted to do just what the Summer Court had done: avoid saying anything about disappearances and even deaths, because they didn't want to start a panic. They had no answers and didn't want to look out of control of the situation. Argus wanted to avoid saying anything to preserve the peace as well, even as he was learning what had happened. If we had answers, if we were on the edge of protecting our people, why shouldn't we grant them respite and relief for a while? If we had none, why not ask our community for help?

But if Argus wanted to keep things quiet, I could trust him. For at least a little while longer.

"Do you want champagne or prosecco for the toasts?" I asked softly.

He brought a hand up to cup my cheek. "Thank you. The Lamarca or Ruffino proseccos. For the clurichaun, the Veuve. And tell them that Baerd is safe."

Not trusting myself to refrain from arguing further, I simply nodded and went to carry out orders, while Argus hefted Baerd upstairs for recovery in his office.

I emerged into a party that had continued apace without me. Kaia's frazzled nerves the only indication that my absence was felt at all.

"Where in Morgana's cavernous tomb have you been?" she practically screamed at me while rounding the edge of the bar with a tray of dirty pint glasses. "I had to call Milo and Tobin to help run drinks for me."

"Long story," I said, grabbing a case of prosecco and peeling the foil away from the cage over the cork of the first bottle. "Champagne toasts for everyone first. Explanations later."

Kaia nodded, trusting that if there was something she needed to know I would tell her. She grabbed a tray and started lining up glasses along the bar. As I poured, Mikka went over to tell our master DJ what was up.

Within minutes, I had three cases of sparkling wine empty, and glasses were being passed around with great enthusiasm.

"All right, friends and enemies," Izolda announced after a selkie sang a subpar version of "Landslide." "The Greenwood Knoll would like to propose a toast."

"A TOAST!" the entire bar roared in response.

Then Izolda nodded to me as I climbed on top of the bar. Light shone on me as expertly as a spotlight, though I knew it was just Izolda's power bending the light just as she'd amplified my voice.

"Thank you all for being here on a special night. Things have been uncertain around here for a bit, I know, and there's a lot we don't know. But there's one thing I do know: there has never been a stronger community of independent fae in all the world. Atlanta fae, when things get tough, we come together. We mourn each other's losses, and we celebrate each other's wins. And while there may have been losses, tonight, we're all here to celebrate." I raised my champagne glass. "Everyone please raise your glasses to Semele Tyne and her newest passenger. We're having a baby, y'all!"

Cheers and cries of "To Mellie!" and "To the baby!" erupted from every corner of the Knoll. Mellie herself stood in a circle of her maenad sisters and wept and accepted embraces and kisses.

As the next karaoke singer advanced on the stage, I climbed down off the bar and immediately began responding to requests for beer, wine, shots, and simple cocktails. I deflected questions about where I'd been with vague mentions of an unexpected issue with inventory and such until Gair cornered me at the edge of the bar.

I didn't even see him until I rounded the edge to deliver a round of whiskeys to some of the gremlins by the stage and ran headlong into his chest, sloshing but not spilling the drinks.

"My fault," he said, sweeping two of the glasses out of my upturned hands and putting them on the appropriate table as if it were his job and not mine.

"Thanks," I said, passing him the other two glasses as well. "Sorry, I wasn't watching where I was going."

Gair smiled at the table of gremlins extending his hands over the glasses. "May I? A gift in honor of the baby?"

They nodded appreciatively as he swiped a finger along the rim of each glass. One of the gremlins picked up his mid-tier whiskey and took a sip. His eyes closed in ecstasy as he moaned back into his chair. "Now, that's the good stuff." He lifted his glass in a toast to Gair. "The child is much honored."

All smiles, Gair followed me back to the bar.

"You're upgrading my drinks now? If they wanted the good stuff, they're supposed to pay Argus for the favor," I teased.

"Vex will never pay for the good stuff, and you know it."

I laughed, reaching down in the cooler for a bottle of white wine for a dryad. "True enough. What can I get you?"

"A straight answer, perhaps?"

His plaintive tone straightened my spine if nothing else. "What do you mean?" I said, avoiding turning around as I poured the wine.

"Mikka told me Baerd was fine, but that he wasn't feeling well and went back to his house early, so she got him a shadow ride with the Hendleys."

"Uh-huh." I avoided his eyes as I passed off the wine to a wooden-looking dryad with gorgeous leaf-green hair in a blunt bob. "Love the new cut, Hazel." She smiled and accepted the drink.

"Siobhan," Gair said, patient but insistent.

"What?" I finally looked at him.

"Baerd hasn't been home in months. He's staying with Leland."

"Oh."

He sighed. "What is going on? Is Baerd really okay?"

I nodded, trying to school my face into neutrality, but no doubt failing miserably. Still, I didn't say more.

"Did something happen to him?" he pressed, his blue eyes searching mine for clues.

I nodded again, sucking on my lower lip to keep in all the things I wanted to say.

His eyes narrowed, and I could see his jawline harden beneath his neatly trimmed red beard. "Does it have anything to do with Hannah?"

I couldn't help it as my eyes darted toward the stairs down to the cellar and back to him. Mab take him, Argus should have known better than to ask me to keep a secret like this.

Gair inhaled sharply. It didn't matter if I intended to tell him anything or not; I'd as good as spelled out the whole night for him. "Right," he said. "I think I may need to explain some things. About where Hannah got mixed up in all of this."

That wasn't the reaction I was expecting, so I bit harder on my lips and nodded again. "That would be helpful."

"Is after karaoke too late? I know you have to shut down the bar and all…"

I shook my head. "No, it's not too late. The more information we have, the sooner we can get to the bottom of all of this."

"I shall see you after the last song, then," he said. "I'll wait out back on the porch."

He stepped away and turned back toward his usual table before I could say anything else. If he had answers, I wasn't about to wait for Argus to give me permission to follow up. He was falling into the same traps that made the palace poison: hoarding truth, controlling the narrative, protecting whatever it was he was protecting.

But he was only my boss. I didn't have to wait for permission to do the right thing.

I was going to get answers.

CHAPTER TWENTY-FIVE

With karaoke finished, the bar cleaned up, and the last of the customers headed out, I finally slipped out onto the back porch. I was surprised to find a few people still lingering around the property. Some were waiting on rides home, but many were content just to linger with their friends and found family a little longer, finishing up conversations and arguments, singing the songs that had gotten stuck in their heads, or just sitting and rocking while looking out at the Chattahoochee sparkling in the moonlight.

Gair waited for me in the same Adirondack chairs where Talisa and I had talked about the missing maenads just a day earlier. He didn't look up as I sat down but continued to stare out toward the woods where the path to the Gate lay hidden in the darkness.

"What happened in the cellar?"

I started and frowned at him. "What do you mean?"

"Despite changing your clothes, you have two people's blood under your nails, you reek of coconut rum, and no one deals with inventory problems for over an hour in the middle of Saturday night karaoke." He looked at me then with an eyebrow raised. "You don't think anyone in that bar missed the fact that you disappeared and came back in a state, do you? Well over half of your customers can taste blood the way you can taste magic."

I started to deny it, but Gair's other eyebrow shot up. Swallowing my protestations, I told him the truth. "Hannah was down there. I don't know why, but she stole things from Argus's private stash, then she attacked Baerd and me and left us for dead before lighting a fire in the cellar."

He nodded solemnly, as if it was exactly what he had expected. Taking a deep breath, he turned his whole body toward me. "I apologize for not coming to you earlier with this. It was an error in judgment, and I regret it. However, in my defense, you have been clear about your desire to stay out of the politics of our community. I only hoped to honor those wishes."

I didn't say anything. He wasn't wrong. When I'd broken with the Court, when I'd given up my claim to the throne and to the role of conduit, I had done my honest best to stay away from any of the power struggles of the Court or individual solitary factions. It would have been improper to step on my sister's authority in any way, when it was only by my renouncing my claims that she'd inherited any of her power. If she saw me trying to encroach on that power or question her decisions, she would not take it well.

The thing is, though, it had left blind spots in my knowledge of my community. Whenever issues of dissatisfaction came up with the Courts, I tended to step away, lest I speak out of turn. It kept me out of trouble but meant I couldn't serve my people fully.

"For the past year or so, a group of us from the Knoll have been meeting to discuss a growing dissatisfaction with the way things work in this world."

That was generic enough to be dangerous, but I seized on a single word. "Us?"

"Yes," he said. "My cluri brothers and I have been among those who most vocally disagree with the power imbalance of the Iron Realm. Complaining about the Courts is a big part of our cultural heritage."

I believed it. With few exceptions, clurichaun and their leprechaun relatives had never pledged themselves to either the Summer or Winter Courts. They prided themselves on being singular and independent and impossible to tame. In truth, I think they just hated following orders, and since their magics were limited to luck spells, currency manipulation, and intoxication, they saw little to be gained in greater magic.

"So, what? You have political meetings at the Knoll?" I would like to think I'd notice big rallies, so this group had to be either really discrete or smaller than he let on.

"Not really so organized at first," he said with a laugh. "Mostly we got together, drank too much, and complained about how to use even our own small magics we had to huddle around Greenwood like it was a campfire on a cold night. But over time, some of us decided we shouldn't have to settle for scraps of influence. That we should do something about it."

"Do something about it? Like, what? Overthrow the entire Court system?" I let out a little of the cynical frustration I'd long felt.

Gair was right. It wasn't fair that the Courts had unlimited access to their own natural magics, while the solitary had nothing but what they could absorb in proximity to the Gates. It wasn't fair that the Courts required unquestioning obedience to pull magic through their Queens. And it really wasn't fair what the Courts demanded of their subjects: arranged marriages or participation in their breeding programs, conscription of individual subjects in territory or power struggles, and tithes of property, money, and even magic.

It bred dissatisfaction.

Mother's Court was more lenient than most, and still, I knew more fae who frequented this bar who had actively chosen to leave Summer than had been born into the solitary life.

"At first, we didn't want to overthrow anything," Gair said. "We just wanted to know if there was a way to increase our own magic, to access more of our natural heritage, without giving up our autonomy."

It finally clicked for me. "You're part of the group that tried to siphon from the Gates?"

Gair flinched. "I wasn't aware you knew about that."

"I didn't," I admitted. "But Argus suggested it. Until we found Nyssa, I had never imagined anyone would do that. That someone would voluntarily let the Gate drain them to access more magic."

He sat back in his chair and considered me. "Why wouldn't people do that? You bleed yourself daily."

"I do it because it is my job. It is how I serve my people, my city. I do it because without someone opening the Gate, our solitary community would be entirely powerless, and because it affects me less than most. But voluntarily? Tell me, what would you do with more magic? Even if I could summon lightning or grow plants or shift into whatever form I wanted, I don't even know how that magic would change my life for the better. I'm happy with my life. What would I do differently?"

Gair just stared at me for several seconds. "Siobhan, I beg you not to take this amiss. But you exist in a very unique sphere of security. Your needs are met, you face no threats, and you exercise great power in a very protected place."

I opened my mouth to protest, but he raised a hand to stop me.

"I know you have had your hardships. You were born to extraordinary expectations, and you were ill-served by your fate in the magic you were given to answer to those expectations. But though you lack great magic, you have been sheltered from ever needing any." He sat forward on the edge of his seat and reached for my hands. I hesitated but gave them to him. He grasped it briefly, then turned my hand over to show my smooth, bronze skin. "You use your glamour to go unnoticed in the human world, but you are able to walk around nearly as you are. That is not true for many of our kind." He gestured to his own purple- and oak-mottled skin. "Some of us use our meager power to pass for human, when we should be able to walk freely." He squeezed my hands and released them. "Your beauty is a single privilege. Your roof over your head, food in your belly, protection from harm or want are others. Believe me, I do not criticize you for not understanding. But know, too, that many would endure a great deal worse to have access to a fraction of your privileges. To live without want or fear or pain."

My mouth felt dry with shame. Shame that I had not known that my friends and community struggled. Shame that I had been too privileged to notice. And shame that I could have helped if I hadn't done so much to insulate myself.

"Please," I said. "Continue."

"The group took turns—"

"Wait," I interrupted. "Who is in this group? You mentioned your clurichaun brothers. But who else was a part of this?"

He looked away from me, out toward the river. I watched as his brows furrowed, he chewed his lips, and his hands began to worry at the wood grain of his chair. "I don't think I can tell you that."

I wanted to grab him and shake him. "Why not? People are dying, Gair, and it may be connected to this political group of yours."

"Because of precisely that. Because of any retaliation that may come from the palace. From Summer, or apparently from Winter. Yes," he said in reaction to my shocked look. "Everyone in town knows the Winter Queen is here. From Romania. Brought her consort. Signed up for a Celine Dion karaoke song."

"Izolda," I said, understanding. The vila was a notorious gossip.

"Yes," Gair said. "But I run in small circles and had still learned of Queen Lada's visit yesterday. Atlanta may be a big place, but it is a small town."

"You can say that again," I agreed. "Okay, you don't want to say who's in the group to protect them. But I can make some guesses. Your brothers, the clurichaun. And I can assume the leprechaun clans?"

He chuckled. "If the chaun are not involved in your local seditious acts, lass, you might as well be crying into your tea at home alone. It's in our nature. But mischief is a common enough past time for those long-enough-lived. I'll not name names, but suffice it that you know many of them. From both of your lives."

That meant there were Court fae as well as my more contrary patrons. That could mean many things, and none of them good.

"So, Argus was right, then. The disappearances and deaths have been accidental as you tried to siphon more magic. Not suicides, but not murders either."

"Not so fast, lass," Gair cautioned. "The Fair Folk—that's what we call ourselves—we were most interested in growing our own individual power. In challenging the rights of the Courts to control the magic of this realm. But only in small ways. We always went to the Gate as a group and were ever careful to keep our sacrifices safe and small. We sought to increase our magic to help our community. All fae deserve a support system, not just those indebted to the Courts."

I wanted to protest that what he wanted was exactly why the Knoll existed. We opened the Gate for all, and we did our best to provide for the solitary fae. Anyone who needed help with food, with housing, with anything they needed, they only had to ask. Every one of us who served at the Knoll would help.

But maybe that wasn't enough.

"For months, we spoke of a better way. Of preserving the freedom of our people, by giving them the means to actually enjoy their magic. But there were those in the Fair Folk who wanted more: to make bigger changes, to challenge Summer's hold on Atlanta."

"They want to overthrow the Queen?" My mouth felt dry, and my heart pounded. "And you went along with it?"

"No. I thought it was just talk," Gair protested. "Some of the humans like Hannah, Jessica, and a few of the maenads, even Baerd and Conlan agreed. The Queens and their throttle on Fairy magic were the main barriers to an equitable society. After much debate and, well, fighting, they left our group, angry that we didn't want to go further. Baerd went with them, but Conlan and I thought their position too extreme. We wanted to focus on helping our neighbors, not leading a rebellion. I had no idea how far they would take things."

He stopped there and buried his head in his hands. I reached out and rubbed his back while he composed himself. Then he looked up and with tears in his blue eyes, he resumed. "Kari was not one of the splinter group. She and Baerd argued constantly about what he was doing. She, like myself and Conlan, believed that the further they pushed things, the more dangerous it would get. She begged him to leave the Fair Folk. To move in with her and focus on building a family. He refused, and she went missing a few days later."

"Do you think the Fair Folk had something to do with it?"

He nodded. "But I couldn't prove anything. Baerd cut ties, and most of them stopped coming to the Knoll. We thought it was over. Then you found Aziz."

"Aziz? Was that the djinn?"

Gair nodded again. "He was one of us who wanted to keep things simple. He thought, though, that he could work within the Fair Folk and moderate their choices."

"And they killed him for it."

Gair sighed. "We don't know that. Not for sure. Lass, ye cannae go around accusing people of murder without proof. There is a connection between the Fair Folk and Aziz. And Nyssa, come to that. Several of her sisters are part of the group."

"And Hannah attacked me and Baerd."

"Aye, attacked you and attacked Baerd. There's no excuse for it, and she should answer for what she did. But you need more information before you go reporting everyone she associated with for the murder of your people."

I sighed. I didn't like it, but he was right. I needed more information: about who was in the Fair Folk, what they were up to, and how they were able to give a human fae powers. I needed to find Hannah before she hurt anyone else.

Gair was wrong, though. I did need to report something to the Court. I'd made a mistake antagonizing Lada earlier. I still didn't have any interest in handing Hannah over to her, but I did need to talk to Bryony. She had to know about the Fair Folk; she could help stop them, without any more bloodshed.

Gair could help with some of that. "Argus has Baerd recovering upstairs in his office," I told him. "Can you go up and talk to Baerd? Try to get him to tell you what the Fair Folk were up to? I don't need names yet, but if we can figure out what Hannah is planning, and if it connects to their actions, we can stop any more unnecessary deaths at the Gate. Find another way."

He nodded. "Aye, I can do that. What will you do?"

I made a small whine. "I have to go talk to my sister again."

CHAPTER TWENTY-SIX

I didn't wait for Argus to come down and stop me. I didn't even head home to change. I stepped in through the back door of the Knoll, reached behind the register to grab my keys, and made for the door.

Mikka and Varon stood directly in front of me, blocking my way out from behind the bar.

"Where you headed, sugar?" Mikka asked, while Varon raised his eyebrows in accusation.

"I have to go to the palace. Bryony has to—"

"Bryony can wait a few hours," Mikka said, plucking my keys out of my hand. "You're going home to bed."

"But—"

"Listen to her," Varon whispered loudly. "She's not going to take no for an answer."

"This can't wait," I insisted, reaching for my keys, only to have Mikka hold them farther out of my reach. "I just spoke to Gair, I know why Hannah attacked us. And I might have a lead on the murders."

Mikka looked at her twin and cocked her head toward the back door. Varon nodded and left for the porch. He was, no doubt, going to follow up with Gair and hopefully bring him up to Argus and Baerd.

"Come on," Mikka said. "I'm taking you home, and—"

"I have to go to the palace!" I shrieked, much louder and in a much higher pitch than I intended. I may have been more tightly wound than I thought.

"And in the morning, I will happily take you there," Mikka said, an understanding half smile tugging on her lips. "But not if you announce it loud enough that the boss and my idiot twin overhear."

"Oh," I said.

"Shiv." Mikka took my hand and pulled me after her as she moved toward the door. "You need to go home for sleep. It's the end of a more interesting karaoke night than most. And we both survived the siren visits of '98."

I cringed. That night a group of Greek sirens, cousins to Argus, came through the Gate for one leg of their world-hopping bachelorette party. Two lilin were stabbed, a pixie was trampled, and a kobold chained himself to the fireplace until one of the visiting sirens agreed to marry him—he was unspecific on which one.

"I can sleep after—"

"You will sleep before," Mikka insisted. "I'm taking you home. And then—" She raised a hand to stop my further protests. "I will accompany you to Court to talk to your sister, sugar. I will follow you anywhere. But I will protect and care for you first."

She walked over to the door and ushered me out to the car.

I had little choice but to acquiesce.

Nour take Mikka for being right. A night of sleep in my own king size was exactly what I needed. I woke the next morning refreshed and clearheaded. I even had time for a long shower and styling for Court.

I half thought Mikka was hoping I would change my mind about going to the palace with a full night's sleep, but she was waiting at

11:30 with the keys and a full tumbler of hazelnut coffee and Irish cream when I emerged from my room.

"Figured a little boost was needed if you're going to face your sister before noon." She grinned with all her teeth bared, and I was happy as always to have her in my corner.

I stepped up to kiss her on the cheek. "You are my best friend, you know that?"

"I'm better than you deserve," she said before winking at me. "Come on. I called ahead to log the official visit and call a Court to observe, and Magdalene said they were already expecting you. Does it freak you out when she does that?"

I laughed. "I swear, Mags has more spies in Atlanta than there are mosquitoes. It means she'll have snacks when we get there."

Mikka took a sip from her own tumbler, which was likely filled with black tea since she didn't care for coffee. "Do you think she knows I like nachos and dumb blondes for lunch?"

"If she doesn't have a pitcher of mojitos and cucumber sandwiches ready to serve, I think there may be bigger problems at hand."

Without wasting any more time, Mikka and I piled into my Honda and drove in silence to the palace. We were already turning onto Riverside Road when my phone rang. I picked up through the hands-free button.

"Hello?"

"What in Mab's name are you doing, Siobhan?"

"Hello, Shiro," I said, giving Mikka in the passenger's seat a look to keep her mouth shut.

She grinned and ignored me. "Shiro, babe, what's shaking?"

"Oh, great," he moaned. "Not only are you actually going through with this, but you're bringing literal fire power with you."

Mikka kissed the air with loud smacks. "I look forward to seeing you there, too, Shiro-san. Wanna snuggle while Siobhan pleads our case to her sister?"

Shiro ignored her. "Why didn't you call me? I could have mediated, interceded. Done something that wasn't entirely noble and stubborn and stupid."

I slowed down as we approached the front entrance of the palace. If I was making an official visit, that meant going through the proper protocols. Taking a left up the asphalt road, I started climbing the hill to the Concordia House Jesuit retreat. "What is stupid? The fact that I'm going to Bryony with what I know the second I learn it? Or the fact that I'm actually asking for her help instead of trying to solve the problem on my own? I would have thought you'd be proud of me for that one."

Shiro went silent for a few moments. "Then, no one's contacted you?"

"Contacted me?" I pulled the car over the cobblestone parking lot and picked a spot far from the entrance of the building. I obviously was not here for a spiritual journey and didn't want to have to interact with any of the Concordia House staff. I'd come through the main area once and been unable to talk myself out of a prayer consultation with the eager priest-in-residence.

"Siobhan, stay where you are," Shiro commanded. "I'll meet you on the path."

Before explaining what he meant, the line disconnected.

A cold pit began to grow in my stomach, but Mikka shrugged. "Should we wait to find out what he meant by all of that?"

If she wasn't worried, then neither was I. I shook my head. "He didn't tell me to turn around and go home." I opened my door. "That's practically permission to go ahead on in."

I slammed the door and started down the wooded path, with Mikka close on my heels. The way was flanked by azalea bushes and leafy ferns, dogwoods and pines, and sparse oak trunks. Roots sprung up along the path, almost as if trying to deter our fast pace through the woods, but though I stumbled a bit, I kept my focus.

My best hope was getting upstairs to talk to Mother directly. She'd hear my case and recognize that the only threat to Atlanta was a rogue group of idealists who wanted to maximize their power. She would gather the group, tell them that she could offer them great magic without giving up their freedom, and she would grant it to every solitary fae in Atlanta with no horrific repercussions.

I know it was unrealistic. Leave me alone. I was raised on Fairy Tales.

My second-best option was that my sister would accept me, hear my case, and work with me to identify the members of the Fair Folk and not kill them outright. She could listen to what they wanted before sentencing those involved in any harm to her subjects to immediate death by internal lightning strike. Not my preferred end.

Still, I charged forward. Toward Court, toward my sister, toward the formal hearing I'd requested before the throne.

It was only Sunday afternoon. With only an hour's notice, most of the Court would still be recovering from Saturday night, but some would be drawn to a spectacle like redcaps to the slaughter. There should be enough of them present to serve as witness to the testimony I'd give. In front of a small group of courtiers, I'd be able to pass off responsibility to Bryony, absolve the Knoll of culpability, and hopefully get some actual protection down on the ground where solitary fae were being threatened.

I'd observed the protocols, and that should be enough. The only hardship was that I had to dress for the occasion.

I looked down at the gown I'd chosen to wear. It was tea length, falling to just above my ankles, with navy lace over an A-line skirt. My sleeves were three-quarter length, and the delicately scooped boatneck brought modest attention to my face and crown of black coils. I'd taken long enough in the shower conditioning and twisting my coils for maximum control. But as I neared the river, I knew they were already starting to expand, sucking up the moisture and humidity and growing as wild as my anxiety.

I skidded to a stop in my kitten heels, as Mikka abruptly darted before me and held up a hand.

A moment later, Shiro came gasping around an oak. He was in court dress; his jacket was open, plunging to sharp points above his legs and up to his collar. The navy open-front jacket was edged in gold with extravagantly broad shoulders trimmed in gold braid. It flared out behind him in deep tails over his tightly tailored leggings that were subtle along the sides, but golden points that descended down his thighs. He simultaneously looked poised for formalities and ready for combat. His expression held none of the confidence of his attire; he looked horrified. "Siobhan, you can't do this. She'll kill you."

"Bryony?"

"No. Lada!" Shiro stood tall and looked directly at me with such intensity, I almost withered under his gaze. "Siobhan, she's issued a challenge. The Winter Queen blames you for the death of her subject. She says the Greenwood Knoll and their army of solitaries are waging war on the Courts. She blames you for the fact that humans are wielding Fairy magic. What in Mab's cursed tongue does that even mean?"

As I was still processing what Shiro had said, how Lada had even learned about Hannah's ability, Mikka cut to the heart of the matter. "Wait, a challenge? Lada wants a duel?"

"With me?" I squeaked, still slow on the process.

Shiro nodded solemnly, his breath finally caught. "She knows you don't have any active power, Siobhan. It's the easiest way to condemn you to death for defying the Courts."

"But I didn't," I protested.

I hadn't defied the Courts. I'd defected decades ago. I'd denied their control over me. But I hadn't defied them.

Not really.

Everything I did was within their parameters. Every pursuit, every aim.

I was obedient.

I just wanted to serve my people. I was a Keeper. I watched the Gate; I preserved the balance of magic; I kept my people safe. I was never built to be a Queen. It was better to pass the legacy onto my little sister, the gifted one.

I had never defied my Court. I'd preserved it.

My facts didn't matter apparently.

"Lada doesn't care. She sees you as an easy target," Shiro said, reaching into a bag at his hip. "She knows that you aren't an active player in the Court. But you're still a piece in play. You are royal, but you're solitary. You're powerless, but you aren't weak. And as a

Keeper, you're one to answer if there's an assault on the Gates. Well, from what she's been saying on the dais all morning, every death that has occurred in Atlanta for the past few months is an assault on the order of our Worlds. Someone has to answer for it." He paused and pulled an item out of his bag. It was a pendant on a long gold chain. I couldn't see what was engraved on the pendant as it spun wildly and flashed in the morning light, but I could guess.

"Shiro, no," I said, taking a step back.

"Shiobhan, she is pinning an insurgency on you. She is claiming that you, as true heir to the Atlanta throne, have rallied an army of solitary fae and humans to overthrow the succession of pure fae Queens. And your sister has granted her right of challenge, since you are the true heir until she ascends."

I could feel a madness seize the knot of fear and anxiety deep in my gut. It twisted and burned and quickly erupted from my throat. "I don't want to be heir!" I screamed. "I never wanted to be a Queen. I don't want followers. I don't want the power or the responsibility."

Shiro dipped his chin. "So you deny that you think magic should be allowed to flow freely to whoever can wield it."

"I—" I began, but bit my tongue.

Of course I'd thought about the free flow of magic. And with what Gair had told me, about people actively sacrificing their blood, weakening themselves to strengthen their friends, I knew there were enough in my city that cared about the free flow of magic to fight to change things.

But was I willing to voice that? To choose an ideal over the life and family I was born to?

Was I born to uphold the status quo? Or was I just a coward, afraid to challenge even what I knew was wrong?

Shiro offered me the pendant again. It was a polished oval stone that was beautifully fused moonstone and carnelian. Though I couldn't see it from here, I knew it was carved with a three-strand braid encircling a three-pointed knot.

It was my mother's pendant and was imbued with her blood, her magic. An heirloom of at least six generations, the Duel Stone was reserved for members of the Atlanta Summer Court. If a challenge was issued to a Queen or one of her descendants, she could use the stone to appoint a second, someone to fight on her behalf. She would choose a champion, anoint the stone with blood, and respond to challenges without risking herself.

It was a privilege reserved for royalty. Which I no longer was.

"You shouldn't have taken that," I said.

"I didn't take anything," Shiro said. "Your mother sent me."

"She—she did?"

Shiro didn't wait for me to protest further. He grabbed my wrist, yanked it forward, and shoved the necklace into my palm. "She's in a precarious situation. She can't stop this, she can barely nail down what year this is, but she wants to protect you. But if it was up to your sister? She'll give you up to defend her throne."

Shiro was right, I realized as I pulled the pendant in close to my chest. Lada was a full Queen, pursuing a legitimate grievance in the realm of another. Mother was unable to respond in her own capacity, but Bryony wouldn't stop Lada from pursuing justice in any legal way she chose. Even if she wanted to save me, and I wasn't sure I could bet my life on that.

"I'll do it," Mikka said, holding her hand out. "I can fight on your behalf."

I clutched the pendant and glared at her. "No. No one is going to fight. There are ways to reject a challenge. No one needs to fight today."

Mikka traded a glance with Shiro, but neither of them said a word. They simply fell in step behind me.

As we approached the palace, the wooded path seemed to disappear. The wood chips laid out between pine barriers gave way to packed dirt, then small undergrowth, then a full barrier. Blackberry bushes with thorns in full summer display seemed to grow up in a wall across what would otherwise be a subtle foot path.

If we had hesitated, we would have been turned away and been forced to circle the marked path three times before we'd have another chance. I didn't hesitate, but I did curse at the illusion of sharp brambles, thick vines, and juicy berries, as if they'd been put there just to infuriate me, personally. A subtler fae would have taken the time to acknowledge the illusion and let it fade before her awareness.

I was rarely that subtle.

A few dozen feet later, I emerged on the pristine front path of the palace. The multicolored river stones were laid in an elaborate mosaic that wound its way up through the carefully manicured lawns. When I was younger, I'd tried to discern patterns in the stones, discover pictures or meaning in them, but they shifted so frequently that a flame and phoenix one minute was a sylph and blustering wind the next and a kelpie sinking below the waves the following day.

I could hear as Mikka and Shiro fell into step behind me. Well, I could hear Shiro's formal heels click on the pavement as Mikka kept pace silently beside him in her soft-soled boots.

As I approached the front walk, though, my determination faltered. There were too many vehicles along the front drive, too many people moving about. There was a crowd forming along the front steps as people jostled to be admitted to the palace proper.

Any hope I'd had that my late announcement might mean I could present my case in a more intimate setting was immediately dashed. It seemed the entirety of Atlanta's fae peerage had come out. I saw the duchies of Decatur, Cabbagetown, Marietta, and Greater Gwinnett all stepping up to the front doors with their appropriate hangers on. They all looked dressed for a party: shimmering chiffon, satin, and silk were embellished with gemstones, jewelry, and more power than I'd seen in any single space since I'd abdicated my throne.

Mikka and Shiro fell in on either side of me, my flanking defense, whether I wanted it or not.

"You don't have to do this," Mikka whispered. She reached out and put a strong arm on my shoulder before giving it a squeeze. "Argus can come tomorrow. When things are less crowded."

I shook my head.

"No, if Lada wants a confrontation, then it is better to get it over with. And better that there are more here to witness what we have to say. I am no enemy of the Courts, even if I'm not subject to them. Let us plead our case and defend our autonomy."

Mikka smiled sadly. "You already sound like one of them."

I shuddered. She was right; it was too easy for me to slip back into my political Court persona. "Curse your tongue. Let's crash their party."

She grinned wildly. "That's more like it."

Shiro shook his head. "I should have left well enough alone." But he fell into step behind us as we climbed the front steps with the rest of the Court's subjects.

CHAPTER TWENTY-SEVEN

While most of the palace obeyed the natural laws of the Iron Realm, the audience chambers were an exception. Located off the main entrance hall was a corridor that exceeded every bound of the physical building. The columns were live oaks with branches that swooped higher than any tree I'd seen in this plane outside of the redwood forests of the West Coast. They created a corridor of life that extended hundreds of paces.

Visitors walked the length of the live forest to arrive at a great arch created by twined oak and willow branches. Most of the time, the branches were filled with rose and wisteria blossoms, giving the entire corridor a perfume that clung to petitioners for days whether their requests were granted or denied. It was Mother's gift, or curse, depending on how you felt about floral scents.

Today, though, the arch was bare. Some optimistic page or maid had placed large vases of roses, wisteria, and hydrangeas alongside the oaks, but given the bare arches that extended over twenty feet above, the extravagant floral displays only drew attention to the lack of natural growth.

Mikka noticed my attention on the flowers. "Your mother is fine," she whispered. "Your sister wouldn't hold Court if there was something really wrong."

I had my doubts, but I agreed. If Bryony was worried about Mother, she wouldn't have opened the palace up to the entirety of the Summer Court; she'd play things closer to the vest.

Or she'd make a play for the throne. I guess I'd find out when we got inside.

I shook away my concerns. "Let's get this over with."

We passed through the arch and entered the formal audience chambers alongside a group of sidhe sisters I knew lived out by the Marietta Country Club. The tall brunette looked over casually but did a doubletake when she saw me. I offered an apologetic smile, but she grabbed her sisters by the arms and tugged them forward and away.

The grand room we entered made even the great hallway seem small. It was as large as Grand Central Station or the entire amphitheater of the Fox downtown, where they'd hosted the *Gone with the Wind* premiere. The ceiling reached impossibly high, held aloft by giant buttresses that extended from wooden ribbed vault alcoves. The alcoves extended to create small ballrooms of their own and were filled with the grandest and most powerful fae of the city. Their glamours wiped away as they entered the arch, so everyone was as they seemed. Stripped of their human illusions, I saw spines and feathers, gills and scales, fur and chitinous exoskeletons. It was beautiful and overwhelming.

And then there was the fashion. At Court, natural but fabulous was the dress code. Dresses were cut away to display wings and peacock tails and gills along the ribs. Pantsuits split along the legs to allow multiple furred tails, jackets opened at the chest to display mottled scales that changed with the mood of the crowd. In the balconies, many fae had eschewed fabric clothing altogether, opting instead to weave Court-appropriate robes of flowers and vines or cloud vapor and fog.

It was in the rafters that the highest ranked fae waited for Court to begin. Looking out over the main, the large private balconies allowed the most prestigious, most noble among the Atlanta fae to watch the proceedings of Court from a distance. They had a perfect view of the ballroom below and the thrones at the far end of the chambers.

In one of the balconies closest to the thrones, I had my own doubletake to see Talisa leaning over the railing. She was in a sumptuous velvet burgundy gown that was low cut and hugged every one of her perfect curves. Her honey brown hair was loose, hanging around a face that looked horrified to see me at Court.

I shrugged an apology, but she whipped her head around to someone who had come up behind her. She stood and listened to the man who held a hand to her lower back as he whispered something in her ear. Then he turned his attention to me, and I recognized him immediately.

Sweet Mab.

Thierry Kellan was gorgeous.

Skin the color of honeyed cream, smooth and flawless. Dark hair short but long enough to be tousled across his head, a whisper of a sharp-cut goatee growing in along his chin and under his nose, a slightly crooked but perfectly proportionate nose, and piercing storm-gray eyes set deep beneath dark and heavy brows. His look was intense, overwhelming.

When he saw me, he smiled, and I nearly fell in love right there. His high, severe cheekbones disappeared as the entire shape of his face changed. The pristine marble of his face pushed aside to make way for teeth and lips and sparkling silver in his delighted gaze.

Thierry Kellan. The most powerful solitary fae in Atlanta, if not the entire New World.

He could almost pass for human, if it weren't for the pure beauty of him. It wasn't the sharpness of his features, looking carved out of living marble. It wasn't the fact that he didn't look a day over thirty despite having been active in human circles for at least the past fifty years in Atlanta.

No, if you had seen a photograph of him, he could possibly even pass for human. But in person, he radiated so much power and magic and life that everyone and everything around him seemed frozen in time. It was like holding incandescent lightbulbs against a bolt of lightning; they possessed the same electricity, but there was no comparison. He was so much more alive than anyone else in the room that he seemed to be the reality against which all other life could be measured.

He was pure fae in a way I'd only ever seen Queens exist. No wonder so many flocked to him.

A small ding pulled my attention from the upper boxes to the far side of the room. There, seven steps above the ground were a pair of thrones. Normally, a single throne towered over the grand space. Mother's throne was carved of oak and accented with holly and walnut branches, while blossoms of mandevilla and clematis climbed along the edges and jasmine curled up and away from the chair back, obscuring where the throne ended and the room began. It loomed large, but delicately cushioned Mother as she frequently tucked her legs up, swung them over the arms of the chair, knelt on the edge, lounged almost to slipping down into a puddle on the dais, and generally refused to remain in a regal upright pose.

The thrones that stood above us now shared nothing with Mother's. They were all sharp, straight lines, carved geometric patterns, and tight confines that would allow for none of the comfortable positions Mother sought. One would sit upright, regal, domineering, or not at all.

What's more important, though, was that there were two of them. Of equal height, they were spare, with no floral or natural adornments They were draped with sable cloth and pillows and were exactly the same in every way.

This did not bode well.

Everyone had heard the subtle ding calling us to attention, and most of the residents of the balconies had found their seats, while those along the floor moved to a good vantage point closer to the thrones. Mikka, Shiro, and I reached the middle of the room when the second ding came, and then a high horn trilled a tune that spread to the farthest corners of the chambers. The murmuring crowd fell silent.

From either side of the dais, apparently seamless walls opened up to reveal large doorways. There was no magic to it; there were multiple anterooms along the front of the throne room, all of them connected so that entrances could be conducted in the most theatrical way possible. Queens usually chose to enter from the center of the room first, took the throne, and then welcomed visiting royals to join them on the dais from the wings.

At the same time, Bryony and Lada entered from behind their thrones. Their matching thrones.

Shiro's moan was under his breath, but clear to both Mikka and me. "Here we go."

The Summer and Winter royals mirrored each other and took their seats of equal size and design, as everyone below the dais waited patiently to see what these evenly matched women had to say.

"Summer's blessings," Bryony said, sitting straight-backed and imperious before us. Her voice was amplified in much the same way we used at karaoke; magic carried her spoken voice to the farthest corners of the room as if she were standing beside everyone. "We are here to welcome a daughter back to Court."

Hundreds of eyes turned to me. It was too much to ask that I had escaped attention. Of course, everyone knew exactly where I was. Only my sister, the one with the crown announcing my fate from the stage, managed to avoid looking at me.

Lada, for her part, was all malevolent grins as she met my eyes directly with a frosty superiority.

Bryony continued. "Siobhan Cambry Illythia, you were missed. We only regret that it took a challenge against your own self to bring you home."

I kept my mouth shut because I had not yet been invited to speak, but it took everything in me not to scream at my sister that she knew better. I dared not question her in front of the formal Court.

She wasn't Queen, but she held the throne.

Bryony continued, her voice amplified though she seemed to speak barely above a whisper. "Though rumors have brought your adherence to fae law into question before, we have never had reason to doubt you. Until now."

There was a brief moment as speculation was allowed to spill across the crowd, but Bryony didn't let the moment stretch. She continued in a dire voice. "In her investigation of her subject's death on our lands, Winter Queen Lada Cassimira has discovered a seditious plot against our Court, led by an organization that was spawned and emboldened in the Greenwood Knoll. The so-called Fair Folk have been accessing the Gate and siphoning power for their own nefarious purposes."

I wondered how long Lada had known this information. Her seemingly spontaneous visit to the Knoll last night might have been just to get the ammunition she needed to issue this challenge. Her even being in Atlanta might have been for this very moment.

"She has further learned that the fae have been arming humans with Fairy magic, sharing their natural abilities, and instructing humans in how to steal magic to aid their crimes."

I couldn't keep silent anymore. "What does any of that have to do with me?"

Bryony finally stopped listing grievances and looked at me. "Siobhan Cambry Illythia, you are accused of fomenting sedition in Atlanta, of providing aid and comfort to those who would do harm to this Court, the Gate, and your Queen, of accessory to the murder of Natara Sakari and of rebellion against the laws of the fae."

All was silent anticipation as they looked between me and my sister.

"Do you deny these charges, Siobhan?" Bryony finally said. "Do you deny that you agree with these sentiments? That you have supported unrest amongst the solitary fae of this city?"

"I have never been disloyal to this Court," I said. "I have never taken action against any Queen. And I have faithfully preserved the Gate as I swore to do in the name of the first Queen. I swore Nour's oath."

"Funny thing. Nour was an oath breaker, too." Lada stood up from her throne and took three steps forward. She stared down at me, less direct malice and more of a dawning recognition. "Her Gates were meant to protect our people, to give fae a future, protected from the threat of the humans. Yet, more humans reside in Fairy now than at any point in our history. Our worlds are blurred, and our people suffer and die out. Nour swore to protect the realms and our magic, but she degraded both. She was a half-blood, as well. Oath breaking comes natural to your kind."

Even the most Court-accustomed fae gasped at that one. The number of pure-blooded fae was perhaps higher in this room than anywhere else in Atlanta, but we were still Summer. Lack of blood purity might be gossiped about, disparaged under breath, and used by the most boorish among us to insult bartenders and former princesses, but to utter such an insult from the throne of the Summer palace was beyond propriety.

Bryony winced, but she didn't stand up for me either. Instead, she stuck to her script. "Lada Cassimira has accused you of sedition and challenged your honor. How will you respond?"

My heart broke, but I smoothed my full skirt and lifted my chin higher. "Is derisive laughter acceptable?"

A titter rose from the balconies as the tension broke briefly. Bryony smiled indulgently as Lada scoffed. "I am afraid that a formal challenge requires a formal response."

"I deny the charges," I said. "I have not engaged in sedition, nor undermined this Court in any way, despite five decades of disagreements with the policies and conduct of the throne." I should have been more careful with my words, but Lada's bigotry had scraped something raw inside me, and I couldn't help picking at the wound. "I have questioned decisions made by this Court, but I have defended its authority and done more than my part to protect this city and its inhabitants. I serve this city, whether it serves me or not. I deny the charges, and my honor does not suffer under challenge from one who questions even the honor of Nour Sitra, preserver of worlds."

Spontaneous applause erupted from one of the balconies and was quickly followed by others scattered across the floor.

An electric cold crackled from the stage as Lada advanced to the edge of the stairs. "You are the reason Natara is dead."

"You decided that before you ever came to Atlanta," I said with more confidence than I felt as her frost descended on me. "I did not kill your lover."

"No, she was merely a casualty in your quest for power."

I wanted to laugh. I wanted to cry. This was the constant struggle around my life, and I still wanted none of it. "Power? I don't want it," I said.

"It is not your choice, Siobhan," Bryony said softly, though her voice still carried to every corner of the chambers. "That's what you've never understood. It's never been your choice." She stood still for a moment, her shoulders slack, as if weighed down with the power that was foisted upon her by my choices.

Oh sister, I thought. *I never wanted any of this.*

It didn't matter.

"The challenge is issued. You deny the charges. The implications of the crimes are vast, but the immediate charge is personal. Your Majesty," Bryony addressed Lada now, "how will you seek satisfaction? Trial? Combat?"

"Yes," Lada interrupted, snarling. "I want blood for blood."

"Is anybody else surprised by that?" Shiro stage whispered to me as he offered me a small ceremonial dagger. "I'm totally shocked by this turn of events."

I shushed him as I accepted the knife but was thankful for the reminder that I wasn't alone here. I had supporters at Court. I had very powerful solitary support. And I had everyone at the Knoll behind me.

I offered up my forearm. Before all, I cut my arm and let the blood well up and drop to the polished wood floor. "I offer blood for your pain, Your Majesty. But you may not take my life's blood for a life I am innocent of. And I will not submit to a death sentence when you know I wield no power."

Lada looked to the ceiling with a new laugh. "You have already designated a second." She lifted a finger and pointed to Mikka, who wore the pendant that Shiro had gifted me. I didn't know when Mikka had stolen it, but no doubt, my aggressive march through the blackberry bushes had anointed it with my blood.

I could taste my magic, subtle as it was, emanating from Mikka.

The irony of someone wielding my magic as her own did not escape me.

Mikka met my eyes, asking either for my permission or my forgiveness. She had claimed the pendant without my consent, but she would not go against me if I refused.

She would fight for me, on my behalf. She would put herself up against a Queen to keep me safe. But more than that, she was willing to put herself on the line for the Knoll. A challenge of this kind had repercussions. If Mikka won her fight, if she even brought Lada to a draw, the suspicion of guilt against me and the Knoll would be suspended until a full investigation by the Atlanta Crown had progressed. Our people would be safe in the meantime.

Mikka was a seasoned fighter. She was strong enough to stand against even a Queen. At least for a time. There was a chance I could intercede in that time and get Bryony to end the duel.

But if I fought for myself? Without an active power, I would die immediately. Lada made that clear. The Knoll would fall, and I would be to blame.

As always, there was no real choice.

I nodded once.

Mikka turned to the throne. "I will fight."

CHAPTER TWENTY-EIGHT

The center of the floor before the throne quickly cleared. Everyone who was not directly involved in the impending duel moved to the alcoves or back toward the entrance, leaving a large open space directly before the throne.

Several members of the Queen's guard stepped up to create a proper barrier, pouring a mixture of salt and fae blood along a carved line that created a magical wall around the dueling space. Only those who were party to the challenge would be permitted inside the circle once the duel began.

For her part, Lada was ready. She stalked within the circle like a caged tiger, tracing a path as she watched me and Mikka confer over strategy. She had removed the full pale green skirts that were part of her Court attire and now stood in her embroidered green corset over stark white leggings with fur-topped camel boots. She looked primed to kill and not shed a single drop of her own blood.

Frighteningly enough, Mikka had the same look in her eyes.

"Meeks, however strong you are, you are not a Queen," I reminded her. "Do not step into that circle thinking you can stron-garm this."

"She's right," Shiro said. "You have to be smart. Lada is not a brawler. She is a Queen. She hits once and expects people to lie down."

"You're the experienced fighter," I continued. "You face down arrogant jerks every weekend. That's all Lada is. Another idiot who thinks their magic makes them a superior fighter."

Mikka stretched her neck from side to side, letting it pop, and grinned at us. "You know, I always wanted to rough up a Queen. But," she trailed off.

"What? But what?" I saw the look Mikka was trading with the Queen, who was waggling her fingers and stretching out her shoulders.

"Did she have to be gorgeous?"

Shiro snorted as I rolled my eyes. "Focus," I said. "You've got fire to her ice. You've got the environmental advantage being in Georgia in summer, but she's got the power advantage, being that, well—"

"She is a Queen. Yeah," Mikka said. "I know." She smiled harder. "Do you know how long it's been since I was properly outgunned in a fight? Last time was back in the Spanish Civil War with Varon and I pinned down in Madrid. There was this gorgon who brought every battle to a standstill and—"

"Maybe we can take this up at another time?"

Mikka grinned without a hint of shame. "Nah. I've got a better one I can tell you about. Ask me about when I bedded three maenads in full mania."

"Nope!" I put my fingers in my ears, turned my back, and stepped outside of the dueling circle, giving her exactly the reaction she wanted to bolster her confidence.

Turned out to the crowd, I looked up for a direct view of Thierry Kellan's balcony. He was nowhere to be seen, but Talisa stood at the center, her brown eyes big and worried.

I smiled at her. I wasn't sure if it was relief that she was here, or an attempt to reassure her, or just delight in seeing a pretty face.

Before I could begin to process the moment, Bryony spoke from the dais. "Challenger and respondent, or rather, designated champion, please come to the floor."

Her words were moot because both Lada and Mikka were already in the arena.

As they waited, the most powerful mages of the Court called up a circle and closed it around the dueling space. With the spells in place, the combatants were sealed inside until the duel was finished, when either the challenger was satisfied, the respondent conceded, or one or both of the duelists were dead. The spells also kept out everyone and everything that might influence the duel. That meant no one could intercede once the duel began, but also that the combatants were limited to what they carried into the arena. Summer, Winter or solitary, Queen or civilian, they were unable to access any conduit to Fairy and call on magic outside of themselves. They were to fight and die by the magic and power they possessed from the moment they stepped inside the circle, to the moment they conceded or life sought release from their bodies.

With the eyes of Atlanta on the center of the chambers, I wanted to step forward and say something, to protest. I wanted to step into the middle of the floor before everyone and scream that this wasn't right. That the real danger to our people, to our way of life, was outside this hall. There were actual threats to our city, and that if we were willing to face them, we could stand together, solitary and Summer. And maybe even Winter.

I wasn't going to let this city fall to outside forces, or threats that came from inside the house. We could be strong. If we stood together.

Then Lada stepped toward me. She ignored the champion that was there to face her, ignored the rules of engagement, and walked directly toward me. She stayed inside the boundaries of the dueling circle, while I stood just outside. But there was no denying her power. The air grew cold, and she was shrouded in fog and illusion.

It hadn't occurred to me until now to consider what kind of fae she was, but the fact that she was an osenya struck me as entirely appropriate for a Queen. Lada was a White Lady, a creature of death, and an empath ruled by her emotions. She wasn't a bean sidhe or a banshee; she wasn't here just to mourn, to give voice to the grief of the people who surrounded her. She felt everything around death: the anger, the outrage, the giddy relief, the exhilaration, and she was empowered when death approached.

In that moment, I questioned whether despite the expert spells and the ancient magic, she could blow past the boundaries of the dueling circle, just with the force of her will and her power. Whether she could pull the full weight of her connection to Fairy through and eliminate Mikka in an instant.

But the moment passed, and Lada turned her attention to Mikka.

The two women took up spots across from each other and waited. Lada stood confidently assured, her chin lifted high and haughty as she shook her blond hair back out of her face. Mikka was bouncing from foot to foot, looking every inch like a boxer waiting for the bell. I could see her struggling not to reach for her magic too soon, but I could see the air starting to shimmer as heat built inside her.

Bryony took to her throne, sat down, and raised a hand. When both of the fighters looked to her, she brought her hand down with a finger slicing through the air. "Begin," she announced, and the air crackled as the spells activated.

Mikka's hands lit up, consumed with flames as she spun balls of fire to hurl at Lada. But Lada vanished in a cloud of fog and mist. The fog spread from where she had stood, filling the dome of the arena. Mikka would have disappeared from view as well, were it not for the intense balls of flame melting away any cloud that approached her. She waved them about as she stalked the arena, looking for Lada.

"Figures a Queen would be too scared to get her hands dirty," Mikka taunted. "Come out and face me!"

At that, a dense tendril of smoke snaked along the ground behind Mikka and twined about her ankle before snatching her backward and bringing her crashing to the ground, face first. Mikka didn't hesitate to twist on the ground and launch one of her fire balls back toward the source of the tendril. It cut a bright path through the fog before shattering against the invisible barrier in a shower of ash and cinders.

Scrambling to her feet, Mikka began prowling again, shoving light and fire into every shadow, but as soon as she lit an area, the fog closed in again, concealing Lada somewhere in the space.

"Coward," Mikka called in a singsong voice. "You're the one who wanted this fight. Are you scared because you're up against someone with active magic instead of the easy target you were hoping for?"

"Ouch," I said softly. "I'm right here." Shiro patted my arm and gave me a look. "No, I know she's right," I said, reading him. "But she didn't have to say it in front of the whole Court."

Inside the arena, Mikka was growing bored with the mouse hunt. She started lobbing small fire balls throughout the dome, spreading them out to uncover as much space as she could to snuff out Lada's hiding spot. It was a clever idea. With enough light, she should be able to spot the Queen and make quick work of attacking her outright.

But Lada was not about to be found that easily. A whispered word slithered through the air, and the fog intensified, extinguishing all of the fireballs, including the ones in Mikka's hands. The entire dome was filled with thick white, and Mikka's muffled chirp of surprise was quickly smothered.

There was a collective intake of breath from the spectators, and many of us leaned forward, trying to see what was happening in the dome. I was practically pressed against the shimmering containment spell, looking for any sign of my best friend.

At once, Mikka was flung up against the barrier, splayed and with a look of horror on her face. Tendrils of smoke had wrapped themselves around her wrists, ankles, and neck, and they were twisted tight enough for the veins on her arms to begin to show. The coils about her neck, though, were not strangling her. I had a moment to wonder why Lada wouldn't go the obvious route with her abilities, when the Queen herself came into view.

She stood just behind Mikka and leaned in to whisper in her ear. All the while, she looked directly at me, her own eyes the white of a blizzard. Mikka's look of horror collapsed into one of anguish, and as Lada's tendrils snaked away, Mikka crumbled to her knees.

"No," she sobbed as her body seemed to close in on itself,

shrinking inward protectively. "No." She began to rock back and forth as she wrapped her arms around her knees. "Oh, sweet Maeve, no."

Lada smiled as she knelt down beside her. The fog in the dome dissipated, and we could all see clearly as Mikka broke down and Lada loomed. "Such a shame." Her voice held sympathy and concern, but there was only malevolence on her face. She held a hand out, palm upward, and a swirl of fog and ice coalesced into a solid shape: a dagger that glowed. With an ivory handle and a wicked blade, it was as real as either woman in the ring. "Such a shame," Lada said again. "If only there was a way to escape the pain."

With that, she put the dagger in front of Mikka. The distant look disappeared from my friend's face as she focused on the weapon in front of her.

"What is she doing?" Shiro said. "Is she actually giving her opponent a weapon?"

"No," I whispered, watching the expression on Mikka's face turn from one of anguish to one of grim determination. "She's attacking."

I threw myself at the barrier. "Mikka, it's not real." I pounded my fists against the magical wall, which rippled but held firm. I didn't care if it was against the rules or not. I couldn't let Mikka go like this. "Whatever she's showing you, whatever you see, it's not real."

There was no sign that Mikka heard me at all, but Lada lifted her eyes and smiled cruelly. "This is your fault, you know." She spoke quietly to Mikka, but I knew the words were for me. "You could have stopped this. It didn't have to be like this." Then she turned her entire attention to Mikka. "You could end it."

Mikka had eyes for nothing but the knife in her hands. She picked it up by the handle, turned her wrist to see the blade flash. She laid the edge of it against her opposite palm. Then with a small movement, she opened up her palm along her lifeline. It was one of the worst places to cut yourself: all the tendons, the nerves, the sensitive skin. Slicing up your palm could bring forth blood, but it hurt like hell.

She didn't seem to mind, watching the blood well up from her shallow cut. Flexing her wrist, she caused more to pool in her open palm. "It's my fault." Mikka looked up but didn't seem to see any of us outside the edge of the dome. "I did this."

Then she slashed upward, a smooth flourish of movement, like a calligrapher swiping ink across the page. Blood welled along her arm, a vertical slash, from wrist to elbow.

A certain suicide.

Lada exulted, clapping her hands and turning up toward Bryony on the throne for recognition of her victory, as Mikka turned her eyes to the heavens.

"Maeve, be with me." Mikka closed her eyes and fell back on her heels.

"No!" I screamed. Pounding against the barrier, I refused the idea that I couldn't go to her. She couldn't die alone. Mikka needed me. I could save her.

I put every bit of power inside of me into the fists that rammed against the wall. Screaming, I knew it would do no good. I had no real magic. My anguish pooled within me with no outlet. I could stitch myself back together, knit together my own flesh, but I could touch no one else with what raged inside of me.

That didn't stop me from pouring myself forward. Every thought, every emotion, every ounce of myself expelled forward at Mikka. My friend.

My brash, loud, confident, beautiful, unquestioning, loyal friend. If I had any power, if I was anything, it made no difference unless it did something now.

The barrier cracked.

I didn't even stop to think. I threw myself at the crack before me and shoved my entire body through the dueling wall, emerging in front of a blinking Lada and a swooning Mikka. Driving myself to my knees in a pool of dark, oxygen-rich blood, I swooped forward and supported Mikka as she fell back, cradling her in my arms.

Her breath was starting to catch as her heart struggled to find blood to pump. It stuttered and jumped. I was losing her.

"Not yet," I swore to her. "Hey, you. You don't get to leave me, yet." I kissed her forehead, trying to get her eyes to focus on me as they stared straight ahead. "Let go of her illusions. Let go of the lies. I've got you. I'm not leaving you."

Her head lolled in my left arm, heavy with mortality slipping away. *No.*

This particular drake should be immortal. Her ending like this was unacceptable.

I snatched her bloody arm to me with my free hand and screamed at it. I had no words. An ineffable sound escaped my lips, torn from the bottom of my stomach and up through every cord and muscle that stretched across my esophagus and throat. It ripped ragged edges through me as it rose, and I poured every ounce of that hurt into my need to heal Mikka. My entire self felt like it was stripped from me in grief, in rage, in need, as I screamed at Mikka to pull herself back together.

At one point in my screaming, I felt a touch on my shoulder.

Lada. Her icy grip left frostbite on my skin as she tried to whisper in my ear, too.

She was going to suggest lies to me, too. To take me down the way she tried to take away my friend.

That wasn't going to happen.

Her touch fueled the fire Mikka's hurt ignited. I seized the feel of her, the imprint of Lada, the taste of caramel and apples, and I pulled as hard as I could, and I shoved every thought and instinct and intention into Mikka. She would not die.

Not today.

Heat. Frost. It was all one.

Until my rage and despair and anguish wore down.

Hours, months, seconds later, I gasped, my face against Mikka's straight black hair, my chin on her shoulder as she slumped forward. She braced against the floor, holding us both up as we heaved breaths and tried to find which way was up and which way was death.

She moved first, turning with her far hand to reach for me, turning to catch me as I fell into her lap as she had been in mine.

"What did you do?" Her voice clear as a bell. I felt along the connection I still held in her. She was whole, her heart beat.

She was alive.

"Hey, Meeks." I smiled. The room rolled, and I thought for a moment I might throw up all the contents of my stomach. But I couldn't quite remember what I'd last eaten. So it obligingly stayed put.

"Sugar. Oh, honey, what did you do?" She cradled my head as I looked up at her, but she turned her eyes to the room.

I had forgotten there was anyone else there.

I rolled my head to see what was happening.

Lada was on the ground, prone, with at least a half dozen healers positioned around her, their eyes closed, touching her, murmuring. Kiral, the consort who had accompanied her through the Gate was holding her hand and whispering to her fervently. Several armored attendants stood arrayed around me and Mikka, swords and spears at the ready.

Bryony towered above us, looking lost, furious, and terrified all at once.

Farther beyond the weapons and dangerous would-be Queens, Talisa and Shiro stood staring, along with the rest of the subjects of the Summer Court.

"Did we win?" I said, before I felt darkness roll up around the edges of my vision, and the Summer palace disappeared.

CHAPTER TWENTY-NINE

I woke slowly in my own bed. The room was empty, and I was bundled under my duvet, dressed in my softest purple t-shirt, black underwear, and nothing else.

Taking a few minutes to remember what had happened, I recovered snippets of what had transpired over the past few hours as I struggled to master consciousness.

There was the anteroom behind the thrones, with its dark wood-paneled walls and grand chandeliers. Bryony was pacing. Lada was on a chaise, attended by healers. Shiro and Mikka were both standing, arguing with my sister.

Mother drifted in.

No. She hadn't?

Had she knelt over me as I recovered on another couch?

"You found it. My special girl."

She was gone. No one had seen her.

That didn't fit. They would have noticed.

Bryony stood firm. "The rules are clear. The magic is clear. One challenger. One respondent. Those rules have never been broken."

Mikka yelled, "Right. The magic is clear. If the circle let her in, she was allowed to be there. Unless your almighty Court magic failed somehow."

Someone entered. A male voice I didn't recognize. "The spells are unbroken."

"See?" Mikka puffed out her chest. "Now, let her go home and recover."

"She nearly killed a Queen. Of the Winter Court." Bryony was close to losing her unflappable cool. I had that effect on her.

"Then focus your efforts on helping her," Mikka said.

Shiro spoke softly. "Your Highness. This must go to your mother."

"Yes," Bryony said. "You're right. But there will be consequences." She was silent for a moment. Then, "I cannot shield her from this. There is more at work here than you understand. Than *I* understand."

"I agree," the male voice said. "Perhaps, we can work together on this issue."

The voices grew distant. Or I did. My cognition faded, and I awoke in a velvety scooped-neck shirt in my own bed.

I sat up quickly and instantly regretted the sudden movement. My head pounded. The room spun. I quickly braced myself with my head bent over the edge of the bed in case I was going to be sick.

Concentrating on breathing and seizing control of the chaos that seemed to be rifling through my skull and stomach, I didn't hear the door open.

"Easy," a gentle voice said as the bed compressed beside me and a hand began to rub between my shoulder blades. "Don't push it. I didn't think you would wake so soon. Though given everything else you've done today, I shouldn't be surprised." The hand on my back settled into a comfortable press against my right shoulder, and I didn't have to look up as I recognized the warmth and subtle taste of her magic.

As a maenad, Talisa was used to enflaming the emotions, but she was experienced enough to influence things in the other direction. Just now she was doing her best to keep my feelings in check, exerting a calming, steady force, as I got my bearings.

I smiled, even as I kept my head bowed. "Thank you."

"My pleasure," she said, and I could hear the smile in her own voice.

I took a deep breath, swallowed, and sat upright. She was ready with a glass of water. As I sipped, I looked at her. Her chestnut hair was soft and waved as it fell about her burgundy gown. She hadn't changed out of her Court clothes, and all I could think was to put my hands in the soft velvet of her dress.

"Are you feeling better?"

I nodded, but the movement made the dizziness return, and I groaned.

"Don't push it," Talisa said. "You've been through a lot."

I started to shake my head, but I immediately thought better of it. "No. I haven't had a headache of my own in fifty years."

"You've also never used your power to heal someone who was near death."

A laugh threatened to escape, as everyone knew I couldn't use my one power on anyone but myself. Then everything that happened in the dueling arena came flooding back. The anguish on Mikka's face, her decisive swipe up her arm with Lada's knife. I could almost taste again the bitter tang of fear I'd felt in that moment, and the resultant fury that anyone would take Mikka from me.

The feel of pushing through the magical barriers: like exploding through a pane of glass or penetrating a membrane. It had felt like stabbing through a thick hide or popping an inner tube balloon: resistant, but ultimately yielding to the right application of force.

And then touching Mikka, essentially rejecting her injury. Feeling the force of Lada's magic, her life force as it coursed through me.

"Oh, Morgana's breath," I swore, realizing the full extent of what I had done.

In the moment, with a dying Mikka in my lap and a powerful Lada attempting to use her magic against me, I had done only what I instinctively knew I could. I had remembered how Lada had used my magic to heal Baerd in the cellar of the Knoll, how she had reached into the gift that nestled inside of me, how she'd bound it up with her own power, and had channeled it into Baerd. She had used my magic and her energy to heal that which shouldn't have been healed.

I had only done the same, channeling my knowledge of my own skills to heal Mikka, and using her power to pull it out of me and into someone else.

Except in the dueling arena, Lada had not been a conduit. She had been cut off from Fairy and had been present only with her own capacity. Considerable though it was, her magic was not enough to break my limitations, reclaim a life, and sustain her own.

"Is Lada—" I couldn't even say the words.

"She's alive," Talisa said, a queer look on her face. "As is Mikka."

I hadn't had to ask that. I knew Mikka was alive, in perfect health. I'd felt every part of her stitch together as her body always should have been. Full of fire and force, full of a purity of magic she hadn't touched since she'd walked freely in Fairy. I'd put that all in her.

I didn't doubt Mikka felt better than she had in decades.

But Lada? I'd taken all of that vitality from her.

"You're sure she's okay?" I turned to see Talisa frowning at me, worry creasing the spot between her brows.

"Mikka went to Argus, to fetch him for the Quee—er, your sister. There was worry there might be fallout from what happened."

"And Lada?" I pressed.

Talisa's hand dropped from my shoulders, and she looked like she would like to put a few inches between us. "Unconscious. But yes, alive. Not that you should care. She wanted to kill you. And any of us foolish enough to try and protect you."

My mouth was suddenly dry, and I licked my lips as I grasped at way to explain what I was feeling. "Tal, I—"

"I don't get you. You don't even ask about the friend who could have died fighting in your place. Your worry is for the royal bitch who caused all of this? After all this time, I had hoped you were one of us, one of the common people, but you're still concerned about your own kind after all. You don't care about us."

She started to get up, but I was seized with sudden strength, grabbed her arm, and pulled her back down onto the bed. With my other hand, I caught hold of the back of her neck and kissed her with all the intensity and longing I had felt in her presence for days. If I could have poured magic and power into her as I had done for Mikka, I would have, but I couldn't seem to remember how I had accessed that ability. Instead, I satisfied myself with telling her through my lips, my tongue, and the subtlest graze of my teeth along her bottom lip.

When I released her mouth, I held tight to her neck, bringing her forehead to mine and looking directly into her eyes. It took her several breathless moments before she opened them. Her long eyelashes fluttered as she brought her green eyes to meet my brown ones.

"I do care about you, Talisa," I whispered. "I care a great deal."

"About me?" Her voice was soft and vulnerable, two qualities I had never associated with the confident, strong, unabashed woman sitting next to me.

I raised my other hand up to her cheek and stroked my thumb along that soft part just under her eyes. "About you. About our community. About the Knoll and Mikka and Argus and everyone that is our family. But right now?" I leaned in to kiss her lips again, focused on her full lower lip as I held her cheek and gripped the finial of her neck with more intensity. Then with barely a hairsbreadth between our lips, I whispered into her mouth, "All I care about is you."

She moaned and returned my attentions, reaching her own hands to my waist and along my rib cage, her fingers splayed but pressed intently into my skin. As we kissed, her lower hand found the edge of my shirt where it fell just above my underwear. Her thumb brushed upward, under the fabric, and traced my waistband gently.

I shifted my weight slightly to lean into her touch and pulled her closer. She leaned farther toward me, and I began to taste the stirrings of her magic. As a maenad, she responded to any heightened emotions, but sex was almost like a drug to her. The taste of balsamic strawberries was heavy on my tongue, and the heady feel of her magic was beginning to affect me as she pulled me into her mania.

I had half a moment to decide whether this was something I really wanted. Another kiss and I might not have the head or heart to refuse.

But the way she felt, the way I felt about her. Why shouldn't I want this?

Taking a breath, I gasped out a question before I dove into all she had to offer me. "Why you? Why did you bring me home?"

She froze for a half a beat. "Because I asked for the honor," she admitted with a laugh. "Shiro had to report to your mother, Mikka had to report to Argus, Thierry was in conference with your sister and Lada's consort. I was there, I was strong enough to bring you home, and, well, I've been wanting to get in your bedroom for a few years now."

I looked around. There was a plain, modern dresser with mirror and assortment of dishes of jewelry, a bookshelf full of science fiction and fantasy paperbacks I'd collected from secondhand shops, and my nightstand with phone chargers and a glass of water. There was absolutely nothing remarkable about it. I spent so little time at home, and when I was here, my bedroom was there only for sleep. I half wished I had invested in decent sheets or pillows, or sex toys.

"I hope it lives up to your expectations?"

She pulled back far enough to look at me from my head down to my waist, taking in the soft but plain t-shirt, the comfortable black underwear, the long, strong legs that were pale from a summer spent too much indoors. Her tongue peeked out to wet the cupid's bow of her mouth before she pressed her lips together and nodded. "Everything I wanted and more."

Then she dove onto me, her hands on either side of my face as she kissed me and pushed me back onto the pillow. I squealed in delight as I fell and wrapped my legs around her form as she pressed into me. My hands sunk into the velvet of her gown, and it was as sumptuously soft as I had imagined. I started to gather it, pulling the long skirt up in soft pleats toward her waist, luxuriating in the feel of it, but she stopped me, pulling up with a stern look.

"No," she said firmly. Her green eyes were swirling with grey magic as she devoured me with her eyes. "If I'm going to service a Queen, I will do so in Court dress."

I moaned as she lowered her head to kiss my cleavage, running a tongue between my breasts. Her hands held my waist firm, but her thumbs began to probe around the fabric, finding soft, sensitive skin.

"Do I have your permission to pledge my fealty to Your Majesty?"

I started to protest, heady from the feel of her fingers slipping beneath my cotton briefs, but the talk of Courts and royalty rubbed against me like velcro instead of velvet. "No, not that," I said. "I don't want anything royal."

She froze and pulled back to look at me seriously. "Siobhan, you brought two Courts to their knees today. Two Queens were left on their backs or scrambling for help. I'm solitary until the day I die, but if I'm going to pay obeisance to anyone, it's going to be to someone who demands nothing and protests when I'm offering her everything."

I kissed her. "I'm not protesting—"

She cut me off with a kiss of her own as she laid her velvet-draped body over top of mine. "You are. Because you never think you're worth what people want to give you." She kissed the tip of my nose and nestled her hips downward, pressing into me in a way that made me squirm. "You don't want to be worshiped, because someone along the way taught you that you were only worth the power that you could wield, the magic you could display." She kissed me harder, grinding her hips into mine, pulling my waist closer, and using her knees to slide my legs outward.

"You are worth more than all of them put together, because of who you are. You show more strength than those who can call forth hurricanes." She pulled my shirt up and kissed my stomach. "You have more power than those who rule cities." She kissed lower. "You are more dignified than any Queen in a hundred jewels." She kissed along my waistband. "You are more entitled to a royal title than any conduit in these realms."

With that, she pulled my underwear an inch lower and ran her tongue along the newly exposed skin, sending shivers all over my body.

"May I express my appreciation for what you have done tonight?

Or may I at least act on the overwhelming desire to taste you and have you screaming as you pull my hair and beg for more?"

With that, she lowered her head and licked along my pelvic bone and downward as I moaned in pleasure.

Then she stopped. "Your permission? To also use my magic?"

"Yes," I gasped, twining my fingers into her hair and tilting her head upward so I could meet her eyes. They were large, wet, and hungry, and the taste of balsamic and strawberries and mint nearly knocked me senseless. "Yes, Talisa. Please."

She grinned as a hand slipped from my waist, down to my thighs, and she sank lower as she slipped my waistband over my hips and lower off my legs. "I serve at your pleasure."

I accepted her worship and firmly refused to think of anything but the present moment from that point forward.

CHAPTER THIRTY

I woke to the glorious smell of Brazilian roast coffee, sausage, and something slightly spicy and earthy. There was also the smell of a thoroughly satisfied maenad and the magic she'd gotten consent to use on me.

My head and heart both reeled from all she'd inspired me to.

Talisa poked her head into my room. She wore my blue robe, and I smiled to realize she'd passed over the purple cotton one with the knee-length hem for the short silky one in my closet. Her legs weren't as long as mine, but the bottom of the hem barely skimmed the tops of her thighs.

When she saw I was awake, she approached, and I took full advantage of the short robe to cup my hand under her bare ass and pull her squealing back into bed. She maneuvered a leg so she sat astride my stomach as she beamed down at me.

"Good morning to you, too." She leaned down and kissed me, her tongue attentive and longing.

"Oh, Mab, come back to bed," I groaned as she disengaged from my mouth for half a second.

She sat up. "One, my name is not Mab. It's 'My Goddess,' so get that right."

I laughed and moaned. "Yes, My Goddess," and I leaned forward to bury my head into her softer regions before she twisted up and out of bed.

"And second," she laughed, as she held up a finger. "I have food on the stove, and I will not burn it for some quick tongue play."

"Who said anything about quick?"

She hopped off the bed and called over her shoulder as she disappeared out the door, "What girl sacrifices breakfast for sex?"

"A maenad," I called after her.

"True!" She laughed, but didn't come back.

I sighed back into my sheets and breathed in the heady potpourri of the two of us. Her strawberry scent was what I noticed most, but I couldn't deny the presence of my own distinct magic: a floral juniper and lemony citrus, effervescent and lively. I hadn't meant to call on any of my power. I hadn't known I could and wasn't sure I wanted to.

After what had happened at the Court, I was almost afraid to touch my magic; I didn't know if what I had done with Lada and Mikka was the one time I would do it, or if it was a new ability. I needed time to explore it safely.

But in the heat of experiences with Talisa, when she had touched something deep inside me, when I'd pulled her to greater heights, when we'd come together in moments that words couldn't capture, I'd reached out and found that power again. I'd touched something beyond me, beyond her, and we had become more than both of us.

Mab's dexterous tongue, I had never imagined reaching such ecstasy with another person. Talisa had taken her time to explore me, to unveil me, and then, true to her word, to worship me. No matter how I begged to attend to her, to explore her in turn, she had refused. "You are more than I could hope for."

I had protested. "If it's what I want? If all I want is to have you helpless on my tongue? The taste of strawberries overwhelming my senses?"

"Is that what my magic tastes of?" She had leaned down and kissed me before twisting and putting her fingers to more vigorous work.

"Then you had better find a way to earn my affections another day." She had paused. "I suggest writhing and moaning as loudly as you want, because I'm drawn to enthusiasm."

I had done as conducted.

And just the memory of it had me twisting in my sheets again.

Interminable minutes later, Talisa returned with a tray of buttered toast, sausages, and scrambled eggs in an unexpected color.

At my raised eyebrows, Talisa explained, "I added curry powder and paprika to your eggs."

She laid the tray across my lap as I beamed at her.

"If anyone earned breakfast in bed," I said. "It's you."

She chuckled beneath her breath. "Oh, then you don't know a lot about maenads. I got just as much out of last night as you did. Probably more."

As she watched intently, I picked up a sausage link and bit the tip of it. Her tongue licked at her own lips, mirroring the places where the sausage entered my mouth. "May I?" she gasped.

I nodded, and she darted forward to lick at my lips, tasting the oil and salt of the sausage. I kissed her before pulling away to chew.

I offered her one of the other sausage links, but she shook her head, simply enjoying the fact that I appreciated it.

"I have coffee to get. Then we can talk?" She didn't wait for an answer as she disappeared out the door of my room again.

Any variation of *We need to talk* is a bad thing. I went and got clothes out of my dresser and slipped them on before Talisa returned. I did try some of the eggs with the curry powder and paprika, and turns out Talisa was not just amazing in bed: the girl could cook, too. A second bite and I moaned almost as obscenely as I had just hours before. Oh, I was in trouble with this girl.

Her eggs were absolutely incredible, flavorful with heat that didn't overwhelm the creamy, butter texture. I polished them off and threw the covers over the disheveled bed, before Talisa returned with two mugs of steaming coffee.

I accepted my mug and sat on the edge of the bed while she went back to perch against the doorway. "Thank you for breakfast," I said, indicating the near-empty plate.

She raised her eyebrows with a smirk. "Glad you liked it."

"And thank you for last night. After everything that happened, I needed a chance to recover."

"I figured." She sipped her drink and seemed to consider me. "What are you going to do now?"

"I don't know," I admitted. "I think I can put things off with Bryony for a few days."

"She does have a Winter Queen to revive," Talisa said cruelly. "Shame about that."

I nodded, feeling little pleasure but quite a bit of relief that Lada was out of commission for at least a bit. "But that leaves her distracted and unable to help with everything else that's going on."

Talisa looked at me over the edge of her mug, sipping slowly. "And what exactly is that? The Winter wretch charged you with inciting a rebellion? Of cultivating a coup? What does that even mean?"

"I don't know everything she knows," I admitted. "But between what Hannah had to say under the Knoll, and what Gair told me, I don't think we can deny that Lada's at least partially correct. There are fae in our city trying to undermine the Courts and their throttle on magic."

"Is that so bad, though?" Talisa asked, moving from her post against my doorframe and settling next to me. The edge of her robe fell open a bit, revealing a wide "V" of silky, white skin. I put my hand on the part of her leg that was still covered, but I was definitely distracted at the thought of laying that "V" wider still and resuming where we'd left off last night.

Talisa smiled at me, and the faint taste of strawberries complemented the aroma of the matching mugs of Brazilian coffee in our hands.

I took a deliberate gulp of my coffee, allowing the scalding liquid to focus me on our conversation. "I think there are better ways to challenge the current system," I said finally.

"Shall we write to our representatives?" Talisa shifted a half inch away as she turned to face me, but it was clear her mind was on anything other than sex. "Siobhan, you can't be this naive. You've *been* a part of the system. You know perfectly well there's no real way to change or even question the absolute rule of Queens. They hold all the power. They hold magic hostage, and we grasp at scraps."

The taste of strawberries increased as her anger flared, and it affected me as quickly as the touch of her skin aroused my lust. "I understand," I said carefully. "And I agree with you. It's not right that anyone should hold such power over the heads of those who can't fight back. But if the string of deaths near the Gate are an attempt to change things, I just think there might be better ways to approach it."

Talisa scoffed and stood again. She set her mug down on my dresser so hard that the coffee sloshed and left a small puddle on the edge. Ignoring this, she began to pace my small room. "You prop the whole thing up as much as any of them. Worse, even, because you pretend to be on the outside."

"Talisa," I started, setting my coffee down half full. "What are you talking about?"

"I'm talking about this game you play," she said, facing me squarely, her green eyes flashing. "You gave up your claim to the throne, gave up access to Summer's power, and live this solitary life. But it's all because you didn't know you had any power. The second you show any signs of having something real, some magic that can do something, you go right back to apologizing for the Courts."

That set my head spinning even faster. "What are you talking about? I have no interest in going back to Court. I don't even know what happened yesterday, but I don't think it really matters."

"You having an active power doesn't matter?" She looked like she wanted to spit. "Like the lack of it wasn't the only reason you left the line of succession?"

"It wasn't," I insisted, ready to tell her all of my moral objections about participating in the monarchy, but I had to stop to close my eyes and give my head a shake. My eyes were having trouble focusing on her. Maybe my performance last night at Court, and my later, more energetic performance in bed were having their effect on me at last. I couldn't seem to focus. "I didn't support the path of the throne, what they were—" I struggled to wet my tongue. "What they were doing. The breeding program, and restrictions." My voice was growing faint even to my own ears.

Talisa took a step forward and towered over me, as I'd somehow fallen back against my headboard.

"What's happening?" I asked. "What did you do?"

There was a shadow of pity that passed over her face before her mouth settled into a hard line.

"We gave you plenty of chances," she said, sipping her mug of my best coffee. "You served the community, always questioned the Court, went out of your way to support those who resisted decrees. There were so many who defended you, you know?"

I felt my legs weaken, my toes already dead and my muscles beginning to quiver. I reached for my mug on my bedside table, but the muscles went weak and my fingers numb. I knocked the ceramic over, and it tumbled to the floor, spreading a dark stain over the light blue rug that laid under my bed. I looked at Talisa's impassive face and knew she was going to do nothing about it. That stain was going to set, possibly for hours, and I'd never get it out.

Finally, I voiced my fear. "Are you serious? Did you poison my Brazilian roast?"

"No," Talisa said, smiling, as she sipped at her mug. "Of course not, Siobhan. I'm not a monster." She gestured to my empty breakfast plate. "I drugged your eggs."

I looked in horror at the clean plate. "But they were—"

"Delicious? Thanks." She beamed. "The spices hide the crastum root and mallan leaf."

My vision was growing hazy around the edges, and the feeling in my fingertips was heavy, cottony, and distant. I fell back into my bed, the world spinning softly around me.

Talisa leaned over me, the look on her face, cruelly, like a concerned lover. "I'm sorry. I gave you every chance. The sex was fantastic. And you taste incredible." She then leaned forward and kissed my irresponsive lips. "But our lots were cast in this matter before we could make our choices." Her lips spasmed as if she would smile or grimace but couldn't decide on an emotion. "I don't think there's a fae in this realm who hasn't realized that."

She swept a hand over my heavy eyelids, sweeping me into a deep and bone-numbing sleep.

CHAPTER THIRTY-ONE

I woke as I was dropped ungraciously on the ground. Jolting pain shot through my hips, and bright sunlight stabbed through my eyelids as I winced. Shooting waves of agony undulated across my temples and circled the back of my skull. I groaned.

"Don't move, lass," a welcome voice whispered. "Keep your eyes closed."

"Gair," I whispered back as I followed his instructions and lay still. "What's happening?"

"They're arguing. Apparently, you weren't part of the plan for today." His voice was low and weak sounding.

"Are you okay?" I said, twisting just enough to get a feel for things. Thoughtfully, Talisa had dressed me in loose yoga pants and a t-shirt again, but she had also tied me up. My hands were bound behind me, and my shoulders were starting to cramp. Thankfully, whatever Talisa had tied me up with was soft and didn't chafe. It felt satiny, and I had a horrible flashback to her in my short, satin blue robe with a loose waist belt.

"I think we have both had better days." I could hear the small smile in his voice and was tempted to open my eyes to see his friendly face.

But the voices that argued raised suddenly, and I stilled as I recognized Hannah in addition to Talisa.

"But we already had one!" Hannah was yelling.

"And now we have two," Talisa said. "I don't see what the problem is. I procured, I delivered. The hard work is done. Now let's get this over with."

"No," Hannah insisted, her voice going high and shrill. "No! You can't change the terms like this. We aren't prepared. Changing things makes it risky."

"Oh, relax." I could hear the exasperation in her voice. Talisa had already moved on in the conversation. "It's not like we're alone today, anyway."

There was a beat of silence. Then, "Are you fucking kidding me?" Hannah sounded livid. "You did this to impress him?"

"No," Talisa began, but Hannah charged on.

"Of course you did. That's all any of this has been about for you. You've never cared about anything but where your next fuck is coming from."

A sudden thud and whump sounded, followed by a gasp of pain or surprise. Probably both.

"Talisa punched her," Gair whispered, reminding me that I probably had better things to do than eavesdrop on my captors' disagreement.

"Not fair," I whispered back. "I wanted to do it."

Gair chuckled softly, but it turned quickly into a cough that sounded wet and pained. He was injured, and I needed to see just how much. I had heard enough to know I was facing Gair and the scene before us. But I needed to know what exactly was happening. "Can they see me right now?" I asked. "Can I open my eyes?"

"They're focused on each other right now. But I wouldn't move around too much yet."

I opened my eyes and found I was in the clearing by the Gate. I'd sat in this exact spot nearly every evening for years, slowly bleeding for my city as the sun set. The stone arch stood quiet as usual, ignored in the heat of the day. There would likely be no crossings to or from

Fairy; everyone would be waiting for dawn or dusk for an easier passage through the Gate.

Hannah and Talisa were in front of the Gate, arguing in lowered voices. A small bag had spilled over on its side, but I couldn't see what it held inside. It was most likely the missing crastum root, mallan leaf, and probably rue and feverfew to thin our blood. I had no doubt there was something sharp to cut our wrists to open the Gate and siphon power.

They were still distracted, so I looked Gair over. He was on his knees but slumped over and breathing unevenly. He was in profile to me, and I could see bruises already forming on his face. But it was the growing wetness on his midsection that concerned me.

"She stabbed you?" I hissed, furious and wildly concerned that a human girl with stolen powers had overcome a full grown clurichaun. It was exactly the sort of danger that Lada and the Courts were worried about.

"After she attempted to seduce me. And then poison me. But I didn't trust her tea."

"I got the poison," I claimed.

"I should have voted for that one," he said, his voice catching as he winced over his movement. "The knife hurts."

As the vise around the base of my head seemed to tighten, I almost objected. But then, I wasn't already bleeding.

I shot a look to the still-quiet Gate. Despite the amount of blood flowing from Gair, the Gate was dormant. I supposed since the blood sacrifice had not been made in the presence of the Gate, it didn't serve as a key to open it.

Despite years of serving as Keeper, I hadn't taken time to understand exactly how the magic worked, how the passage was invoked. I'd spent years, kneeling here, opening the Way, sharing as much power with my community as possible, giving my blood and draining my energy; and I'd never spent any time wondering how it worked. It shamed me to know that these others, these opportunists who only cared about how they could use the gift of magic already knew more than the Keepers about how to wield it.

"Hello, princess," Talisa said, turning and catching me alert. "See anything you like?"

No longer worried about attracting attention, I wiggled to sit up. The motion sent spasms through my contorted shoulders and made my head pound even harder, but I ignored that, squashing it down with anger. "What are you hoping to accomplish here, Talisa? Even if you absorb all the power you can from this side of the Gate, no matter how many vials of blood you collect, you won't have a fraction of what you need to overcome the Courts. You can't overthrow a single Queen with a few stolen elemental powers."

"Oh?" Talisa raised her eyebrows. "Perhaps you need a demonstration of what we've discovered." She turned to Hannah. "Hannah?"

Hannah scowled at Talisa. "Seriously? I'm not a show dog."

Talisa rolled her eyes, lifted her hand, and a huge bolt of lightning jumped upward from her palm. The resultant crack knocked both Gair and me backward and left a taste of ozone in the air.

In no world that I knew could a maenad wield raw electric power like that. It was evidence enough that she had uncovered something.

Hannah was equally cowed by Talisa's display, so she stood tall and spread her hands. A gust of wind gathered and began to swirl around the clearing. It grew in intensity, and then flames of fire began to lick around the edges. Gair and I began to sweat as the swirling fire tornado spun faster and the base of the cone shrank closer and closer.

Finally, Talisa waved a hand at Hannah, who let her arms fall. She gasped and bent double, her hands shaking.

"You need to practice," Talisa sneered.

"I practice all the time," Hannah insisted, but she was out of breath, and she seemed unsteady. She looked like she was going to throw up, and I felt pity for her.

"Talisa, this isn't right," I said.

"Neither is hoarding the powers of fairy according to birthright, or royal status." Talisa walked over and pulled me to my feet, wrenching my arms farther back and causing my migraine to spike. "This world is broken. As much as the fae pride themselves on being better than the humans, on taking care of our own, it's all still based on the oppression of the weakest among us. The Courts hoard power, and powers. If we have a chance to equalize things between the solitary and Summer, if we can find a way to share the wealth of magic without giving up everything to get it? Then I'm going to deem your sacrifice worth it."

"Giving up everything?"

"Pledging ourselves to the Courts means giving up our freedoms just to access our natural abilities. There's nothing without the ability to choose where you live, who you spend your life with, how you choose to procreate or not!" She screamed that last bit with a desperation that I'd heard from my own voice once upon a time.

But I'd never sacrificed anyone but myself for the freedom I craved. "So you're just going to kill a whole bunch of solitary fae? The very people you claim to want to help?"

"We're not just—" She stopped herself. "I don't have to justify myself to anyone. Especially not to you." She pulled me forward toward the Gate. Though my legs seemed to be working perfectly, I made her drag me.

"What do you mean, 'especially not me'?"

That pulled Talisa up short. "Are you serious? We all heard you at Court. Insisting that you and the Keepers at the Knoll would be first to hunt down any who opposed their majesties."

I goggled that anyone could have misinterpreted my words. "Any who threatened the lives of the solitary, my people!"

"Your people?" Talisa spit at me, and flecks of her saliva spattered on my cheeks and eyelids as I flinched. "We are not your people, you self-righteous fuath! You lied to us. You pretended to be one of us, a victim of the Courts. You sheltered with us, sought our pity. We should have known better. No one gives up as much power as you had. You've been loyal to your mother all this time. Probably lived down among the people to hunt out those who opposed you so you could root us out when you took the throne." She laughed bitterly. "I almost respect the ruthlessness. But why hide your powers?"

Though none of her accusations were accurate, I felt small. How many of the solitary who came to the Knoll, those I had hoped to befriend, to help, saw me in the same way? A privileged royal slumming it with the disenfranchised. "I didn't hide anything," I said, my voice small and not even convincing myself. "I could never do before what I did yesterday."

From her back waistband, she pulled a gleaming dagger and held it between my lips, forcing me to open my mouth or risk getting cut. "By Nour's forked tongue, if you lie to me again, I will cut yours out." She put pressure, and the blade bit at the corners of my mouth, causing twin trickles of blood to fall down to my chin.

The Gate responded instantly, shimmering and coming to life. The tiny offerings of my blood weren't enough to open the Gate, but I could feel the power of Fairy reaching out to find me and my unwilling sacrifice.

"Heal that," Talisa ground out as she pulled the dagger away. "Or would you like to deny again that you have the power?"

I glared at her but did as she asked. I licked my tongue along the corners of my mouth, tasting the raw copper of it before I asked the delicate skin of my lips to repair. A slight tingle and it was as if nothing had happened. I also used the opportunity to finally ease the headache that was still lingering, but I couldn't wipe it away as cleanly. The combination of herbs Talisa had used to poison me was still having its effect.

"Why hide that?" Hannah asked from behind me. "Why hide what you can do?"

Turning my head, I marveled that I had forgotten she was there. This poor human. I'd tried to help her once before. I'd thought of her as vulnerable among the fae, as powerless. When she was the one hunting us.

I laughed, a pained gasp of irony. This poor broken girl.

"I didn't hide anything," I said honestly. "I didn't know I could do what I did until I did it. Until it was stolen from me, and then forced from me. I can heal myself, but I'd never affected anyone else before. It wasn't an active power."

"As someone who couldn't even cast a glamour until Tally gave me the means to do it," Hannah said, "I wouldn't dismiss anything you can do as unimportant." Her eyes darted between us. "Michael Phelps turned his exceptional oxygen capacity into the most gold medals of anyone before. Your useless power? Still makes you a superhero in most of this world."

All was quiet for a moment as we considered what Hannah said. The implications of it.

Before it could sink in, though, Gair coughed, a wet sound that ended in a groan.

I started to move toward him, but Talisa caught my arm and whirled me around. The look on her face stopped me colder than Lada's frost. She looked at Gair's blood, his obvious suffering, and smiled. Then she looked at me, her eyes narrowed. "Oh, of course. Hannah. You may be short-lived and as disposable as a tissue, but you have your moments."

Hannah looked terrified, but she stammered out a questioned "Thanks?" anyway.

Ignoring her human friend, Talisa steered me over to Gair and with a strong grip on my shoulder, she shoved me down to my knees. "Heal him."

The wound in Gair's midsection was dark and wet, still actively bleeding. He needed help, but I didn't know how to do it. I didn't even understand what I'd done to Mikka, how I'd saved her. Whether it was Lada's power that made it possible, or if I could do it without her.

Still, I owed it to Gair to try.

I reached out to something, some power that might allow me to touch him. To heal myself, I had only to think of the hurt, to touch that part of myself with my mind, like stretching a muscle. I would flex it or relax it, and it would respond with fitting itself back together, healing.

Thinking of Gair, of the way he felt, the way even his magic tasted, I reached out for him. I thought of his unassuming but confident spirit, his subtle humor, his love of his community. I tried to center on the feeling he evoked in me, of a sweet but subtle ache, like he was too good for me, the feeling of this stoic, brilliant, distant being, who saw good in others, and was patient enough to let them show it. I tried to touch his overflowing concern for others. I pulled hardest at the taste of pine and wine, trying to pull the essence of his magic onto my tongue. I reached for his blood, concentrated on the feel of my own midsection and tried to extend it to the lanky, beautiful, caring man before me.

Nothing.

I couldn't feel him. I couldn't extend my power beyond myself.

My magic was as it had always been: impotent, fruitless, and confined to my useless body.

I tried to feel angry, to call on the power of rage to touch him the way I had with Mikka. I tensed every muscle in my body and focused on the betrayal of someone I had invited into my bar, into my home, into my Mab-cursed bed drugging me and attacking innocent people. And I still couldn't find the power I needed.

Nothing. I couldn't find the magic to heal him.

"I don't know how," I whispered, apologizing more to Gair than to Talisa. He was pale, and a fine sheen of sweat had begun to bead across his forehead. If the cut had been shallow, he might have survived. If it had avoided major organs or arteries, he might have already begun to heal himself. As a creature of fae, he might not even have required surgery or healing magic if the stab wound in his gut had simply severed flesh and muscle.

But from his deteriorating condition, the gray color that was seeping into his complexion, and the deep black of the blood that leaked from him, without a miracle, there was nothing I could do. He was going to die. Slowly.

"Gair, I'm so sorry," I said to him, my throat thick with emotion.

Gair grimaced, but he nodded weakly, as if to say it wasn't my fault. It wasn't my fault I couldn't access my feckless powers to save him. That he was going to bleed out because a greedy maenad and human thought they could steal the powers of the fae and the hurt wouldn't matter.

"Such a shame," Talisa said, as she wrenched me back to my feet with a tug so violent, I thought she might want to pop my shoulders out of socket.

The movement was so sudden, the satin material that bound my wrists stretched and cut into my hands, but as Talisa got me to my feet, I felt the knot give a little. I hid my surprise by looking down at the ground, and then at Gair.

He'd lost focus. He was staring straight ahead, leaning over his knees, and as he swayed, I knew he was about to topple over to his side.

"Catch him," I said, suddenly, and to my surprise, Hannah moved to cradle Gair as he slumped over.

Talisa scoffed. "Let him be. We can use his blood to hold open the Gate a bit longer. What's left of it anyway."

Hannah looked at her in horror, but she didn't say anything in protest.

Talisa seemed to take nothing of this in as she dragged me forward to the Gate. I was reminded exactly how strong maenads could be as she maneuvered me as easily as if I were a child. She wrenched my bruised arm, and my entire body followed. Then she turned me and held me in place, just a grip on my bicep. If she had wanted to, she probably could have ripped my arm from my body with barely a thought.

We stood facing each other, eye to eye. I searched her, looking for any sign that she might hesitate, that she might feel some regret for what she was doing. That there might be something real between us that would change her mind.

She merely stood there, her expression empty.

"Well," she said. "Let's get this over with, shall we?"

She took a deep breath as she stood before me and brought the dagger to my neck.

I whimpered. So many of the other victims had been sacrificed with cut wrists. I had harbored hope I might be granted the same.

But no. She was looking into my eyes, holding the dagger.

At least her attention wasn't on my hands. I gave them a twist that pinched so hard I nearly yelped.

Talisa gave no indication she noticed my movement. She pressed the blade to my neck and gave the slightest amount of pressure. I struggled to free myself, tugging at my wrists.

Then, a scream came from off near the woods.

Talisa looked, but with a blade to my throat, I didn't dare move.

The voice I heard froze me in my tracks.

It was Mellie, the pregnant Maenad. "Talisa. What are you doing?!"

CHAPTER THIRTY-TWO

Mellie stood there in a long white bohemian dress covered in ruffles, a rolled-up blanket under one arm, a small basket held in her opposite hand. Her expression was one of horror and disgust.

"Talisa, what is happening? What are you doing?"

Talisa stood frozen, her back to Mellie, almost as though one of her girls hadn't caught her in the act of murder. "Mellie, go back to the Knoll." She spoke without dropping the dagger and without turning her head. "We can discuss this later."

"Are you—" She stopped and took in the rest of the scene: me, terrified with a blade to my throat, Hannah holding an unconscious and bleeding Gair, and her mentor and friend refusing to turn around. "Siobhan, are you okay?"

I opened my mouth, but Talisa pressed with the knife, cutting me. The feel of my skin splitting was familiar enough that I stopped and shut my mouth. I had to stop myself from healing the shallow cut, though I desperately wanted to keep my blood inside my body at the moment.

I could feel the Gate waking farther behind me. After so many years, it knew me, knew my blood, and I could feel it reaching for me.

"Go back, Mellie," Talisa said again. "I will take care of this and join you in a half hour."

"What is this? What are you taking care of?" Mellie took a step forward but stopped as Talisa turned her head while keeping a firm grip on my arm and the dagger against my neck.

"Mellie, I need you to trust me. I have only ever kept you safe. That was my vow to you when you first left the Summer Court and joined my troupe. It is my vow to you now. I will do what is necessary to keep you and your child safe. Now I need you to go back to the Knoll and forget you saw anything here."

Mellie's eyes widened, and she looked like she was about to do exactly as asked. But then her eyes lighted on Gair again, where Hannah was laying him down gently. Hannah stood slowly and began to approach Mellie, though Talisa didn't seem to notice her movement.

Turning back to Talisa and me, Mellie seemed to put things together. "Is this about the deaths? The missing fae?"

I opened my eyes wider, trying to tell her as much as I could, but terrified of moving and pushing Talisa to do what she was set on doing.

Mellie gasped and looked harder at me. "Siobhan?" She shook her head. "No, Talisa, there's no way. Siobhan couldn't have done that." Damn, apparently she'd come to the wrong conclusion.

Talisa turned back to me, a smile on her face. She raised an eyebrow to me. "Semele," she again spoke over her shoulder, keeping her attention on me. "I can't let her go. Not after what she's done. But I promise, I won't let her hurt anyone else." She puckered her lips and gave me a mock kiss.

I could do nothing but glare. I felt like a fool. How could I have fallen for her act? The honeyed words and strawberry kisses. I would die because I couldn't see that underneath all her charm and seduction, she was as ruthless as any Court royal.

"Okay," Mellie said, her voice uncertain. She knew something wasn't right, and I begged her to trust that instinct.

In the end, though, her trust of Talisa, of her leader, won out. They were sisters, and no connection I could have made with her would have beaten that. I was as good as a stranger, just another solitary half fae. We weren't family. We were barely members of a community. Just a random collection of people who just happened to disagree with the same system of royal governance.

It obviously wasn't enough to forge a life-saving connection.

Tears pricked at my eyes, and I blinked rapidly.

It was fine. I couldn't rely on someone else. I'd have to save myself.

I began once again to twist my wrists, tugging harder at the ties, until one hand finally popped free.

Schooling my face to impassivity, I kept attention on Talisa and Mellie. If I could get a hold of the dagger, I could turn this thing around.

"If you're sure?" Mellie said. She took an uncertain step backward. Her head was tilted with concern as she waited for Talisa to look at her. "Do you want me to call for someone?"

Talisa's smile faltered, but she turned her head once again, not enough to actually look at her girl, or to take her attention off of me, but enough to call over her shoulder. "I've got it under control, Mels. Can you order me a double Manhattan? I regret that I'm the one who's going to have to tell Argus what happened."

Mellie nodded, but still looked incredibly uncertain. She took a step backward and stumbled back into Hannah, who was waiting.

"Oh," Mellie said, her voice a low exhalation of pain and surprise. Talisa whirled, forgetting me for a moment. I could do nothing but stare at what was in front of us.

A sudden red spot appeared on the side of Mellie's midsection, staining the innocent white of her ruffled dress.

Mellie staggered a step forward, and immediately fell to her knees, revealing a solemn Hannah wielding a knife of her own. The long steel dripped with blood.

"I'm sorry," Hannah said, as she took a step back. She didn't look sorry, though. She stared directly at Talisa, as Mellie fell forward on her hands. Mellie's back was bloody, the wound spreading rapidly across her white dress, bleeding enthusiastically as it seeped from her body.

Talisa dashed forward, leaving me reeling before the Gate that sprang to life, fully open now and bleeding power and magic into this world. It was if it had been waiting for a big enough sacrifice, as if it had waited to taste the life draining out of Mellie.

"What have you done?" Talisa screamed at Hannah, as she rushed to hold Mellie. "Hey, it's okay. Hey, Mels, Mellie, you're okay. Hannah! Do something."

"I did," she sneered downward. "Removed a witness, made a sacrifice, and provided a strong source of blood all at once. Just as I was taught." She held a bowl forward. "Don't let it go to waste."

Talisa struck the bowl away. "She is pregnant. A baby! For the solitary fae. Do you even know what that means to us?"

Hannah curled her lip at Mellie who was already swooning from blood loss. "Two for the price of one?" She shrugged her shoulders and laughed. "Maybe the magic in her blood will be more potent. Worth finding out, isn't it?"

With a scream of mindless rage, Talisa dropped Mellie and lunged forward, her dagger ready to attack Hannah. But Hannah had learned her lesson. She had her stolen magic ready to defend herself. A wall of wind buffeted Talisa backward.

She stumbled, but an enraged maenad is an unstoppable force. She immediately charged again.

I didn't wait to see how a fight between the two progressed. I ran to Mellie and pulled her away before the over-powered fighters trampled her and made matters worse.

I laid the pregnant maenad on her back, hooked my arms under hers, and heaved. A trail of blood showed our path, and already a pool gathered beneath her body. Hannah must have punctured something vital: a kidney or liver or something worse. I kept pulling. Toward the Gate.

The Gate responded. Somehow, I could feel the magic more intensely, as her sacrificial blood approached. The taste of green overwhelmed me. It was as if the rich, verdant air of Fairy was reaching out through the Gate, hungry to reclaim the life that was ebbing away before it.

"Mellie," I said. "Hey, I'm here. I've got you. Don't give up yet." I reached out for her, trying to feel her power. Even the apple and honey taste of her magic was faint. I tried to pull the taste onto my tongue, to forge a connection with her. But as with Gair, I could find nothing to hold on to.

"Siobhan?" She looked up at me, her eyes already distant. "I don't…" She paused to wet her lips. "It hurts." She closed her eyes.

"No, no, Mellie stay with me."

Darting a glance up, I knew I would find no help from Talisa. She tried to lunge at Hannah through a wall of fire as vines ripped at her. I spared a thought to wonder how many fae had died so those two could have those abilities, while another part of me wondered how long that stolen magic could last. Even with the Gate open.

I didn't have time to find out.

"Mellie, hey. I've got you. We can fix this." I didn't know how, but I wasn't willing to give up on her. If I hadn't been able to help Gair, how would I save her?

"Stay with us, Semele." The voice that came over my shoulder was low and in its own pain.

It was if I had summoned him. Gair had somehow crawled over to us, his stomach wound still tacky and wet.

He put a hand on my forearm as I pressed it over Mellie's exit wound in her stomach. "You can do this," he said. "I saw Baerd after you'd healed him. You can do this."

"No," I said. Tears of frustration forced from my eyes as I blinked rapidly. "That was with Lada's help. I tried. I tried with you. I can't do it. Alone, I can't heal anyone but myself." I would have given anything if I could heal Mellie, or Gair or anyone. But when I reached for the power, when I tried to reach outside of myself, I hit a wall. They would both die, because I wasn't fae enough. I was only half of what they needed me to be.

"You can, Siobhan." Gair leaned against me, his chest along my back, as his hand on my arm strengthened. His other arm came around my side and helped guide my other hand over the first, both palms downward over Mellie's injury. I could taste the distinct flavor of his red wine and pine-flavored magic as he helped me, pouring luck and drunk confidence into me. "You can do this. You can do anything. You just have to believe in yourself. The Gate is open. Draw on its power, the way you did through the Winter Queen."

"I don't know how," I said. But that wasn't true. Maybe it was the effect of his heady magic or maybe it was the familiar taste of red wine, good for celebrations, for courage, but my apprehension and fear slipped away. I knew exactly how to do this.

I closed my eyes and let the verdant magic of Fairy fill me. I breathed it in and felt my cells rejuvenate, replenish, stretch, and grow. Then I breathed out.

And instead of releasing it into the world around me, as I always did, I directed it into my power. I breathed the eternal, life-giving magic into my will, and I pressed it outward, down, into my hands that touched Mellie. I breathed out every bit of light and life in my body and pushed as hard as I could, willing it into Mellie's slowing body.

As I got ready to take another deep breath in, to take in more magic through the Gate, I could feel something foreign. There was another breath, another heartbeat. No, another two heartbeats. They were slow, and one was small and new, but they were there and tasted of apple and honey.

I flooded my lungs with another breath and pulled with every ounce of my control on the green magic of Fairy. I could feel its smooth, almost slippery texture as the green parsley taste of it overwhelmed my senses. Then as I exhaled, I pressed outward as hard as I could, pushing the magic, the green life energy through my hands and into the woman who lay before me.

Twice more I repeated the process, flooding Mellie with the power I could taste but not harness. Her breath was slowing as the life ebbed out of her, and I couldn't believe that I was going to lose her.

As her breath slowed and mine deepened, we met. We inhaled as one, the maenad and me. And my magic caught her.

In an instant, I could feel all of her injury, the ripped flesh, the punctured liver leaking dark bile and rich blood into her body and the ground, the heart that skittered as it lost blood and oxygen.

I could fix this.

On my next inhale, I pulled at the edges of her wounds, wrapping them up and pulling them together, skin seeking skin, muscle fibers into muscle, blood vessels sealing their ragged edges as they closed and repaired. On exhale, I flooded her body with oxygen-rich blood and magic, restoring what she had lost and granting her more power than she had known.

The next inhale restored vitality to every part that had given up function to help her: brain, heart, lungs, and womb all flushed with restored and renewed life. My exhale gave her the renewed energy to come back to us, restored and whole.

Semele Tyne gasped before the Greenwood Gate, whole and refreshed.

As she sat up, Gair sagged. His hands on my arms slipped down, and he fell onto my back, his head heavy and lolling to the side.

"Help me with him," I begged Mellie as I struggled to ease him onto the ground.

Mellie didn't hesitate, pulling herself to her knees and taking some of his weight as we rolled him over. I pulled open his shirt as Mellie eased his head down. He was completely unconscious, and his breathing was growing labored as the effects of his magic faded. I might be too late.

Refusing to give up, I took a deep breath and felt for the magic from the Gate. The green energy of Fairy was beginning to shimmer with an obscene purple glow. Mellie looked up and gasped, recognizing the sky of Fairy seeping through the Gate, drawn by the promise of death.

Except no one was going to die here.

Heedless of the consequences, I reached for that purple glow and tasted it, drank it in, gulped at it with my full consciousness. It had the bite of anise with just a touch of sweet, herbal complexity. I got up on my knees, reaching physically with my hands and with that part of me that touched magic. I needed as much of that raw power as I could get.

Breathing deep, I gulped it down, pulling it into my cells and letting it power me. It flowed through my blood, in and around my spirit until I felt like I was buzzing, glowing with the pure life of it. I breathed in until I could take no more, and then I directed my attention to Gair.

A loud pop sounded, and my breath left me with a whoosh, not directed but explosively coughed out as my left shoulder caught fire.

Mellie screamed and dove backward as I fell forward. I tried to catch myself, but my left arm was useless, and I nearly tumbled on top of Gair. It took me several seconds to realize I'd been shot, the bullet passing cleaning through just beneath my shoulder blade and out the front, leaving my upper arm a bloodied mess. I pulled myself up, my left arm dangling uselessly as I turned to face the threat.

Hannah was walking toward us, a gun raised and pointed directly at me. Talisa was nowhere to be seen, but if Hannah was the one menacing us, I could assume Talisa had lost the fight. Hannah, though, was limping and seemed to be much worse for the disagreement. The side of her face was red and chapped with burns, and her right arm was one big bruise, already purple and swollen.

It didn't keep her from holding her weapon steady and trained on me. "Siobhan, I'm going to say this once. If you don't listen, I will shoot the maenad and the clurichaun both. My father was a Marine and taught me to shoot at an early age. I do not miss. Do you think you can heal head shots?" She looked genuinely curious about the answer.

I swallowed hard but began healing the wound she'd given me anyway. With as much magic as I'd taken in, it should take me only a few seconds. If I could buy that time and get to Hannah before she hurt anyone else, I had to do it. "I'm listening."

She gestured with her chin toward the archway. "There are bowls at the edge of the Gate. I want you to collect the blood that is flowing from your wound."

"I will give you as much of my blood as you want," I said, already stepping over Gair to get the bowls. "But can I heal you first?"

That surprised her, and she actually lowered the gun for a second. "Can you what?"

I brought the bowl to my shoulder and collected the already slowing blood. She would be disappointed in the amount I collected, and I had to distract her. "You want my blood to heal yourself, right?"

She nodded, a skeptical frown on her face.

"Smart. It will take you a while to figure this power out. It's taken me most of my life to figure out what I can do. If you're in as much pain as I think you are, then it might be better for me to heal you myself."

She brought the gun up quickly. "You're trying to trick me." As she looked at my shoulder, it became clear that the gunshot wound had already stopped bleeding.

"Smart girl," I said as I hurled the bowl of my blood at the armed human. I closed my eyes to pull in as much power as I could with a gasp and pushed it fully into Gair at my feet.

Three sudden pops, and I looked in horror to see how badly Mellie and Gair were hurt.

Mellie was cowering face down on the ground farther away, while Gair was unchanged.

But the purple of the Gate flared brighter than ever, as my hands came to the center of my pain, the ragged meat of my stomach where I'd been shot.

I stumbled, reeling and dizzy, and unable to keep my feet.

I only had enough time to think "No" before I took a breath in, pulling on my magic and tumbling backward.

For better or worse, the purple glow of Fairy reached out and pulled me in.

CHAPTER THIRTY-THREE

As I passed the threshold of the Gate, the magic I had worked so hard to pull in came flooding into me. I was more alive, more real than I had ever been as the raw power of the Gate consumed me entirely.

I expected to pass through the Gate into Fairy, to emerge on the other side to see the purple sky and verdant fields of my ancestral home. The purple glow remained as I hung suspended between the worlds. Trapped inside the Gate.

My body burned with the power around me. That impossible shimmering purple color was everything. It wasn't something I could even claim to see. It simply was.

I didn't even think as I used the full strength of the magic that was in me and threw my power out, trying to reach Gair somewhere on the other side of the Gate. I could still heal him.

My magic found him, anchored me to him and the Iron Realm. Time stood still as my every atom thrilled and quivered with the power of unleashed magic.

I tried to pull on my connection to Gair to pull me back to Earth, to drag myself back to my world. Then I attempted to let it go, to release my magic into Gair so I could pass through to Fairy.

I could do neither.

I was suspended, trapped between the Iron Realm and the Eternal Realm as my body burned, and the wound at the center of me seemed to open and fold me up inside of it. My blood flowed, and I could not even sense my body enough to stitch it back together. I was nothing. I was everything. I was burning up.

It was unlike anything I'd ever felt. Not quite power, for power was strength according to rules. Not just energy, though it pulsed through me filling me with more energy than I'd ever known. No, it was *magic*: pure, unadulterated chaos, flowing around and through me as I screamed and burned.

I tried to push it outward, to direct it away, but it flowed ever inward, like an unending wave, a tsunami of chaos and impossibility, of everything and nothing, tumbling me in and over myself, until I thought I would go mad.

I must pass through. No one is meant to stay inside the Gate. It is not a place. It is a passage, but it is not itself a place. If I stayed another moment in this liminal space, this in-between threshold that was neither Fairy nor Human, Eternal nor Iron, I would break. I would shatter and keep shattering, infinitely breaking and being remade.

Torn apart, shredded, reborn, firing, fired, on fire. I was everything and nothing, a thousand voices and personalities and no one at once.

Desperate and losing what remained of me, I threw every ounce of myself in every direction. Grasping with the tattered remnants of my mind, I reached for Mikka, Argus, Mother and Bryony, Gair, Mellie and her baby. I reached for my father, secreted away in Fairy, never aging, never dying as humans are meant to do. I reached for any anchor, anything I could tether myself to and pull myself ashore.

And I found something. It wasn't out there in one of the realms. It wasn't some connection, some person out there waiting for me to come home. It was all of them and none of them. It was everything they meant to me and what I meant to them.

It was me. Half fae, half human. It was me. I belonged to both realms.

Though I'd lived most of my life in the Iron Realm, I was still fae, a creature of the Eternal. I could reach through the Gate and touch that Realm any time I wanted. I could pass through, because it knew my blood and welcomed me as one of its own. And the Iron Realm knew me, too. Atlanta was my home and my queendom.

More than that, I was a Keeper. The Gate was my responsibility and my privilege. I had given more of my blood to this Gate than any being, living or dead. This was *my* Gate. And it would not hold me captive.

I stopped fighting its embrace and opened myself to it as it was trying to open itself to me.

At once the burning stopped. My wound stopped trying to consume me, too, turn me inside out. It stitched together at once. I felt charged, changed, accepted, whole. I shivered with climax as the chaos found a home inside of me. I didn't control it, but neither did it control me. It flowed freely, exploring and caressing in and through, around, and past me.

Accepted and claimed, it released its grip but never released me. I would carry it with me.

A door opened, and it throbbed with a slow but steady assurance. I had a lifeline, and I just had to follow it home.

I stepped through.

Hannah stood with the gun just barely lowered, still smoking from the three bullets she'd put in me.

No time had passed between me falling through the portal and the eternity I'd spent there. The Gate still glowed purple and throbbed with the slow beating of Gair's dying heart. My anchor had kept me from drifting away.

Hannah's mouth fell open as I emerged, my t-shirt torn to shreds and covered in blood, but with smooth unblemished skin beneath. As I advanced on her, she quickly raised the gun again, but I reached out a hand and closed my fist over it, crumpling the hot metal like it was made of paper.

I tossed the weapon aside and considered Hannah. "What do I do with you?" I asked genuinely. I couldn't let her go, after all she'd done, but I couldn't hand her over to the Summer and Winter Queens either. She was human and would suffer the brunt of their rage. They would take out the cost of the lives lost in her blood. But they would keep her alive until they knew all who had conspired with her.

She might deserve to be punished, but she didn't deserve all that Lada would do to her. She didn't even deserve what Bryony would do.

Hannah looked like she was going to plead for her life, but without a word, she turned and fled for the path. I couldn't let her go, so without quite knowing how I did it, I reached out for her mind and whispered that she should sleep. Hannah collapsed at the edge of the tree line. Her head hit the ground with more force than I had intended, but another thought, and I found the small bruise at her temple. Soothing it away, I knew she'd be fine.

I could deal with her in my own time.

"Siobhan!" Mellie's voice turned me back.

Gair.

The Gate no longer throbbed, and the light inside it was fading, closing as his life swept away.

I dashed and knelt, ready to heal my friend, my anchor. I seized his hand and placed another on his chest. I was ready to make use of this new power now that I knew I had it. I could heal him.

Gair's eyes were closed, and his mottled skin had grown pale, but with whatever was inside of me, I reached for him, sought to connect with the sure heartbeat that had guided me home. I would pour it all in. Now that I knew I could do it, I was ready. But as I took a breath in, he let his out.

One moment. One moment of time, and we were out of sync.

With everything I had, I threw my thoughts to his, feeling for connection with him, with his spirit, his magic, anything I could find. But there was nothing.

Behind me, the Gate sealed.

I took another breath. Gair did not.

Feeling frantically with my power, I could not find enough blood left to stitch him back together, to convince his heart to beat, to power his lungs for just one more breath. He'd given it all to the Gate, to me. There wasn't enough for him.

"Can you—" Mellie's words died when she saw the stricken look on my face as the magic of the Gate faded.

Gair was gone. The taste of red wine and pine, of currants and plums, of faint tobacco and earth was nowhere to be found.

He had still been here. When I'd come through. He'd been the anchor that guided me back, helped me find myself and this world. If I had gone to him immediately. If I had ignored Hannah and the idea of punishing her. If I had healed him first.

"I could have saved him," I said softly, though I wasn't entirely sure that was true. He'd used the last of his strength and magic to help me save Mellie. Then he'd faded quietly away as I'd struggled with Hannah.

I fell back on my heels and began to weep as Mellie crawled to me. She held me as I sobbed, and the subtle but unmistakable sweet rot taste of death began to fill the air. But the flavors of balsamic and strawberries overshadowed the red wine taste I searched for.

CHAPTER THIRTY-FOUR

Wednesday, we closed the bar to the public and held a wake for Gair. Though Argus offered to help cover the bar so I could grieve with the rest, I'd known he wouldn't last the night without lighting the new waitress on fire.

"Joshilyn," I yelled, early in the evening.

"It's Jocelyn," she corrected me for the sixth time.

I ignored her again and handed her a tray of glasses and a fresh bottle of Macallan for the Clurichaun clan at the center of the room. "Drop this with the clurichaun, give the bottle to Leland. Then come straight back and get the champagne for the maenads at table three. I'll pop the cork this time." When I'd let her open the bottle at the table as was proper, she'd managed to shoot the Mab-cursed thing at Gary the nine-foot-tall barguist with the sharp teeth. Argus had had to give him a raw steak on the house to keep him from eating her.

"Right," the spacey maenad said as she bobbled the tray and nearly dropped the expensive bottle of whiskey. "Which one is Leland again?"

I sighed. We had just opened the doors and only had about twenty people in the building. If she was struggling this much already, we were in for a long night.

"The one in blue and green," I said. The clurichaun were all wearing their traditional family tartans and had been taking turns raising toasts to their fallen friend. The group seemed small without Gair, and without Baerd.

According to Argus, after Baerd had woken up, he'd refused to talk. He had said nothing about the Fair Folk, about Hannah or even Kari. By morning, Gair had come to collect him and they'd departed together. It was the last time anyone had seen either one of them. Gair had died because I failed him, and Baerd had disappeared. His cluri brothers were devastated by the double loss. Free whiskey was the least we could do for them today.

"Got it." Jocelyn went over and began distributing fresh glasses to the gathered mourners. She only dropped one glass, and the large ball of ice rolled across the floor to the front door.

Varon scooped it up and came to drop it in the dish tub behind me. "Maybe we were better off with her flaking off to Panama City."

I hated to agree with him. It turned out that Jocelyn's disappearance had nothing to do with Talisa and Hannah's fae sacrifices. She'd just gotten it into her head one sunny day that she'd like to spend the weekend at the beach. A weekend had turned into a week when she met a cute guy, but when he'd revealed he was married, she'd flown into a rage and forced him to drive home to beg his wife to take him back with jewelry, flowers, and a puppy that Jocelyn had picked out herself. The maenad had then gotten the wife's number and promised to check in monthly. If the guy messed up again, Jocelyn had the wife's word that they would devise a suitable punishment together.

With that good a story, it had been hard to deny Jocelyn a second chance. "She's doing better," I defended. "At least she hasn't spilled the drinks on anybody yet."

Varon rolled his eyes. "You just guaranteed she will. I'll go get the towels."

Mikka clapped her brother on the shoulder as he brushed past her to the back, and I thought she might come over to talk. She just nodded to me and turned her attention back to staring off into space.

What happened at Court had affected her more than she seemed willing to admit. The past few days, she'd been quiet and withdrawn.

I knew I had to give her time to process, but I hoped she'd come to me when she was ready to talk about what she had seen in the dueling circle. Whatever Lada had shown her had shaken her hard. It might take some time for her to get back to flirting and fighting.

Argus came over from the subdued group of maenads in the corner. "Can we get a cheese plate to the meanads? And your girl requested extra olives stuffed with bleu cheese." He gestured to Mellie, who was centered and trying to engage the group in conversation.

They were here to mourn Gair, but I knew many were shedding tears for Talisa as well. We'd found her body at the riverbank, where Hannah's stolen magic had blown her. Her gorgeous auburn hair was singed and burned away, and her moss green eyes were brackish and grayed. I'd wept until Varon had to carry me away.

I couldn't explain how I could still grieve so intensely over one who'd betrayed me, who'd tried to kill me. She'd caused so much pain, hurt so many. And yet, she was so full of life, conviction. She'd seen beauty in me and in others, and she'd fought for her people. Our city was dimmer without her light.

And with her dead and Baerd gone, Hannah was the only certain source of information about the Fair Folk and what they might still have planned for our city. I had no illusions that the group was finished just because of what happened to Talisa and Hannah. I only hoped they would lay low long enough for Hannah to start naming names. From what Gair had said, there were maenads and clurichaun and others in the group. Which meant that it was likely some of the Fair Folk were in my bar right now, waiting for drinks and food.

"One cheese plate with extra stinky olives, coming up," I said. I rang it up in the system for Meara and rolled my shoulders back. My fingers had begun to tingle, and I needed to stretch my legs. "Hey, boss?"

Argus looked up from the round of lagers he was preparing.

"Can I take a break to go back to the Gate? My session earlier was rushed because of the wake, and I kind of just—"

"Want to get away from the sob fest for a minute?" He looked around. The early stages of wakes were always so subdued and mournful. As people began to trickle in and drink more, the mood would change. Brothers would exchange stories, friends would share memories, and everyone would celebrate the lost life, instead of standing around moping. As it was now, I was going to fall apart if I had to stand around watching people cry for the man I failed to save. The man who died helping me find my power.

"Yes, please," I said, feeling my eyes prickle.

Argus grunted and jerked his head toward the door. "Scram. Get yourself together. Take as long as you need."

I was nearly to the door when a tremendous hand came down on my shoulder and spun me around. Argus enfolded me in his arms and pulled me close. He laid his chin down on the top of my head and sighed.

"You're not alone in this, *louloudi mou*. You know that? Your family here will protect you no matter what."

I looked over his tree-trunk arms and saw Mikka, staring off into the distance, her eyes haunted and bruised.

"I know," I said.

But at what cost?

Outside, the early evening was cool and quiet, full of the hums of frogs and cicadas. The sun had sunk below the horizon, but it wasn't full dark yet. The sky glowed with a hazy yellow, and the fireflies lit up the trees with luminous mating signals. Traveling the path felt like walking among the stars as they sang to me in chirps and trills.

I closed my eyes and continued along the path, feeling the Gate waking up. A floral juniper and citrus taste bubbled up in my senses, like a French 75, celebrating my return. Why the Gate tasted like my own magic, and why I recognized it as my own I could not yet explain.

Why it opened to me without sacrifice, without blood, and without draining my magic, I could.

"Hello," I whispered as the Gate opened its arms to me. It was like coming home. She was happy to see me tonight and a little disappointed it had taken me so long between visits. "I'm sorry," I said. "But I'm here now."

The Gate responded with a pleasing purple glow that washed over me and released into the city. The magic was stronger now, spreading farther and faster, even without my bloodletting. I needed to hold it open shorter times, and just as much magic passed through, spreading over the city. I wondered if the solitary fae had noticed, and whether they wondered at the change.

I knew Mother would have noticed by now. I had not spoken to her since the duel, had not been able to ask her if she had visited me in the audience hall anteroom, or if she had even been aware of the duel. Was she aware at all of what was happening in her city? Was she in her own head enough to even understand it?

Bryony certainly wasn't responding to my requests for an audience with her or Mother.

Her knights had come to claim Talisa's body, but no one would believe that Talisa had been acting alone. Investigations were being planned to root out the Fair Folk in the solitary community, and they would likely start at the Knoll.

At least for the moment, though, I was cleared of suspicion. Mellie had testified to my attempts to save her and Gair and defeat our assailants. Even Lada had hesitated to question the pregnant fae, and the Court had accepted that the human accomplice was at large.

In truth, Hannah was currently the unwilling roommate of Mikka and Varon. The drake twins had a spacious five-bedroom house in Marietta, with a mother-in-law suite that was perfect for holding dangerous fugitives.

Argus had demanded blood oaths from the siblings that they would not kill her before he called in the Grey Meranti to put up wards specific to the human, confining her to their basement rooms. She'd been unhappy about the arrangement; Mikka said she'd taken a butcher's knife to the couch the first day and left cotton and foam stuffing all over the place. Argus agreed to pay the cost of any replacements when she finally got over the destructive phase of her confinement, and the twins were mollified for the time being.

We hoped Hannah would eventually talk to us, give us information about who she had been working with in the Fair Folk, who was calling the shots, and what they might have planned. I had little hope that they were the only dangerous members of their group, and I worried that there was more grief waiting before we got the answers we were looking for.

My questions could wait, though.

I sat down on the cooling grass in front of the Gate, the dappled purple light dancing over me like moonlight refracting off the gurgling river beside us. It set my body tingling, like the very space between my cells was excited at what was about to happen.

I don't know if I imagined it, but it felt like the Gate was excited, too.

"All right," I said softly. "Let's see what we can do."

I reached out with my consciousness, feeling first the trees at the edge of the clearing and the river, then up to the Greenwood Knoll. I could count the people inside. I could taste the mix of their magic.

I could feel how to use their magic. In my hand, I called up a small flame and watched it dance for a moment before snuffing it out.

"Farther." My mind reached out, beyond the Knoll, out past the dryads at the edges of the property, past the mansions of Riverside, out into the city. Sidhe, nixies, lilin, shadow spirits and sylphs, I could feel them, I could taste them all.

There was the palace. I could feel my mother, hazy but there. The overwhelming vanilla of my sister.

Beyond, there was someone who tasted of watermelon and salt. I breathed in and released a small cloud of rain a few feet ahead of me. There, a hint of coconut and lime. A bird of paradise flower blossomed to my left. Coffee and cream, and my skin shivered with the touch of a lover kissing up my inner thighs.

So long as the Gate was open, if her magic could touch them, I could as well. I could find them, savor their magic, sample everyone like they were ingredients of a tasting flight.

It was utterly intoxicating.

I couldn't wait to see what chaotic cocktail I could shake up.

End of Book One

FAE GLOSSARY

Ala or hala (pl - ale or hali) – winter fae. Powers include weather manipulation, possession, and psychic manipulation. Known to drive mortals to madness. Hostile to men and dragons.

Alven (pl – alvens) – water fae. Prefers lakes, ponds, and rivers to salt water. Powers include shape-shifting and water manipulation.

Banshee or Bean Sidhe (pl – banshees) – non-elemental fae, related to Bean Nighe and Bean Tighe. Evoke strong emotions when they sing or cry. Powers include prophecy and emotional manipulation through vocal control, psychic consumption.

Barguist or barghest (pl – barguists) – non-elemental fae, shapeshifter. A strong natural creature with massive claws, teeth, and horns. Powers include invisibility, shapeshifting (into the form of a large dog or human).

Basilisk (pl – basilisks) – water and serpent fae. Powers include great strength, speed and agility, poison, and ability to petrify with a look.

Bean Nighe and Bean Tighe (pl – bean nighe and bean tighe) – As bean sidhe age and their vocal control wanes their powers of emotional diminish, but their powers of prophecy grow. As they age into later stages of their lives, they tend to retreat into their homes where they are less likely to encounter unpleasant views of the future, though this is not a rule.

Boggart (pl – boggarts) – non-elemental fae, shapeshifter. Very territorial fae. Powers include invisibility, luck and fortune manipulation, psychic influence, and short bouts of physical strength.

Brownie (pl – brownies) – non-elemental fae. Small physical stature. Very territorial fae, they often commit to homes, where they can live for generations of other inhabitants. Powers include invisibility, telekinesis, and luck manipulation.

Clurichaun (pl – clurichaun) – non-elemental fae, cousins of leprechaun. Powers include manipulation of luck, emotions, and psychic stability. Have an affinity for alcohol and can inflict experiences of drunkenness, including the depression and mania that can come with it.

Daione Sidhe (pl - daoine sidhe) – royal fae. Descendants of Mab's fae line. Make up majority of Court fae in both Summer and Winter Courts. Easily pass for human without needs for glamour. Can be elemental or non, but often possess great access to power regardless of affinity. Powers range greatly.

Diwata (pl- diwata) – tree fae. Territorial over large areas. Communal fae that attach to groves and forests, building families around a given territory and tending to the trees that grow there. Powers include flora manipulation, particularly of trees.

Djinn (pl – djinni) – fire fae. Powers include fire manipulation, enhanced speed and physical strength, invisibility, teleportation, and possession.

Dobie (pl – dobie) – non-elemental fae, cousins of brownies. Small physical stature. Unattached to territory, but partial to humans and can attached to people and families. Powers include invisibility, telekinesis, and luck manipulation.

Dragon (pl – dragons) – fire fae. Large physical stature. Powers include fire manipulation, great physical strength, and durability.

Drake (pl – drake) – fire fae, cousins to dragons. Less powerful than their cousins, but still boasting fire manipulation, great physical strength, and durability.

Dryad (pl – dryad) – tree fae. Territorial over singular trees. Communal fae, living in large groups of other dryads. Powers include flora manipulation, particularly of trees.

Encantado/encantada (pl – encante) – water fae. Strong affinity for water. Musically inclined, often great singers. Powers include shapeshifting, psychic manipulation and consumption, breathing under water.

Fuath (pl – fuaths) – water fae. Large physical stature. Solitary creatures. Powers include water manipulation and psychic consumption.

Gancanagh (pl - gancanagh) – sex fae. Known as love talkers. Powers include seduction, shapeshifting, and psychic consumption.

Ghillie Dhu (pl – ghillie dhu) – tree fae. Strong affinity for all flora. Powers include flora manipulation.

Gorgon (pl – gorgons) – serpent fae. Powers include physical strength, precognition through psychic manipulation, and ability to petrify with a look.

Gremlin (pl – gremlins) – metal fae. Related to kobolds. Strong affinity for stone and metal work, particularly machinery. Powers include great strength, durability, and technopathy.

Harpy (pl – harpies) – weather and bird fae. Winged fae. Powers include wind manipulation and psychic consumption.

Hobgoblin/hob (pl – hobgoblins/hobs) – non-elemental fae. Fertile fae line. Powers include dexterity, tirelessness, telekinesis, and invisibility.

Huldra (pl – huldrae) – water fae. Typically solitary. Powers include invisibility and minor water manipulation.

Iele (pl – iele) – air fae. Communal fae, drawn to large groups. Powers include speed, invisibility, and vocal manipulation.

Ifrit (pl – ifrit) – fire fae. Powers include fire manipulation, physical strength and durability, teleportation, and possession.

Incubus (pl – incubi) – sex fae. Strictly male term for lilin. See lilit.

Kappa (pl – kappas) – water fae. Powers include water manipulation, shapeshifting, strength, and psychic consumption.

Kikimora (pl – kikimory) – non-elemental fae. Powers include sleep inducement and psychic manipulation.

Kitsune (pl – kitsune) – fox fae. Powers include shapeshifting (into fox form), precognition, superior intelligence, and psychic manipulation.

Kobold (pl – kobolds) – stone and metal fae. Related to Gremlins, Strong affinity for stone and metal work, particularly stonework and mining. Powers include great strength, durability, and earth and stone manipulation.

Lilit (pl – lilin) – sex fae. Descendants of the Lilith fae line. Nongendered term for incubi or succubi. Hunts using pheromones, can feed on fae and humans alike. Powers include seduction, possession, psychic and emotional manipulation and consumption.

Maenad (pl – maenads) – sex fae. Strictly female term for a race of sex fae. Powers include psychic and emotional manipulation.

Monaciello (pl – monaciellos) – non-elemental fae. Powers include invisibility and luck manipulation.

Nymph (pl – nymphs) – nature fae. General term for a number of elemental races. Affinities can include flora, earth, water, air, fire, and stone. Powers vary but can include elemental manipulation, enhanced strength, and durability.

Ogre (pl – ogres) – non-elemental fae. Often considerably large physical stature. Powers include great strength and durability.

Osenya (pl – osenya) – non-elemental fae. Sometimes called a White Lady. Powers include precognition, and psychic manipulation and consumption.

Red cap (pl – red caps) – non-elemental fae. Pejorative term for a family line of hobgoblins, though the term was later embraced by the line. Powers include dexterity, tirelessness, telekinesis, and invisibility.

Selkie (pl – selkies) – seal fae. Strong affinity for water. Can transform into human form by removing seal skin. Powers include shapeshifting (into a human from seal form) and luck manipulation.

Shadowman/woman (pl – shadowmen/women) – non-elemental fae. Ability to wield darkness and shadows as substantial elements. Powers include telekinesis, psychic manipulation, and consumption.

Sidhe (pl – sidhe) – see daoine sidhe.

Siren (pl – sirens) – water fae. Power is located in voice. Powers include psychic and emotional manipulation through vocal control, psychic consumption.

Strega (pl – strega) – non-elemental fae. A secretive family line descended from Nour. Powers vary.

Succubus (pl – succubi) – sex fae. Strictly female term for lilin. See lilt.

Sylph (pl – sylphs) – air fae. Powers include wind and air manipulation and invisibility.

Valkyrie (pl – Valkyries) – non-elemental fae. Powers include great strength, durability, speed, agility, and stamina.

Vila (pl – vila) – air fae. Powers include precognition, seduction, psychic manipulation, and consumption.

This book is a work of fiction. The people, places, and events are products of the author's imagination and any resemblance to reality is entirely coincidental or meant with a nod and a wink. But the cocktails are real, lovingly tested, and should be enjoyed responsibly.

I wrote *Summer's Blood* during the first year of the COVID-19 pandemic, when I was spending a lot of time at home with my family. During a week, I would binge read entire urban fantasy series, make up cocktails in the evening, and then write. I wanted to write something fun and easy and kind of just for me, so I dashed off a draft of a story about a fairy bartender who would protect her patrons with only her ability to taste cocktails and the community she built around her. The first draft was messy and poorly developed, so I shoved it into the deep recesses of my hard drive and then promptly forgot about it.

Somehow, Falstaff Books publisher extraordinaire John Hartness convinced me that it was a decent idea, (his exact words: "Sounds fun. Can you make it a series?") and I should rewrite it with the thought that people might want to read it one day. The book you have now is because he had faith in my ability to transform a handful of ideas into a well-balanced cocktail of story. Thank you, John, for recognizing me as a Misfit years before I did and for encouraging developing my bad habits into productive creative tools.

For those interested in recreating some of the cocktails in this book, here are some select recipes inspired by locations and characters in *Summer's Blood*. If you want more, come follow me on my website www.saratbond.com or my TikTok channel (tiktok.com/@ saratbond) where I regularly pair cocktails with my favorite recent reads.

$\sim$

Cocktails for SUMMER'S BLOOD

Summer's Blood – STRAWBERRY GIN FIZZ

For my title cocktail, I wanted something cool and refreshing and optimistic. It should be bubbly, smooth, and easy to drink when everything around you feels like too much. This is inspired by my writing sessions in a hammock in my front yard, working out how Siobhan protects the life she's worked so hard to build.

- ¾ oz strawberry or raspberry simple syrup
- 1 ½ oz gin
- ½ oz lime juice
- 4 oz club soda

To make strawberry simple syrup: Combine 8 oz strawberries, 1 cup water, 1 cup granulated sugar in a saucepan. Bring to a boil, then reduce to a simmer. Cook for twenty minutes. Strain strawberries and chill liquid for an hour until cold.

Shake first three ingredients together with ice. Strain into highball glass over ice. Top with club soda. Garnish with strawberry or lime twist.

Greenwood Knoll – GIN BASIL SMASH

The Greenwood Knoll is an oasis in a city that often feels like too much. Atlanta is simultaneously painfully slow moving and demandingly rushed. The Knoll is somewhere the solitary fae can relax, regroup, and reclaim a moment of peace. This drink, like a mint julep, is meant to be enjoyed on a porch in a rocking chair, while you take a moment for yourself. It's a slowdown, when rush hour on 285 makes you feel like you're getting nowhere.

- 4-6 basil leaves, more for garnish
- ¾ oz simple syrup
- ¾ oz lemon juice
- 2 ½ oz gin
- Splash club soda (optional)

In bottom of lowball glass, muddle basil leaves and simple syrup. Top with ice, lemon, and gin. Shake or stir until cold. Strain into glass. Top with club soda if desired. Garnish with extra basil.

Character Drinks

Siobhan, former fairy princess turned bartender – FRENCH 75

I'll be honest: Siobhan is my main character, so she gets my favorite cocktail. Also, it's straightforward, easy to make (which any bartender appreciates), and immensely drinkable. It's not too sweet, it's good at any time of day, and it's something consistent almost no matter where you order it. The French 75 is a standby cocktail that you can rely on and always enjoy. If Siobhan strives for anything, it's to be exactly that.

- 1 oz gin
- ½ oz lemon
- ½ oz simple syrup
- 3 oz champagne
- Lemon twist

Mix first three ingredients over ice. Strain into champagne glass. Top with champagne or prosecco. Garnish with a lemon twist.

Lloyd, the Incubus – AMARETTO SOUR

Lloyd is one of the first characters we meet. He's smarmy, sticky sweet, and artificial. A proper amaretto sour is balanced and uses fresh lemon and lime juice. This ain't that. This drink should be closer to something you drink when you are too young and foolish to know better. It should be sweet enough to taste like tomorrow's hangover.

- 1.5 oz amaretto
- 1.5 oz sweet and sour mix
- Lemon-lime soda
- 1 orange slice, maraschino cherry

Mix first two ingredients together. Add ice and mix. Pour into rocks glass. Don't even bother straining. Top with lemon-lime soda. Garnish with an orange slice and at least three maraschino cherries.

Shiro, Summer Court scribe – FRENCH CONNECTION

Shiro is everything Lloyd is not. He's classy, refined, a true gentleman, and possibly a little pretentious. He would insist on a proper French cognac (no Hennessy for him) and Italian amaretto for this drink, served over a single large ice cube made with distilled water. It's still about as basic and straightforward as drinks come, as Shiro ultimately strives to be.

- 1 ½ oz cognac
- 1 oz amaretto

Stir both ingredients together and pour over ice in a rocks glass. Garnish with a lemon twist.

Talisa, big sister of the maenads – STRAWBERRY BALSAMIC MOJITO

As maenads pride themselves on the fact that they can never be tied down or controlled, it takes a lot to unite this clan for any amount of time. They'd all agree, though, that Talisa is the big sister that directs them and moderates their worst impulses. (Though do not call her the mom friend!) She's got a strong presence but is always up for a good time, so this assertive take on a mojito is perfect for her. She's grounded and assured—the kind of girl who will get the party started and make sure you get home safe and hydrated to go out again the next night.

- 3 strawberries
- Bunch of fresh mint
- 2 oz gold rum
- ½ oz simple syrup

- ¼ tsp white balsamic vinegar
- ½ oz lime juice
- Splash soda water

Muddle strawberries and mint in bottom of collins or highball glass. Add liquid ingredients and crushed ice. Mix, then top with crushed ice. Top with soda water. Garnish with half a strawberry or sprig of mint. Add a small crack of white pepper for extra flavor.

ACKNOWLEDGMENTS

Writing is a solitary endeavor, but living as a writer never is.

Thank you to my family for being my unending support system.

To my best friend and partner, my husband James: you are the love of my life, and there is no one I would rather be weird with. Thank you for walking beside me, lifting me up, and leaning on me on this journey. Let's do this for a few more years?

Alex and Evie, you are some of the most amazing humans I know. Thank you for encouraging everything that makes your mom a little different and forgiving the moments my work takes me away mentally and physically.

To my parents, Beth and Joe, you gave me earth to ground my roots, water to grow my strength, wind to spread my wings, and fire to light my way. Thank you for nurturing every element of my journey.

To Kate and Rachel, those without sisters will never know what a comfort, what a security, what a blessing it is to have someone like you in their lives. At the end, you are more than just friends, more than just family; you are a part of me. You are both so incredible in such different ways, and I am so proud of you and all you have accomplished. I miss you like crazy.

To Sarah Sover, I have no idea how I'm surviving without seeing you every week, but I know I'd be better with you. I am so thankful for you and so proud of all you have accomplished. I am honored to be on this publishing journey with you and chasing after your glowing footsteps. I'll fight for you whenever you ask (and maybe sometimes even when you don't).

To John Hartness and the entire Misfit family at Falstaff Books, my convention families: you are my sanity. Whenever I get lost in the madness that is writing, y'all send out a flare to guide me back to our weird little reality. Found family recurs in my stories, because y'all are the ones that see to the truth of me. You remind me why I write the stories I do. Thank you from the bottom of my heart.

To my friends who have beta read, posted reviews, and mixed me drinks when I'm supposed to be taking it easy but am secretly writing in the corner, I love you so much. Thank you for standing by me when I'm absent even when I try to be present. Thank you for reading my words, for accepting my absences, and for supporting my struggles.

And Jordan, I owe you so many more stories. When I think of giving up, I remember what I've promised, and I get back to work. Thank you. As long as I have stories to tell, I won't stop writing.

And to my readers, thank you for giving me a chance to entertain you. There's more to come, and I can't promise I won't try to break your heart next time. But I'll make it worth it.

ABOUT THE AUTHOR

An unapologetic extrovert, science fiction and fantasy author Sara Bond has lived many lives, dabbling in political research, campaign management, and even a short, lucrative career in high-end fashion retail. Writing about the fantastic and improbable allows Sara to cut through the lies we tell ourselves to better uncover the deeply personal and political stories about how we reconcile our inner truths with our communities, our pasts, and our deepest selves.

(That's just fancy talk to say she uses fiction to uncover truth.)

Born and raised in Atlanta, Sara now lives in Seattle with her husband and two children who moonlight as advanced agents of chaos. Visit her website at www.saratbond.com for her latest projects, essays, and even a book review and cocktail pairings blog series.

FRIENDS OF FALSTAFF

Thank You to All our Falstaff Books Patrons, who get extra digital content each month! To be featured here and see what other great rewards we offer, go to www.patreon.com/falstaffbooks.

PATRONS

Dino Hicks
John Hooks
John Kilgallon
Larissa Lichty
Travis & Casey Schilling
Staci-Leigh Santore
Sheryl R. Hayes
Scott Norris
Samuel Montgomery-Blinn
Junkle

www.ingramcontent.com/pod-product-compliance
Lightning Source LLC
Chambersburg PA
CBHW050029120726
47903CB00006B/1970